BY THE SAME AUTHOR

The Majat Code
Blades of the Old Empire

The Princess of Dhagabad
Ivan-and-Marya
The Goddess of Dance
The First Sword
Mistress of the Solstice

ANNA KASHINA

The Guild of Assassins

THE MAJAT CODE
BOOK II

**ANGRY
ROBOT**

ANGRY ROBOT
A member of the Osprey Group

Lace Market House	Angry Robot/Osprey Publishing
54-56 High Pavement	PO Box 3985
Nottingham	New York
NG1 1HW	NY 10185-3985
UK	USA

www.angryrobotbooks.com
Epic romance

An Angry Robot paperback original 2014

Cover art by Alejandro Colucci
Set in Meridien by Argh! Oxford

Distributed in the United States by Random House, Inc., New York

ISBN 978 0 85766 527 0
Ebook ISBN 978 0 85766 528 7

Printed in the United States of America

9 8 7 6 5 4 3 2 1

To VKB

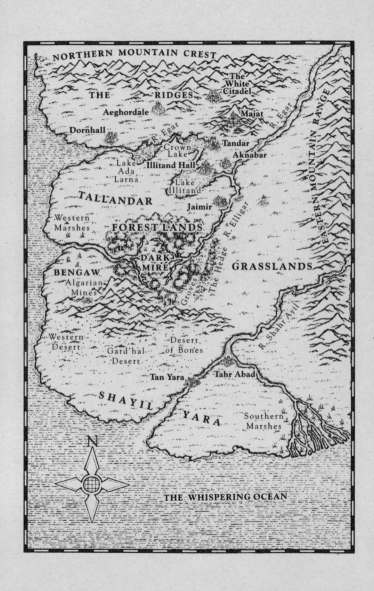

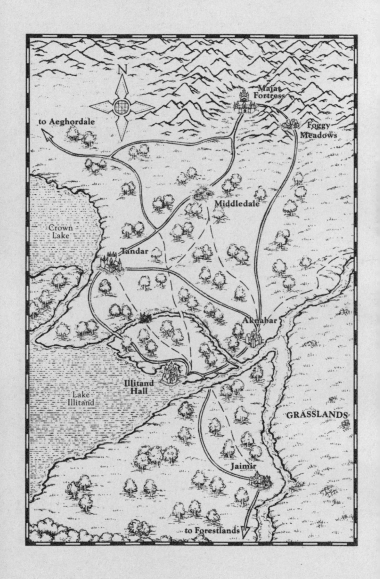

1
A LOOK BACK

Oden Lan, Master of the Majat Guild, Assassin of the Diamond Rank, forced his face into a calm mask as he stared at the object in his hand – a four-pointed throwing star, the large diamond set into its center glittering so brightly that it hurt his eyes. The intricate lines of the golden inlay at the base of the blades spelled a word in the ancient runic language, used in the Majat Fortress as a token of the Guild's unique ancestry.

Black.

In the Majat dialect the word was pronounced "*Kar*" and sounded similar to the star bearer's name.

Kara.

Oden Lan's face twitched. It had been hundreds of years since the Majat Guildmaster had to arrange an assassination of one of his own, an elite warrior of the Diamond rank. The fact that he had to do it because Kara had betrayed her duty for the love of the sleek, blue-eyed Prince Kythar of the ruling House Dorn made things worse. The Majat Warriors were not permitted to love. If they had been, Oden Lan himself would have never watched Kara grow up from a little girl into the most incredible nineteen year-old their Guild had ever seen, without letting her know how he felt about her. And now, he would never have the chance. She was dead, killed at Oden Lan's orders by another of the Guild's best.

A rustle of footsteps brought Oden Lan back to reality. He closed his fingers over the token in his hand, suddenly aware of the early morning chill creeping under his cloak, and the smother of the looming walls that made the courtyard adjoining the Guildmaster's tower seem dark and hollow, like a deep stone well.

"This had better be important," Oden Lan said into the gloom of the low archway.

A hooded figure separated itself from the shadows, its long, dark robe shuffling over the paving stones.

"Forgive the interruption, Aghat," the newcomer said in a deep, soft voice.

Oden Lan looked at him with curiosity. The way the stranger used the Guildmaster's rank as a form of address suggested familiarity with Majat customs, yet Oden Lan was certain he had never seen this man before. Finding an outsider, unannounced, in the Guildmaster's inner sanctum was so preposterous that Oden Lan couldn't even find it in his heart to feel angry. After all, no one in his right mind would come to the Majat Guildmaster, the man in command of the most impressive military force in the history of the known world, with bad intentions.

"Who are you?" he said.

"A friend." The man stopped halfway across the courtyard and pushed back his hood, allowing the Guildmaster a good look at his face.

He had heavy, gaunt features, his prominent eyebrows

looming over deep eye sockets. His graceful posture spoke of warrior training, not sufficient, perhaps, to stand up to a Majat of a gem rank, but good enough to defend himself in a tight spot. His bulging robe suggested hidden weapons, perhaps a sword or saber strapped across the back. But the most unusual thing about him was his eyes – so pale brown that they bordered on yellow. From the shadows of his eye sockets they stared at the Majat Guildmaster calmly, without the fear or reverence that Oden Lan was used to seeing in the faces of his visitors.

"What do you want?" the Guildmaster demanded.

The man shifted from foot to foot, his calm look acquiring a touch of curiosity, as if he were studying a strange animal.

"I bring news of one of your Guild members," he said. "A Diamond, Kara."

Oden Lan's hand holding the throwing star clenched so tightly that the blades cut into him, piercing the skin. He kept his face steady, shoving the bleeding hand into his pocket before the strange, yellow-eyed man could see it.

"I believe," he said, "that I have all the news of Kara that I need. If you have nothing else to say–"

"She's alive."

In the silence that followed these words the quiet rustle of the morning breeze seemed as loud as the howl of a hurricane.

Oden Lan stared at the man, trying in vain to quiet his racing heart. *"What* did you say?"

The stranger's lips twitched into a smile. "I'm afraid, Guildmaster, that the man you sent to do the job, Aghat Mai, failed to fulfill your orders."

Oden Lan took a deep breath.

Alive.

Could it possibly be true?

It didn't seem likely. Mai, a Diamond whose incredible skill had made him a legend in the Guild despite his young age, couldn't possibly fail. Even less so would he disobey a direct order. The reports had been clear about this. Mai had used his famous blow, the "viper's sting", on her. A blade between the collarbones. Instant death.

Unless…

Oden Lan felt a chill creep up his spine.

"Tell me more."

The man bowed his head. "She and Aghat Mai are both at the King's court. I've seen them myself. Aghat Mai has resumed his duty as the head of the King's bodyguards – following your orders, I believe. As for Kara, she's spending her time getting closely familiar with the royal heir, if you know what I mean."

Oden Lan hesitated. Now he was beginning to think that the man was crazy. What he was saying was impossible. Mai was one of their Guild's best. If, for some unknown reason, he had failed to kill Kara the first time, he *couldn't* possibly just stay around her without trying again.

He should have this man executed for prying into Guild affairs. Yet, something kept him from calling the guards.

"Perhaps there's been a mistake?" he asked carefully.

"It was my impression that the Diamond Majat don't make such… mistakes."

"I was referring to you."

The man held his gaze with calm confidence.

"I wasn't there when they fought, and cannot be certain what happened, but I saw the two of them afterward, fighting side by side. In fact, Aghat Mai took considerable risks to save Kara's life."

Oden Lan hesitated. This seemed preposterous. Yet, the stranger was clearly certain of his words.

"You seem to be extremely well informed," he said.

The man bowed. "I pride myself on having good sources of information, Aghat. But I can see that you still don't believe me. Please, don't take my word for it. Ask the Jade who was on this assignment with Aghat Mai – Gahang Sharrim, if I am not mistaken."

Oden Lan lifted his chin. For how unremarkable he was, the yellow-eyed man *did* seem to be well informed.

"Not that it is any business for an outsider," he said, "but since we are having this conversation, I don't mind telling you this. Gahang Sharrim brought back Kara's armband, and reported on a successfully completed assignment. In fact, he seemed to be quite proud of it."

"Question him again, Aghat. Ask him what kind of blow Aghat Mai used to kill her."

"What does that have to do with anything?"

"I heard," the man said softly, "that Aghat Mai is rumored to have invented several special blows, which made him quite famous in your Guild. One of them is called 'viper's kiss'. Am I correct?"

Oden Lan froze. No outsider could possibly know this. This man was either a spy or–

He should call the guards. But the thought that, despite everything, Kara could still be alive, continued to hold him in place. He *had* to know.

"Go on," he said.

The man smiled with the calm confidence of one who has the situation well in hand.

"This blow," he said, "looks exactly as deadly as the 'viper's sting', entering the body in exactly the same spot between the collarbones, but by a skillful tilt of the blade it merely sends a person into a deep coma, until the victim can be revived by a special pinch on the pressure points. The wound is still serious, of course, but with proper care it could be easily treated."

Oden Lan's skin prickled. It would have taken a hell of a lot of skill for Mai to use "viper's kiss" against an equal opponent. But if he had managed to execute it on Kara, it was indeed indistinguishable from the "sting" on the surface. Even Sharrim, Mai's partner in the assignment and the best of the Guild's Jades, could have been easily fooled.

But why would Mai do such a thing, knowing that sooner or later the truth would come out? And how could this yellow-eyed stranger possibly know this?

"How did you come upon this information?"

"This is not important, Aghat," the man said. "The important question is whether or not I am right, isn't it? Call in Gahang Sharrim. Ask him."

"I fail to see how this would help," Oden Lan said. "I heard Gahang Sharrim's report. You, on the other hand–"

The man waved his hand in dismissal. "I am not your problem, Aghat. You have treason brewing in your very midst. I came here with humble hope that bringing you this information could be considered a gesture of goodwill, and that in future you would consider me a friend."

Oden Lan gave him a long look. It felt surreal. There was no way he, the commander of the most powerful military force in existence, the man feared by kings, was having a personal conversation with a stranger, far too well informed in Majat affairs to be allowed to walk freely within these walls. And yet, something in the stranger's face, in the way he held himself, put his suspicions to rest. This man couldn't possibly be an enemy if he freely came forth with this kind of information, could he?

"What you are suggesting is ridiculous," he said. "But given the graveness of the accusation, I will question Gahang Sharrim again."

He signaled and a Majat guard appeared from the shadows at the edge of the courtyard.

"Take this man to the guest quarters. Keep him safe. Master–?" He turned to the yellow-eyed man with question.

"Tolos," the man supplied.

Oden Lan nodded.

"Until we talk again," he said, "Master Tolos."

He turned and strode away.

The Jade, Sharrim, had curly red hair, a freckled face, and a perpetual expression of childlike wonder that seemed odd in someone with his reputation as the best archer among the Jades. His superior, Gahang Khall, a pale man with straight black hair and piercing eyes, made a chilling contrast as the two of them stood in the Guildmaster's study with the solemn look of men well aware of due praise for a job well done. Looking at their silent forms, Oden Lan had trouble believing

Master Tolos's accusations. Yet now, after summoning the Jades to his study, he had no choice but to proceed.

"Tell me how Kara died," he said.

The men raised their eyebrows in puzzled silence.

"Is there a reason for–" Khall began.

Oden Lan lifted his head. "I choose not to take your words as doubt that I would ask you *anything* without reason, Gahang."

"But I already told–" Sharrim put in.

Oden Lan turned, his gaze forcing the younger man into silence. "Tell me again."

Sharrim swallowed, his face losing several shades of color. "After we received our orders, Aghat Mai and I caught up with Kara after a ten day chase. Aghat Mai engaged her, and when she was distracted, I shot her in the forearm. Then I stood down, like Aghat Mai instructed me."

"He instructed you to stand down?"

The Jade's face continued to show puzzlement. "He told me to stand down after the first hit. He said that one light wound would give him all the advantage he needed. And it did."

Oden Lan hesitated, searching Sharrim's eyes and finding nothing but honest pride in the successful assignment. He was beginning to feel like a fool. He swore to himself to have another conversation with Master Tolos after this was over. Now that the yellow-eyed man was out of the way he no longer seemed so friendly or trustworthy. What possessed Oden Lan to believe such ridiculous accusations of two of his best warriors?

"What happened afterward, Gahang Sharrim?" he asked.

"After my arrow hit, it took mere minutes for Aghat Mai to get through. Kara lost a sword from her injured hand. Then, he struck her down. Death was instant, Guildmaster. Almost no blood."

As before when he heard this, Oden Lan felt giddy. He summoned all his strength to appear calm.

Instant death.

When this was over, he was going to make an example of Master Tolos, to show everyone what it meant to pry into Majat Guild private affairs. How *dare* this yellow-eyed man come here to suggest such preposterous things and stir up wounds that hadn't yet had time to heal?

"You told me before that Aghat Mai used 'viper's sting' on her, Gahang Sharrim."

"Yes, Guildmaster."

"How do you know?"

The Jade hesitated.

"We all learned what it's like, Guildmaster. It's Aghat Mai's signature blow. A deep stab between the collarbones, tilted left and in to go straight through the heart."

Yes, that was how "viper's sting" was supposed to go. Oden Lan had never tried it, but he had heard enough talk in the Fortress five years ago, after Mai, a newly ranked Diamond at the time, had used it on his first kill. Mai had also used the other one, "viper's kiss", during the same assignment, to harmlessly get the victim's bodyguard out of the way. Mai's fame had spread like fire. Not many people in the history of the Guild had blows named after their token rune. *Viper.*

Oden Lan strained his memory to recall the details. There *was* a way to tell between the two blows, just not an easy one.

"You said there was no blood," he said slowly.

"Almost none, Guildmaster. A splash, no more."

A splash. Oden Lan's heart quivered, but he kept his face straight. "And what did Aghat Mai do immediately after the fight?"

"What do you mean?" Sharrim looked lost.

"Try to recall exactly, Gahang. *What happened immediately after the fight?*"

Sharrim licked his lips.

"I– I approached the body and checked that she was dead," he stammered, trying to speak faster under Oden Lan's urgent gaze. "There was no pulse. Then Aghat Mai sent me off to find her armband."

"He sent you off?"

"Yes."

"Why?"

Sharrim hesitated. "I was under his command. I didn't question his orders."

"Didn't you wonder why he stayed behind?"

"He– he said he'd collect her weapons."

"And what did he do when you walked away?" Oden Lan prompted.

"He leaned over her, and…" Sharrim paused, his face going pale.

Oden Lan waited. After a moment Sharrim spoke slowly, his narrowed eyes looking into the distance.

"He hit some points on the neck. Her body shook. I saw it as I left. And then, Aghat Mai said something to the boy, Prince Kythar Dorn. After Aghat Mai left, the Prince wrapped Kara's body in a cloak and held her in his arms."

"He told the Prince to hold her, so that he could keep her warm," Oden Lan said. "Didn't he?"

Sharrim's blue eyes were suddenly dark like Khall's. His face lost its innocent expression and became cold and distant.

"I don't blame you, Gahang Sharrim," Oden Lan said. "You couldn't have known."

The two Jades went so still that they seemed inanimate.

"You may go," Oden Lan said.

"What do you intend to do, Guildmaster?" Khall asked quietly.

Oden Lan turned to him, keeping his face so straight that it hurt.

"I'll do what I have to, Gahang Khall," he said. "Just like I've always done."

2
MESSENGER

Prince Kythar Dorn narrowed his eyes watching the lonely rider approach the castle at a slow walk. The man's dusty travel cloak and his plain gray lizard-beast mount made him inconspicuous enough to pass unnoticed. Yet, something about his muscular shape made Kyth's skin creep as he watched the man come around the last bend in the road onto the wide stretch leading up to the gate. He glanced at Kara standing by his side and saw her neck tense as she, too, watched the stranger approach.

It must be the weapons, Kyth decided. Two sword hilts sticking out above the shoulders suggested that the man was not only highly skilled with blades, but could use both hands equally well. A crossbow adorned the man's saddle next to a full quiver, and his cloak, folding away at the belt, revealed an array of throwing knives impressive enough to compare to those carried by the Majat of the Royal Pentade of the King's personal bodyguards. In fact, only the top gem ranks of the Majat carried such a set of weapons. Could it be–?

Kyth threw another glance at Kara. Her posture was tense and graceful as she watched the man approach the castle gate. Her violet eyes glowed like precious amethysts in the setting of her chocolate-brown skin that seemed even darker in contrast to her pale golden hair. She wore it short, its soft waves resting against her cheeks. On top of her beauty, she looked no less deadly than the approaching rider, her own weapons in full view.

"Do you know him?" Kyth asked quietly.

She shook her head. "I haven't seen him before, but I'm pretty sure he's from the Majat Guild."

Kyth turned to look down into the front castle courtyard, where the activity told him that the rider had been spotted and his arrival expected. The Kingsguard formed a line in front of the gate and the two Diamond Majat stationed at court, Raishan and Mai, stood behind them with impassive looks.

"You must stay out of sight, Kara," Kyth said. "If he sees you…"

She nodded.

"Let's get out of here," Kyth urged.

"Give me your cloak. I want to see what happens."

Kyth took off his cloak, its black and blue colors of the Royal House Dorn adorned with a crown on the left shoulder, and wrapped it around her. The movement brought them close, so that for a moment he inhaled her barely perceptible scent of wild flowers and sensed her warmth against him. His pulse quickened as he caught her brief smile. Then she flicked the hood over her face and receded into the shadows beside the tall protrusion of the castle wall. Together they watched events unravel in the courtyard below.

The newcomer rode through the gate and dismounted in a quick, fluid move that left no doubt of his Majat training. He stepped toward the greeting party so fast that his shape blurred. Seeing him next to the two Diamonds made Kyth wonder. Could he be–

A Diamond?

Kyth held his breath, watching the three men below exchange quiet words, too distant to hear. They each looked so different. Mai's slender build, smooth skin and soft blond curls made him appear much too young for his high post as leader of the Royal Pentade – and far too good-looking to be trustworthy. Raishan with his short brown hair and regular face looked unremarkable next to him, his high rank identifiable only by his powerful grace and the ruthless glint in his slanted gray eyes. The new Majat was of a heavier build, his black clothes far less elegant than Mai's. He had curly hair cut closely to the scalp and black eyes so large that they seemed painted, their whites shining with a pearl glow against his dark skin.

The newcomer exchanged brief words with the two Diamonds, then took out a folded parchment and handed it to Mai. There was a pause as the Pentade leader unrolled and read the letter, then another brief one when he lowered it and looked at the messenger with unseeing eyes. Then Mai carefully folded the parchment, put it away into a pocket inside his shirt and strode out of the yard.

"He's in trouble," Kara whispered. "Because of me."

Kyth bit his lip. It had been Mai's decision to spare her life and face the consequences. Besides, Mai was one of the best warriors in the Majat Guild, and was perfectly capable of taking care of himself. But he didn't say any of this to Kara. She had been cast out of her Guild because of her decision to protect Kyth, and he knew that no matter how casual she tried to be about it, it hurt her deeper than he could ever imagine. There was nothing he could do to make it better.

Kyth watched Raishan run up the narrow stairs of the battlements, closely followed by the white-cloaked shape of Magister Egey Bashi, the second-in-command in the Order of Keepers. The Magister was a middle-aged man, whose grim looks and heavy muscular build suggested that his title had to do with more than scholarly activities. During the past months, Kyth had learned to fully trust this man, rumored to be much older than he appeared, and much wiser than he pretended to be. As Kyth saw the two men rush toward them with grim faces, his momentary relief gave way to a deep pang of anxiety.

The speed of Raishan's approach made the wind rise in his wake. He came to an abrupt halt in front of Kara after collision seemed inevitable and spoke, the unevenness in his voice betraying more emotion than his face.

"You must stay out of sight, Aghat. This man has come from the Guild."

Kara took a moment to answer, her violet eyes meeting Raishan's in an unspoken exchange. "Is Aghat Mai in trouble?"

Raishan's eyes darted to Egey Bashi.

"I'm sure he'll be all right," the Magister said. "The Majat messenger seemed quite friendly. From what I know about your Guild, if there was a problem he would have attacked on sight."

Kara continued to look at Raishan. "That man's a Diamond, isn't he?"

"Aghat Xandel," Raishan confirmed. "I know him. Both he and I trained together in the Outer Fortress."

"And the letter he brought was from Master Oden Lan?"

Raishan nodded.

"He *knows*," she said quietly.

"We can't be sure," Raishan said. "I didn't see the letter. Aghat Mai read it and put it away without showing anyone. But Magister Egey Bashi is right. If the Guildmaster knew what happened, we should have seen a bigger outburst, shouldn't we?"

"Why else would Master Oden Lan send a Diamond?"

"I could imagine many reasons," Raishan said. "For example, the King could have sent him. Do you know of any such plans, Your Highness?"

Kyth shook his head.

"I think we'd have heard if that had been the case," Egey Bashi said.

Kara's face froze into an unreadable mask. "Did Aghat Xandel say anything?"

"Not much," Raishan said. "He gave Aghat Mai the letter. And, he said he has another one for the King, to be delivered personally. Aghat Mai went to arrange for security before the audience could be granted."

"That might take some time," Egey Bashi said. "The King has other things on his mind."

His grim tone made everyone pause.

"What other things?" Kyth asked.

The Keeper gave him a dark look. "A messenger from the Aknabar Monastery arrived this morning.

Things don't look good up there. In fact, it seems that the Kaddim Brotherhood has taken more control of the Church than we first thought. I believe there's no choice for the King but to send armed forces down there."

"Armed forces? To the *Monastery*?"

"The messenger was a very frightened man," Egey Bashi said. "He brought news that Father Bartholomeos has been imprisoned. He also brought a parcel containing the head of the late Chief Inquisitor, Brother Valdos. Dipped in tar and quite rotten, but still recognizable. There was a note with it. '*From the Conclave to the King*', not quite in those words, but with far fewer niceties than warranted, I'd say. And now, a response from King Evan is definitely called for."

There was shocked silence.

"But… But the priests aren't even supposed to wield weapons!"

"I assure you, Your Highness. The head had definitely been severed with a weapon. A very sharp one."

"You think the Kaddim Brothers did it?"

"I am certain of it."

Raishan shook his head. "It's hard to imagine how a dark order of Ghaz Kadan worshippers could possibly take hold of the Church. The Kaddim and the priests serve opposite sides, don't they?"

"You forget, Aghat," the Keeper said. "The Kaddim are capable of mind control. Only a certain type of magic could make people immune to it, and the Church has spent centuries eliminating magic in their midst. If you ask me, something like this was bound to happen, sooner or later."

Kyth nodded. The Kaddim Brothers could wield a

disabling mind control power that bent people to their will. To his knowledge, his own magic gift, the one he hadn't even fully mastered yet, held the only way to resisting it.

It was good that his father had managed to gather enough support on the High Council to abolish the anti-magic law, but the effects of this law being in place for centuries couldn't be ignored. For all he knew, the Dark Brotherhood overtaking the Church might not be the only outcome, even if it was hard to imagine a worse one.

He shivered, meeting Kara's gaze.

"This is bad," she said.

"All the worse, it seems," Raishan put in, "because right now the King can't afford to risk any disagreement with the Majat Guild. Which is why you must stay completely out of sight, Kara. If Xandel is here to negotiate your return to the Guild, things might get ugly."

"If Mai had killed me like he was instructed," Kara said, her eyes fixed unseeingly on the distant lake view, "we wouldn't be guessing right now. And, none of you would have anything to fear from the Majat Guild."

Kyth reached forward and placed a hand on her shoulder. She tensed under his touch and for the first time he realized she was shivering.

"It's not your fault," he said quietly.

She turned and looked at him, her shivers lessening, her gaze slowly becoming calm and detached as she hid her emotions behind an invisible shield.

"Whether or not it's my fault," she said, "it's too late for regrets."

Regrets. Kyth hoped she wasn't talking about him,

but there was no way to tell. Worse, whatever she meant, there was nothing he could do about it. He looked searchingly into her eyes, but she turned away.

"I believe I'll be speaking for many of us," Raishan said carefully, "if I say that I'm really glad you're alive, Aghat Kara."

"I'll second that," Egey Bashi said.

She smiled, but her gaze remained distant.

"Let's hope I can justify some of it by making a difference. We should go and find out more about Aghat Xandel's mission. Shall we?"

"As long as you stay carefully hidden," Egey Bashi pointed out.

"I will, Magister." She wrapped Kyth's royal cloak tighter around herself and moved to the stairs leading down from the battlements onto the castle grounds, but Kyth caught her by the arm.

"It's too risky for you to appear anywhere near the throne room right now," he said. "Why don't you and Raishan go to the Keepers' quarters and wait? Magister and I will go to the throne room and find out what's going on."

Kara gave him a brief glance and he imagined that in the shadows of the hood he saw her smile.

3

AN AUDIENCE

As Kyth and Egey Bashi entered the long gallery leading up to the throne room, they saw Alder's towering figure up ahead. Kyth's foster brother was standing beside a niche, waving his hands in the air. As they approached, Kyth realized that Alder wasn't alone. Their friend, Ellah, deeper in the corner, was shaking a five hundred year-old tapestry depicting a scene of the royal hunt vigorously as if she were trying to tear the precious hanging off the wall. Her face was contorted into a disgusted grimace, her white cloak of an apprentice Keeper hanging off one shoulder to reveal a dark dress underneath.

"What happened?" Kyth asked, running up to them.

"One of Alder's spiders!" Ellah panted. "It ran loose!"

Kyth looked at Alder's left shoulder, which usually served as a perch for three live spiders, each larger than a man's hand. He could see only two, their hairy legs giving off a faint cracking noise as they crawled around in agitation at all the bustle around them. The third spider was missing.

"Why did this thing..." Kyth paused, catching his foster brother's displeased look. He forced himself to remember that the spiders were a token of Alder's status as the emissary of the Forestlands at the King's court, bestowed upon him by Lady Ayalla the Forest Mother herself. It was utterly wrong to call them "things", or even to think of them as deadly monsters, even if their venom was potent enough to dissolve a man into a pool of goo. After all, the spiders never attacked without command and even showed a kind of fondness for their owner.

"Be careful!" Alder snapped, rushing past Kyth to the wall. Ellah hastily scrambled back. Moving with great care, as if handling a precious ornament, Alder picked the huge spider off the tapestry and placed it back onto his shoulder.

Kyth suppressed a shudder. Ellah let out a breath and stepped away, straightening out her hair and outfit and keeping a clear distance from Alder and his frightening burden. The look of exasperation in her hazel-green eyes spoke without words.

"It's lucky that we ran into you two," Kyth said. "Ellah, can you come with me and Magister Egey Bashi to the throne room right now?"

"Why?"

Out of the corner of his eye, Kyth caught a smile of approval on Egey Bashi's face. Ellah's gift of truthsense, discovered recently by the Keepers, was an invaluable aid in court intrigue. There was nobody like Ellah to uncover hidden intentions and unspoken threats.

"A Diamond Majat just arrived to see the King," Kyth told her. "Kara thinks he's here because of her. She believes Mai is in trouble. We have to find out."

The four of them exchanged glances.

"Let's go!" Ellah said and darted forward toward the double doors of the throne room. Kyth, Alder, and Egey Bashi followed.

The guards on duty stood to attention as Kyth and his friends approached. Two servants wearing blue and black royal livery held the doors open for the Prince and his small suite and closed them behind with a muffled thud.

Everyone was already assembled in the large vaulted chamber. King Evan Dorn sat on his throne, the royal colors of his cloak accenting the deep blue of his eyes and the raven-wing shine of his long black hair, barely touched by gray. Kyth couldn't help but smile when he caught his father's gaze. The King looked so striking – a handsome, majestic man even in his late forties. Kyth often heard that he looked just like his father, but he always found it difficult to believe.

The Royal Majat Pentade stood around the throne like statues, the only movement about them the glint of the rank gems in the broad metal bands clasped over their left upper arms. The four Rubies surrounded the King in a protective ring. Their Diamond leader, Mai, kept to the shadows at the side, his position against the wall giving him the best view of the entire chamber and into its most distant corners. His black polished staff, whose wooden tips concealed two retractable blades, protruded from the strap at his back, a weapon even more deadly because of its inconspicuous look. Kyth noticed how Ellah's cheeks lit up with color as Mai glanced her way and, not for the first time, wondered how this sleek youthful man had such a strong effect on women without showing any apparent interest in any of them.

The elderly lords of the Royal Visory sat in a semicircle that made the throne on its elevated platform in front of them seem like a stage. Slanted sunbeams shining through the tall arched windows illuminated their ornate robes and graying hair. As Kyth and his companions made their way in, heads turned to give them respectful nods and mildly curious glances before returning to the action in the center of the chamber.

The new Diamond was kneeling in front of the King with a grace that left no doubt of his high Majat ranking. His outlandishly huge eyes studied King Evan with calm indifference as he held out a glittering throwing star in his outstretched palm.

"His token," Ellah whispered. "He's here to offer his services to the King."

Kyth froze, straining not to miss a single word.

"Aghat Mai's term on the Pentade is not up for another year, Aghat Xandel." The King's voice had a ringing timbre that betrayed his exasperation. "His service has been exemplary."

The new Diamond slightly inclined his head.

"We are all proud of Aghat Mai, Your Majesty," he said. "This replacement has nothing to do with the quality of his service. However, since I share Aghat Mai's high rank, I assure you that I am equally qualified to perform the Pentade duties."

The King let out a sigh. "We are on the verge of war, Aghat. I think you'll understand my reluctance to let my personal bodyguard be replaced at such a time, even with someone who is equally qualified. Not without a truly compelling reason."

Kyth's heart sank. If Mai was being replaced without an obvious reason, it quite likely meant that the Majat Guildmaster had found out about Kara. Which meant that, unless something was done about it, things could quickly get out of hand.

Kyth glanced at Mai, searching for an indication of what was going on, but Mai's blue-gray eyes remained calm, showing no surprise or alarm, or even awareness that the conversation concerned him at all. Kyth knew the Diamond too well to be fooled. Mai was the kind of person who wouldn't flinch even if an entire Cha'ori hort was charging down on him. He acted only when there was something he could do, and never looked upset about anything he was powerless to change. In fact, the very calmness in the Diamond's face finally settled Kyth into absolute certainty that things were about to go terribly wrong.

"I assure you, Your Majesty," the new Diamond, Xandel, said, "our Guildmaster has reasons of utmost importance for this replacement."

"What reasons?" Evan asked.

"This letter from our Guildmaster might clarify things, Your Majesty." Xandel held out a folded piece of parchment. A Ruby of the Pentade handed it to the King, who unrolled it, his eyebrows slowly rising as he ran his eyes through the page.

"I don't think my gift can help much," Ellah whispered. "He's speaking the truth, but he isn't really saying anything, is he?"

Kyth felt a hand on his shoulder and turned to look into Magister Egey Bashi's dark eyes.

"Go get Kara and Raishan," the Keeper whispered. "Meet us in the gallery behind the throne room."

He pushed between Kyth and Alder and stepped into the aisle leading up to the throne.

All heads turned toward the new disturbance. Egey Bashi kept a measured pace as he walked forward, his white Keeper's robe with an embroidery of the lock and key on the left shoulder wavering with his steps. He approached and knelt on the floor beside Xandel, the solemn expression on his face suggesting that no force in the world could possibly budge him from his current place.

The new Diamond gave him a dark look. Kyth marveled at the way Egey Bashi pretended to ignore it.

"Magister Egey Bashi," King Evan said. "What a surprise. How may I be of service to you?"

"I came to seek an audience, Your Majesty," the Keeper said.

The King threw a restrained glance around. "It may have escaped your attention, Magister, but I am a little busy at the moment."

Egey Bashi remained kneeling. "I have a matter of utmost urgency to discuss, Your Majesty. In fact, I must ask you to grant me a private audience. I understand that for reasons of security Aghat Mai will accompany you, of course." His eyes darted to the Pentade leader.

"What, now?" King Evan asked.

"*Now*, Your Majesty."

Kyth grasped Ellah's wrist.

"Let's go," he whispered.

Trying to move as quietly as possible, they slid through the double doors at the end of the chamber and out into the hall.

Kara and Raishan stood by the window in Mother Keeper's guest chamber, the tense set of their bodies betraying the restlessness of caged predators. As Kyth, Alder, and Ellah rushed inside, Kara turned toward them so fast that her shape blurred. Her eyes fixed on Kyth with silent question.

Kyth glanced past her to the slight, white-robed woman occupying a tall armchair by the fireplace. Mother Keeper, whose tranquility suggested a wisdom of years that couldn't possibly be guessed from her smooth, ageless face, returned his gaze with quiet curiosity.

"He came to replace Mai," Kyth said, failing to find a way to soften the blow. He kept his eyes on Kara, noticing the way her neck went tense for a brief moment and her gaze became distant, fixing on the shadows in the corner of the room.

"Magister Egey Bashi is talking to my father and Mai right now," Kyth went on. "He said we should get Kara and Raishan and meet them in the gallery by the throne room."

Mother Keeper rose from her chair.

"Why?" she asked, her deep caressing voice holding concern.

Kyth hesitated. In his hurry to fulfill the Magister's instructions, he had never bothered to ask what the plan was.

"I don't know. But I think he hopes to prevent it somehow."

Kara glanced up. "There's only one way to prevent it. I must go with Mai and take the blame."

"*You*?"

"I don't think you should do that, Aghat," Raishan said. "If you show up at the Guild, they'll kill you."

"But they might spare Mai's life if he brings me along."

"They *might*, if the Guildmaster happens to be in a forgiving mood. But I wouldn't count on that, Aghat. He feels very personally about the whole thing."

She shook her head. The calm set of her face told him that she had made her decision and no one could possibly sway it.

"If you go," Kyth said, "you will negate everything Mai fought for when he spared your life."

Her full lips folded into a grim line. "He put his life on the line for me."

"It was his choice to make."

She looked away. "I don't expect you to understand."

He sighed. He *did* understand. It was just that letting her give herself up was unthinkable. He couldn't possibly allow it to happen.

"I don't mean to sound too dramatic," Raishan said, "but I'm sure you are aware of the kind of punishment warranted by Aghat Mai's disobedience? If he is indeed being recalled because the Guildmaster knows what he has done–"

She shrugged. "Whatever our Guildmaster chooses to throw at Mai, he stands a much higher chance if I fight by his side. Two Diamonds would be extremely hard to beat for warriors of any skill."

"With the abundance of ranked warriors in our Guild…" Raishan stopped, spreading his hands in a wordless gesture.

"I hope it doesn't come to that, Aghat Raishan. If Mai brings me along, he would at least partially be making up for his mistake. Aghat Oden Lan would likely accept my surrender, and, if he does, he would be more or less obliged to spare Mai's life. He would be foolish not to."

"He might surprise you," Egey Bashi said under his breath.

Kara shook her head. "Mai is one of our best. The Guild simply cannot afford to lose him. I'm sure, if I give myself up and credit Mai with bringing me back, our Guildmaster would grab the chance to erase the whole thing and give Mai full pardon – in exchange, perhaps, for a nominal punishment to keep up appearances."

"I'm sure you know that, at the very least, there are no guarantees," Raishan said.

She shrugged.

"You're playing very dangerous games, Aghat Kara."

"Mai shouldn't be the one to pay for my actions."

Kyth bit his lip. Kara had violated her orders to save Kyth's life. In the end, he was the one responsible for all this mess.

"If you go back to your Guild," he said quietly, "I'm going with you."

Her eyes gleamed as she looked back at him. She was about to speak, but at that moment Mother Keeper stepped between them.

"Forgive the interruption," she said. "But if Magister Egey Bashi wanted you to meet him in the gallery, shouldn't we all be on our way?"

"Right." Kara flung the trailing edge of the cloak over her shoulder and strode out of the chamber. The rest of them followed.

4
THE GALLERY

King Evan glanced at the parchment in his hand, marveling at the way the Majat Guildmaster managed to write an entire page of text without putting any information into it beyond what his messenger was able to reveal in a few short words. He lowered the letter and looked at the two men standing motionless in front of him. They looked nearly exact opposites – Magister Egey Bashi, a dark, heavily built man with a scarred face, wearing a pristine white Keeper's robe, and Mai, a slender youth in dashing black, his skin so smooth that even the young maidens at court envied it. Both men stared at him with blank expressions that warned Evan of the difficult conversation he was facing.

"What's the urgency, Magister?" he asked.

The Keeper cleared his throat. "Forgive me, Your Majesty. I wanted to prevent you from taking any irreversible steps. I hoped if you and Aghat Mai could discuss the situation…"

The King glanced at the parchment again. Beneath the irritation he often felt when talking to the Keeper, he was inwardly grateful for the interruption. Letting Mai go was the last thing he wanted to do. On top of the Diamond's superior skills and his unique ability to resist the Kaddim's mind control magic, he had developed a special bond with his bodyguard. Mai was one of the very few people he could trust with his life. He could think of no other man he would rather have by his side.

"What's this all about, Aghat Mai?" he asked.

Mai held a pause. His gaze, clear like a smoothly polished mirror, warned against any attempts to pry.

"I understand your concern about letting me go, Your Majesty. But Aghat Xandel is quite competent. He'll do a fine job on the Pentade."

Evan leaned closer, trying in vain to catch some feeling in Mai's blue-gray eyes. "You know bloody well this is not about competence, Aghat. I choose my men carefully, especially my personal bodyguards. In these uncertain times, I want *you* on the Pentade, and that's that. If I were to let you go, I'd want assurance that you'd be coming back."

The pause was longer this time. "I'm afraid, Your Majesty, that won't be possible."

"Even if I pay triple to hire you by name?"

"I can't really speak for the Guildmaster but I strongly believe it wouldn't work. Not in this case."

"Why not?"

A shadow ran through Mai's eyes, a wave that rippled the mirror surface of his clear gaze.

"I'm being relieved of duty," he said.

Evan stared. "You're too young to be relieved of duty, Aghat. You're – what, twenty-four?"

"Twenty-five, last week."

Evan gave him an appraising glance. The man looked no older than nineteen. His slender body, sculpted of lean, wiry muscle, emanated force that seemed to make the air around him tingle. A touch of arrogance in his gaze spelled quiet challenge, enclosing him like invisible armor. He was one of their Guild's best, a spearhead of the deadly force that made the Majat a supreme power throughout the lands. There was *no way* someone like Mai could be relieved of duty in his prime years and be unavailable for further assignments.

"I know for a fact that Diamonds serve on assignments well into their forties, Aghat. The previous Pentade leader – Aghat Seldon – was forty-seven when he retired. You're too damn valuable to your Guild to be relieved of duty at your age."

Mai smiled. "Normally you would be right, Your Majesty. But this is a special case."

"Enlighten me, Aghat."

Mai kept his silence.

"If you don't tell me," Evan said, "I'll ask others. Perhaps Aghat Raishan, or Kara, could offer more information?"

Alarm glinted in Mai's eyes.

"Not Kara," he said.

"Why not?"

"She can't get involved in this, Your Majesty."

Evan raised his eyebrows, but before he could speak further the doors at the back of the gallery opposite to the throne room burst open, admitting Kyth with a large group in his wake. Evan saw Raishan and Mother Keeper stride beside him, followed by Alder, Ellah, and finally Kara, wrapped head to toe in a blue-and-black royal cloak. She threw off her hood as she walked, her violet eyes gleaming as she approached with a purposeful stride.

The airy gallery suddenly felt as crowded as an outer audience hall on a busy morning.

Kara stepped past the King and halted in front of Mai. Their gazes locked.

"He's here because of me, isn't he?" she said.

Mai's eyes narrowed as they flicked to Raishan and Egey Bashi. Then he turned back to Kara, his face once again acquiring an expression of serenity.

"He's here on Guild business," he said.

She continued to hold his gaze. "Are you being recalled?"

Mai folded his arms on his chest in a slow, deliberate gesture.

"I fail to see how this is any of your business."

"You are not thinking of going, are you?" She leaned closer, the air around them so charged it caused Evan to take an inadvertent step back.

Mai glanced at Raishan and Egey Bashi again, but the two men responded with calm stares.

"Like I said," Mai continued, "none of your business. No offense, Aghat Kara."

Kara nodded with the grim expression of one whose worst fears had been confirmed. "I'm coming with you."

"No, you're not."

She lifted her chin. "Is there anything you can do to stop me?"

Mai's eyes flared. His hand darted to his back, flicking his double-bladed staff out of its sheath. Almost simultaneously, Kara drew her two narrow swords with a long silken sound.

Before anyone else could react, Raishan darted forward, throwing himself between Mai and Kara. In the ensuing silence, the three Diamonds glared at each other.

"Stand down, both of you," Raishan said. "You're not planning to fight each other, are you? Not in the presence of the King and the royal heir, I hope."

Mai held still for a moment. Then he slowly sheathed his weapon. His eyes slid over Kara, who stepped back and withdrew her swords. For a brief moment Mai's gaze softened before resuming its tranquil, impenetrable expression.

"You'll have to kill me to stop me, Aghat Mai," Kara said.

"This has nothing to do with you."

She held his gaze. "Prove it. Show me the Guildmaster's letter."

He slowly relaxed his arms. A distant smile creased his lips. "My correspondence with the Guildmaster is private, Aghat. It doesn't concern you."

"Look me in the eye," she said distinctly, "and *swear* that this letter doesn't concern me."

"It doesn't concern you."

"You're lying."

"You're out of line, Aghat. I'm your senior and my correspondence with the Guildmaster is none of your business."

She smiled. "I'm no longer a member of the Guild. Your seniority means nothing to me, Aghat Mai."

Again, his gaze wavered before returning to tranquility as he looked at her.

"You may think that all Guild business revolves around you, Aghat," he said. "But I assure you, you're wrong."

"He knows I'm alive, doesn't he?" she asked quietly.

There was a pause.

"Like I said. You'll have to kill me to stop me from coming with you, Aghat Mai." She turned and strode out of the gallery. After a moment Kyth turned and ran after her.

"Would somebody care to tell me what all that was about?" Evan asked as their footsteps died away in the hollow stone passage.

Raishan and Mai exchanged a glance, but kept their silence.

"*I'll* tell you, Your Majesty," Egey Bashi said.

Mai shot him a warning glance, but the Keeper ignored it.

"Do you remember, Your Majesty, how keen the Kaddim Brotherhood was to capture Prince Kythar, to ensure that his power to resist their mind control magic did not threaten their plans?"

"Yes." Evan felt puzzled. The explanation wasn't going the way he expected.

"That time, Kara was able to acquire resistance to the Kaddim. With her fighting skill, this made her a serious obstacle to the Brotherhood's plans. As long as she remained by Prince Kythar's side, her protection made the Prince invincible to any Kaddim attack. So, they devised a plan to remove Kara once and for all."

"A plan, Magister?" Evan still had no idea where this was going.

"Yes, Your Majesty. A very devious and complex one, too. One of the Kaddim Brothers, Nimos, who was somehow able to gain very detailed knowledge about the way the Majat Guild operates, forced Kara to disobey her orders and abandon an assignment. She did it to save Prince Kythar's life. The way it was presented to the Majat made it look as if she disobeyed her orders because of her love for the Prince. As a result, the Majat Guildmaster had no choice but to send a killer after her – Aghat Mai, who had been specially trained for the task."

Evan listened, captivated. He noticed Mai's narrowed eyes, betraying emotion so uncharacteristic for his normally calm and composed bodyguard. Clearly the Keeper's words were true – and for some reason they were affecting Mai much more than anything else he had ever observed. His skin prickled. The Majat Guild's affairs had always been too complex for an outsider. How could the Kaddim figure them out?

"With the help of another Guild member," Egey Bashi went on, "Aghat Mai was successful in overtaking Kara and defeating her in battle, but he chose to disobey his orders and spare her life. He made it seem as if she were dead, but the blow he struck her with wasn't fatal, and he was able to revive her later on. This was a violation of his assignment and the Majat Code. I believe that he is now summoned back to the Guild to pay for his disobedience. Aren't you, Aghat Mai?"

A long, charged glance passed between the two men.

"Is this true, Aghat Mai?" Evan asked.

Mai shifted from foot to foot.

"With all due respect, Your Majesty, I fail to see the reason for this conversation." He slid a cold glance over the Keeper. "I am being recalled by orders from our

Guildmaster. The Majat Guild has sent my replacement for the Pentade to fulfill our obligations to the crown. That's the end of it. The rest doesn't concern you. Or the Magister, for that matter."

"It concerns us all very closely, Aghat Mai," Egey Bashi said. "For a very simple reason. You and Kara are the only two Diamonds who can resist the Kaddim's mind control powers. We are at war, and both of you are critical to our chances of winning it. If one, or both of you, go back to your Guild to be killed, in order to uphold the Majat Code, it would be a bloody waste; one that we can't afford at the moment."

"Kara's not going."

"Like she said, you can't do much to stop her, Aghat. Can you?"

Mai's eyes darted to Raishan with an expression that, for a fleeting moment, seemed like a plea.

Raishan shook his head. "I won't take sides in this one, Aghat Mai. I'd hate to see either of you die, and I can't possibly overlook the fact that with Kara's help you do stand more of a chance."

"Against the entire Guild?"

"I was hoping it wouldn't come to that."

Mai smiled. "That's because you haven't read the Guildmaster's letter."

"I see."

"Can't you refuse to go?" Evan asked.

Mai's smile faded. "If I do, I'll renounce everything I am. Given that it's only my life that's at stake here, I'd rather not."

"So, you'd rather go there and face certain death?"

"I'll take my chances."

"From what I heard just now," Evan said, "there won't be much of a chance."

Mai's gaze became distant.

"I don't think our Guildmaster fully understands what he's up against. The Kaddim Brotherhood is set to destroy everyone, and recent events suggest the Majat Guild is not immune to its powers. I must make sure Aghat Oden Lan is aware of this, whatever he chooses to do to me afterward."

Evan stared at him in disbelief. "How can you think like this, Aghat Mai, when they're effectively ordering you to return and be executed?"

"My life's not important, Your Majesty. Not when the integrity of our Guild is at stake."

He looked calm as he said it, as if there was nothing out of the ordinary in his assertion. Looking into his impassive face, Evan could see no room for further argument.

"If that is the case," he said, "I tend to agree with Aghat Raishan. With Kara's help you do stand more of a fighting chance."

"If she gets involved in this," Mai said quietly, "there will be no return."

"It seems to me she's already involved."

Mai shook his head. "Her situation is unprecedented. No one's ever survived in her circumstances. My guess is, as long as she remains free, the Majat Guild has no idea what to do with her. But if she follows me back to the Guild..." His gaze darkened, but before Evan could catch the emotion that passed within, there was a barely perceptible glint, as if invisible shutters inside his eyes slid into place, hiding Mai's feelings behind an expression of calm tranquility.

"I violated my orders," Mai went on, "so that she could live. If she goes with me and dies protecting me, all this would be for nothing. You'll lose a prize fighter who can help you against the Kaddim. If no one else here sees it this way, maybe you would, Magister?" He turned to the Keeper.

Egey Bashi shook his head. "I'd hate to lose either one of you. If you really must go, Aghat Mai, then I'm the one who should be going with you to explain the situation to your Guildmaster."

Mai smiled. "I heard you tried, when he gave the order to kill Kara."

"True," the Keeper said grimly. "He feels quite personally about her, doesn't he?"

"Yes, he does." Mai exchanged a glance with Raishan.

"But we have to do *something*," Egey Bashi insisted.

"In this particular case, Magister, the best thing you could do is let me go, and make sure Kara stays behind. I've sent a messenger raven to the Guildmaster to explain the situation in advance of my arrival. There's a chance he will listen. And if not, you'll at least have Kara to fight on your side."

"Do you really think you have a chance, Aghat?" Egey Bashi asked.

Mai averted his gaze.

"I didn't think so. From my personal experience, Aghat Oden Lan can be quite stubborn, especially when he feels personally about something."

"All the more reason to make sure Kara doesn't get anywhere near him. Not until he's had a chance to relieve his anger by punishing someone else."

"You."

Mai's lips twitched. "I have a plan."

"A good one, I hope."

"As good as it can be, under the circumstances."

"Why don't you share it with Kara? Maybe she'll agree to stay behind?"

Mai let out a barely perceptible sigh. "Not as good as that, I'm afraid."

Egey Bashi shook his head. "If *you* can't prevent her from coming, Aghat Mai, what do you suggest *I* do to stop her? Unlike you, I can't even stand up to her in a fight for more than, oh, three seconds?"

Mai shrugged. "Perhaps you can persuade Aghat Raishan to help?"

"I will not take sides in this one," Raishan repeated. "This is between you and Kara, Aghat Mai."

Mai's face became stern. "Fine." He turned to Evan. "I'll need my token back, Your Majesty. If I may, I suggest we go back into the throne room so that you can give it to me and accept Xandel's, or things might get out of hand."

Evan ran his gaze around the silent faces.

"I hate to lose you, Aghat Mai," he said. "But if you insist there's no other way, let's go back to the audience chamber and finish the show, shall we?"

5

ARCHERY

Kyth followed Kara all the way to her room and paused in the doorway, looking inside.

"Come in," she said. "And close the door before somebody else sees me."

The room was small and bare. Light finding its way through a small window did little to illuminate simple furnishings that consisted of the bare necessities with no embellishments of any kind. A sleeping cot stood by the wall next to a large trunk, two chairs, and a weapon stand in the corner. Kyth had been to this room before, and like before he couldn't stop wondering how Kara could possibly find such a place acceptable for living.

He sat in the indicated chair, watching her sweep through the room, collecting things into her travel pack. Her face was drawn and composed, showing deep concentration on her task. She looked so distant that his heart ached. He knew that their relationship, while it had lasted, was too good to be true, but it still hurt to see how quickly she retreated back into her Majat world at the first signs of trouble. As she darted around the room gathering her scarce belongings, she looked worlds away.

"Do you really have to go with him?" Kyth asked.

"Yes."

"Why?"

She paused and turned to face him. She seemed calm, but knowing her well, Kyth recognized the air of detachment that spoke of turmoil within.

"I owe him my life," she said. "It's a debt I must repay."

"By getting yourself killed?"

She lowered the shirt she had been folding. "I won't get killed. Mai needs my help, that's all."

"Your Guild has issued a death warrant against you. What do you think will happen when you go back there?"

She shook her head. "If Mai goes there alone, it will be worse."

"But what if he's telling the truth? What if this has nothing to do with you?"

She walked over and stopped directly in front of him.

"Do you believe that yourself, Kyth?"

He rose from his seat so that their faces were level. He ached to put his arms around her, to hold her. He hoped there was a way to make it all go away. But deep inside he knew she was right. Mai was being punished for sparing her life. And she was about to commit herself to sharing this punishment.

He swallowed, holding her gaze. "No."

She nodded and turned away, but he reached forward and caught her by the arm. She slowly turned back to him, their faces so close that he felt her warmth and the barely perceptible smell of wild flowers emanated by her skin.

Her closeness made his head spin. He couldn't bear the thought of losing her.

"Is there anything I can do to make you stay?" he asked quietly.

She ran her hand along the side of his face. His arms responded on their own accord, enfolding her, pulling her close. She rested her face against his shoulder, cradled in his embrace. For a brief instant it seemed as if everything were all right, again. Then she drew back.

"Remember when I told you I'm different, Kyth?"

He nodded. She had told him early on, when he made his first advances and she had tried to warn him off. He knew she believed it, but it never made sense to him.

"Of course you are different. You are the most amazing woman in existence."

She shook her head. "I'm a trained killer, Kyth. I may look to you like a normal woman, but I'm not. For a brief moment when we were together, you made me very happy. But you know, as well as I do, that it can't possibly work out between us. This life – it just isn't for me."

His heart quivered. "It *can* be. If you give it a chance."

"No."

"Why?"

"Because," she said, "I can't renounce what I am. Even if my Guild casts me out, I can't stop being a Diamond Majat."

He leaned forward, looking searchingly into her face. "Are you telling me everything?"

She frowned. "Yes. Why?"

He swallowed. "It's because of Mai, isn't it?"

She stepped back, watching him, wide-eyed. "Are you jealous?"

Kyth frowned. "No. It's just... You do care about him, don't you?"

"Not the way you mean."

"Which way, then?"

She sighed. "I admire his skill. And... I owe him. It's just like any other debt, but with higher stakes. I can't possibly stay behind when Mai is going there to face punishment for saving my life. If one of us must die, it has to be me."

"But—"

Her quick glance stopped him. "I'm sorry it has to be this way, Kyth. But I'm going, and that's that. Believe me, it will hurt less if we say our goodbyes now rather than dragging it out."

"No. You got into this whole ordeal because of me. If you truly must go, then I'm coming with you."

"Don't be ridiculous. Your kingdom needs you. Your power is the only hope against the Kaddim. Besides, there's nothing you can do against the Majat Guild."

"And you can?"

"I don't know. But the Guild is the only home I've ever had. They gave me my life. They can take it away if they really must." She turned away, shoving things into her pack.

Kyth sat down on her bare bed, watching her. He felt numb. His mind just couldn't possibly enfold everything that was happening. The woman he loved, breaking up with him so that she could run off with another man to face certain death.

"Mai seemed very determined not to let you go along," he said. "If you go with him, he'll just keep fighting you all the way. You might kill each other before you even reach the Guild."

She shook her head. "I'll find a way to convince him. Once he sees there's no return, he will accept me. And you – you must help me."

"*Help* you?" Kyth raised his eyebrows. Helping her to run off to her death was the last thing he wanted to do.

"Don't talk to anyone of my decision, or try to use anyone's help to stop me. Just accept it. Please?" She slid forward and sat next to him, clenching his face in her palms, turning it to her. "Will you?"

He swallowed. "You are asking me to help in what I believe is equal to suicide."

"If you don't help, Kyth, I'll do it anyway. You must know that by now."

He exhaled slowly. "I do."

She quickly leaned forward and brushed his lips with hers.

The touch sent warmth through his body – and, just as suddenly, the realization of what was happening hit him full in the face. She was leaving him. She was going to die. She had made up her mind, and there was nothing he could possibly do to stop her.

He swallowed. "All the times we were together... You felt the same way I did. I *know* it."

She sighed. "I felt happy with you, yes. But I now know for certain that it wasn't meant to be. I hope you can accept that. I always told you, no promises, remember?"

"Yes." She had said that, just like she had told him how different she was. It's just that Kyth had never believed it. To him, she was always, above all, a beautiful woman, and the moments they spent together made Kyth the happiest man in the world. If she felt the way he did, how could anything else matter at all?

"Forgive me," she said. "I never meant to hurt you." She stepped away, once again picking up her half-finished pack. "Goodbye, Kyth. And, thank you. For everything."

Kyth could barely feel his way as he stumbled out of the side door into the castle's garden. His hands clenched into fists until they felt numb, his entire body shivering with the effort of holding back tears.

He could not bear the thought of losing Kara. Her resolve to return to her Guild and face punishment, his inability to sway her decision, left him shattered. But worse than that, the fact that she broke up with him just didn't make sense. They had been so happy together. Or so he had thought.

Was she really as different as she tried to make him believe? Was she incapable of loving anyone?

Or, was it that Kyth was not the right man for her all along?

The thought stung him as he blindly wandered along the garden paths. The gleaming waters of the Crown Lake shone unbearably bright through the slits of the outer castle wall. He had always loved watching the lake and the ever-shifting colors reflecting off the water. But now, his gut wrenched as he glanced that way. The last time he and Kara had been sitting together was on top of the wall overlooking the lake, watching the sunset. Only a few days ago, but it felt like an eternity. Would they ever be able to do that again?

He steered deeper into the grove of apple trees, but their whispering shade brought no comfort. His thoughts were going in circles. He was losing Kara. She was going to die. And even if, by a miracle, she survived, she may no longer choose to be a part of his life. It stung even more to think that everyone else, starting with his father, would feel nothing but joy at such a turn of events. A crown prince could never marry a hired guard, even one released from her former duties. The kingdom had enough trouble dealing with the fact that Kyth was the first royal heir in history to possess magic, a feat that, until recently, had marked him as an outlaw and an ungodly abomination. It had taken a lot of effort on his father's part to change this law, and some of his subjects were still coming to terms with it. To marry a former Majat warrior would be taking things too far.

Kyth had always believed things would work out somehow. He loved Kara with all his heart and could never think of any other woman in his life. Even now, when she had decided to leave him, he couldn't imagine he would ever recover enough to be with anyone else.

A movement ahead caught his eye. He froze, peering through the greenery into the sunlit glade adjoining the back palace wall.

Inadvertently, he had wandered too close to the archers' practice range. And it was occupied. As he watched, an arrow whistled past and hit the very center of the bullseye.

Kyth narrowed his eyes. The feathers on the arrow shaft looked unfamiliar, green and yellow. Who could this possibly be?

He carefully edged through the bushes, heading for the archer, invisible behind the protrusion of the wall. As he rounded the bend, he stopped, gaping.

A slender young woman with long auburn hair stood by the wall, taking aim. She held a Lakeland bow so long that, when raised, it reached down to her knee. He couldn't see her face, but the colors of her dress, green with a thin yellow trim, left no doubt of her identity. Lady Celana, heiress of the rival royal house Illitand. After her father, Duke Daemur Illitand, had temporarily fallen under Kaddim influence, she had been staying at the Tandarian court in his place, serving on the royal council with fervor, in an attempt to diminish her father's mistakes in the eyes of the King.

Kyth knew Lady Celana to be highly intelligent, with a grasp of politics that went far beyond her tender age of seventeen. But he had never seen her do anything physical. To think that she was also an adept archer...

He watched the royal lady release the arrow, which hit the target very close to the first one. Then he gently cleared his throat.

Lady Celana spun around with unladylike speed. Her startled expression slowly relaxed into a smile as she recognized Kyth.

"Your Royal Highness." She sank into a deep curtsey.

"Forgive the interruption, my lady," Kyth said awkwardly. He had been raised in a Forestland village to protect his identity, and even after all his time at court, he still found it difficult to get used to all the bowing and curtseying from high nobles.

She lowered her bow and watched him with a chilling intelligence he had always found disconcerting. Her eyes missed nothing as she slid her gaze over his face, likely bearing the trace of recent tears, his ripped sleeve, which had caught on a rose bush as he stalked unseeingly through the grounds, his aching hands, their knuckles still white from the force with which he had been clenching his fists, now slowly relaxing by his sides. She was in no hurry to start the conversation, for which Kyth felt inwardly grateful. He was in no mood for court pleasantries.

"I had no idea you were an archer," he said.

She smiled. "It's just a passtime, Your Highness. The weather was too fine to stay indoors."

"I– I seem to have taken a wrong turn in the garden," Kyth said. "I should leave you to it."

She curtseyed again. "Pray be careful, Prince Kythar. If you had come out into the open on the target side of the range…"

Against reason, he smiled. "Having witnessed your skill, I am certain I was in no danger, my lady."

She blushed and lowered her eyes.

"You are too kind," she murmured.

Kyth bowed and made his exit, back through the thicket toward the castle wall. Trying to keep his eyes away from the sweeping view of the lake, he circled the wall all the way to the front courtyard and back into his quarters. To keep his promise to Kara, he was supposed to act like nothing was going on. He was due in his father's council chambers in half an hour to discuss the message from the Monastery, and he had no intention of showing up there on the verge of tears, wearing disheveled clothes.

Strangely enough, the thought of his encounter with Lady Celana brought another smile to his face as he made his way upstairs. He was not used to women blushing so deeply at his compliments, especially not those as smart and level-headed as he knew Celana to be. Was it possible that she liked him?

He dismissed the thought. It hardly mattered. Besides, he had more pressing things to deal with.

6

REINCARNATE

In the red sunset glow the courtyard shadows bled with deep, velvety darkness. Low sunbeams licked the roughly hewn stones of the Great Shal Addim Temple, throwing the shadow of its jagged outline across the inner Monastery grounds. From his position by the wall, Kaddim Tolos could easily observe activity without drawing attention to himself.

Dozens of eyes followed the pacing figure of the Reincarnate with the reverence of the newly converted, the row of black-robed shapes against the walls of the courtyard so still that they appeared inanimate. Even the sight of the dead body lying motionless at his feet couldn't possibly command as much fear as his wiry figure, enfolded in a private aura of chill.

Tolos followed the Reincarnate's gaze down to the dead man. Kaddim Nimos, one of the most valuable members of the Brotherhood, struck down by an unfortunate blow that was never supposed to happen. It was amazing to see how death could rob anyone of their commanding presence, reducing even the most powerful of men to a pale, drawn shell, a useless inanimate object. This transformation seemed even more incredible for the Kaddim, who could then be resurrected to their former glory. Tolos hoped that it wasn't too late in this case. They needed Nimos for their plans to succeed. Besides, a Kaddim Brother's life was too precious to lose in something as simple and trivial as a sword fight.

"How did he die?" the Reincarnate asked. His voice had the same quality as his movements, its deep sound entrancing listeners like the coiling dance of a poisonous snake.

The figures closest to the Reincarnate exchanged nervous glances, their searching gazes venturing further, toward Tolos's silent figure standing at the side.

Cowards. Can't they do anything without me? Tolos stepped forward and bowed his head.

"His death was instant, Cursed Master," he said, keeping his voice appropriately low, yet clear enough to carry through the hollow stone courtyard. "A blade between the collarbones."

The Reincarnate prodded the dead man's head with the tip of his boot. The head rolled sideways, exposing the gaping wound at the base of the throat. There was no blood around the narrow triangular entrance wound. The blade had gone deep enough to reach the heart.

"Kaddim Nimos was not only a great master of his Gift," the Reincarnate said. "He was also a formidable swordsman."

He raised his head and met Tolos's gaze. It was unnerving to see the man's irises, whose bloodshot redness filled his eyes with an inhuman glow. Tolos knew that his own eyes, whose pale brown bordered on yellow, were equally unnerving to some of the weaker members of the Brotherhood, but he could never fully understand how they felt, outside the rare moments when the Cursed Master himself graced him with a direct look. He felt a chill run down his spine as he returned the gaze.

"The man who struck him down," he said, "was a Majat of the Diamond rank."

The Reincarnate nodded. The setting sun chose that exact moment to slide behind the main dome of the Shal Addim Temple, submerging the courtyard fully into shadows. In the dusk the Reincarnate's eyes glowed like coals.

"Aghat Mai."

"Yes, Cursed Master."

The Reincarnate threw another thoughtful look at the body by his feet.

"The Majat are becoming a problem. How was he able to withstand our power?"

Tolos sighed. The fight at the Illitand Castle had been a disaster, with the Kaddim warriors pitched against three combat-effective Diamond Majat who appeared to be immune to Kaddim mind control. It was not supposed to have happened this way.

"We don't know, Master," he said. "We are still investigating. We believe Prince Kythar Dorn had something to do with it. His ability to resist us can apparently be passed on to others."

The Reincarnate shook his head. "His ability is a problem indeed: one that we are hopefully about to address once and for all."

"Indeed, Cursed Master," Tolos mumbled. "As soon as the Majat are out of the way, we should have no trouble dealing with the Prince and his ability."

"*He who commands the Majat commands the Empire*," the Reincarnate said quietly.

Tolos raised his eyebrows. "I beg your pardon, Master?"

The Reincarnate chuckled. "An old saying, Kaddim. Yet, it couldn't be more true. The Majat's political independence, combined with their military strength, has made them a dangerous weapon. Their alliance, if they ever choose to form any, could guarantee victory in any war. Yet, their desire for independence in this case should become their undoing. The strike we are planning will strip the Majat of their power once and for all."

"With Our Lord's will, Cursed Master," Tolos said.

The Reincarnate nodded. "Have you delivered the news of Aghat Mai's treason to the Majat Guild?"

Tolos bowed. "Yes, Cursed Master."

"And I believe you've also sent the message to the King from the Conclave?"

Tolos bowed. "As you instructed, Master."

The Reincarnate's red eyes lit up with a gleam of interest. "Whose head did you send him, Kaddim Tolos?"

"The Chief Inquisitor, Brother Valdos."

"I thought he was one of ours."

"He proved... meddlesome, Master. I felt he was too much trouble alive. Besides, Kaddim Farros's men could handle the inquisition much better. His Power to Kill–"

"Inquisition is not about killing, Kaddim Tolos. It's about keeping a man alive for as long as necessary. But these are minor things, of course. We have bigger plots to unfold."

"Indeed, Master."

"Good. Then, things are in motion. How did the Majat Guildmaster take the news?"

Tolos suppressed a smile. The Guildmaster's reaction had been priceless, a triumph to the Kaddim's plans. Talking to him had been one of the most enjoyable missions in decades.

"Aghat Oden Lan is beside himself with fury. He sent a messenger to the King's court right away."

The Reincarnate nodded. "I trust Kaddim Xados is still on the inside at the Majat Guild, doing his job?"

"He is," Tolos said quietly. "I spoke to him when I was there. He believes if Aghat Mai takes the bait, the conflict could potentially be amplified enough to bring down most of their top Gems. Added to the fact that the parcel we sent to King Evan will likely drive him to the Majat for help..."

"It all hangs on a delicate balance," the Reincarnate said.

"Indeed, Cursed Master." Tolos glanced at the body sprawled at the Reincarnate's feet. "Kaddim Nimos was always the one to fine-tune these details. His help would be instrumental in putting the final touches to our plan."

The Reincarnate nodded thoughtfully, his eyes sliding over the dead man.

Few outside the Brotherhood were aware that the Kaddim power did not grace similarly each of its leaders. Nimos's strength had always been the mind magic, an ability not only to communicate with other members of the Brotherhood but also to sense people's thoughts and, occasionally, to pry into the minds of others and influence their decisions. There was no one like Nimos when it came to playing mind games. This was how he was able to gather invaluable information about the Majat Guild and, eventually, find a way to infiltrate it, by placing their man into a key command post about ten years ago. Few of his talent had survived the bloodbath that had marked the decease of the Old Empire centuries ago.

The Reincarnate bent over the corpse to continue his inspection. "You preserved him well, Kaddim. He died weeks ago, yet the revival will be easy."

Tolos smiled, lips only. One of the things he was valued for was honesty. He would never take the credit due to another.

"Kaddim Haghos took care of the body," he said. "I was in charge of our escape. Prince Kythar Dorn managed not only to resist us and protect the others, he threw our power right back at us. His Ghaz Alim is far too strong."

The Reincarnate lifted his face and gave him a long look. "His ability is perhaps the only thing that could threaten our plans for the Majat. We must prevent him from fully developing his powers before we take care of him."

Tolos nodded. "The Prince is immersed in his love affair with the Diamond, Kara. Once she falls victim to our plans he will be so heartbroken he will pose no threat."

"We will see the new dawn of the Empire soon, Kaddim."

Tolos bowed. "*Adi Kados*, Cursed Master. We cherish your wisdom."

"*Adi Kados*," echoed a murmur through the courtyard.

The Reincarnate dismissed the ceremonial hail with a wave of his hand. He knelt down on the ground beside Nimos's body and lifted the lifeless head, holding it between his palms. Then he leaned over and touched the pale lips with his.

It looked like a kiss, sickening in ways that went beyond the mere fact of a wiry, middle-aged man engaged in an intimate act with a dead body. Nimos's limp form shuddered as the Cursed Master bore onto him with a force that could be mistaken for passion by an unknowing observer. The air around them crackled.

Tolos watched with a mix of disgust and fascination. No one in the Brotherhood, besides the Reincarnate, possessed the true Power to Resurrect, which was why it had taken weeks to revive Nimos from his unfortunate death. He felt relieved as he finally saw the pale fingers of the corpse's hand twitch. Nimos's eyes opened, revealing the blackness without irises that made the Kaddim's gaze so frightening in its own way, no less than that of Tolos or the Reincarnate himself.

The Cursed Master drew away and rose to his feet, absentmindedly brushing the dust off his robe. Tolos hurried forward and helped Nimos up from the ground.

"He will not be able to speak until his throat heals," the Reincarnate said calmly.

Tolos forced his eyes away from the gaping wound.

"Take good care of him," the Reincarnate said. "And try not to get anyone else killed. That time vortex you summoned to pull everyone out of the Illitand Hall was an impressive tribute to your special power, but it did spend a lot of our resources. I must return to the Bengaw Outpost as soon as I can to replenish them. I hope you and Kaddim Nimos can complete what you started and that you will have good news upon my return."

Tolos bowed, watching the Reincarnate stride out of the courtyard. Then he gestured to the nearest cloaked figures, who took Nimos by the arms and carefully led him away.

Their work on bringing down the Majat Guild, started over a decade ago, had seen many setbacks, including the most recent ones, when two of the Guild's best Diamonds were able to acquire resistance to the Kaddim's mind control. Tolos hoped that the Kaddim's recent scheming had set their plans back on track. With luck, both Kara and Mai were on their way to answer the Guildmaster's summons, and King Evan was about to respond to the message from the Monastery the only way he could. Nimos, once fully recovered, would help to finish the rest.

Soon, the Majat Guild would be so crippled they would be unlikely to ever recover to their former glory, and the kingdom of Tallan Dar would finally cease to exist. He could not wait to see this happen.

7
PLANS

When Kyth entered the small council chamber adjoining the throne room, he was surprised to find it nearly empty. Besides his father, only three people sat around the small table by the window overlooking the stunning Crown Lake sunset. Kyth kept his back to it as he lowered into a chair opposite Mother Keeper, Egey Bashi, and Raishan.

The Majat Pentade was absent. Kyth knew why his father wanted to exclude them from the gathering, but he could only imagine what kind of an argument it must have caused.

"This isn't a formal council," King Evan said in response to Kyth's questioning glance. "And thus I only asked the people I can fully trust to be present."

Kyth nodded, even though he couldn't stop wondering. His father and Magister Egey Bashi had always been at odds, even if grudgingly respectful of each other. As for Raishan, he pledged no loyalty to the crown and was bound by the code of his Guild. Yet, under the circumstances, Kyth, for one, appreciated his father's decision to include Raishan in this gathering. The Diamond was the only man who could stop Kara from carrying out her insane plan to follow Mai to their Guild. He was also a reasonable and dispassionate man, likely to listen to Kyth's arguments in favor of such interference. True, Kyth had promised Kara to keep her decision secret, but he would never consider keeping such a foolish promise if he thought he could save her life by breaking it.

"Here, Kyth," Evan said. "Read this." He thrust a piece of parchment into Kyth's hands. Its spidery writing said:

As Your Majesty is undoubtedly aware, the Conclave does not consider outside appointments by the crown. Your wish to appoint the renegade priest Brother Bartholomeos the Holy Father of the Church was duly noted and we are grateful to Your Majesty for sending him our way. The renegade has now taken his rightful place in the Monastery dungeons and will await the decision of the Holy Justice regarding his fate.

We are duly informing Your Majesty of our intention to hold a new election by the Conclave at our earliest convenience and will keep you fully apprised of the proceedings and their outcome.

Signed:

the members of the Holy Conclave

Gurath 23rd, the Great Shal Addim Temple, Aknabar

"It is a wonder," Egey Bashi said darkly, "that they bothered to use any pleasantries at all when writing this letter."

"If you call the severed head they sent along a pleasantry, Magister..." The King spread his hands in a wordless gesture.

"I think," Mother Keeper said quietly, "it is quite clear that *this* Conclave is no longer run by the priests."

The King stared unseeingly into space.

"I see only one possible course of action," he said. "We must assemble an army and go to the Monastery to dislodge this hornets' nest and rescue Father Bartholomeos."

Mother Keeper shook her head. "The people of Tallan Dar would never support it, Your Majesty. They would never believe rumors of the Dark Brotherhood to be a sufficient reason to lead an open armed force against peaceful servants of Lord Shal Addim."

"*Peaceful*?" Evan threw another glance at the letter. Only now Kyth noticed a rust-colored splotch staining the corner of the parchment. He hastily placed the letter back on the table.

"You are right, of course, Your Majesty," Magister Egey Bashi said. "But common folk don't know that. If you were to lead such an army, this would result in a revolt."

Evan frowned. "Do you suggest I do nothing?"

Mother Keeper shook her head. "Not at all. A response is warranted, and fast. But I think our only chance would be to send a small force of highly skilled warriors to rescue Father Bartholomeos." She glanced at Raishan.

"The Majat."

"Yes."

"How many?"

"How many can the crown afford?"

The King sighed. "Not enough, I'm afraid, even though I am willing to empty our treasury for this cause. If only Aghat Mai and Kara would agree to fight on our side. Their skill – as well as their ability to resist the Kaddim – could make all the difference." He looked at Kyth, but the Prince averted his eyes.

Seeing no response from his son, Evan turned to Raishan. "Can't we still try to convince either of them?"

The Diamond shook his head. "Aghat Mai has already left, Your Majesty. He seemed pretty determined."

Evan shrugged. "I must confess I still can't quite understand his decision."

"Aghat Mai is a man of duty," Raishan said. "He has always put the Guild above all else. For him, it is unthinkable to do otherwise."

Egey Bashi's lips twitched. "You forget that his current predicament resulted from disobeying his orders in the first place."

Raishan's face darkened. "I spoke to him about it. While personally I am glad that he chose to spare Kara's life, I have to say that it was very unlike Aghat Mai to do a thing like that."

"And how did he explain it?"

"In a strange sense, he believes he has done what's best for the Guild."

"I hope Master Oden Lan sees it that way."

Raishan sighed. "For Master Oden Lan, this has become personal. Far too personal for him to see straight."

Egey Bashi shifted in his seat. "Yes. I wouldn't want to be in Aghat Mai's place when they face each other over this. And, I can't escape the feeling that we should do our best to help this situation. We simply can't afford to lose a Diamond of Aghat Mai's skill, who is able to resist the Kaddim."

"Do you know how he and Kara managed to acquire this resistance?" the King asked.

The Keeper threw an uncomfortable glance at Kyth. "I am not exactly sure, Your Majesty. I believe that it comes from their deep ability to focus their minds."

"Can other Majat be taught this?"

The Keeper kept his eyes on Kyth, making the Prince feel disconcerted. *What does it have to do with me?*

"Perhaps, Your Majesty," Egey Bashi said. "I guess we'll never know without trying."

"Can it be used as a bargaining chip with the Majat Guild? We can offer that, if they accept our alliance, we could teach them to become resistant to the Kaddim. This way they would likely lend us more warriors than the crown could afford."

Egey Bashi tore his eyes from Kyth and turned back to the King. "It's a possibility, Your Majesty. But I believe Prince Kythar's skill is the key to our resistance. He is the only one who can always resist their powers and, on occasion, protect others."

I was also able to transfer this resistance to Kara. Kyth remembered how she first acquired the ability, defending him against an ambush in the castle courtyard. The memory stung him with new pain. She had been so close to him then. He believed that their love for each other had protected both of them – if indeed she had ever loved him. But he still wasn't sure how Mai had been able to do it. Certainly not because of Kyth's love for him.

"I can protect one person from their power," he said. "But I'm not sure I can teach anyone to be resistant when I'm not around."

Mother Keeper looked at him thoughtfully. "Perhaps, Your Highness, you can learn this with time – or at least learn to protect more people at once?"

Kyth thought about it. This possibility had haunted his dreams for quite a while, since he had first encountered Kaddim Tolos and his men. "Maybe. But I have no idea how."

Mother Keeper nodded, as if it was a done deal. "The Keepers can help you to develop your gift, Your Highness. In the meantime, the Majat Guild does not have to know that you have not mastered it to the full."

Kyth stared. "Are you suggesting we *lie* to them?"

The woman slid a calm glance over him and briefly met Egey Bashi's gaze. "It's called 'diplomacy', Your Highness." She turned to the King. "If I may, Your Majesty, I suggest you send Prince Kythar, along with representatives of the major powers in this kingdom, to bargain with the Majat."

Kyth opened his mouth to object but closed it at the look of enthusiasm in his father's eyes.

"Do you really think it can work?"

"I don't see why not, Your Majesty. I hope Magister Egey Bashi could also be included in the embassy. His experience with the Majat is unmatched, and he can also help to develop Prince Kythar's ability during their travels. If I may, I suggest you also send Prince Kythar's foster brother Alder, who is an emissary from the Forestlands. This way the Prince's request will be backed by more representatives throughout the kingdom. It would also be prudent to send Ellah, whose gift of truthsense makes her indispensable in any negotiations."

The King nodded. "Anyone else?"

"Lady Celana Illitand."

"But she–"

"–is the heiress of a major royal house whose claim to the throne is second to yours, Your Majesty. Her cooperation would be invaluable, especially since she is also, as I heard, well read and very intelligent. You will find no better scholar of the kingdom's law and politics, except, perhaps, Magister Egey Bashi himself."

"She's only seventeen!"

"All the more valuable, Your Majesty. The Keepers call this tactic 'smoke screen'. She could be in the midst of action, giving Prince Kythar advice when no one else expects it. Who would suspect anything intelligent from a maid of seventeen?"

The King shook his head. "If any harm should come to her in my care, it would mean war."

"If this embassy does not succeed, we are doomed anyway, Your Majesty. The Majat are our only hope. Remember the saying: 'He who commands the Majat commands the Empire'? It couldn't be more true in this case. We can only win this war if we can combine Prince Kythar's ability to resist the Kaddim with a Majat fighting force."

The King frowned. "The risk is too great, Mother Keeper."

"Think about it, Your Majesty. A small party like this can make it through the lands virtually unnoticed, and Aghat Raishan is more than capable of providing the necessary protection. And once they arrive, Aghat Oden Lan will have no choice but to listen. Even in his madness he is well aware of the danger posed by the Kaddim."

The King leaned back in his chair. "You are asking a lot, Mother Keeper. You want me to send my only son—"

"—into the safest stronghold in the world, Your Majesty. If you wish for his safety, no place could possibly be better than the Majat Guild."

"Last time he was there it didn't quite work. Besides, if what I heard about Master Oden Lan's feelings for Kara is true, my son may not be the most welcome sight in the Fortress."

Mother Keeper turned and met Kyth's eyes. "On the contrary, Your Majesty. If I'm not mistaken, the Guildmaster would likely take pity on the Prince."

"What do you mean by that?" Kyth demanded.

"She's left you, hasn't she?" the older woman asked quietly. "She broke up with you so that she can follow Aghat Mai to the Guild."

Kyth felt as if she had hit him in the gut. As long as he was the only one who knew the truth of what had happened in Kara's room behind a closed door, it felt as if it wasn't real, as if things still might change. By saying it out loud, Mother Keeper had just made it all true. Kara was no longer with Kyth. Whatever her decision, he had no claim to her anymore.

It hurt to think about it. It hurt so much that he couldn't even find enough fire to get angry at Mother Keeper for throwing it out into the open like this, in front of Egey Bashi and Raishan; in front of his father, who met the news with an inappropriately hopeful look.

Kyth let out a sigh. In the bigger picture, these things didn't matter anymore. And if Kyth could indeed lead this embassy, and fast, perhaps he could manage to trade his offer of protecting the Majat against the Kaddim for Kara's and Mai's lives?

He turned to the King.

"Let me do it, Father," he said. "We must act without delay for me to secure an alliance with the Majat Guild."

8
PURSUIT

Kara pulled her horse to a stop, peering into the tracks ahead. Mai had been covering an amazing distance each day, especially considering the fact that he had been avoiding the main road, leading the chase almost entirely over raw terrain. He was also being tricky, keeping mostly to the rocks so that his trail would be especially hard to follow. If, at the start of her chase, she had been secretly hoping to catch him by surprise, the last few days left her with no doubt that he knew she was following and was doing everything possible to prevent her from overtaking him. It took all she had just to keep up, without any signs of gaining on him.

She peered closer. There. A barely perceptible trace on the stone marked the hoof print she was looking for: a horseshoe with a slightly chipped surface, right near the middle. She smiled. If he kept this kind of pace over the rocks, his horse would lose its shoe in no time. And then, there would be no way for him to prevent Kara from catching up.

She urged her gray mare on, patting the tired animal on the neck. Just a couple of hours before dusk, and then they could finally have a good night's rest.

She raised her head from the trail and looked around. The glimmering shape of the Crown Lake at her back had disappeared days ago, giving way to the duller landscape of the Ridges' outcrops. She could see the snowy mountain peaks rising in the distance ahead, their gleaming white caps floating over the bluish haze at the horizon. Gray splotches of boulders rose out of the open fields spreading to either side of the trail, with patches of coarse silvery grass growing in between. Here and there she could also see the groves of mountain hazels, fleshy bushes huddled together against the bitter gusts of mountain wind. She could bet Mai spent each night hiding in one of those. Yet, with the way he kept off the main road, it was difficult to find which one.

The air here smelled of pine and wild aemrock, stirring up memories. She had grown up with these smells, roaming the Ridges' wilderness for as long as she could remember, until the Guild took her under their control. She shivered at the memory, fighting an unbidden sting in her eyes. The Guild's training had been cruel, yet it was the only home she had ever known. And now, she was unlikely to ever live there again.

She shook off her sadness. Life at court had made her soft. With the challenges she was facing she couldn't possibly afford to feel emotional at a simple gust of wind.

She urged her horse toward the hazel outgrowth looming up ahead. The sun was setting. This would be as good a place as any to spend the night.

Magister Egey Bashi set a punishing pace. Kyth welcomed it, since it provided good distraction. He secretly wished they could arrive at the Majat Guild before Mai and Kara, to have another chance to talk things out and possibly soften whatever welcome was waiting for them there, but that was too much to hope for. Still, he was glad of the strenuous marches each day that kept his mind fully occupied, even if he couldn't help feeling guilty every time he watched Ellah and Lady Celana dismount in the evening and get into their saddles in the morning.

Even the presence of Ellah and Alder, the people he had grown up with and always thought of as part of his family, could not ease the emptiness in his heart. Kara was no longer a part of his life. Worse, she was heading toward what would likely become her execution. And, despite the rush, Kyth and his party seemed to have no way of catching up with her.

Lady Celana had been surprisingly agreeable to the trip. She also looked amazingly fit in her pants outfit, riding a horse like a man, with her long Lakeland bow flung over her shoulder. Kyth had never imagined she would be such good company on the road. Yet, her presence brought him no comfort either. Worse, he found her longing glances disconcerting. If she truly cared for him, he pitied her. But he couldn't escape the feeling that the affection she showed him was more of a political nature. It must be, for he failed to see what a dashing lady like her could possibly see in him, besides the fact that he stood to inherit the throne. Everyone spoke of her as a woman with a highly calculating mind.

On the fifth day of travel they set camp in a hazelnut grove, one of those so abundant along the road from Tandar to the Ridges. Raishan and Alder busied themselves with the fire and Egey Bashi took a kettle to the nearby spring to fill it with fresh water. Kyth unrolled the blankets, watching Ellah and Celana talking quietly by the horses. He felt a sting of pain as he remembered the last time he had camped here. Kara had been with them then. They'd even kissed when they went into the grove to collect wood. It was when she had first told him how different she was, but he hadn't believed her. Had she been right all along?

A quiet chuckle on the other side of the glade drew Kyth's attention. He turned, feeling the small hairs on the back of his neck stand on end.

A robed man emerged from the shadows and walked toward them across the glade, leading a lizardbeast by the reins. As if in a nightmare, Kyth recognized his slight, bird-like features, disheveled brown hair standing in a halo around his head, his eyes, so dark that they seemed to have no irises, like the eyes of an owl.

Nimos.

"Long time no see, Your Highness," Nimos said.

Kyth's skin prickled. "It *can't* be you."

Nimos's smile widened. "And yet, here I am. Just like old times."

Kyth swallowed, half aware of Raishan, Alder, and Egey Bashi crowded by his sides.

"I *saw* you die."

"Isn't this a pleasant surprise?"

"More like a bad dream all over again."

Nimos cocked his head to one side, running a glance around the group. "I think of it more as an old friends' reunion. We have so many memories to share, haven't we?"

Ones I'd rather forget. Kyth drew himself up. "I can protect Aghat Raishan from your power, and he will kill you."

Nimos's smile widened. "Haven't you learned, Your Highness, that killing me simply doesn't work? I have been killed before by Aghat Mai, as you were kind enough to remark on just now. I assure you it wasn't the first time, either."

A chill crept down Kyth's spine. He knew the Kaddim Brother was deliberately trying to unsettle him and he hated to admit it was working. The thought of this man coming back from the dead after Mai's perfect blow was just too frightening to dwell on.

Grass rustled behind him and he saw a slender figure with flaming red hair step up to his side. *Lady Celana.*

Nimos turned to her in surprise.

"I read about Kaddim resurrection in the old chronicles," Celana said, keeping Nimos's gaze. In the sudden silence her voice rang clearly through the glade. "Even though you can indeed make a complete recovery, the experience is quite strenuous and requires considerable skill from other members of your Brotherhood. If Prince Kythar and Aghat Raishan cannot kill you forever, they could at least put you through the inconvenience again, and hopefully spare us the trouble of your company for quite some time."

Kyth looked at her in surprise, which was reflected in Nimos's eyes as he continued to stare. It was compelling to watch the discomfort her words caused the Kaddim Brother, even though he put on a great show of hiding it.

Nimos stepped back, folding into an elaborate court bow.

"My dear Lady Celana, I have no choice but to bow before your wisdom. What a change from the innocent young lady I had the pleasure of encountering in your father's castle."

She smiled but did not reply, her calm gaze smoothly reflecting his disconcerting look. Somewhat deflated, Nimos turned back to Kyth.

"All I wanted to do, Your Highness, was to express regret at my former actions and to share your joy that Aghat Kara is still alive. You know by now that I have, shamefully, been plotting her execution. Yet, when I learned what Aghat Mai had done, I felt so relieved. She truly deserves to live, and I am so glad that my plans for her did not work. You see, when I was planning this, I was not aware of Aghat Mai's feelings for her."

Kyth's heart missed a beat. *His feelings for her?* That couldn't possibly be true. As far as Kyth knew, Mai *had* no feelings for anyone. He was just a highly skilled man who always did the right thing. This was what made Mai so trustworthy. And yet... to think that Kara ran away from Kyth to join the man who had *feelings* for her...

He caught Egey Bashi's gaze. The Keeper's frown did nothing to reassure him. Did Egey Bashi know about this? Was Kyth the only one oblivious to what was going on? He glanced at Ellah, who, he knew, could sense if Nimos was telling the truth, but her face was carefully blank.

Nimos is just trying to disconcert me. He forced down his racing thoughts. Even though he hoped, against reason, that Kara would survive her ordeal and come back to him, at this moment in time it hardly mattered. He should focus on the upcoming bargain with the Majat Guild, which hopefully could include Kara's and Mai's lives. He should not give in to unreasonable jealousy.

He met Raishan's gaze. "Are you ready, Aghat?"

Raishan nodded and drew his sword. Nimos backed away.

"No need to get violent, Your Highness," he said. "I only came to apologize for the past, that's all. And now I'm leaving, with promises not to bother you for the rest of your trip." He jumped into the saddle and threw his lizardbeast into gallop, disappearing around the bend of the road.

Egey Bashi sighed, watching the retreating dust cloud. "Here we go again. Another ride to the Majat Guild, with Nimos at our heels."

"Let's just hope this trip ends better than the last one," Raishan mumbled and busied himself with the preparation of the meal.

9

WORTH DYING FOR

Kara slid down from her saddle and picked up the cracked horseshoe. Her heart leapt. In this wilderness, without the horseshoe, Mai couldn't possibly have gone very far. He was very fond of his horse, and she knew that, urgent or not, he wouldn't drive it hard enough to risk an injury.

A search of the tracks ahead confirmed her suspicions. A set of prints indicated the place where Mai had noticed the loss and dismounted. She saw some of his tracks going backward, likely in an attempt to recover the lost horseshoe. He must have been hard pressed indeed not to notice it right away. From here, his prints went parallel to the horse's, showing that he had continued on foot, leading his horse over the terrain. Furthermore, the three-legged horse track indicated that he must have wrapped a cloth around the bare hoof to prevent further injury.

She raised her head, surveying the surroundings.

The light of the setting sun painted the landscape with deep fiery strokes. Long shadows crept off every rock in sight. Ahead of her she could see a hazel grove, with the gleam of a brook running through.

She smiled. She was willing to bet Mai was camping in there right now, trying to find a temporary replacement for the lost shoe. The nearest blacksmith lived in Middledale, a day's travel ahead. Without a shoe, this was a considerable distance to cover.

She urged her horse onward, keeping to the shadows, until she spotted a faint wisp of smoke rising through the hazel crowns on the distant end of the grove. Good. She hoped he was sufficiently occupied not to keep watch on this side of the tree line.

When she reached the hazel shade she dismounted and let her horse wander, using all her stealth to creep to the campsite without making a sound. In the gathering dusk, she paused at the edge of the glade and looked into the circle lit by the campfire.

Mai was sitting with his back to her, carving a piece of wood with his boot knife. She noiselessly drew her weapon before approaching further, not sure how he would react. Then, she cautiously stepped into the glade.

Mai's shoulders went still, forcing her to an abrupt stop. Yet, he did not turn around as he spoke. "You may put away your weapon, Aghat. Unless, of course, you're here to kill me."

She relaxed and lowered the weapon to her side, but did not sheath it. "You know I have no intention of harming you, Aghat Mai."

He slowly turned around to face her. His eyes gleamed with mischief.

"I didn't think so. Why don't you come and sit by the fire, then? I am guessing you must have had a strenuous trip."

Kara still held her weapon out as she approached and settled on the other side of the fire, keeping a clear distance.

"Thank you, Aghat," she said. "But my trip was actually quite relaxing. By the way," she took out the horseshoe, "I think I found something that belongs to you."

His eyes darted to the shoe and back to her face. He didn't reach out to take it.

"I assume there's a price to pay for it," he said.

"Yes. Your promise to take me along."

He sighed. "We've been over this, Aghat. The price is too high, and you know it."

Kara shrugged. "Have it your way." She put the shoe back into her pack. "It's quite a ride from here to Middledale," she went on, "but it takes a lot longer on foot. I think I'll just ride ahead and warn them of your arrival before continuing on to the Majat Guild." She glanced at the sky. "In fact, it's not that late. I think I still have a few hours of travel ahead of me."

He leaned back, the disbelief in his gaze mixing with amusement. "Where's your horse, Aghat?"

She smiled. "Close enough to mount it at very short notice." She raised her weapon just a bit, to make sure he didn't think of anything foolish.

Mai's shoulders shook with silent laughter. "You certainly know how to bargain, don't you?" He reached forward and held out a hand. "I'll take the horseshoe, thanks."

She held his gaze. "You do promise you won't try to disable me or run away from me?"

"Do I have a choice?"

"None."

"I thought so."

She waited, holding the shoe just out of reach.

He sighed, glancing at her wearily. "I *promise*. You don't think I'd try a cheap trick like that, do you?"

She didn't respond as she handed him the horseshoe. He took it out of her hand and examined it. It was badly cracked, but she knew it could be fitted to the hoof to enable him to ride, at least as far as Middledale.

Kara sheathed her weapon and took off her pack, settling by the fire across from him. She helped herself to some of the tea from the kettle. It was too bitter, by the taste of it brewed some time ago and kept over the fire too long. She gulped it down anyway, then took out two food rations and offered him one.

He shook his head. "I already ate, thanks. Besides, I wouldn't dream of depleting your supplies."

She smiled. "We're traveling together now, remember? We can share."

He threw her another amused glance before returning back to his work on the horseshoe.

"You are quite something, aren't you?" he asked at length.

Kara smiled, stretching out her legs. It felt good to relax her tired muscles after the last few days of crazy riding.

"I try to be."

He raised his face to her. "Is there anything I can do to convince you to reconsider?"

She shook her head. "No. The only thing that would convince me is reading Master Oden Lan's letter and seeing with my own eyes that you have been recalled to the Guild for a reason unrelated to me."

For a brief moment his face lost its amused expression. His hand darted into the opening of his shirt to shove something deeper into the inner pocket. She caught a glimpse of the folded parchment, feeling a chill run down her spine. His expression told her so much more than words ever could. And now, she absolutely had to see what was in that letter and to understand how bad things really were for her and Mai.

She finished her ration, then walked over to the edge of the glade and whistled through her teeth. After a short moment, her horse appeared from the direction of the brook. She patted it and took time to unsaddle and brush it, then brought her saddle and bedroll to the fireside.

Mai was already lying down on the other side of the fire. As Kara settled down, he slowly relaxed into his bedroll.

"Good night," he said and closed his eyes.

She sat for a while watching him. After a few minutes his breath became even, indicating that he was asleep. She waited a while, then got up to her feet and crept over to him. She used extra stealth to move smoothly, so that she would be all but invisible against the flickering firelight. As she approached, she filled herself with inner stillness to prevent him from sensing her presence, and leaned over, looking at his outstretched shape.

The night was warm and he had no cover over him. His shirt, open down the front, revealed the upper part of his lean, muscular chest with a small star-shaped scar at its center. From this angle she could no longer see the parchment he had tucked inside, but she knew it was there, stashed into the deep inner pocket. If she could just reach in there without waking him up–

She paused, looking down on him. He appeared fast asleep, his breath even, his body completely relaxed. His staff lay next to his hand, his long fingers resting over its black polished wood. If he woke up, he would be ready to instantly spring into action. But there was no reason to wake him. She was certain she could do what she needed without disturbing him, if she was careful enough.

She crouched next to him, so that her body was parallel to his, weight spread along the ground. Supporting herself on one hand, so that she could stay in position without making any excessive movements, she carefully reached into the opening of his shirt. She moved slowly, so as not to disturb any of its silky folds as she reached further inside to the secret pocket against his body.

She sensed a barely perceptible twitch of muscle and froze. She stayed still, but there was no more movement from him, his breath as even as before. After a long moment she dared a look.

He hadn't changed his position, but his eyes were now open, looking at her with a mocking expression – alert, as if he had never even been asleep.

"Sorry," he said. "I was trying not to disturb you, but I just couldn't help it. It was too much for a man to bear."

There was laughter in his eyes as he slowly and deliberately ran his gaze down her crouched shape, making her painfully aware of the awkward position she was in. She knew he was purposely trying to get her off balance, but she still couldn't help blushing.

She tried to ignore it and kept very still, watching him. She knew she couldn't move. With the twisted position she had gotten herself into, she was completely in his power. He could break her wrist inside the shirt before she had time to get it out of his reach. To withdraw her hand, she had to be sure he was going to let her do it.

He seemed to be in no hurry as he continued to watch her with a disconcerting look. His eyes became dreamy, but they also held mischief that kept her in check.

"When I agreed to travel together," he said, "I had no idea we were going to have such a good time."

She held still. Their faces were so close that she could smell his skin, a faint fresh scent of mountain pine. He moved his eyes down her body with a slow, appraising look as if he were actually able to see through her clothes. She struggled to stay calm and keep the blush away, but it was just too hard.

He made sure she was fully aware of the way he looked at her, before he finally relaxed back into his sleeping cot.

"You can take your hand out," he said. "I'm not going to touch you. I have to say, though, that I'd much rather you continued with what you were doing. It feels so good."

She forced the blush away as she slowly pulled out her hand and sat back on her heels, looking down at him. Her shoulder was stiff, but she wasn't about to show it. His mocking gaze continued to scrutinize her, making her feel too exposed. She knew he was doing it on purpose, and she was not going to give in to it.

"Where is the letter?" she asked slowly.

He shifted to a more comfortable position.

"Now, Aghat," he said, "you don't expect I would keep it where you saw me put it? That would be almost as foolish as thinking you could sneak up on me like this."

"Where is it?" she insisted.

He ran a slow, deliberate glance down his own outstretched body, and looked back to her face, his intense gaze holding an unsettling mixture of seriousness and mischief. She knew what he was doing, but it was difficult to resist. She felt the annoying blush creep back into her cheeks as she forced herself to keep his gaze.

"Why don't you search me?" he suggested. "There're a lot of places you could check which are even better than the inside of my shirt. Just make sure you don't miss any."

She didn't want to look, but her eyes moved on their own accord down his body, sprawled in front of her with a lazy grace that she knew could turn into action in the blink of an eye. She fought a blush, hating herself for allowing him to get her disconcerted so easily, just by looking at her. But, if he was playing these games with her, she was going to pay him back with the same coin. She forced her eyes back to his face, giving him her best innocent look.

"I'm sorry," she said. "It was indeed foolish, to think that I could sneak up on you, Aghat. I just... I really wanted to see the letter."

She put sincerity into her voice as she said these words, letting her gaze drop down to the ground and slowly rise back to his face in a look that she knew made her seem childish and vulnerable.

He seemed to have bought it. His gaze softened and his face slowly lost its mocking expression.

"Why don't we just forget it?" he suggested. "It's late. I'm sure you can hold your curiosity until morning, can't you?"

She nodded and turned to get up to her feet, but kept her eyes lowered, watching him out of the corner of her eye. When his gaze moved away and his body relaxed, she spun around with the speed that made the air around her whistle, aiming her fingers at the two spots at the base of his neck, right above the collarbones.

His shape blurred as he shifted out of the way, her fingers landing harmlessly off the pressure points. His hands flew up and caught her by the wrists. She twisted out of the hold, but he grabbed her again, throwing her over his head and landing on top with all his weight. She gasped, struggling to recover her breath as he pinned her down to the ground, holding her wrists away from her body.

"Don't you ever give up?" he asked.

She didn't respond, relaxing against his hold so that she didn't have to spend unnecessary strength. He was bigger and heavier, and he spread his weight over her in a way that made it difficult to move. She paused for a few breaths, forcing herself to relax so that she offered no resistance at all as he held her down. After a moment she sensed his grip weaken. She concentrated. Letting her strength carry her, she charged, her body turning from a completely relaxed state into a ball of muscle in a split moment. She kicked her legs up to dislodge his weight and pushed off with her feet to twist sideways out of his grip. As

he moved to match, she flung her body the other way,
sliding through the resulting gap. He reacted, but she
was faster this time. She tossed her weight sideways
against him, forcing him to spin over, and went for his
neck again, a left-handed blow that whizzed through
the air with the speed of an arrow. He parried, but
his block wavered, unprepared for the strength of
the attack. She went for the gap and he fought back.
As they rolled over, he tried to pin her down with
his weight again, but she twisted out of the hold and
threw him sideways, landing on top.

They stayed in that position for a long moment,
breathing heavily. She balanced her weight over him,
pinning his arms down just above the elbows, with
his hands locked over her wrists. She felt the play of
his muscles under her and braced herself, trying to
anticipate his next move. But he showed no intention
of throwing her off. Instead, he slowly released his grip
and dropped his hands away. She held on, suspecting a
trap, but he relaxed, spreading his arms out and laying
back against the ground. His chest heaved as he steadied
his breath and she felt the tension released throughout
his body, pinned underneath her.

She was glad for the break as she stayed on top
of him, changing her grip to hold him by the wrists,
leaning over him so that she could catch her own
breath. Her hands still felt numb from his earlier grasp,
tingling as feeling slowly returned to her fingers.

She looked down at him. His shirt had opened
wider from the fight, the sculpted muscle of his chest
so impressive even in his relaxed state. Seeing him at
this angle made her feel too aware of his body against

hers. She knew it was the wrong thing to focus on in a fight, but it was so hard to forget the way he had looked at her earlier, his bold gaze reaching under her clothes. She clenched her teeth, angry at herself for falling for such a simple trick. Men had tried this on her before, but it had never worked. There was no reason it should be any different now, however good he was at this tactic.

The position they were in was awkward. He showed no intention of continuing the fight, and yet she couldn't afford to let go. If he used the gap to spring into action again, she would be in trouble. He was bigger, and he would definitely try to use his weight against her, just like before. She had to save her strength to counter it. She balanced her weight on top of him, enjoying a short rest and trying to force her thoughts away from how close their bodies were, every inch of his muscle toned against hers.

She waited for another long moment, but nothing happened. Finally, she glanced at his face.

His blue-gray eyes held none of the mockery he had showed before. He looked at her with a mix of fascination and longing, so intense that she shivered. As she made contact, she could no longer turn away.

Her mind screamed caution. Was this a trick? Or did he just show her a possibility she had never considered before?

And why did she suddenly feel so tempted to believe it?

Her tired arms didn't want to hold her anymore. She needed rest, and she tried to tell herself that was all it was as she leaned down into his chest until his face was mere inches away. His gaze trapped her, the promise in his eyes so overwhelming that she felt her head spin. Was she imagining it?

Was he trying to trick her?

She turned up her face. Inadvertently, her lips brushed against his. *Dear Shal Addim, I didn't realize we were so close.* She shivered, dizzy with his barely perceptible smell of pine, with the way he looked at her, with the feeling of his body toned against hers. *His lips. Did I do it on purpose? Or did he?* It didn't seem to matter anymore. Even if it was a trick, she no longer cared. The pull was so strong that she couldn't possibly resist it.

Her mind retreated as she leaned down and kissed him.

His arms closed over her, moving against her back in a slow, powerful caress. She shuddered and drew deeper into his embrace, strong enough to break every bone in her body if she didn't match it with the strength of her own.

It was a violent feeling of passion beyond control that came out of nowhere and crept up on them unawares. They struggled in each other's arms, hovering on the border between roughness and tenderness. It was fierce, but after a while it no longer seemed enough. They broke apart to pull off their clothes, so that nothing could possibly be in their way. She got on top of him and he drew her into his arms. She grasped him, drunk with the warmth of his smooth skin against hers, with the way his body yielded to her touch until there was nothing left between them.

He was so strong it was frightening, a lethal fighter at the edge of control, and this thrill of danger drove her on, making it impossible to hold anything back.

She moved on top of him until she found his hardness below and opened up to let him inside. She shivered as he entered her, digging her fingers into his skin, arching her back so that he could go in deeper. A moan escaped through her clenched teeth and her head fell backward, letting it out.

His hands lifted her as if she were weightless. He shifted her and rolled over, so that he was now on top, thrusting into her. She wrapped her legs around him, urging him on.

The world around them was slowly collapsing, leaving nothing but his body moving against hers, his strength that made this wild passion seem breathtaking, like a fight, an ultimate form of closeness that transcended life and death in its perfect balance. He was like her, an unmatched warrior, a lover whose passion was the essence of his incredible skill. She sensed him as if he were a part of her, every move, every beat, every thrust that left her gasping for more until she was breathless, and beyond, into a void that left her disoriented. She shuddered in his arms, but his hold was steady until, in a last thrust, he released all of his strength into her. She gasped and screamed, grabbing on, her fingers digging into his flesh, their bodies intertwined so much that they felt like one.

The world shivered and went still around them. There was nothing left.

He lifted her against him, rolling onto his back and easing her on top. She relaxed over him, unable to move or even fully understand where she was. His arms enfolded her, gentle and tender as he held her close against his chest, his warmth easing her shivering as she clung to him with the last of her weakening senses.

She didn't remember how long it was before she was able to move again, to lift herself up just enough so that she could see his eyes, the deep tenderness in his gaze making her breath catch in her throat.

This wasn't supposed to happen. It went against their entire training and who they were.

And yet – it felt so *right*.

She lifted up higher against his chest so that she could look him full in the face.

"What just happened?" she whispered.

"Something worth dying for," he said quietly.

She looked at him for a moment longer, then relaxed against his body. She felt so weak that it seemed that she needed his strength next to her just so that she could keep on breathing. He put his arms around her, holding her and gently stroking her hair.

She didn't know what would happen now or what they were going to do. But she knew that she was never going to let him get killed. Whatever the future held, they were bonded now. If he died, she'd have to die too.

10
A LESSON

"Just think, Your Highness," Egey Bashi said. "What makes you capable of resisting the Kaddim power?"

Kyth thought about it.

"Focus," he said. "Their power seems to make everything scatter. I am not doing it on purpose, but somehow I feel that by staying focused I can make it flow around me without affecting me." He thought some more. "It feels like a blade," he said. "A very sharp blade over the top of my head that slices their power like a net, making it fall to the sides without enfolding me."

The Keeper nodded thoughtfully. Everyone else sat around watching in fascination, except Alder, who crouched at the side of the glade over his spiders. They ate fresh meat and could catch and kill small rodents. Kyth preferred not to dwell on what was happening right now next to his foster brother.

"I know the feeling," Ellah said. "When I use my gift, I see colors, blue if someone says the truth and red when they tell a lie. It took many lessons with Mother Keeper to bring this ability under control."

Kyth frowned. He couldn't control his gift much. Except for the fact that he was always immune to the Kaddim, his ability just came and went, seemingly on its own. The Keepers told him his power was in elemental magic, a rare ability that had all but disappeared since the times of the Old Empire. True, he could sometimes focus the power of the wind or water to aid his swordplay, but overall it wasn't as impressive as it sounded.

"What about when you protect others?" Egey Bashi asked.

Kyth glanced at Raishan. He and Mai were the only two people he had ever protected from the Kaddim to enable them to fight. "It's kind of the same," he said. "I imagine an invisible spearhead I can control, which cuts through their power like a knife through a net. It takes effort to slice their power away. When I first tried to do it I had no idea it would work so well."

Lady Celana cleared her throat in that special way of inborn royalty, drawing everyone's eyes without saying anything or making any loud sounds.

"Prince Kythar," she said, "was able to draw away all the Kaddim troops during the battle in my father's castle. It looked quite different from what you describe, Your Highness."

Kyth raised his eyebrows. He'd almost forgotten about that incident – not because it was insignificant, but because it was too traumatic to think about. Back then, the Kaddim had cornered and almost killed Kara. And Kyth hadn't been able to do anything to save her, until it was almost too late. He shivered as the memories flowed in.

The person who had saved her back then was Mai, who was somehow able to overcome the Kaddim power in the middle of the fight. Kyth had no idea how he was able to do it. And now, unwittingly, he remembered Nimos's words. *His feelings for her...* Could Mai have overcome the Kaddim because of his *feelings for Kara*?

Was this why Kyth was immune too?

He forced away the thought. Nimos was their enemy, trying to wedge discord among them. He would never give in to that.

"You are right, my lady," he said to Celana. "That was different. That time, I was able to use the Kaddim power the same way I use the elements – to help me fight. I focused their power against them. No imaginary blades involved."

It was fascinating to watch how this refined royal lady blushed every time he looked at her directly. Did she really find him attractive? He found it hard to believe. She looked so much more impressive than him, her heart-shaped face, porcelain skin, and clear green eyes accented by rich auburn hair, its waves flowing around her head like a flame. Even her riding outfit, a plain pants suit of deep forest green, looked like an exquisite royal gown, simply because of the refined way she wore it. Next to her, Kyth in his plain clothes – as well as just about everyone else in the group – looked downright shabby.

"Still," Egey Bashi said. "It's all part of the same power. We must identify a common element in all this, and develop it. Aghat Raishan," he turned to the Majat. "What did it feel like to you when Prince Kythar protected you from the Kaddim?"

Raishan appeared to consider it.

"It did feel kind of like a blade," he admitted. "As if I were enfolded in a fog and then a blade descended and cut the fog away."

Kyth nodded. "Yes, fog sounds right. Except I could see the strings this fog consisted of, making it seem more like a very thick and wooly spider's web." Inadvertently, he glanced at Alder crouching on the ground. His eyes slid further, to the furry shapes crawling at his feet. The spiders were nearly as big as the rodents they ate. He shivered. Being the emissary from the Forestlands came with a price; he just hoped his foster brother was happy with it.

"I wonder," Raishan said, "how Kara and Aghat Mai were able to acquire this resistance on their own?"

Kyth's heart quivered as the subject was brought up again. He glanced at Egey Bashi, expecting to see a puzzled look. His heart sank as he met the Keeper's intense gaze.

"You know, don't you?" he asked quietly.

The Keeper nodded. "Yes, to the extent I can pry into a Majat's mind. Their training develops very deep focus on its own. It takes less for a Diamond Majat to cover the gap and acquire the necessary level of focus to resist the Kaddim. Much less so than for an ordinary person."

His feelings for her. Kyth forced Nimos's words to quieten in his head. "Can Raishan learn to do it too?"

"I hope so. This is why we are rushing these lessons, Your Highness. If you and Aghat Raishan can work this out by the time we reach the Majat Guild–"

Ellah's look cut him off.

"There's something you are hiding, Magister, isn't there?" she said. "You know more about it than you lead Kyth to believe."

The Magister frowned. "Whatever else I know is not relevant here. I know lots of things. Telling the Prince everything I know would do nothing but confuse him."

Ellah shook her head. "No, I can sense something different, Magister. The way you sound... it seems like a lie. Sorry."

Egey Bashi sighed. "Your training is good," he said. "But you are wrong in this case. I am not lying. It's just that, in some situations, knowing all the details can only make things worse, believe me."

"Worse?" Kyth asked.

"Can't we just leave it be, Your Highness?"

Kyth shivered. "It's about feelings, isn't it? What Nimos said about Mai. He was telling the truth, wasn't he?"

Egey Bashi's shoulders sagged. He didn't hurry to break the silence.

Kyth's eyes darted to Ellah. "*Was* he telling the truth?"

Ellah hesitated. "I don't think my ability to sense the Kaddim–"

"Was he?"

"Yes."

Kyth receded into his seat. He felt numb and angry, as he looked back at the Magister.

"You knew, didn't you? And you weren't going to tell me."

The Keeper sighed again. "Telling you wouldn't have served any purpose, Your Highness. Besides, it's not even important."

"*Not important*?"

"Kara does not share these feelings. She is not aware of them. And, knowing Aghat Mai's self-control, it is very likely she never will be."

Kyth felt a weakness in his stomach. Deep inside, he knew Egey Bashi was right. And yet, thinking of Kara out there, chasing a man who had feelings for her, seemed like too much. He prayed Mai was moving too fast for Kara to catch him on the road.

Egey Bashi sat up. "I guess now that we're talking about it, I can explain further. The only thing I know so far that could give a Diamond the necessary focus is being in love. Kara was in love with Prince Kythar when she first encountered the Kaddim. The way it was described to me, how she initially wavered under their power and then recovered, suggests that she probably realized it in the middle of the fight." He looked at Kyth, clearly hoping for a reaction Kyth was unable to give. She *was* in love with him. She *had been*, once, before she broke up with him so that she could run off with a man, who... who...

Kyth's lips twitched. "What about Mai? He wasn't immune to the Kaddim when I first defended him against them. I know he wasn't pretending. They nearly killed him that time. They would have cut off his arms if I hadn't interfered in the nick of time."

Egey Bashi shrugged. "Not that it matters, Your Highness, but I think I witnessed the moment when he realized he was in love – during the fight in Illitand Hall, when he stepped into the stream of Kaddim power to save Kara."

"In love," Kyth echoed. *His feelings for her.* Nimos was right all along. And Egey Bashi *had known* about it and hadn't said anything.

The Keeper watched him intently.

"I fail to see why this upsets you so much, Prince Kythar," he said. "She acquired her resistance to the Kaddim because of her love for *you*. I don't think you have any reason to worry on Aghat Mai's accord."

Kyth lowered his eyes. Most likely this was true. And yet, the way Kara looked at Mai, the way she receded into his company whenever she needed comfort, had made him feel disconcerted on more than one occasion. Mai had a way of stirring these feelings in many women, but to Kyth's knowledge there was never any reason behind it, besides Mai's natural glamor that women of all stations somehow found so irresistible. His apparent lack of interest in women was what made him trustworthy in Kyth's eyes where Kara was concerned. To know that he was *in love* with her...

He felt intensely uncomfortable now, with the way everyone was looking at him uneasily, but worst of all was Lady Celana, whose deep green eyes held such compassion that he felt he had earned it already. He had nothing to worry about, he told himself. Mai's station in his Guild made it impossible for him to act on his feelings, even if he ever dropped the control that made him such an unmatched fighter.

It was all Nimos's fault. The Kaddim had stirred up these doubts in Kyth's mind. It felt no better to think that this was probably the main reason for his appearance on the road, to wedge this doubt and force Kyth to think of Mai as a rival.

For this reason alone, he should control his feelings and never let himself act differently toward Mai. Besides, all these doubts were probably foolish. Kara had never given him any reason to think she fancied Mai – or anyone else for that matter. While Kyth knew he was not her first man, he believed himself to be the first she felt bonded to, and they would share this bond no matter what the future held.

"Let's all get some sleep," Egey Bashi said. "We need to start early tomorrow."

Raishan glanced at the sky. "Tomorrow we should reach Middledale."

Alder looked up from his spiders. "I hope we can spend the night there. Their inn is built on hot springs and has a private bath in every room."

Kyth could see both Ellah and Celana lift their heads in anticipation. A bath *did* sound good after nearly ten days of non-stop riding.

But the Keeper only shook his head. "Tomorrow's the last day of the Lantern Festival. Every house and inn in town will be fully occupied. I believe we should camp just before reaching town." He noticed the ladies' forlorn expressions. "We can go there in the morning to make a short stop for a bath without spending the night."

Raishan nodded. "True. I once passed through Middledale on an assignment during the Lantern Festival. Despite the enormous credit the Majat Guild runs with their inn, I had to sleep in the stable."

Egey Bashi rose and went to the heap of bedrolls, picking out his own.

"If we sleep early both days," he said, "we should make perfect speed."

Kyth nodded. It made sense, just like everything else Egey Bashi had said this evening. In all the time he had known the Keeper, he had learned to trust him unconditionally. Only someone like Nimos could wedge doubt into this trust, and he was determined not to let the Kaddim Brother's words affect him.

If only he could be certain the Keeper was right about everything else. He looked at the terrain ahead, thinking of Kara, out there by herself, following Mai into their Guild. Was she as tired right now as he felt?

Did she manage to overtake Mai and ride with him?

He forced the thought away.

11
THE LANTERN FESTIVAL

Kara woke up at dawn. At first she couldn't remember where she was. It was a strange feeling – one she hadn't experienced for years – of waking up from a sleep so deep that it took her a few moments to gather her thoughts.

She was lying naked on a sleeping cot, wrapped in a long, silky cloak down to her toes. Its cloth was black, and at first it didn't seem familiar. Then she caught the smell, a barely perceptible scent of mountain pine. Her heart raced as she inhaled it.

She sat up and looked around. The camp was empty, but a thin wisp of smoke rose from the firepit, suggesting that somebody had already spent effort to start a fire. Her clothes were folded in a neat pile next to her head. She grabbed them and pulled the cloak tighter around herself.

A movement from the direction of the brook caught her eye. As she watched, Mai emerged from behind the thin line of bushes looking neat and elegant, quite undisturbed, except for damp hair and a slightly drawn face. He returned her gaze with an air of guarded silence, as if waiting for her to make the first move. They were silent for a moment, looking at each other.

"I didn't hear you get up," she said.

A smile slid through his lips, but his eyes remained in shadow. She had a feeling he expected her to say something else, but he had already moved away and busied himself with the fire.

She got up, careful to keep the cloak tight around herself, and walked over to the brook. Finding a deeper pond of water, she took time to wash herself, submerging into the cool, transparent pool to soak off the dreamy feeling of last night. She felt strange. She still wasn't sure what had driven her to behave the way she had, but it was hard to let go of the memory. She could easily lose herself in it if she allowed her thoughts to flow.

She cut them off. Stepping out of the water, she dried off in the cool morning breeze, then dressed up and walked back to camp.

Mai was sitting across from her, attending to the fire. As she approached, he looked up with the same guarded expression.

She folded up his cloak and put it down over his bedroll, then sat across from him, holding his gaze. He handed her a mug of tea and she took it, unthinkingly sipping the tart, hot liquid, too strong for her taste.

She felt so confused. What happened last night wasn't supposed to happen, she told herself again and again. Despite how good it felt, it wasn't meant to be. He was her senior in the Guild, and their training made any bonds all but impossible. What she had with Kyth had been pleasant but wrong, and people had suffered for it. And now–

Mai wasn't looking at her, but she sensed how alert he was of her every move.

"About last night…" she said.

He looked up. Their gazes locked.

"I– I shouldn't have…" She paused, unable to go on.

His gaze wavered. "It was my fault. I lost control. Please forgive me."

She felt a lump in her throat, but ignored it. It wasn't meant to be. They weren't meant for this.

"We both lost it," she said quietly, "didn't we?"

His gaze was unreadable as he looked up at her. It seemed that he was about to say something, but then fell silent.

"It can't continue," she said, her voice sinking to a near whisper. "We both know it mustn't happen again."

A shadow stirred in his eyes, a barely perceptible movement that for a moment made him appear vulnerable. His direct gaze made her heart quiver. Then he sat back, subsiding into calmness.

"I toasted bread," he said. "Why don't you have some?"

She took a warm crispy piece from him, conscious to keep clear of his hand. She wasn't sure she could handle it if she touched him. And, she couldn't afford to lose her mind again. They were headed toward certain death, all because of her. All because of her inability to control herself before.

They ate in silence, the calmness around him almost palpable, like an invisible armor. His gaze slid over her with outward indifference, but she still sensed the intensity inside.

"I feel I must ask you the same question again," he said. "Is there anything I can do that would convince you *not* to come with me?"

She met his gaze. "My answer's still the same. The only thing you can do is to show me the Guildmaster's letter to *prove* your return to the Guild has nothing to do with me."

He reached into his pack and took out the folded parchment. Keeping his eyes on her, he threw it into the fire.

She gasped and rushed forward, but before she could even take a step, his staff was in his hand, pointing her way. He slid a hand over it and a blade sprung out toward her, its steel point hovering near her throat.

There was a dangerous glint in his eyes as he kept her gaze. She swallowed, glancing down at the blade that almost touched her skin. Seeing it this way brought back bad memories. Last time, when he defeated her and made everyone believe she was dead, his blade hit her at exactly the same point, between the collarbones. *Viper's kiss.* She suppressed a shiver. "Viper" was the name of Mai's token rune in the Majat Guild. He had invented that blow. And now, when she learned what his real kisses were like, she was having too much trouble dealing with it.

This is madness. Stop it. Focus. She glanced at the parchment. The fire turned it over, licking the crumpling surface with long red tongues. The sharp letters of the Guildmaster's handwriting melted away in front of her eyes, slowly consumed by the flame.

She didn't want to fight Mai again. Not with real blades. But even if she fought him now, she would never make it in time before the letter burned.

She met his gaze.

"If you can't even let me see it," she said quietly, "I must assume the worst."

He threw a side glance into the fire and withdrew his staff, flicking the blades back into their sheaths. A distant smile creased his lips.

"You can assume whatever you want, Aghat," he said. "But I suggest you leave it be. It's really not worth it."

"If it wasn't worth it, there would've been no harm in me seeing it, would there?"

He grinned. "Perhaps not. But then, we would have missed all the drama. Wouldn't that be a pity?"

The drama. She felt a blush rise into her cheeks as she remembered last night.

"At least," she said, "you can now stop questioning me about staying behind."

His eyes showed regret.

"If we assume, for argument's sake, that they are really going to kill me," he said, "there's nothing you could do by siding with me against out entire Guild. If you come with me, you'll die. It will be a waste."

"That bad, eh?"

He didn't respond.

She stepped forward and paused just short of reaching him. His closeness was dizzying, but she forced herself to distance from it, looking into his eyes.

"I'll stay behind," she said, "if you do."

He went very still. "You know I can't. If I do, both of us will have to run forever."

"You are doing it for me, aren't you?"

He smiled. "Honestly. It concerns me too, doesn't it?"

"But it all happened because of me in the first place."

His brief glance stirred with a gentleness that made her heart quiver. "It happened because you chose to do the right thing. So did I. We both made our choices. I wish you'd stop feeling as if it's all your fault."

"And you expect me to stay behind?"

"I don't believe you can help by coming with me."

She lifted her chin. "You underestimate me, Aghat Mai. Don't you?"

He softened, a wave of warmth washing over her as she met his gaze, caressing like a touch of summer wind.

"I know exactly what you're worth," he said. "That's why I will do anything in my power to stop you from coming."

She smiled, feeling lightheaded from his closeness, from the way he looked at her.

"There isn't much you can do to stop me," she said. "Is there?"

He held her gaze, the smile suddenly gone.

"Of all the bad things I can imagine happening to me at the Guild," he said, "watching you being killed stands pretty high on the list. In fact, I don't think I can imagine anything worse. And, as we both know, it's quite likely to happen if you insist on coming."

"How about getting killed yourself?"

He shrugged. "Comparatively speaking, that possibility doesn't bother me at all."

"It bothers *me*." As she said it, she realized with surprise how deeply she meant it. It was unthinkable to imagine that he would die, because of her. "And I intend to prevent it from happening."

His lips twitched into a smile, but his eyes were in

shadow. "You'll be risking your life against very heavy odds. I'm not worth it."

"As you once said to me," she said quietly, "this is my call to make. Not yours."

After they fitted the cracked shoe to the hoof of Mai's horse, the ride to Middledale was uneventful, even if much slower than normal. With no more need to hide his tracks, Mai agreed to return to the main road. They rode quietly side by side, enjoying the warmth of the sun and the fresh mountain wind, fragrant with the smells of aemrock, pine, and ice from the distant snow caps.

It felt so easy to ride next to Mai. His horse obeyed him without any visible signals, matching Kara's speed down to a single beat. He sat relaxed in the saddle, emanating calmness – a special technique of stilling the mind that helped so much to restore upheaved balance. Kara knew she should do it too. Yet, she couldn't resist riding on her emotions for just a bit longer. In a week or so she was likely going to die. Could there be so much harm in enjoying her feelings just a touch more than appropriate?

In all her life, she had never imagined being close to a man. All her training had been directed against it, teaching her to channel her emotions, to project an aura that warned men from getting close. Kyth's innocence had originally cut through this shield, catching her by surprise. He was the only man she had ever met who saw a beautiful woman where everyone else saw a deadly fighter, and his admiration had swept her away into his fairytale world, where her training did not matter and where she could think of herself simply as a woman. With Kyth, she had been living somebody else's life – one, she now realized, she would never be able to fully fit into.

It was so different with Mai. He knew exactly what she was, and he shared her training down to the last detail. He never saw her for anything else. With him, she could fully be herself. And yet, it was hard to understand how all their training, all the ruthlessness they both were capable of, could go hand in hand with the tender passion of the previous night.

Better not to think of it too much, she finally decided as she, too, subsided into her trained aura of calmness. What happened between them was no more than a fighting incident, and she should never think of it any other way. Top ranked Majat were trained to channel their sexual energy into their combat skill. Both she and Mai had learned it well, that was all. And if they took it a little bit too far this time, no harm done.

By the early evening, wisps of smoke up ahead signaled their approach to Middledale. Kara narrowed her eyes, peering into the domed roofs drowning in the greenery. The gusts of wind carried a mild smell of sulfur. The town was built on hot springs, providing luxurious accommodations and rooms with private baths, drawing tourists from all over the kingdom.

She knew that no blacksmith could shoe Mai's horse until morning, which gave them an opportunity to spend the night in the local inn. After days of camping in the wilderness, she couldn't help but look forward to it.

The streets of Middledale were so crowded that Kara and Mai were forced to dismount and lead their horses, pushing through the thick throngs. Garlands of colored lanterns floated overhead, and here and there they could hear the popping of firecrackers exploding into the night sky.

"The Lantern Festival," Kara said above the noise. "I forgot all about it. Today should be the last day, I believe."

Mai only nodded as he pushed his way to the inn, a large multi-domed building enfolded in sulfur-smelling fumes, its walls and roof richly covered by lichen.

A harassed-looking stable boy took their horses and led them into a side stall. Mai stayed behind to ensure the horses were well cared for and Kara went ahead to make arrangements for the night.

Warm fog enfolded her as she stepped into the inn's common room. She paused, letting her senses adjust. She had never seen this inn so full. In the flickering light of lanterns hanging overhead she could see row after row of occupied tables, people laughing and talking. The festive mood showed in the ringing timbre of the elevated voices, in the rich colors of clothing, in the fumes of the best ales and meads floating in the air.

A large basin of bubbling water dominated the center of the room, the biggest hot spring that fed most of the baths in the inn and ensured that its patrons needed no other heat source even on very cold days. It felt good to feel the warmth on her face after the biting chill of the breeze outside; she didn't even mind the humidity that clung to her skin in a mist of tiny droplets and made her hair curl against the side of her cheek. She tucked it behind her ear as she pushed her way to the counter.

The innkeeper, a slim man with pale eyes and a large damp towel hanging over his shoulder, paused as he saw her approach. His eyes widened as he recognized her.

"Mistress Kara?" The man licked his lips nervously and twitched the corner of his towel.

The Majat Guild paid many inns throughout the kingdom to ensure their Guild members received the necessary support on their assignments. She knew she could expect a warm welcome.

She smiled. "Hello, Master Olren."

He bowed, looking at her with awe. She was used to it from those who knew about her ranking and had at least some understanding of the Majat Guild. Last time she was here she was still an active member of the Guild. She felt a pang of regret at the thought and forced it away.

"My companion and I will need two rooms for the night, next to each other, if possible." She couldn't risk getting separated from Mai. If they stayed close together, she could at least keep an eye on him and make sure he didn't slip away. Of course, he had given his word. Besides, his horse was in no shape to continue until a local blacksmith could attend to it. Still, it didn't hurt to be careful.

The innkeeper used the corner of his towel to wipe his damp forehead. His face wore an unsettled expression.

"I'm sorry, Mistress," he stumbled. "Today's the last day of the festival. All our rooms are full. Unless..." He paused, looking past her shoulder. She turned to see Mai walking toward them.

"Unless what?"

Master Olren briefly lowered his eyes. "Um, I was going to offer you one last option. It's a two-room suite with a separate bath chamber. We had a last minute cancellation, and it is far too expensive for our regular patrons. Nothing for you to worry about, of course. But..."

"But what?"

"I... um... I didn't realize your companion was a man."

Kara shot a quick glance at Mai. A two-room suite with a separate bath might work out even better. After camping together in the wilderness they could hardly be bothered by the lack of privacy. Besides, the suite still gave them two rooms to sleep in, but in addition it also made it much easier for her to keep an eye on him. In fact, if she took the outer chamber between him and the door, she could sleep soundly, in the certainty that he would never be able to sneak out without her knowledge.

"A suite would be fine," she said, sliding a questioning glance over at Mai and receiving a nod in response.

"I– I only have one key," Master Olren stammered.

"That's quite enough, thank you." She reached over and took the key before Mai could grab it, putting it in her pocket.

"Room eighteen at the end of the west corridor," Master Olren said. "I hope you will be comfortable there. The maids will prepare it while you are having dinner." He gestured to a table by the wall and waved to the serving girl, who rushed over with a tray containing a pitcher of brew, a half-loaf of bread, mugs, and steaming bowls of stew.

12
HOT SPRING

The suite was even bigger than Kara had imagined. In fact, the outer chamber would have been quite enough to sleep a very large group. But there was also the back room, with a luxurious bed that beckoned with its freshly ironed sheets. The maids blushed and giggled as they looked at Mai, and made a lengthy show of arranging a bouquet of wild aemrocks in a vase before leaving them alone.

Mai threw down his pack and surveyed the large space.

"You take the bed," he said. "I can sleep out here."

She shook her head. "I will sleep between you and the door, thank you."

He grinned. "Don't you trust me, Aghat?"

"No." She pushed a chair to the wall and put down her own pack, reaching inside for a fresh change of clothes. A gust of warm moisture from the side door carried the faint smell of sulfur, telling her of the location of the bath. After the strain of the last few days, she felt she really needed one.

"You want to wash first?" she asked.

He shook his head. "You go ahead. I'll do it later." He stepped past her into the bedroom. In a moment he reappeared with a long bath towel and tossed it to her across the room. She caught it as she fished the key out of her pocket to lock the door. He watched her from the inner doorway with an amused expression.

"You really think I'll run away from you?"

"Now that we're so close to a blacksmith, I can't risk it."

"I thought I gave you my word."

She shrugged. "No harm in making sure, is there?"

"I suppose not." He disappeared into the bedroom. She checked that the door was secure and put the key away before walking into the bath chamber.

The large stone basin was built level with the floor, with a few wide steps descending into the turmoiling water. It looked like this chamber had a spring of its own, its water less sulfuric than that in the inn's common room, boiling with tiny bubbles that rose to the surface in smooth domes.

This suite must have been very expensive if no one else took it even on such a busy day. It was a good thing that the Majat Guild had such unconditional credit in so many places.

She left the door open a crack so that she could catch any activity by the entrance and stepped into the bath. The water was hot, and, as she submerged into it, it felt so good to her tired muscles. The tiny bubbles made her skin tingle, the swirl of the underwater currents pressing against her with a gentle massage. She lay back and relaxed, enjoying every bit of it.

She took her time before emerging out of the tub and wrapping herself in the bath sheet. The air was too damp to don her clothes, but fortunately the sheet was large enough to wrap securely in. She did not want Mai to think she was provoking him in any way, especially after what she had told him that morning. Most likely he wasn't even interested, she reminded herself. What happened in the heat of a fight rarely had any connection to real life.

Mai was in the bedroom, with the door open, inspecting his gear. He had taken off his shirt. She paused, taking a private moment to gape.

His muscular torso was so perfectly sculpted that even Kara, used to seeing fit, half-naked men engaged in strenuous physical activities, couldn't help feeling amazed. She hoped her awe wasn't obvious as she tore her eyes away, turning her attention to her own gear. Dear Shal Addim, how could the mere sight of a man possibly affect her so?

Inadvertently her thoughts wandered to the previous night. She would never forget it. The hardness of his muscles against her, his warmth, his strength, his maddening scent... She shook her head. This was a dangerous path and she should do her best to stay clear of it.

She noticed a movement out of the corner of her eye and spun around to face Mai. He stood a few paces away wearing only his breeches, a bath towel thrown over his shoulder.

"If you're done, I'll take a bath now," he said.

She nodded, hoping her flustered state wasn't too obvious.

He left the door open. She made sure to keep her back to it, avoiding any possibility that she could see him naked. Once or twice she paused in her task of setting out her gear, struggling to quiet her unsettled mind. What was happening to her? How could she have allowed herself to get so far out of balance?

A dark cloth thrown over the back of a chair caught her eye. Mai's shirt. Before she knew it, she had stepped over and picked it up. She should return it to his room. He may need it.

Unwittingly, her hand holding the shirt lifted higher, bringing its silky folds up to her face. His scent enfolded her, a natural smell of mountain pine and fresh river water, clean, and so sensual that she felt her head swim.

Most men she knew smelled of sweat, not altogether unpleasant but very down-to-earth. Mai's natural smell was so different. She couldn't get enough of it. She inhaled deeply, glancing toward the bathroom door to make sure he couldn't see her.

Her thoughts raced. They were alone, under lock and key. If something were to happen between them, no one would ever know. And if anyone did, would she really care? They were both headed for their execution. If she was meant to die so soon, she wanted to make sure she died with no regrets.

Most likely Mai wasn't even interested anymore. But in that case he would just say "no", wouldn't he?

Wrapping her sheet tighter around herself, she crossed the room in a few strides and stepped into the foggy warmth of the bath chamber.

Mai turned and looked at her. She paused in the doorway. His body, submerged in the low vapors rising from the water, seemed tenser than expected for someone taking a relaxing hot bath after a day of riding. As she stepped closer, he turned around in the bath, watching her with a guarded look.

She continued to approach, holding his gaze. When she came within a few paces, he reached for his bath sheet heaped at the side of the basin and stood up, wrapping it around his waist with a quick move as he stepped out of the tub. His naked torso glistened with water, his slim body so graceful and powerful that it was hard to concentrate. She forced her eyes back to his face.

"What happened last night…" she began.

He stood very still, watching her. She couldn't read his expression at all.

"I'm finding it hard to let go," she said quietly. "Are you?"

His gaze wavered. "I don't want to do anything to hurt you."

"*Hurt* me?"

His lips twitched. "In all likelihood, my chances of surviving this are low. I don't want to do anything that would make it more difficult for you to forget me."

She stopped mere inches from him, looking into his face.

"Too late for that."

He looked at her with wonder. "Is it?"

Unwittingly, she lifted her hand and ran her fingertips down his cheek. His skin was smooth, but she could also feel the barely perceptible stubble of a clean shave. A ripple went through his body as she made contact.

"Yes," she said.

She kept his gaze as she released her other hand, letting the bath sheet she was wrapped in slide all the way down to the floor.

He swallowed, his eyes sliding down her body with an entranced expression. She could see his muscles tense, a fascinating sight. Then he lifted his eyes to her face.

"I don't want you to do things you'll regret."

"What makes you think I'd regret them?"

"Won't you?"

The air around them was so charged that it seemed to crackle. She felt dizzy as she inhaled his scent, even more potent now when he was so close.

"You must be joking," she said.

"I must be dreaming," he whispered.

She took another step forward, closing the distance. As their bodies touched, she felt a shudder go through both of them, so intense that she gasped.

He swept her up in a powerful embrace and she clung to him with a fierceness more overwhelming than anything she had felt before. His kisses left her disoriented, her mind slowly slipping away into the grasp of his dizzying scent, the hardness of his muscle, his skin, so smooth and hot that it almost burned. He scooped her into his arms and she held on, lightheaded from his closeness and his incredible strength. She floated in his arms as he carried her and then lowered her onto a soft surface, silky sheets caressing her skin.

She gasped and stifled a scream as he entered her, a sensation so intense that she almost came undone. He drove into her, again and again, until her body shook, letting loose the last bits of her weakening mind. The scream that she held inside found its way to her eyes and poured out in a flood of tears that streamed down her cheeks as she grasped on to him with the last of her strength. His movements were fast and powerful, driving her to new heights of ecstasy. She sobbed and dug her fingers into his skin, unable to hold on much longer and yet powerless to let go.

His last thrusts as he released into her made her lose herself so completely that she forgot everything around her. She couldn't remember who she was or what was happening to her anymore. All she knew was his body against hers, so strong that she couldn't imagine life without holding on to it. She floated in a void, his arms around her, powerful and gentle at the same time. Her face was wet with tears and he kissed them away, holding her close. She gave in to his hands, submerging in his caress.

He held her as she drifted into sleep, curled in his arms. She could never leave the safety of his embrace. She never wanted to.

When she woke, a little later, he was lying next to her, leaning on one elbow, watching her. Her heart quivered as he smiled down at her.

"Don't you ever sleep?" she asked.

He shook his head. "I'm still dreaming. And if I fall asleep, I might just wake up. I wouldn't want to risk it."

She ran her eyes to the dots of blackening bruises on his chest and arms, where her fingers had dug into his skin with a force she couldn't control. She gently brushed over them, feeling his muscles ripple from the touch.

"I've hurt you," she said.

His eyes followed the movement of her hand. When he looked back at her, his gaze stirred with such feeling that she felt her heart race.

"I wish they'd never heal," he said. "This is one memory I'd like to cherish for the rest of my life."

She ran her fingers up his chest, watching his skin rise in prickles at her touch. *Why can't we do this all the time?* The thought came unbidden, followed by another, more sensible one. Whatever possessed her to pursue this madness had to stop, and soon. Being with him was impossible on so many levels that it was useless even to dwell on it.

She sighed and dropped her hand away.

"We must sleep," she said. "Or we'll have no strength to ride tomorrow."

In the dim light it seemed to her that his face showed regret, but he nodded and lay down beside her, closing his eyes. She watched him for a moment, but her tiredness got the better of her and she sank into a deep sleep.

Kara awoke to the sound of rapping on the door. She sat up. Mai was already on his feet, a towel wrapped around his waist. His warning glance froze her in place.

Morning sun shone into the room, illuminating the havoc of sheets and towels around the disheveled bed. Kara felt her cheeks warming up, remembering how they had spent the night. Whether it was friend or enemy outside the door, they couldn't possibly allow this person to see it.

Mai slid into the outer room, his staff in hand. She jumped out of bed and wrapped a sheet in a secure knot around her chest to be ready for action as well, if needed.

"Aghat Mai?" a familiar voice called from outside.
Raishan.

Kara's heart missed a beat. Raishan's assignment at the King's court was to protect Kyth. If he was here, it meant Kyth must have acted on his threat and followed her.

She felt weak. She couldn't possibly face Kyth after what had happened between her and Mai. Not *now*.

"Just a minute, Aghat Raishan," Mai said in the outer room.

Crouching behind the door Kara saw him fold away her scattered clothes, covering them with her cloak and fishing the room key out of her pocket. He turned and met her gaze. She nodded, then shut the bedroom door all the way and leaned down to peer through the key hole.

Raishan was alone. He stepped inside and ran a quick glance around the room. His eyes paused on Kara's cloak heaped over the chair and on the tightly shut bedroom door, then slid over the finger-shaped bruises on Mai's shoulders and chest. Kara felt her cheeks burn as Raishan's eyes returned to Mai's face with an impassive expression.

"I assume Kara's with you," he said.

Mai nodded.

"I'm here with Prince Kythar and Magister Egey Bashi," Raishan said. "As well as several other emissaries sent by the King. We are on our way to negotiate with the Majat Guild. Frankly, even though I had hoped to catch you and Kara on the road, I never believed we could do it."

"My horse lost a shoe," Mai said. "For the past two days I could only travel at a very slow walk. I cannot continue without first visiting a local blacksmith."

Raishan nodded. "We're ordering breakfast. Perhaps you and Kara can meet us in the common room?"

"We'll be along soon."

Raishan's eyes flicked to the bedroom door again. Kara felt angry at herself for being so flustered about it. How she spent her time was no one's business, especially after she was officially expelled from the Guild. Raishan could guess whatever he wanted. It was Kyth she was much more worried about. She really couldn't bear to face him right now, knowing that he would see right through her.

She leaned back against the wall, hearing the creak of the closing door and the click of the key turning in the lock. After a moment Mai reappeared and stopped in the doorway, looking at her.

"I assume you heard everything," he said.

She nodded.

"One last bath?" she asked.

"Sounds like a good idea."

She followed him into the bath chamber. The steaming stone basin was big enough for at least four people, definitely enough for two to relax without disturbing each other. However, to Kara's surprise, she realized that relaxation was very far from her mind.

She should be exhausted after last night. She should be worried about facing Kyth, only a short time from now. How could things have possibly gone so far out of control?

Mai dropped his towel at the edge of the bath and she saw that he was erect again. When he noticed her look, he lifted an eyebrow with a subtle question as he stepped into the water.

Wordlessly, she undid her own sheet and followed him. He held out a hand to steady her, and she used his shoulders for support as she eased over him, guiding him inside. Grasping him tighter, she moved up and down, feeling his hands clasp her underwater, helping her rhythmical motion. She tried to slow down, savor it, but her movements accelerated on their own accord. A moan escaped her lips as she closed her eyes, giving in.

His hands moved up, finding the exact spots to build her excitement, until she could no longer hold it in. As she shook in his arms in a violent release, he came with her, his quiver inside her bringing the sensation to a new height. His kisses drowned her cries as she clung to him, no longer able to tell them apart.

Spent, she lay over his chest with her head on his shoulder, building up strength to lift up and finally let him go. He gently stroked her back, his touch calming and not arousing anymore. She knew he was doing it on purpose, and she was grateful for it. This madness had to stop. They couldn't possibly continue like this.

"You are so perfect," she whispered.

"So are you," he said.

Afterward, they finished their bath and donned their clothes and gear. Together, they made their way to the inn's common room.

13
ARGUMENT

Egey Bashi lifted his head, watching Kara and Mai enter the room. He saw how Kyth's face lit up when he saw her, and how his eyes darkened for a brief moment as they slid over Mai. However, as the two Diamonds approached the table and lowered into the last two available chairs, he also noticed more. The way Mai and Kara avoided looking at each other, yet moved in perfect unison, as if aware of each other's thoughts. The way Kara blushed and turned away as she met Kyth's eyes. The way Mai didn't look at Kyth at all.

Egey Bashi peered closer. A small bruise darkened Mai's skin inside his shirt, very close to his neck. It could be a punch mark from a fight. But if the Magister didn't know better, he would have thought it looked suspiciously similar to a love bite.

His eyes widened as he glanced at Raishan. The Diamond had been the one to seek out Mai and Kara in the inn. He had probably entered their room. Had Raishan noticed something too?

Raishan's impenetrable look confirmed his suspicions. Egey Bashi looked at Kyth again, seeing the Prince's eyes narrow as he, too, must have noticed the subtle signs. Kyth knew Kara very well. It was too much to believe that the Prince could stay ignorant for long.

"I made arrangements to have your horse shod, Aghat Mai," Egey Bashi said, aware how his voice cut through the building tension around the table. "I hope you don't mind."

Mai turned to him, as though seeing the Magister for the first time. His face looked drawn, as if he hadn't had enough sleep. His damp, neatly combed hair suggested that he had just taken a bath. Egey Bashi cursed silently. While ordinarily this was none of his business, tension between Kyth and Mai was the last thing they needed right now. Things were heading toward a disaster, and he wasn't sure if he knew anything humanly possible to avert it.

"Thank you, Magister," Mai said.

Egey Bashi nodded. "We plan to ride out as soon as possible. Since, fortunately, we were able to catch up with you and Kara, we hope both of you will agree to continue this trip with us. We are, after all, heading to the same place."

Mai glanced at Kara. Egey Bashi couldn't help noticing how, when their gazes met, it seemed for a moment that they were alone in the room. Their eyes locked on each other for an extra instant, as if having trouble separating.

Egey Bashi cursed again, thinking of the conversation he had had with Kyth at the last campsite. Back then the mere possibility that Mai was attracted to Kara threw the Prince off balance even when he firmly believed that Kara would never reciprocate. And now, even if Egey Bashi tried very hard, he couldn't imagine a worse turn of events. Given the Keeper's inclination for pessimism, this state of affairs seemed a very hard one to achieve.

"I think it is a good idea to travel together, Magister," Kara said. "If you'll forgive me, I need to go and check my horse." She swept past the Keeper and left the inn before anyone could rise.

Kyth sat for a moment looking after her.

"I'll be right back," he said.

Mai lifted his head, watching Kyth hurry outside in Kara's wake, but he didn't comment or move to follow. Egey Bashi let out a sigh. Perhaps this was the best way. If this trip were to continue without major incident, Kyth and Kara needed to talk things out, the sooner the better.

Kyth overtook Kara halfway to the stable. She paused, waiting for him to catch up. Kyth looked searchingly into her eyes, seeing her drawn face, her distant look, and the special set of her shoulders that made her look relaxed and tense at the same time.

He was sure something terrible must have happened.

He had to know.

He stopped in front of her, seeking out her gaze. "Did you and Mai...?"

Her eyelids trembled. "I don't expect you to understand." She lowered her eyes, her fingers absently twirling a string of her pack.

A sinking feeling in the pit of his stomach made him instantly nauseated. It was as he suspected. Her expression told him as much.

"Try me," he managed.

Reluctantly, she raised her eyes back to his face. "Things got a bit out of hand."

"*Out of hand*?"

She sighed. "Remember when I told you I was different?"

"Yes."

"I know you never believed me. But I did really mean it. I am not like you, not at all."

Kyth continued to look at her in disbelief, feeling as if the world around him was slowly going awry. True, she had told him all that before. She also told him that she was leaving him, which meant that, even if she did find love with someone else, she had committed no betrayal. And yet, up to now, he hoped her only motivation was to do her duty. Hell, she had told him this much. Had she lied? Had she had feelings for Mai all along?

"The Majat training," Kara said, "discourages any emotional bonds. However, we are encouraged to explore the physical ones, during our training. We do it to overcome the discomfort that could get us disconcerted in a fight – say, if it gets too physical against an attractive opponent. In such situations, sexual inexperience can become a serious handicap." She paused as if waiting for Kyth to ask a question, but he kept his silence. "Later on, we are taught to control our sexuality, channel it into weaponry. In the end, it adds to our skill. In the heat of a fight, it's often difficult to tell the difference."

Kyth shook off his stupor. "You did it with Mai in the heat of a fight?"

"Yes."

Blood rushed into Kyth's face. "He *forced* himself on you?"

Her gaze wavered. "No. It wasn't like that at all. I... It just... happened, that's all."

Her look told him questioning her further would be useless. Kyth took a breath to quieten his racing heart. He didn't want to venture his thoughts into what had happened between them. He also couldn't escape the feeling that she wasn't telling him everything, but he let it be for the moment. He still couldn't wrap his head around what she had told him.

"And it doesn't mean anything to you?"

She sighed. "You know you weren't my first man, right?"

Kyth nodded, at a loss for words. He knew, of course. She was not a virgin when they first made love, but in some ways she had seemed like one. She had been so detached, so distanced from any physical affection that it had taken a while for him to break down this barrier and convince her to let him close.

"You knew that, yet you never questioned my prior experience, did you?" she said.

"No."

"Can't we just leave it at that?"

He slowly let out the air he was holding. "Was it the same with Mai as what you had before with other men?"

Her hesitant expression made his gut wrench.

"It's something that definitely wasn't supposed to happen between two people of our training," she said at length.

He continued to hold her gaze, suppressing the sting of tears in his eyes.

"I did tell you," she said, "that things between us weren't likely to work out. Even if I survive. I am just too different from you. In your world, I am not a normal person, not a woman who could make you happy. You deserve better."

His lips twitched. "Isn't that for me to decide?"

"Look," she said. "I'm likely heading to my execution. As I told you before, I cannot let Mai do this alone. This hasn't changed, regardless of what happened between us. I wish you would just let this go. Please. We have bigger things at stake."

He nodded, trying to control his trembling lips. *I will not cry. I will not.* "I understand. I try to. I just cannot possibly give up hope."

She shook her head. "Sometimes you have to. That's the only way to allow other things into your life."

He clenched his fists until they hurt, forcing back tears. Was he truly losing her?

Had he lost her already?

"Kyth," she said. "If we're to travel together, we have to make it work. All of it. The fate of your kingdom – all our lives – depends on it."

He nodded again. She was right. And yet, could he ever bear to look Mai in the face and not hate him? Could he bear the thought of traveling together with *this* hanging over their heads?

"I'll go prepare my horse," she said. "I'll be back shortly. Will you be all right?"

Kyth nodded. As she turned and walked away, he stood still, looking after her.

He felt dumbfounded. He believed she probably meant what she said, but her hesitation when he had asked if what happened with Mai was the same as her prior experiences kept haunting him. She said they hadn't meant for it to happen, but Kyth just couldn't feel convinced. *She* hadn't meant for it to happen, he was sure of it. But what about Mai?

He caught a movement behind him and spun around. *Mai.*

Kyth's eyes narrowed. Seeing the Diamond face to face made his hatred boil. Everything Kara had said, everything he had been thinking on the road even before his worst suspicions were confirmed, rushed into his face with a strength that threw him momentarily off balance.

"You… *bastard*," he blurted.

Mai kept his gaze with an unreadable expression.

"*How could you?*"

Mai didn't respond. He just stood in front of Kyth, watching him.

Gloating, are you? Kyth's hand darted to his belt, drawing his sword. He thrust it at Mai's chest, but the Diamond leaned out of the way in a quick, easy move.

Kyth concentrated. He used his gift and drew in the force of the wind, focusing it on the tip of his sword as he sent it around in a sneaky spin, straight at Mai's heart. The Diamond stepped aside, so fast that the wind whirled around him. He no longer looked as if dodging Kyth's blade was so easy. His face acquired the deep concentration that Kyth usually saw in a fight, his eyes following the tip of the sword that kept whistling around with speed and precision far beyond Kyth's regular skill.

"Draw your weapon!" Kyth demanded.

Mai ignored his words. He kept his arms relaxed at his sides as he danced between Kyth's thrusts. Kyth called in more wind, increasing the speed.

He knew he probably couldn't stand up to Mai for long in a weapon fight, but if Mai refused to defend himself, Kyth was bound to come through sooner or later, if he managed to maintain his concentration and his command of the wind. Yet, knowing Mai's skill, he knew it was going to take a very long time.

He lowered his sword.

"You think I'm not good enough to fight you?"

Mai came to a standstill, surveying him.

"Actually, you're not."

"Have it your way." Kyth raised his sword again. He hated to admit that, despite using his gift, he was already getting tired. This knowledge filled him with even more anger. Why did Mai have to be so damned perfect in every way?

"That's not the only reason I won't cross blades with you," Mai said. "We have no quarrel."

Kyth stared, once again lowering his blade.

"Are you out of your mind?"

"I don't own her," Mai said. "Neither do you. If I agreed to fight you over this, I would be admitting I had a right to her, wouldn't I?"

Kyth narrowed his eyes. "True. You have no right to her."

"And you think you do?"

Kyth lifted his sword again, pointing its tip at Mai's throat.

Mai surveyed him calmly. This time he did not try to dodge the blade.

"If you strike me down, would that make you feel better?" he asked.

"Yes." Kyth clenched his teeth and pressed the tip of his sword against Mai's skin.

Mai held his gaze. "Go ahead, do it."

Kyth's hand wavered. He lowered his sword.

His heart raced. He *hated* Mai, but he just couldn't do it. Not this way, when Mai was refusing even to lift a finger in his defense.

"You think you understand everyone, don't you?" he said. "You think you can play with people the way you want."

Mai raised his eyebrows. "What do you mean?"

Kyth's lips trembled. "You made such a show of your sacrifice. You made everyone fuss over saving you. You lured her to follow you and then... then you *seduced* her so that you can be bloody sure she will help you fight. And now, she is heading into serious trouble because you just couldn't keep your hands off her, could you?"

Mai's gaze wavered. "If you convince her to stay behind, I'll be in your debt forever. There's nothing I want more than to see her walk away from this."

Kyth paused to control the annoying twitch at the corner of his mouth.

"I've seen the way you treat women. You use them as your tools. And now, you found the ultimate tool and are doing everything you can to make sure she doesn't leave your side."

Mai didn't respond, but a glint in his eyes suggested to Kyth that he was treading on dangerous ground. He didn't give a damn.

"I know you think you have feelings for her. But if you truly cared, you would never have done this, not when you knew that being close to you can only draw her deeper into trouble."

"I didn't ask her to follow me," Mai said quietly.

Kyth clenched his teeth. "If you hadn't been so bloody *comforting* to her all the time, if you hadn't made sure she felt so eternally *grateful* to you for saving her life, she may not have."

Mai shifted from foot to foot. "Are you going to kill me or not?"

"You think something will stop me?" Kyth raised his sword, but a firm hand grasped his shoulder. He spun around and came face to face with Egey Bashi. Raishan stayed at his back, his narrow eyes darting around to take in the scene.

"Kyth," the Keeper said. "Your Highness. Leave Aghat Mai alone. Killing him won't make things better."

"Actually," Mai said, "it might. If I'm dead, Kara would have no reason to return to the Guild, would she?"

"If you're dead," the Keeper retorted, "she would be far less likely to handle whoever your Guildmaster decides to send after her. Come, Prince Kythar. We must prepare for the road."

Kyth shrugged, throwing the Keeper's hand off his shoulder. Then he turned and strode away. He saw Raishan fall into step in his wake, but he didn't care.

After they were gone, Egey Bashi turned to Mai.

"That was foolish, Aghat," he said. "I've always held you in the highest regard for your ability to think clearly. Of course, in this situation it may no longer be applicable."

Mai's eyes held a distant look as he watched Kyth's retreating back.

"He is right, you know," Mai said quietly. "I was the one who let things get so far out of hand. And now, as if the situation wasn't bad enough, I've made it so much more difficult for everyone."

The Keeper sighed. "Have you ever thought, Aghat Mai, that some things in life are simply outside your control?"

Mai did not respond. He stood so still that if it wasn't for the breeze touching his hair he would have looked like a statue.

"I've watched you, for a while now," Egey Bashi went on. "Ever since you learned to resist the Kaddim. I can personally vouch that you did everything humanly possible to hide your feelings. Some things just happen, that's all."

Mai shook his head. "I could have kept myself in line. I let my control slip, once. And now she is paying for it with her life."

"Regardless of what happened between you two, she would have gone with you till the end, and you know it."

Mai met his gaze. For the first time Egey Bashi saw the Diamond look vulnerable, a young man in his twenties with a burden on his shoulders far beyond what anyone should ever be asked to bear.

"How could I possibly know it?" Mai asked quietly.

"Because, like you, she puts her duty above all else. Do you think she could have stood by idly and let you get yourself killed, when she believes it is all her fault?"

"It's not her fault."

The Keeper shrugged. "You believe it's yours, don't you? Well, she blames herself, too. You two are more alike than you care to notice. The sooner you get this into your stubborn head, the better."

Mai's eyes lit up with amusement. "I don't believe I remember ever being called stubborn, Magister."

"I pride on being the first in many things, Aghat."

"Perhaps you can help her see how futile it is for her to come with me to the Guild? I think both Kyth and I are far too close to get the message across without messing things up even more."

Egey Bashi shook his head. "I tend to agree with Aghat Raishan on this. We don't want to lose either you or Kara, and you definitely stand more chance when you are together."

"Are you always so calculating, Magister?"

The Keeper frowned. "Isn't everyone?"

"No."

"Like you said, Aghat Mai, you are too close. I can only hope when the time comes you can still keep a cool head. And now, we must return to our group. We have things to discuss."

14

THREATS

When Egey Bashi and Mai returned to the common room, things seemed as settled as they could be under the circumstances. Kyth sat at the table with a glassy look, staring unseeingly into space. Raishan and Alder held a quiet conversation, which seemed like a distraction more than an exchange of information. By the looks of it, it wasn't quite working.

"Where're the ladies?" Egey Bashi asked, settling into his chair.

"They went to take baths," Alder said. "And Kara is still in the stable checking her gear. I think." He glanced at Kyth.

Egey Bashi nodded. "Good, this gives us some time to discuss plans. Aghat Mai, can you tell us exactly what your current orders from the Guild are?"

Mai shrugged, settling into his seat with the grace and ease of a cat reclaiming its favorite spot by the fireplace. Egey Bashi was glad to see the Diamond's composure back, even though the prominent way he avoided looking at Kyth was still quite noticeable.

"It's exactly as I said to the King, Magister. I'm being recalled."

The Keeper shook his head. "I cannot believe, Aghat, that with everything that's at stake you chose to return to your Guild and face certain death."

"What makes you think I face certain death, Magister?"

"Don't you?" The Keeper lifted his eyebrows.

Mai shook his head. "It's not about me, Magister."

The Keeper sighed. "It's about your foolish sense of honor that is driving your actions now, when they really should be driven by your conscious mind."

Mai leaned back into his seat.

"Do you know an old saying, Magister? 'He who commands the Majat commands the empire'?"

"Yes."

"If I'm not mistaken, your mission right now is to convince the Majat to protect the King against the Kaddim."

"How do you know this, Aghat?"

Mai shrugged. "This is the only reason anyone ever sends embassies to the Majat Guild. Isn't it? Besides, I spent enough time at King Evan's side to be able to guess what he is most likely to do."

This time he did glance at Kyth, but the Prince was looking away, too absorbed in his own emotions. Egey Bashi reminded himself to have a conversation with Kyth some time soon. If they hoped to win the war against the Kaddim, this rivalry couldn't possibly continue.

"Your point, Aghat Mai?" he asked.

"Has it ever occurred to you, Magister, that the King is not the real target for the Kaddim?"

"What do you mean?" Egey Bashi felt genuinely puzzled. He *had* thought about it, as a matter of fact, but hearing it from Mai was disconcerting. Despite his youth, this man seemed to be far more proficient in politics than Egey Bashi had ever given him credit for. He really should pay closer attention.

Mai leaned forward. "Think about it. All the threats, all the scheming, making sure that King Evan and everyone on his side feel as if they are out of time and must act immediately to save their kingdom."

Egey Bashi nodded. "They do have to act, and you know it, Aghat."

"Yes. And what is the first thing everyone does when faced with a superior force?"

"They hire the Majat to aid them."

"Exactly. No one even fights wars anymore. In fact, the Majat are normally reluctant to pitch top warriors against each other, with very few exceptions. So, it all comes down to the timing and the amount of gold everyone is willing to put up front. But the result is still the same. The Majat, not the powers who hire them, are the real centerpiece of the action. Whoever can get there first and hire more Majat to their side wins by default, without any fight. Except that no one in this kingdom and the surrounding lands can afford to hire more than a few."

"Isn't that why your Guild prospers?"

"Normally, yes. But it also has a flip side. The Majat Guild is a wild card that can turn the tide of a war. So, if anyone wants, say, to defeat all kingdoms at once and ensure absolute victory, they would first have to get the Majat out of the way."

"The Kaddim," Egey Bashi said slowly.

Mai nodded. "Yes, the Kaddim. If they want to restore the Old Empire, they simply can't afford to play hiring games. For centuries, the Majat has stood in the way of any attempt like that, simply by being there. We don't take sides. As long as we are strong, we will always be a problem for the Kaddim."

The Keeper leaned back in his chair. He had been thinking the same thing, but he still couldn't believe that Mai had also thought it through, possibly in more detail.

"The Kaddim are using careful plotting to weaken the Majat Guild from the inside," Mai went on. "And they are targeting the tip of our force. The Diamonds. First Kara, because she became immune to their powers. Now, me. In all likelihood the Kaddim, or their envoys, have been the ones to inform our Guildmaster of my disobedience. I want to make sure he is aware of that before he proceeds to carry out my punishment."

"Do you think it will make a difference?"

"It should, if he is truly thinking of the good of our Guild, Magister. And if not... I must make everyone realize it, before it's too late."

"By getting yourself killed?"

"If that's what it takes."

Egey Bashi shook his head. "Aren't you taking too much upon yourself, Aghat Mai?"

Mai held a pause. "The real outcome of the battle with the Kaddim will be decided at the Guild, Magister. Not in Tandar or in Aknabar. I can't possibly allow the Majat Guild to fight this battle on the enemy's terms. If they do, my life won't be worth much anyway."

Egey Bashi continued to look at him.

"Do you really think Aghat Oden Lan will listen to you?"

Mai shrugged. "Only one way to find out. I sent a raven ahead to explain the situation and tell him I must talk to him as soon as I arrive. It should get his attention, if he has not gone completely insane. At the very least, he'll hear me out. And if, after that, he still wants to do all these things to me…"

"What things?"

Mai grinned. "In his letter, he elaborated on what he is planning once I arrive at the Guild."

"And what is that, if I may ask?"

Mai's grin widened. "It went on for quite a while, but it essentially came down to torturing me beyond recognition and hanging whatever was left of me from the tallest tower in the outer city to let me rot alive. He said he will leave me hanging there forever, as a reminder to anyone else who ever thinks of disobeying orders again."

Egey Bashi frowned in disbelief. "And he thought you would follow such an invitation?"

"As the alternative, he promised to recall all available Diamonds from assignments and send them after me and Kara, with orders to bring us back and skin us alive in front of the entire Guild. It went on from there. He said he would do all this if I didn't report to the Guild in three weeks. Which really doesn't leave me much time to spare."

Raishan's wide eyes betrayed his shock. "He said such things in his letter?"

Mai nodded. "Yes, in quite colorful detail. He was clearly insane when he wrote it. To be honest, that prompted me to hurry more than I originally meant to. We cannot leave the Guild in the hands of a man in such a state of mind. I just hope his insanity was temporary."

"He really cares about Kara," Raishan said quietly.

Mai's gaze wavered, and Egey Bashi saw a faint touch of color rise to his cheeks. He noticed Kyth's intent look before the Prince glanced away. *What a mess.*

"You don't really think that–" Raishan began, and stopped, as if struck by a sudden thought.

Mai met his eyes. "Yes, Aghat, I do. The person who orchestrated this present state of affairs *knew* about Master Oden Lan's feelings for Kara. As well as too many other things about our Guild which should not be known to outsiders."

Raishan frowned. "But who could it possibly be? It takes many years to gain this kind of trust."

"Exactly. The Kaddim must have a man on the inside. Worse, this man was likely in place for as long as the Kaddim have been conceiving this plan, which could be more than a decade, for all we know."

"Aren't you giving them too much credit, Aghat Mai?" Egey Bashi said.

Mai glanced at him. "In our training we are taught not to underestimate our opponents, Magister. If you assume the worst, you are always prepared. Of course, I hope I'm wrong in this case. But I can't possibly risk being right and not acting on it."

At that moment, Kyth sharply lifted his head, looking at the door. Egey Bashi turned and saw Kara walking toward them. He noted how Mai kept still, not turning his head or otherwise acknowledging the disturbance.

Kara looked calm and composed, her clothes neat, her short hair resting against her cheeks in a golden wave. If Egey Bashi didn't know better he would have never guessed anything out of place was going on. She chose a seat between Alder and Raishan, briefly glancing at the three spiders on Alder's shoulders. They were still, dozing after what Egey Bashi knew was quite a filling meal this morning at the campsite. He marveled at the way everyone in the group was able to put up with these frightening pets.

"What did I miss?" Kara asked.

Raishan shrugged. "Not much, Aghat. We were just discussing plans."

"And?"

"We should press on to reach the Majat Guild as soon as we can. Prince Kythar has a negotiation to conduct."

She nodded, her face reflecting the obvious thought that this explanation carried no information whatsoever.

"I've seen Ellah and Lady Celana on the way here," she said. "I think they're done with their baths. Should we get ready to move?"

The road was wide enough for three riders to ride side by side, but their group gradually separated into pairs. Kara rode at the back next to Magister Egey Bashi, behind Kyth and Alder. In the distance ahead she could see Mai and Raishan riding in the lead, with Ellah and Lady Celana in their wake. Kara was glad that with the position she chose in their formation she had very little possibility of seeing more than a glimpse of Mai. In addition, being at the rear allowed her to sort out her feelings without anyone watching her closely enough to guess what was going through her head. The only person she could possibly worry about was Magister Egey Bashi, who probably understood everything involved better than she did, and wasn't known for prying. She was grateful for his silence, for the way he kept his eyes firmly ahead, without ever glancing her way.

She felt utterly confused. After letting her thoughts revolve again and again, she still wasn't quite sure what drove her to forget herself so much with Mai. There was only one thing she clearly realized. While their lovemaking had been passionate, nothing had been said or done to suggest that their relationship was anything more than physical, a fighting incident that got out of hand and stretched a bit beyond the appropriate. She knew from her training that no matter what significance people tended to put on it, sex was no more than a form of exercise that could allow fighters to release some of their tension. Diamonds rarely needed it, but in the end it was all the same.

It felt exactly this way for her and Mai, she told herself. What she experienced was no more than an ultimate form of enjoyment that stemmed from the top skill they both possessed. It came rarely to warriors of their rank, but perhaps for a more practical reason than anyone realized. With very few exceptions, Diamonds never fought each other, in training or otherwise. The possibility of two Diamonds of opposite sex wrestling on the ground with no one to witness it was far too remote.

She shook her head. When she made the decision to attack Mai over the Guildmaster's letter, she never thought of the way things could get out of hand besides the obvious, of injuring each other needlessly. She

thought she could control it, but what she had told
Kyth was true. Diamonds were taught to channel their
passions into their skill, and in the heat of a fight it was
often hard to tell the difference. The rest was just due
to unique circumstances, that's all.

Her cheeks warmed at the memory. Perhaps this
time it had gone a bit too far, back at the inn. She
shouldn't have pursued it. Yet that was understandable
too. She was acting on the knowledge that in less
than a week they were both doomed to die and it was
likely her last chance to do anything pleasant. Mai had
probably thought the same. Even though some of Mai's
words implied that, like her, he found the experience
enjoyable enough to cherish the memory, she was
certain that the drive was purely physical on his part.
As well as on her own, she told herself firmly. She had
never enjoyed exploring her sexuality on Majat orders
as much as other trainees, and this was her chance
to see what it could have been like. She was curious,
nothing more. And she *did* have the fun of her life.

Mai couldn't possibly have any feelings for her. She
knew his reputation with women. If Kara had been
known for her reluctance to take sexual partners during
her training, Mai had been very much the opposite.
Before he got his Diamond ranking, his trainers had to
fend off women who literally tried to force their way
into his quarters, day and night. He must have had
dozens of lovers before completion of his training sealed
in his ability to channel all his energy into weaponry.
Even at the King's court she saw ladies of all stations
swoon over him, despite the fact that he didn't so much
as glance their way.

Her heart raced at the memory of the tenderness with which he looked at her, his sparse words suggesting he cared about her feelings, the way he held back every time until she showed him very clearly what she wanted. Thinking back, she was amazed to realize that in each of their encounters, including the very first one, he had never made any advances or even provoked her in any way, except by indicating with subtle body language that the possibility was open. Without exception, she had been the one who had taken the initiative. And now, the best she could do was to forget it all as soon as possible. She had had her fun with him to the full, but any further relationship between them was simply impossible.

She distanced her thoughts, subsiding into trained calmness, raising her face into the stream of fresh wind. In only a few days they would reach the Majat Guild. She needed to use the time to prepare for what was coming.

15
ELEMENTAL MAGIC

At every campsite during their travels, Kyth had made a point of taking extensive training sessions with Egey Bashi, trying to develop his skill, but after Kara and Mai joined their group he insisted on making these sessions private, with only Egey Bashi and Raishan present. Under the Keeper's guidance, he learned to call the invisible blade on command, drawing strength from his surroundings even when no flow of wind or water was there to aid him. He was now aware that elemental power filled the air all the time, suspended all around him. This knowledge helped him not only to master his skill of summoning the invisible blade, but also to improve his weaponry, where he was making considerable advances in his practice fights with Alder and Raishan.

He was making no progress, however, in teaching Raishan to develop the necessary focus to resist the Kaddim on his own. If what it took Kara and Mai was being in love, he saw no possibility in it. More, even though he gradually came to terms with Mai's company and forgave Kara for what she had done, he couldn't help feeling shattered whenever he saw her. She wasn't with Mai; he understood it now. But she wasn't with him either, and that was so difficult for him to deal with.

He found unexpected comfort in the company of Lady Celana. The royal lady had a rare ability to sit quietly by his side, sharing the silence without prying into his thoughts. He wished he could learn this from her, aware how his prying glances caused Kara more discomfort than he meant. The way Celana could just sit quietly next to him was amazing, her very presence soothing and calming to his turmoiled mind.

She possessed rare knowledge of the kingdom's history, and her stories often let his mind wander away from the painful present to the distant and fascinating past. He learned that mastery of elemental magic had been an ancient feat of the Dorn royal line, which his family had kept carefully hidden for generations after the instigation of the Ghaz Shalan anti-magic law. He had no idea how Celana came upon this knowledge, but it made sense to him. More, her fireside stories about his Dorn ancestors helped him realize another thing about his gift. He should be able to extend his powers to protect hundreds, thousands of people. If only he knew how. It seemed impossible, wielding a single imaginary blade.

"Perhaps you should start by trying to protect two, my lord," Celana suggested one evening when they were all sitting around the fire sipping tea.

"Two?" He frowned. "What difference would it make?"

She smiled. "It could, if you had two Diamond Majat fighting on your side."

Kyth nodded. Back at Illitand castle, if he could have protected both Mai and Raishan at the same time, the fight would have gone much better from the start. At the very least, Mai wouldn't have had to face the Kaddim on his own, and perhaps he wouldn't have had to find a way to resist them by realizing that he was in love with Kara... The thought made Kyth's lips twitch, and he subsided into grim silence.

"You say when you use your skill you imagine wielding a blade, don't you, Your Highness?" Lady Celana continued. "Perhaps if you think of it as sword play, you could consider expanding this skill in the same way, by learning to wield this blade against more opponents?"

Kyth looked at her in surprise. How could she possibly know these things?

He saw a sudden interest in Egey Bashi's gaze, and the way all three Majat nodded knowingly as if what she said made perfect sense.

"A wise suggestion, Lady Celana," the Keeper said. "Perhaps we have been going about Prince Kythar's training the wrong way."

"What do you mean?" Kyth asked.

"We are training you in weaponry, and in calling up invisible blades, to perfect your skill. But we have been focusing all your training on one opponent. We overlooked the fact that maybe expanding your attention is what's required."

"But..." Kyth glanced at the Majat who were all listening to the Magister with expressions that suggested there was nothing to it. "If I'm not even good enough to handle one opponent, how could I possibly handle more?"

The Keeper smiled. "To protect Aghat Raishan and Aghat Mai against the Kaddim, you did not have to learn to fight as well as they do, did you?"

"No." Fighting like a Diamond seemed impossible. Kyth knew that this ability not only had to be trained since birth, but also required special inborn qualities, similar to those of his gift. All the Majat had the same training, but only a few ever achieved the highest gem rankings.

"Same here. You don't have to be *good* at fighting multiple opponents, only at being able to divert your attention to covering more ground."

Kyth nodded. In a way, it did make sense. Yet, his practice fights with Raishan had already been draining. Could he handle more?

Egey Bashi glanced around. "I have to admit I have no skill in this type of training. But I assume the Majat do it at some point, right?"

Raishan nodded. "Yes, we do have these mêlées from early on, with multiple trainers attacking one person. It can get wicked at times."

Kyth saw a quick smile slide over Mai's face, as if answering a pleasant memory. He shivered. Mai may have thought it fun to have a wicked fight with multiple trainers, but Kyth wasn't sure he was up to it. He remembered how, once, he tried to fight multiple Kaddim warriors. Fun was the farthest thing from his mind that time. They had almost killed Kara during that fight, until, on the verge of the fatal blow, she had managed to acquire resistance to the Kaddim power. Kyth shivered. She did it back then because of her love for him. And now...

He suddenly became aware of the preparations going on around him. The glade was being cleared of gear and packs, Ellah and Celana retreating to its edge.

"Wait!" he called out. "I didn't say that—"

"Don't worry, Your Highness," Egey Bashi said. "The Majat will use sticks in place of swords. The possibility of them injuring you is remote."

The Majat? Kyth felt a chill run down his spine as he saw Kara and Raishan at the edge of the glade measuring out lengths of wood, a bit thicker than a riding crop and about an arm long. Mai was doing something with a rope.

"You must be out of your mind, Magister," Kyth said.

Egey Bashi smiled. "I'm certain they know how far to drive you, Your Highness, and they do understand the stakes. You don't mind fighting Raishan one on one despite his skill, do you?"

I trust *Raishan.* Kyth looked around. He trusted Kara too. He knew she would never do anything to harm him. But Mai—

Mai approached, holding out a thick rope with knots, two tied at one end very close by and another on the opposite side.

"Here," the Diamond helped Kyth fit his hand between the two knots. "This is the first step of the exercise. If you can use this rope to prevent us from getting through—"

"You want me to fight you with a *rope*?" Kyth asked in disbelief.

Mai shrugged. "It gives a better range. This will teach you to keep your attention on multiple opponents. Don't try to *attack* any of us, or you'll lose focus. Use the rope to keep a distance."

Kyth clenched the rope. He wished it was anyone but Mai instructing him right now. While he had learned to put up with the fact that Mai was in their traveling party, talking to him was another matter. The Diamond seemed oblivious to it, receding into the quick, efficient mode he always had when his skill was involved.

He thinks it is all right, Kyth thought. *If he had something to hide, he wouldn't be talking to me this way.* Yet, he knew he could never trust Mai. Not after what had happened before.

The Diamonds took positions on three opposite sides of the glade. Standing in the center, within the circle of light from the camp fire, Kyth couldn't see them at all.

"Remember," Egey Bashi said. "This is not a regular fight. Try to use your gift to aid you."

I will need all the aid I can muster. Kyth raised his rope, giving it a few experimental swings. Mai was right. It did have a good range. The knots tied on both sides of his hand also allowed for a better grip, and the larger knot at the other end made it heavier, easier to wield.

"We'll try to attack you from three sides," Kara said. "Use the rope to deflect our sticks and prevent us from touching you."

Kyth nodded, raising the rope.

He spun it around his head in a wide circle, thinking that by doing this he should at least be able to feel their approach. He focused on Mai, advancing from the front, and barely caught a glimpse of another shape sliding at his side before all three sticks touched his chest, very close together. All three Diamonds were standing in front of him.

Heck, he didn't even see them *move.*

"You tried to attack me," Mai said. "Didn't you?"

Kyth swallowed. He did. He had let his feelings take over. Yet, he knew that in a big sense Mai was not his enemy. In a *real* fight, he might hate his opponents even more, even though he doubted it was possible. He had to distance himself from it.

"Use your gift," Egey Bashi said.

Kyth nodded and raised his rope again, watching the Diamonds retreat back to their original positions.

This time his rope caught on wood, and he felt its edge retreat, but the other two came through, almost as quickly as before. He lifted his eyes and met Mai's gaze. How the hell did he always end up facing *him*?

Perhaps because you're trying to seek him out. He took a breath. Some time, when all this was over, he would love a chance to have it out with Mai once and for all, but it was useless to wish for something that wasn't going to happen.

He relaxed and let in the wind, stilling his mind to all other thoughts. This time he could see three shapes moving around him, with less speed than he knew they were capable of, but still faster than he could possibly follow without using his gift. He felt his rope connect several times before the points of the three wooden sticks touched his chest, one by one.

"Better," Mai said. "Let's do it a few more times. Perhaps if we do this enough we can try it once with a real weapon before we reach the Guild."

Kyth nodded and raised his rope again, preparing for the worst.

At the end of the hour Kyth could barely stand upright. The Majat took away his rope and folded it away, all three of them neat and composed as if they had spent their time resting and not dancing around the glade in their devilish play. Kyth collapsed on the ground near the fire, watching Ellah and Alder bring their packs and resume their seats next to him.

"I heard Raishan say we'll reach the Majat Guild in two days," Ellah said, watching the others in the distance spread out the bedrolls. "I wonder what will happen when we get there."

Kyth's eyes followed Kara. He hoped they could manage to include her freedom in the bargain, assuming the Majat Guildmaster would even be interested in what Kyth had to offer. He had never seen the man, but the things he heard about him, especially when Mai quoted the letter he received, suggested the worst. He hoped that, with the help of Egey Bashi's diplomacy, he would be able to connect with the Guildmaster's compassionate side.

16

THE ULTIMATE CHALLENGE

Kara lowered her reins, urging her horse into a fast walk. The Majat Fortress rose in front like an ornate monolith carved out of the terrain. Built on the relatively flat ground in the middle of the large valley, it was positioned in a way that afforded its inhabitants the best possible view, making sure no one could ever approach it unnoticed. Kara's heart quivered as she ran her eyes over the signal towers, each of them hiding a watchman ready to raise an alarm, and over the large gate ahead, swinging open to greet their arrival.

On the last stop each of them had donned their official gear, rearranging their procession into a ceremonial order. Kyth rode in front next to Egey Bashi and Lady Celana. His black-and-blue royal Dorn cloak draped down his back, his neatly combed hair crowned with a thin golden circlet that signified his status as the Crown Prince. His face was grave. Kara had never seen him look so composed and majestic – a true royal heir, fit one day to take over the kingdom.

Lady Celana looked like his match in every way as she rode next to him. Her deep green cloak with a golden trim was covered by a wave of her loose auburn hair, which gleamed like gold in the beams of the afternoon sun.

They looked like a couple, symbolising the union of the two rival royal houses. If this was truly going to happen some day, their marriage would seal the kingdom's power for centuries to come. Kara knew that King Evan strongly supported this possibility. She wished Kyth could truly find happiness with Lady Celana, even though the thought of him marrying someone else caused a feeling of regret she tried not to dwell on. She shook her head. She had never thought it possible for her feelings to get muddled up so much. She almost welcomed the thought that in the near future she would have other things to worry about.

Magister Egey Bashi had donned his white Keeper's cloak, with the emblem of lock and key on its left shoulder. Ellah rode in his wake, wearing a similarly fashioned cloak without any ornaments, indicating her apprentice status. Her gift of truthsense was known only to a few. While it was precious during negotiations, her official role here as an apprentice Keeper in training left much more flexibility to use her gift without alerting the other side.

Alder completed the line up as he rode next to Ellah in his patched green Forestland cloak, with the spiders perched on his shoulder. They were still, and Kara hoped they would remain so until they gained access inside. The spiders were lethal weapons, and if the Majat knew about them they wouldn't take kindly to it.

Kara took care to stay close to Mai and Raishan, each wearing a diamond-set ranking armband glistening on their upper left arms. She had no Majat regalia to wear, but she knew that once she entered the Fortress she would be instantly recognized.

The greeting party assembled in the outer courtyard made her heart quiver. Two dozen Jades, crossbows in hand, lined the walls. The tall man with straight black hair and piercing eyes wasn't supposed to be here at all, not for the simple job of receiving visitors. Gahang Khall, the head of the Jades, marched up to the newcomers, his eyes sliding over Raishan, Mai, and Kara with an impassive expression.

"I am Prince Kythar Dorn," Kyth said, "on the embassy from King Evan of Tallan Dar to the Majat Guildmaster."

The Jade bowed, his eyes never leaving the Diamonds in Kyth's wake.

"Master Oden Lan has been notified of your arrival, Your Highness," Khall said. "He has ordered accommodations prepared for you. However, we have Guild business to attend to before we can let Your Highness into the Fortress. It won't take long. If you can dismount and wait here, please." He gestured toward the side area of the courtyard.

Kyth threw a quick glance at Egey Bashi, then at Kara. She nodded, trying to appear nonchalant despite the sinking feeling in her chest.

Mai and Raishan were dismounting and Kara hurried to follow, keeping a few paces behind as Khall led them through the gate into the courtyard ahead. Her eyes darted around the circular space about fifty yards across, surrounded by a tall wall with gates on all sides leading to other areas of the compound.

As soon as Mai, Raishan, and Khall passed through, two Jades guarding the entrance barred her way.

"Guild members only," one of them said.

Kara looked past his shoulder. With a sinking feeling she realized that all the gates in the next courtyard were closed, leaving Raishan and Mai with nowhere to go.

Khall stopped by the far wall, two dozen Jades with crossbows fanning out behind him. He turned to Mai and held out a hand.

"You must surrender your weapon, Aghat Mai," the Jade said.

Mai didn't move as he calmly returned Khall's gaze. "I will surrender my weapon to the Guildmaster, Gahang Khall," he said. "I believe he's expecting me."

The Jade's piercing eyes lit up with a predatory glow. "He *is* expecting you, Aghat Mai. And he gave me explicit orders. You will surrender your weapon, or die."

At his signal, the wall above the courtyard darkened with human shapes. A line of archers circled the courtyard from above and raised their bows, pointing them down at the group below.

Khall stepped back, leaving Mai and Raishan surrounded by two lines of ranged weapons, aimed and ready to fire.

"For the last time, Aghat Mai," Khall said. "Surrender your weapon."

Mai did not move.

Raishan pushed past, stepping between him and the Jade. "You are out of line, Gahang Khall. Aghat Mai is a standing member of the Guild and he outranks you. You have no authority to take away his weapon."

The Jade's eyes narrowed. "I have my orders, Aghat Raishan. I also have orders to kill anyone who stands in my way. Please step aside."

Raishan raised his hand and drew a sword from the sheath at his back.

Khall backed off, signaling with his hand. The archers at the top of the wall took aim and released their arrows. Their dark cloud descended on Raishan at high speed. The Diamond spun around like a streak of lightning, his sword almost invisible as it whizzed through the air. As he cut down the arrows Khall signaled again, and the crossbowmen along the walls of the courtyard fired at short range.

Raishan swept his sword again, but he wasn't fast enough this time, unprepared for the new attack. One of the bolts came through and hit him in the chest.

A gasp echoed through the courtyard. The Jades lowered their weapons, staring.

Raishan released his sword and stumbled, his legs twisting from underneath him as he folded down to the ground. He fell on his back, the tip of the bolt sticking out of his chest. Blood gushed out of the deep wound, soaking his shirt. His face went creamy white. His eyelids trembled and closed, and his head lifelessly rolled to the side.

Mai looked at Khall in shocked stillness.

"That wasn't necessary, Gahang," he said quietly.

Kara's heart raced. In all the Guild's history no Diamond had ever been harmed by their own. Diamonds were the spearhead of the Guild's power, unique and priceless fighters that everyone cherished and awed. To have a Diamond shot down by the Jades on the Guildmaster's orders...

Shaking off her stupor, Kara pushed forward between the two Jades blocking her way. They didn't resist, their eyes fixed on Raishan's still shape. She swept to his side and crouched beside him, reaching to feel the pulse on his neck. It was still there, but weak and uneven, showing that the Diamond was barely alive. With quick movements she drew her belt knife and cut off a flap of Raishan's shirt, pressing it to the wound.

The Jades from the gate were slowly approaching, uncertainty written all over their faces. Their shock told her shooting Raishan hadn't been part of the plan, which left some hope that the Guildmaster was not entirely out of his mind. Still, if Khall had orders that enabled him to open fire on a Diamond, things were bad indeed.

She could see the rest of their party gaping into the courtyard through the opening. She briefly met Egey Bashi's gaze, then Kyth's, his eyes wide with terror. She quickly looked away, afraid that he might see the hopelessness in her face and do something foolish. Guild business took precedence over everything else, and even the royal heir wouldn't be spared if he tried to interfere.

"Get Aghat Raishan to the medical barracks," she told the Jades. "Quickly!"

Their questioning eyes darted to Khall. The leader of the Jades nodded and signaled. More Jades rushed in from the entrance courtyard, lifting Raishan and carrying him out of sight.

Mai raised his face to Khall, steel glinting in his eyes. The Jade calmly stared back, and Kara imagined she saw a shade of smugness in the depth of his piercing gaze.

"It seems, Aghat Mai," he said, "that you're not taking our warning seriously. I will say this one last time. Surrender your weapon, or die."

Mai drew his staff.

"Let's see," he said, "how good your archers are, Gahang."

Khall looked at Mai in disbelief. "You will fight all of us by yourself, Aghat Mai? Would you rather die than surrender your weapon to me? That seems foolish."

Mai smiled. "I already told you, Gahang. I will surrender my weapon to the Guildmaster – and only to him. If you're talking of foolishness, it's at least as foolish for you to risk your men when all you need to do is call Aghat Oden Lan. Things are already way out of hand. I'm sure under the circumstances he'll understand."

Khall threw a quick glance at the Guildmaster's tower looming in the distance at the edge of the Inner Fortress. The tense set of his shoulders told Kara that, while the Jade did hesitate at Mai's words, whatever lay up in that tower frightened him more than the threat of a direct attack on their Guild's best Diamond. She used the moment of confusion and stepped up to Mai's side. Mai acknowledged her with a brief glance.

"I wish you'd stayed out of this, Aghat," he said quietly.

Kara didn't respond, her eyes darting around the walls. She counted twenty-four archers and an equal amount of crossbowmen down on the ground. She knew that whatever their odds of deflecting the arrows, they stood much less chance against the crossbows.

Khall's face contorted in anger as he noticed the new addition to the standoff.

"This is Guild business, Aghat Kara," he said. "You have no place here."

She drew her swords.

"As far as I understand, Gahang," she said, "you've just thrown all the rules to the wind. However, my presence here might give you an additional excuse to call the Guildmaster. Whatever your orders are about Aghat Mai, I'm sure he will want to be informed as soon as possible that I'm here."

Khall hesitated, then signaled. She saw a movement through the gate on the inner side, indicating a messenger dispatched to the Inner Fortress at a very fast run.

"Kara," Mai said quietly. "Get out of here while you still have a chance."

She glanced at him, surprised that he had used her name. He had never called her simply by name before, and now, in the face of deadly battle, it felt so intimate that her heart quivered. He wasn't looking at her, his eyes darting along the circle of archers at the top of the wall.

"If I do," she said, "they'll kill you."

"If you don't, they'll kill us both. That would be a bloody waste."

She smiled. Against reason, she felt excitement rising in her chest, her muscles warming in anticipation of the upcoming action.

"Aren't you giving up too easily, Aghat Mai?"

He glanced at her again. His eyes gleamed with mischief, his excitement matching her own.

"You're crazy," he said. "But I guess you probably know that."

"No crazier than you."

He edged closer to her. They stood back to back, so that their shoulders almost touched.

"When I bare my blades," he said quietly, "all hell will break loose."

She nodded, checking her footing, toning up her muscles. She sensed him brace next to her.

"Ready?" he asked.

"Yes," she said quietly.

"Then," he said, "let's dance."

She heard the click as he sprang the blades out of the ends of his staff, followed by the whizz of arrows and crossbow bolts descending at high speed. Excitement filled her as she whirled her swords, creating an impenetrable wall that stopped all arrows in midflight, sending them in a shower of splinters down to her feet. She could feel Mai on the other side creating a similar shield, rotating his staff with a force that made the air around it whistle.

She could see the surprise on the Jades' faces turn to disbelief as they sent more and more arrows down on them. A bolt penetrated her defense, stinging as it grazed the skin of her forearm, but she ignored it, focusing on maintaining her speed. Their lives right now depended on their ability to hold on.

One by one, the Jades were lowering their weapons. The crossbowmen stood down first as they ran out of bolts. The archers were also stepping back, one by one.

Through the crackle and whizz around them, Kara heard distant orders, barked at high speed. The flow of arrows ceased.

She lowered her blades, sensing Mai by her side do the same. Both remained tense, ready to spring into action again at any moment.

A movement on the wall above them turned into major turmoil as a tall man in a black cloak ascended the narrow space and stopped, looking down at them.

The Guildmaster.

Kara's heart quivered as she saw him. This ruthless man had always been the closest she had to a father, personally overseeing her training, encouraging her, urging her on. And then, this man had ordered her execution.

His eyes narrowed as they slid over her with an impenetrable look and fixed on Mai by her side.

"Aghat Mai," he said, his voice ringing through the yard. "Gahang Khall tells me you are refusing to surrender your weapon."

Mai kept his staff lowered, taking a barely perceptible side step that partially shielded Kara from the Guildmaster's view.

"I had hoped I could do it in a personal audience, Aghat Oden Lan," he said. "We have things to discuss."

Oden Lan shook his head. "We have nothing to discuss, Aghat Mai. You have done wrong. Have the decency and courage to admit it and give up quietly."

Mai lifted his chin. "I have done *right*. And in the depth of your heart you know it, Aghat Oden Lan."

The Guildmaster's eyes narrowed. "Surrender your weapon to Gahang Khall, Aghat."

The Jade took a step forward, but Mai's short glance stopped him.

"If I surrender my weapon now, I'm as good as dead."

Oden Lan pursed his lips. "You sealed your death warrant when you made your choice to disobey your order, Aghat Mai. It was good of you to answer your summons and come here yourself, so that you could spare us the trouble of searching for you, but it doesn't change a thing."

"Yes, it does," Mai said. "I came of my own will and walked freely into the Fortress."

"So what?"

"By the Code, this leaves me the right to issue an Ultimate Challenge."

A whisper ran through the rows around the Guildmaster as dozens of eyes clashed on Mai.

Khall stepped forward. "An Ultimate Challenge can only be issued against a Diamond, Aghat Mai. By the Code, you can't challenge the Guildmaster. Who is it that you wish to challenge?"

Mai slid a quick glance over him and turned back to Oden Lan.

"I challenge the Guild," he said.

Oden Lan looked at him in disbelief. "You wish to fight the entire Guild?"

"Yes."

The Guildmaster shook his head. "If you had learned the basics of Majat history, Aghat Mai, you would realize how futile that is."

Mai kept his gaze. "I know my history, Aghat Oden Lan."

"Then, you must know how such a challenge has ended before."

Many glances slid up the Guildmaster's tower where the rusted iron rings were still sticking out of the weather-beaten stone. Kara had read the chronicles too, how the challenger had been chained up there and used for the Jades' target practice, starting with the extremities. They said he had still been alive when the arrows finally severed his limbs two days later, sending him down to his death fall. She suppressed a shiver, doing her best to maintain her confident posture.

"I know," Mai said.

"And you still insist on going through with this outrage?"

"Yes. Somebody in this Guild should have the courage to stand up for what's right."

Oden Lan leaned forward. "You will face the entire Guild alone?"

Kara stepped forward to Mai's side. She saw Oden Lan's face twitch as he finally looked her way. His lips quivered, as if suppressing a sting of pain.

She knew how he felt. It hurt her too, to see him like this. But there was no going back.

"Aghat Mai is not alone," she said. "I join his challenge. You may pretend I don't exist anymore, Aghat Oden Lan, but I am here, and I will stand by his side as long as I can hold a weapon."

His eyes narrowed.

"By the Code—"

"—none of the Guild members can help him," she finished. "But I am no longer a Guild member, am I? The Code never bothered to prohibit outsiders from participating in the Ultimate Challenge. So, here I am, an outsider, willing to stand up to whatever you choose to throw at us, Aghat."

In the ensuing pause the courtyard went so still that even the gusts of the low breeze seemed too loud. Everyone held their breaths, looking at the Guildmaster.

"Very well," Oden Lan said. "The challenge begins tomorrow. You may sleep in a cell in the east courtyard. Under lock. No aid will be given to you in your preparations. At sunrise, your lives are forfeit."

A whizz of a lone arrow cut through the silence. Mai's hand shot up, catching it in front of Kara's face. They both spun around, searching for the source of the attack.

A man stood at the opposite side of the circle, on top of the wall. Streaming sunlight illuminated his freckled face, blue eyes opened in an expression of childlike wonder. He held a lowered bow with an arrow fitted in. Then, his face contorted in anger as he raised his bow again.

"Sharrim," Mai said quietly.

Kara recognized him too. The Jade who had been sent with Mai on the assignment to kill her. She shivered at the memory. He was a superb archer, their Guild's best. Back then, he had wounded her in the arm. And now, she felt the memory sting as he aimed his bow at her.

"Stand down, Gahang Sharrim!" Khall barked. "We're in ceasefire!"

Mai's shoulders stiffened as he brought the arrow to his face.

"What is it?" Kara asked quietly.

"Black Death. The arrow's coated with it."

Kara's skin prickled. Were any other of the arrows the Jades shot at them earlier poisoned too? She had minor scratches, and her forearm burned where the crossbow bolt had grazed over it – a light wound, but if the bolt had been coated with Black Death...

A new arrow whizzed through the air, aimed at Kara's face. She shot out her hand to catch it, but another, sneaky one followed right behind it.

As if in a bad dream she saw Mai step into the way of the arrow, shielding her. His body shook as the arrow hit, piercing through his shoulder.

Blood rushed into Kara's face. Supporting Mai with her left hand, she used her right one to draw two throwing knifes, balancing them in her palm. Stepping around Mai, she sent them forward in a sneaky spin, the force of the blow making the air whistle with a low hum that echoed clearly through the courtyard.

The daggers spiraled through the air in perfect unison, as if connected to each other. She knew it was nearly impossible for a man of any skill to deflect them, or even to see that it was two blades flying in place of one. Any disturbance to one of the daggers sent the other in an unpredictable direction. Only a few in the history of their Guild could master this shadow throw, and Kara had always prided herself on being good at it, even though she had never before used it on a live target.

Sharrim saw it coming, but he clearly did not realize the danger he was in. His hand darted to the sheath at his back, drawing a curved saber. It hit one dagger as it approached, sending the other off at an angle, straight into his chest.

Kara heard the thud as the Jade hit the floor, followed by shouting and running. She didn't bother to look as she turned back to Mai. He swayed, his face ashen pale. Kara steadied him, fighting a sinking feeling in her heart.

He wasn't supposed to get hit. Not after a ceasefire, after they deflected whatever their Guild's best Jades were able to throw at them in an impossible standoff.

And now, there was no hope left. Even if the wound wasn't deadly, it made it unthinkable for Mai to fight tomorrow. But if the arrow was also coated with Black Death...

It was a slow and potent poison that caused delirium, followed by violent agony and a painful death within a few hours. There was no known antidote. She could sense its bittersweet smell on the arrow point protruding from Mai's shoulder.

"Would you like to withdraw your challenge, Aghat Mai?" Oden Lan asked. "Under the circumstances, I will let you do it and surrender instead, to face your punishment."

Mai met Kara's gaze. She slightly shook her head.

Mai steadied himself against her arm and stood straight, turning to face the Guildmaster. She knew what this show was costing him, but she kept it to herself, standing still by his side with a smile on her face.

"The challenge stands, Aghat Oden Lan," Mai said.

The Guildmaster looked at him for a moment in disbelief. He did not look at Kara at all.

"So be it," he said. Then he turned and strode away.

17
WOUNDS

Egey Bashi watched Kara and Mai led away, surrounded in a protective ring of the Jades. Mai was using Kara's arm for support, but it took a man closely familiar with both of them to see the effort it was costing to keep him upright.

Kara marched with her head high under the stares of the crowd. Egey Bashi admired her for her composure. He knew that without Mai she did not stand a chance in hell of surviving what was coming tomorrow. Yet, he also knew that even with Mai's skill they were likely doomed.

Still, he had to do everything in his power to help.

He looked at Kyth.

"Perhaps you could try to meet with the Guildmaster tonight," he said. "Not much hope, of course, but if he does see us, something we say might help find a way out of this situation."

Kyth nodded. "I already sent a request, but the initial response was not encouraging. I don't think they even relayed it to him. I'll try again, of course."

Egey Bashi shook his head. Tomorrow this Guild might be witnessing the biggest bloodbath in the history of the Majat, at least in the count of the top gem ranks that were likely to perish in the mêlée. Raishan's injury added to the numbers. He needed to see if he could do something, at least about this one.

"With your permission, Prince Kythar," he said, "I need to attend to something urgent." He signaled for Ellah to follow and set off in the direction he had seen the Jades carry Raishan earlier.

They slowed down as they approached the medical barracks. The Majat Guild had some of the best doctors for taking care of wounds, and Egey Bashi knew that over the years they must have developed many potent substances to make healing effective, but he also knew that the Keepers were far ahead of them. The small vial he was clutching in his hand could heal Raishan in no time, even if the wound was very grave. But it couldn't be done unless the Diamond's life was out of danger, and it certainly had no power to bring him back from the dead. The Magister had to hurry.

Inside, he easily guessed where to go by a trail of forlorn Jades lining the corridor and crowding in the doorway ahead. Egey Bashi made sure Ellah was keeping up as he pushed through into the room.

Raishan lay on a table in the center, his pale face showing no signs of life. Several men in medics' uniforms bustled over him, and the middle-aged doctor with graying hair and thin, long fingers, gave quiet orders as two of his associates tied a white coverall over his clothes. The tart, metallic smell of blood filled the room. Egey Bashi heard Ellah stifle a half-gasp, half-sob as she pushed into the room in his wake.

When Egey Bashi stepped up to Raishan's side all the action in the room halted, the concerned expressions around them turning to disbelief, then suspicion. The Keeper kept his eyes on the doctor. Master Lestor, if he wasn't mistaken. In Egey Bashi's dealings with the Majat Guild he did his best to put names to many important faces.

He felt somewhat relieved. Lestor was the best doctor he knew outside the Keepers' White Citadel. He was also a reasonable man.

"How deep is the wound?" he asked.

Lestor surveyed him for a moment with an appraising glance, as if deciding whether to have him thrown out or let him speak. Egey Bashi hoped his expression was sufficiently determined to convince the doctor to settle on the latter option.

"Magister Egey Bashi," Lestor said. "I'm about to remove the bolt. Perhaps this conversation can wait until after that?"

Egey Bashi took out the small vial and held it up.

"This substance," he said, "can cure deadly wounds in a matter of minutes, helping them to disappear without a trace. It causes excruciating pain, but I doubt Aghat Raishan in his condition would even notice."

Lestor's gaze wavered, his eyes flicking to his patient and back to the Keeper.

"I fear," he said, "the bolt might have penetrated the lung and its point definitely sits very close to the heart. Can your substance handle that, Magister?"

Egey Bashi let out a sigh. "He has to be alive and in no immediate danger before we can apply the substance."

The doctor nodded. "I thought so. Perhaps you can step aside and let me do my job? If Aghat Raishan survives this surgery, I will welcome any cure you can bring."

Egey Bashi gestured to his side. "Ellah is an apprentice Keeper who knows how to use the substance. I will leave her here. If the cure is warranted she'll know what to do." He met Ellah's frightened gaze and placed a calming hand on her shoulder.

"It will be all right," he said quietly. "Master Lestor is the best. He will do everything possible to save Aghat Raishan's life."

Leaving Ellah in a chair in the corner of the room he stepped outside and proceeded to another room down the hall, also attended by the Jades. As he strode in, he was met with more suspicious glances but no one tried to stop him as he approached the bedside.

Sharrim lay very still, but he was clearly awake, his eyes following the Magister's approach with caution. Two medics bustled over him, dressing his bleeding chest wound. The bloodied throwing dagger lay in a metal dish on a side table and the Magister glanced at it with interest. By the look of it, the dagger had gone in at an angle, to about two thirds of its length, twisting toward the right side, which was probably what saved Sharrim's life. It was a hell of a throw, one Egey Bashi had only heard about but never thought possible to witness in real life.

"I'm glad to see you are going to live, Gahang," Egey Bashi said. "For a moment out there I feared the worst."

The Jade's gaze wavered and to his surprise Egey Bashi saw a tear standing in the corner of his eye.

"I never meant to hurt him," Sharrim whispered. "I..."

"You wanted to kill Kara, didn't you?"

Sharrim nodded. "It was our assignment to kill her, his and mine, together. His failure is my responsibility too." His lips trembled. "I was so angry with him when I learned what he'd done. I couldn't forgive him for deceiving me. But when I saw him today..." A tear rolled down his cheek as he subsided back into his pillow. A medic by his side glanced up at Egey Bashi with irritation.

The Keeper crossed his arms on his chest, thoughtfully looking down at the wounded man. He'd seen Mai stir up this reaction in women many times over. But to see a man feel this way was strange.

"How much Black Death do you put on your arrows?" he asked.

Sharrim looked at him in surprise. "Why?"

Egey Bashi leaned closer. "If you want me to try to help Aghat Mai, I need to know."

The Jade nodded earnestly, causing another irritated glance from the medic. "Ten drops," he said. "I coat the arrowhead and two inches of the shaft. This way even when the arrow goes through it still leaves enough poison to..." His lips trembled again. "What have I done, Magister?" he whispered.

Egey Bashi lightly patted him on the shoulder.

"Don't think about it, Gahang," he said. "Just focus on getting well. I appreciate your help."

He turned and strode away.

Doctor Lestor stood outside Raishan's room, surveying the crossbow bolt in a small dish pooled with blood. His arms were bloodied up to the elbows and splotches of it stained his white coverall. He raised his eyes in response to Egey Bashi's silent question.

"He's lost a lot of blood," he said. "And he's barely hanging on. I asked your apprentice to wait until his condition is stabilized."

Egey Bashi nodded. "If you need my help, please don't hesitate to call me. Aghat Raishan and I worked together on many assignments. His life is very precious to me."

"As it is to all of us," Lestor said. "This was a nasty incident getting out of hand, and everyone here is deeply regretting it. I assure you, Magister, I will do everything it takes."

"Are you also going to treat Aghat Mai's wound?" Egey Bashi asked.

Lestor lowered his eyes. The Keeper watched him with a sinking heart.

"Aghat Mai's life is forfeit," the doctor said at length. "By the Guildmaster's orders. If I did anything to help him, I would share his fate."

"But…"

The doctor's eyes showed regret.

"I share your feelings, Magister. Believe me. This is all such a waste. And now, come tomorrow, we will lose two of the best fighters our Guild has ever known in this senseless challenge – along with Shal Addim knows how many others, if this fight indeed goes through as planned."

"And you will just stand by and let it happen?"

The doctor sighed. "Following orders is the price we all must pay for being the Majat. The best I can do is treat Aghat Raishan before I receive orders to the contrary. Given the Guildmaster's feelings in the matter and the circumstances of Aghat Raishan's injury, I wouldn't be surprised to see such orders forthcoming. I am trying to do my best to give him a chance."

"But Aghat Mai–"

Lestor's glance cut him off. "Even if he was in top shape, I see no way he and Aghat Kara could win this challenge against the entire Guild. But I also know more. Gahang Sharrim's arrow that shot Aghat Mai was coated with Black Death. Even my skill cannot save him now."

Egey Bashi nodded. He knew better, but telling that to the doctor would serve no purpose except to put him into a precarious position.

As he strode back to the guest quarters, he heard hasty footsteps behind. He turned, watching a lean, wiry man with large dark eyes approach. A crossbow protruded from above his left shoulder and a suffused green jade glistened in his armband.

"Magister Egey Bashi," the man said. "I overheard you back there, talking to Gahang Sharrim, and later to Master Lestor. Is there anything you can do to help Aghat Mai?"

Egey Bashi stopped, looking at the man keenly.

"Why?"

"I…" the man hesitated. "You probably know what I'm risking by saying this, but I don't believe it would be right to stand back and let current events run their course. Not if anything can be done about it."

Egey Bashi peered into his eyes, seeing nothing but honesty in the man's urgent gaze. He was impressed. With people like this, the Majat Guild had hope indeed.

"You're a good man," he said.

The Jade lowered his eyes. "I love my Guild, Magister. I cannot possibly stand by injustice."

The Keeper nodded. "Do you know where Kara and Mai are kept?"

"Yes, in a cell by the east courtyard. They're under lock. The whole courtyard has been ordered off limits until tomorrow's challenge."

"Do you think you can find your way in there?"

The Jade hesitated. "I can always go into that courtyard to check on security, yes. I cannot get the key to their cell, though."

"Can you get anything to them?"

The Jade nodded. "The cell is protected by a grate, large enough to pass things through."

"Good." Egey Bashi rummaged in the pouch at his belt and brought out another small dark vial, similar to the one that he had just left in Ellah's care – his private stash even Mother Keeper did not know about. He pushed the vial into the Jade's hand. "Give them this. Aghat Mai should know what to do – if he is still conscious. If not, tell Kara to coat the arrow shaft with this liquid and pull it through."

The Jade's hand quivered. "Master Lestor believes Aghat Mai will die of poison. I heard your conversation. Do you know something he doesn't, Magister?"

"Yes, I do, Gahang, even though I'd appreciate it if you keep this knowledge from circulating. Aghat Mai is far more resistant to Black Death than anyone else.

With the amount he had, he should be able to recover by morning, assuming that his wound is treated within an hour or so."

The Jade put the vial into his pocket with great care.

"You should also give them some lanterns," Egey Bashi said. "It's getting dark and Kara will need all the light possible to do what's needed. And... I'm not sure how Majat prisoners are kept, but it would of course be good to make sure they have food and water. They need to replenish their strength. Walk with me; I'll tell you more details."

The Keeper parted with the Jade at the entrance courtyard, watching the man retreat in hasty steps. He hoped this man would do what he promised. So fortunate that, back in the Grasslands during their fight with the Kaddim, Egey Bashi had used a small dose of Black Death on Mai, to treat a seriously infected wound. Very few knew of the medicinal properties of this poison – or the fact that small doses of it made a man resistant to Black Death for life.

He hoped, with the Jade's help, Mai would give a nasty surprise to their Guildmaster by appearing in the arena in top shape tomorrow. This still didn't leave much chance for him and Kara to win the challenge, but at least it somewhat improved the odds.

18
SHADOW MASTER

Oden Lan looked out of the window of his study over the rows of warriors assembled in the courtyard below. Even though many of the top gems were out on active assignments, the display still looked impressive. Over two hundred people, the deadliest fighters in existence, formed row after row, the gems in their Majat armbands glistening in the torchlight.

The Fortress housed thousands of ranked Majat, but it was senseless to throw all of them into the challenge. Only the top gems could stand up to Kara for any length of time, given appropriate instructions. She had no chance with what the Guildmaster had in mind. With Mai out of the way, the challenge was bound to be a very short one.

Oden Lan knew he had to go down there and address the troops, but seeing the display from above enabled him to think through the battle plan in more detail before giving them specific instructions. He watched the trainers rush between the standing warriors, checking weapons and gear.

"Impressive, isn't it, Aghat?" a voice said from behind.

Oden Lan turned to watch the old weapons keeper, Abib, enter the room and approach at an unhurried walk. He silently stepped aside, letting the man stand next to him by the window with a good view of the courtyard.

Abib had been one of the few in the Fortress left from the old guard, trained at the time when Oden Lan himself had gotten his Diamond ranking. Abib's quiet humor, the ever-shifting expressions of his long, animated face, had always been comforting. And now, despite his stern composure, Oden Lan was glad of the company.

He had mourned Kara's death once before, and then lived through the relief that she was still alive and through the knowledge that, despite that, he was unlikely to ever see her again. And now, he was about to order his best warriors to do everything in their power to bring her down, and then witness her execution with his own eyes. He almost wished that he was the one to face an impossible fight tomorrow, and that it was his life that was forfeit, not hers. Being a Majat Guildmaster had always suited him. And now, he was finding it more of a burden than he could bear.

"You can still stop this madness, Aghat," Abib said quietly. "It's still in your power to pardon them. They don't have to fight to the death against the entire Guild."

"*Pardon* them?" Oden Lan sharply lifted his head. Against reason, Abib's words hit him harder than they should have. He had always prided himself on doing the right thing, no matter what. This meant giving no consideration whatsoever to his personal desires, even if doing so killed him inside. What could Abib possibly know about the sacrifices it took to uphold the Code? His lips twitched in a bitter smile. "You know that if we let their disobedience go unpunished we will throw away everything our Guild has built over centuries."

Abib shook his head. "These are not regular circumstances, Aghat. Like it or not, the lands around us are at war, and we must stand united."

"We *are* united," Oden Lan said. "Look at that force down there. They are the best warriors in existence and they all follow my command. Nothing can possibly stop us."

The weapons keeper's lips twitched into a distant smile.

"If you let this unravel, the ranks down there might look far less impressive only a day from now. You are pitching two of our Guild's best against them."

"One," Oden Lan said. "I see no possibility Mai can appear in the arena tomorrow. With the kind of wound he received, he's as good as dead. He will be, by morning, or so Gahang Khall tells me. He knows exactly how much poison Gahang Sharrim puts on his arrows."

"And you'll stand there and watch Kara face them alone?" Abib turned and looked into his face. "Come, Aghat, I know you don't want to do this."

Oden Lan's lips twitched. "It's not about what I want, Abib. If I did what I wanted..." He paused, his face contorting into a grimace.

"What is it, Oden Lan?" Abib asked quietly.

The Guildmaster clenched his teeth. "Mai. He… He *touched* her. I know it. I can see it in their eyes."

Abib chuckled. "Come now, Aghat. You can't possibly be upset about that. Have you forgotten what Mai was like in his teens? One way or another, he probably laid his hands on every woman between thirteen and thirty who was attractive enough to catch his eye and resourceful enough to find her way into the Inner Fortress. And if he missed any, it certainly wasn't for lack of eagerness on their side. Don't you remember how bad it was? It almost threatened his training, having all these women follow him like snakes follow a charmer, especially after it became clear he was going for the Diamond ranking."

Oden Lan shot him a side glance. "It's different now. Mai is not in his teens anymore. He's a grown man responsible for his actions. And Kara…" He paused again, controlling an annoying twitch of his mouth.

Abib shook his head.

"They're both young, healthy, and very attractive," he said. "And, through your orders, they are stranded together in an incredibly tight spot. Can you blame them for having some innocent fun?"

"*Innocent*?"

"Come now, Aghat. We teach them to channel their passion into fighting, but we never forbid our ranked warriors, especially Diamonds, to have this kind of pleasure if they feel they must. In fact, such things have proven invaluable in providing us with new stock for the gem ranks. Kara and Mai are a perfect match, both in combat styles and in how talented they are. They're the best our Guild has seen in centuries. What's wrong with them being together, eh?"

Oden Lan's face became a mask.

"He... He doesn't take women seriously. To him, it's all a game. And, she is not one to be played with. He's *wrong* for her."

Abib looked at him with amusement. "And who isn't?"

Oden Lan regarded him in cold silence.

"No one," he said. "She's a Diamond. She's meant for a different fate."

"She *was* a Diamond, and one of your best, until you sent killers after her, Aghat. Most likely, she only has hours left to live if you don't do something about it. You can't possibly let your jealousy destroy her, can you?"

Oden Lan measured him with his gaze. It was good that he and Abib were old friends. He would have likely had to strike down any other man who said such a preposterous thing to his face.

"It has nothing to do with jealousy, Abib. They were the ones who chose their fate. She – when she decided to abandon her assignment to help that boy. He – when he violated his orders and spared her life. They deserve to die. And they will. No one will stand in the way of justice as long as I'm the Guildmaster."

"You call that justice, Aghat," Abib said quietly. "I call it blindness."

"You've said enough, weapons keeper," Oden Lan said coldly.

"Not yet, Aghat. I have one more question. What about Raishan? Was it part of your justice to get him shot?"

Oden Lan pursed his lips. "Raishan made a choice too. He sided with the traitors of our Guild and tried to interfere with my direct orders. As far as I'm concerned, he's one of them."

"You are mad, Aghat Oden Lan," Abib said. "I will not stand by your actions."

Oden Lan's heart raced as he stepped back, looking into Abib's face.

"You have only one choice, old man," he said. "Either you take back what you just said, or you're an outcast too."

Abib held a pause.

"Given the circumstances," he said, "I'll take it back for now. Thank you for giving me the chance, Guildmaster."

He turned and strode out of the room.

After the weapons keeper was gone, Oden Lan spent a while looking into the courtyard below. Then he rang the bell on his desk and nodded to the man who appeared noiselessly in the door.

"Send him in," he said.

In a few moments he heard the rustle of feet on the stone steps. The door opened and closed, letting the newcomer into the study.

The man that stood in front of him was clad all in black. Even his face was covered with a mask, a black cloth with slits for the eyes: the mark of the Anonymous from the Inner Fortress, protecting the identity of one of the most important men in the Guild.

Oden Lan had not seen this man's face in years. And now, after all this time, he wasn't even curious anymore.

The Shadow Master was not one of the best warriors of the Guild. His value lay in his unique ability to spot the weaknesses of the top warriors that other trainers might miss. He was also a strategist, who knew the exact fighting style of every top gem. But, more importantly, his job was to oversee the Diamonds' shadow training, where one Diamond in the Guild was taught the exact fighting style and weaknesses of another, in case it became warranted for the Guild to bring this Diamond down. Seeing the Shadow Master now brought bad memories. Mai had been Kara's shadow, trained to kill her if needed. And now, despite this ability, he had chosen to spare her life and ultimately to commit her to this senseless challenge.

"I would welcome any suggestions, Shadow Master," Oden Lan said.

The man nodded. "How many top ranked warriors are currently in the Fortress?"

Oden Lan glanced outside the window, then at the list on his desk. "Four Diamonds," he said, "not counting Aghat Raishan. Thirty-six Rubies. Over a hundred Sapphires. The Emerald Guards. And the Jades, of course."

"Which Diamonds?"

"Jamil, Rand, Lance, and Shebirah."

"You assume Aghat Mai won't be able to fight?"

"I don't see how he could possibly do it. In fact, I assume we won't be seeing him at all – except his corpse, which I fully intend to put on display after this is over."

Shadow Master nodded. "Four Diamonds shouldn't have a problem finishing her off. Send Lance first. Kara's main weakness is in the fact that being smaller and lighter than a man, she would have more trouble against head-on attack with brutal force. Lance is good at it. He is bigger and heavier, and he is brutal enough for the task. Have the other three Diamonds cover him and distract her, if needed. It should be a fairly short fight."

Oden Lan shivered. Lance was indeed a brutal man who wouldn't hesitate to kill even his own mother if charged with the task. He wished every one of his Diamonds had been so reliable.

"Have the Rubies stand by as a precaution," Shadow Master said. "And a ring of Jades around the top. Whatever happens in the arena, after she exhausts herself, the Jades will have no trouble finishing the job."

Oden Lan nodded. Now that they were actually talking about it, he couldn't help the unpleasant quiver in his stomach at this calm discussion of the fastest way to kill Kara. The reason he was so angry at Mai was not only because the man had disobeyed his orders and stirred up Oden Lan's jealousy by getting closer to Kara than Oden Lan could only dream of. The worst of it all was the fact that, through Mai's actions, Oden Lan was now forced to witness and orchestrate Kara's death.

Perhaps Abib was right and he should give her, if not a pardon, at least a chance to surrender. But in the end it was all the same. He had no choice but to have her killed. Doing otherwise would violate everything he believed in.

"I must go down into the courtyard to address the troops," he said. "Gahang Khall is already waiting down there. I'll send him and the Diamonds to your quarters afterward for detailed instructions."

He swept his cloak back over his shoulders and descended the spiral staircase leading to the inner grounds in smooth, springy steps.

19
THE KEEPERS' CURE

The Jades locked the prison door and left, making a lengthy show of putting the bars into place and clicking the numerous locks. Kara watched them from the depth of the cell, throwing frequent glances at Mai crouching in the corner. He was sitting on the floor with his back to the wall, leaning heavily on his uninjured arm, watching her with wary eyes. In the dim light his face looked drawn, exhausted.

It was to their advantage to make the Jades believe Mai was near death, but only if in the end he could recover and surprise them tomorrow. Kara didn't believe it was possible. He had taken a poisoned arrow for her. There was no way he could survive this. He was going to die, all because she was too slow to defend herself. She was having a hard time coming to terms with it.

As soon as the Jades were gone she swept to Mai's side, easing him into a more comfortable position. She knew she should at least get out the arrow. But in the dim light of the waning sky coming in through the open grate of the doorway, she was likely to do more damage than good. Still, she couldn't possibly have him sit through the night with an arrow in his shoulder.

"Sorry," Mai said. "How stupid of me to get myself shot."

Kara swallowed a lump. She shouldn't cry, she knew. She should maintain all the composure she could. Tomorrow she was going to give their Guild the show of a lifetime, a fight that would go down in history for centuries to come. It wouldn't make a difference in the end, but she was going to make damned sure Mai's death had a meaning and that she went through with what he had started.

It crossed her mind that she would be fighting her former comrades, and that this whole thing was madness orchestrated by a devious enemy. If the Kaddim's goal was to bring down the Majat Guild by taking out the warriors of its top gem ranks, they were succeeding, and there seemed to be no way for her to stop it.

She could refuse to go through with the challenge, of course. But then she would be throwing away everything Mai had fought for. After everything he'd done for her, she couldn't possibly betray him. She owed him her life, and she was going to pay this debt in spades.

"Let me take the arrow out, Aghat," she said.

He shook his head. "We both know nothing you can do could possibly stop the inevitable. You should rest. You need your strength."

She ignored his words, looking for a brighter place where she could put him to do her work. But at that moment she heard a click of a distant gate opened and closed. Footsteps echoed on the cobblestones and she saw a tall man with a crossbow on his back striding through the courtyard toward their cell.

She kept outwardly calm, but went tense inside, ready to spring into action. Did the Guildmaster stoop so low as to send a spy to them?

He probably wanted to know how bad Mai's wound was. And she was damned if she was going to give him any clue.

She kept to the shadows as the man approached, peering into the darkness of the cell.

"Aghat Kara?"

She strained her eyes to see him more clearly. The newcomer was a young man with short wavy hair. His strong jaw and full lips threw long shadows in the waning light. She was certain she had never seen this man before.

"Yes?" she said.

"Is Aghat Mai all right?"

She glanced at Mai, slumping by the wall. "He's just fine. Why?"

She imagined she saw the man's shoulders sag in relief. From this distance she could see his armband, its dim, suffused stone accented by the sharp glint of the metal around it. She couldn't make out the stone's color, but she could guess it all the same.

"You're a Jade," she said. "Which, at the moment, makes you an enemy. I strongly caution you to approach no further." She took out a throwing dagger, shifting just a bit into the light and making a show of weighting it in her hand. The man hesitated, the fear in his face suggesting that he might have been one of those in the courtyard who had witnessed her shadow throw.

He took off his crossbow with slow, deliberate movements, and laid it on the ground in plain view.

"I brought you a package," he said, "from Magister Egey Bashi. May I come closer so that I can give it to you, Aghat?"

She frowned, doing her best to hide her surprise. A package from Magister Egey Bashi was the last thing she expected. Was this some sort of a trap?

The Jade straightened up and held his arms out to the sides. A small vial glistened in his hand.

Kara stiffened, feeling her skin creep.

"It's a healing elixir," the Jade went on. "He said Aghat Mai would know what it is. If he's conscious."

She shot another glance at Mai.

"I'm quite all right, Gahang," Mai called out. His voice was calm, but she knew how much effort it was costing him to speak like this.

"I'm so glad to hear that, Aghat Mai." The cautious glance the Jade gave Kara showed that he wasn't fooled. She stared back, hoping that her expression didn't betray anything at all.

"This liquid," the Jade said, "will heal his wound completely, without a trace. You have to put it all the way into the wound, though. Did the arrow go through?"

"Yes," she said. There seemed to be no reason to deny something he apparently knew so well.

"Have you taken it out yet?" the Jade insisted.

"No."

"Break off the feathered part of the shaft, coat the rest with this substance and pull it out through the wound, slowly. It should be enough. That's what the Magister said. He also said that you should treat your own wounds, if you have any. Even if they're scratches. You'll need all your strength for tomorrow."

She nodded. Then she reached out and carefully took the vial from his hand.

"I have something else for you too." The Jade took a bag off his shoulder and held it out, working to fit it through the narrow grate.

"You'll need light to do this," he said. "There're two lanterns in there, fully fueled. Enough to burn until dawn, even though you probably won't need that long. And a flint, in case you don't have one. Also, there's water and food rations."

She met his gaze. From this distance she could finally see his eyes, watching her with a mixture of awe and concern. She knew she would remember him if she saw him again.

"Why are you doing this?" she asked.

He hesitated. "My crossbow shot down Aghat Raishan. I didn't think he deserved to be shot, but I followed my orders. I did my best, along with the others, to shoot down you and Aghat Mai. When Gahang Khall gave the signal, I was certain you were as good as dead." He swallowed. "I've never seen such fine swordwork. You and Aghat Mai are the best our Guild has seen in centuries. I can't just stand by and let you two get killed. If you're doing this, you deserve your best chance."

"You do know that if you're discovered you'll be in a lot of trouble?"

He held her gaze. "I don't intend to be discovered. But if I am, I'll answer for my actions. Dying by your side would be an honor, Aghat."

She smiled. "I don't intend to die. Neither does Aghat Mai." She wished she could believe it, but she made certain her voice sounded confident and easy, as if there were nothing to it.

If she could heal Mai's wound it would ease his suffering. It would make his death as easy as possible for someone shot with Black Death. But it still left no hope that either of them would survive. She bit back the thought, her smile so stiff that it hurt her cheeks.

"Magister Egey Bashi also asked me to tell you one more thing," the Jade said. "Aghat Mai will not die because of the poison. Its effects should wear off completely by morning. Black Death can't kill him. I'm not sure why."

Her eyes widened, the sudden rush of hope making her head spin. It took her a moment to find her voice.

"He said that?"

"Yes, he was very certain. He said he talked to Gahang Sharrim and found out how much poison the arrow was coated with. Aghat Mai should tolerate it well. But, the Magister also warned that Aghat Mai might become delirious for a while, even violent. Black Death does it to people; I heard it, too. This elixir causes terrible pain and at the heat of his delirium Aghat Mai might go berserk, if the wound is not treated very soon. Please be careful."

Kara let out a breath. "Thank you, Gahang."

"I wish I could help you more."

This time her smile came from the heart. "You've done enough. I won't forget it."

"You're not asking my name."

She shook her head. "No. You're risking enough without telling me your name. When this is over, I look forward to being properly introduced. Now, go, Gahang, before someone discovers you here."

She waited until the tall slim figure disappeared under the low archway. Then she unclenched her fist and looked at the dark glass vial in her hand.

She knew what it was, even though she had never had a chance to see it in action. The liquid in this vial could make damaged flesh grow whole in mere minutes, without so much as a scar. This elixir was once used on her own mortal wound, so that it healed without a trace while she lay unconscious.

She shivered with relief. If she did everything right, Mai would survive. He might be in shape tomorrow to fight by her side. Against reason, this knowledge filled her with hope, as if facing their entire Guild side by side with Mai guaranteed them victory.

At least she would not have to watch Mai die in her arms. Not tonight.

Kara returned into the cell and lit both lanterns, placing one on the shelf above Mai's head and the other on the floor next to his wounded left arm. Her own arm was stinging whenever the sleeve touched the long gash grazed by the crossbow bolt, but she ignored it. It was nothing but a deep scratch and wasn't even bleeding anymore.

Mai's eyes had a feverish gleam as he watched her movements. The poison was taking hold. She hoped she could finish the worst of the healing while he was still aware of his surroundings and that it wouldn't be as bad as the effects of Black Death were rumored to be.

She took out a knife. He drew up against the wall, then slowly relaxed as awareness settled in. He was losing control, and it was frightening to watch.

"Did you hear everything?" she asked.

He nodded.

"I'm going to cut the shaft. Then I will coat the arrow with this substance and pull it through."

He tried to lift up higher against the wall and winced, subsiding back into place.

"You must not move when I'm doing it. It's going to hurt, far more so than from just pulling the arrow through."

"I know." He looked up at her, a smile glimmering in the corners of his mouth. His face was hollow, so pale that he looked like a ghost.

"You've been through this before," she said. "Haven't you?"

"Yes." His voice was a near-whisper as he watched her movements with an entranced look.

She took a vial of disinfecting liquid from her pack and wiped her hands and the blade.

"Ready?"

He nodded.

She leaned over him, cutting away his blood-soaked sleeve, trying not to disturb the arrow protruding from his shoulder. One by one, she peeled off the strips of the sleeve, leaving his arm and shoulder bare. The wound was still oozing, blood caking around the entry point.

She reached forward and grasped the shaft, sliding her knife across in a clean, precise cut that snapped the feathered end right off.

He stiffened.

"Are you all right?" she said quietly.

He slowly relaxed his shoulders and leaned back into the wall.

She reached for the Keepers' vial. His eyes followed her movements. The thought of causing him excruciating pain made her quiver inside, but she knew she had to go through with it, and quickly, if she wanted him to make his best recovery.

The liquid was thick and stayed on like glue when she carefully brushed it onto the arrow shaft protruding from his shoulder. She was careful not to let her movements disturb the shaft too much, or to touch the skin around the wound. Then she screwed the lid back on and put away the vial.

"Ready?" she whispered.

He looked up at her. "Be careful not to cut yourself on the arrowhead. I'm not sure how much poison's still left on it."

She clasped his shoulder, holding him in a half-embrace as she reached behind him with her free hand toward the protruding arrowhead on the other side.

"Wait," he said.

She paused.

"I can feel the poison taking hold. If I snap and go berserk, you must promise you'll knock me out."

She swallowed. "The healing will take much longer if I do."

He turned and met her gaze within her half-embrace. His eyes were feverish. She could feel his hot breath on her skin.

"Promise me," he insisted. "I don't want to risk hurting you."

"I promise," she said quietly. Then she grabbed the arrow and pulled.

He gasped as the shaft moved through the wound, and she felt him shudder in her hold. She tightened her embrace, keeping him in place. When the arrow was through, she threw it aside and used her free hand to pull the wound closed on both sides.

Each of her movements shook him with a spasm that echoed in her body too, as if she were the one being hurt. Knowing his usual composure, she could only imagine what the pain was like. Tears stood in her eyes, but she took care not to let it affect her actions.

After she had done what she could, she eased him against the wall, keeping her hands on his shoulders to support him, ready to restrain him if needed. His eyes looked feverish, his pupils dilated from the pain so much that instead of their normal blue-gray they seemed black. He was no longer shivering, but she could see in his drawn face how the pain was draining him, robbing him of his strength. Dear Shal Addim, how long was this going to take?

"Are you feeling any better?" she asked quietly.

A ghostly smile creased his lips. He was beginning to look delirious, from the pain or the poison, she couldn't tell.

"With you touching me," he said, "I feel I'm in heaven."

She swallowed. "Don't joke. I know how much it hurts. I can feel it."

"I'm not joking."

She looked into his eyes searchingly. His pupils were still dilated. He was in pain, but he smiled as he met her gaze.

"I know you think I'm delirious," he said. "And you're right... I can feel it too. It's much harder in this state to control my words and actions. Normally, I wouldn't try to tell you how your touch makes me dizzy... like I'm dreaming and never want to wake up. Your skin... it smells like wild aemrock. Even if I held you in my arms all the time I could never get enough of your scent... If all it takes is some pain to have you touch me like this, I hope it never stops."

She went very still, peering into his face. He was definitely driven by the poison. His eyes had a feverish gleam and she could see the skin of his bare arm ripple as he shivered. His wound was closing, but she could still see the entry point, with dry blood caked around it.

The look in his eyes was so unsettling, a mixture of tenderness and longing that made her heart quiver.

"When I am with you," he said, "you make me feel complete. It's like... we are meant for each other... Do you ever feel the same way?"

He was looking at her when he said it, but she wasn't sure he could actually see her. *Dear Shal Addim.* She had heard that people in delirium said the strangest of things. Yet, she had also heard that delirium only forced people to speak their mind, revealing something they would never say otherwise.

Could he possibly mean any of this?

Like we're meant for each other. Do I feel the same way?

"I know I am not supposed to fall in love," he said. "But with you... I just couldn't help it."

Her skin prickled.

In love.

Did he have any idea what he was saying?

Would he remember any of it?

Mai's head rolled, his body shifting restlessly in her hold. She peered into his eyes, relieved to see them returning to their normal blue-gray as the pain receded. She let out a sigh, dropping her hands away from him and sitting back on her heels.

His eyes were feverishly bright. Even though he was talking to her, she wasn't sure he was aware that she was actually here.

"I... I never meant to act on my feelings for you," he said. "But that time... when you fought me and you got so close... I couldn't possibly resist it... I should have controlled myself. I shouldn't have shown you how much I wanted you... And later, I shouldn't have provoked you... If I had stayed away..."

Provoked me. She had always felt she had been the one provoking him. He did show her during the fight that he was open to the possibility, but he never took any further steps until she drove him to it. And yet... back in Middledale, when he had taken off his shirt and left it where she could find it... when he had left the door to the bath chamber open, as if inviting her inside...Was he aware of the effect he had on her? Was it possible he did all these things on purpose, hoping that she would go after him?

Dear Shal Addim.

She suddenly realized that the thought that he might have controlled himself and stayed away filled her with dread. If he had, she would never have known what it was like with him. She would have missed the most enjoyable moments of her life.

"You are so innocent," he said, "and I... I took advantage of it. And now... I've confused you. I should have known better. You are probably regretting it... I know I should be regretting it too, but I can't. You've given me happiness beyond my wildest dreams. I always hoped... I could save you by laying down my life... I just never thought you would end up sharing my fate."

His eyes held such longing that she felt a lump in her throat, unbidden tears rising to her eyes. Whether or not he was aware of what he said, whether or not he would remember any of it tomorrow, she felt she was hearing something he never wanted her to know. And yet... If he meant any of it, it concerned her so closely. She felt a tingling in her stomach, as if falling, at the mere thought he could actually be telling the truth.

She picked up his hand and pressed it to her cheek. She wasn't sure he could understand what she said, but she wanted to say it anyway.

"I don't regret a thing," she said. "Given a choice, I would do the same, over and over again. And now... the only way you can save me is by staying alive. Promise me you'll do everything you can to survive."

His eyes focused on her face. For a moment he seemed almost sane.

"I promise," he said.

She shivered. Could he understand her? Was his delirium over?

She peered into his eyes, searching for glimpses of sanity, but saw none. He looked dazed as his gaze drifted to his hand she was still pressing against her face. His palm shifted in her hold, cupping her cheek, tracing it with his thumb in a gentle caress. As she released his hand, he brushed it through her hair to the nape of her neck. She gasped. She had never realized how sensitive it was back there, his touch echoing through her like a charge of lightning.

He had always been so controlled around her, never initiating any intimacy unless she drove it first. And now, the delirium of the poison was stripping away his restraint. She felt as if she was prying, witnessing a private side of him she wasn't meant to see. Against reason, it felt even more arousing to see him like this, when his superb self-control was no longer governing his actions.

His eyes trapped her, his hand on her neck warm and light, and toned in a way that made it unthinkable for her to escape his hold, even if she wanted to. She melted into his touch as his fingers found the right spots. She couldn't tell if he was aware of what he was doing, but it felt so good that she didn't care. She vaguely wondered at the wisdom of being so close to him, so that if the poison drove him berserk she would be vulnerable to his attack. But, danger or not, she wouldn't move from her current position for anything.

His other hand caught her wrist. His lips brushed the tender skin on the inside of her arm as he rested it over his shoulder. He pulled up her sleeve and planted a kiss in the crook of her elbow, inhaling deeply.

Inadvertently, her hand slid into his hair, caressing him. She sensed his shiver as he pushed away from the wall, kneeling in front of her. His hands moved down her back, trapping her in a half-embrace, his touch sending pleasure spiraling through her every nerve. *Dear Shal Addim, how does he know exactly where to touch me?* She briefly closed her eyes, weakness spreading from the pit of her stomach, her body yielding to him even before she could give it any conscious thought.

And now, with this hold, he had her trapped completely, so that if he lost control and tried anything violent, in her dazed state she couldn't possibly defend herself at all. The thought of being in his power was so arousing. His closeness was like a spell, robbing her of her own self-control. Perhaps she was poisoned too?

He lifted his face to hers, mere inches away, his breath making her skin tingle with anticipation. His pupils were dilated again. She could see reason in his eyes surface and recede, as if he was struggling with consciousness, holding back, finding the strength to let her go.

She held still, trying to quiet her racing heart. Her entire body wanted him to go on, but her mind was screaming caution, telling her to stop. He was delirious, about to become violent from the poison. She would be crazy to allow him to have his way with her in this state, when he couldn't possibly control his actions.

She could sense the last bits of his control slipping away as his touch became more powerful, his hands claiming her in a way they never had before. Yet she marveled how, even in this semi-conscious state, he still held back, as if trying to give her a choice.

Perhaps it was this hesitation, more than anything else, that drove her on, making her feel as if, despite his daze, despite the danger he posed in this state, the choice was still hers. And, as she thought about it, she realized that she had made her choice already. No matter what he was going to do to her, she couldn't possibly stop.

She felt a thrill in the pit of her stomach, as if stepping over the edge into an abyss, as she yielded to his embrace. His eyes lit up with a deep carnal glow as his muscles flexed and hardened, pulling her into his arms.

We shouldn't be doing this here, was her last sensible thought. And then his scent enfolded her, his hands so strong and passionate in their near-violent caress that she couldn't possibly hold back anymore. She responded, no longer sure which one of them was driven by the poison. Her mind was clouded just like his. This was madness, and she couldn't possibly resist it.

She had only a vague memory of how she ended up with her clothes off, with him upright and inside her, driving into her with a strength that sent her over the edge again and again, until she could no longer tell which one of them was convulsing and if this was ever going to stop. She didn't know how much time passed before she came back to her senses and realized that they were still in the prison cell and that she was now sitting in his lap, naked and open, with his arms around her. He still wore all his clothes and that made her feel even more vulnerable, a feeling she had never believed possible to experience with any man. She turned and shifted her weight so that she could relax against his chest, inhaling his pine scent, never wanting the moment to end.

You make me feel complete, he'd told her. She suddenly realized that it was exactly how she felt around him. Complete. They made an invincible pair. Nothing could possibly happen to them while they were together.

20
WEAPONS KEEPER

Mai had his eyes open, but showed no awareness of his surroundings. Kara knew this was an effect of the poison too, an apathy that followed the violent stage. If Black Death were to run its normal course, he would eventually drift off and die, without ever waking up. She prayed that Magister Egey Bashi was right and that wasn't going to happen.

She eased him down onto a cloak she spread over the floor. Her clothes were scattered around the cell, ripped but still usable. She put them on and lay next to him, resting her head against his shoulder. Exhausted, she dozed off.

She woke what felt like minutes later from a distant click of the courtyard gate, followed by hasty footsteps over the cobbles. She slid off along the wall, to the edge of the moonlit circle falling from the grate into the cell. From this position she could see the newcomer without betraying her own actions.

As she watched the tall, slightly stooping figure take shape against the dark outline of the distant gateway, she saw a movement in the darkness to her right and spun around to see Mai, sitting up, watching her intently.

"Are you back?" she asked quietly.

He nodded.

She let out a small sigh of relief. "It may be better if you stayed hidden. Let whoever is coming think you're near death."

He nodded again and subsided into the corner, lying back down onto his cloak. She saw his hand resting next to his staff, relaxed, as if the closeness were merely accidental.

He was putting on a good bluff. If he were shot and dying of poison, he would probably look just like that. Looking at him brought an inadvertent blush to her cheeks. Did he remember what had happened? Or was he so delirious he was not even aware of his actions? If so, perhaps it was for the best. And yet, the things he had said to her just couldn't leave her mind. Had he meant any of it?

The approaching man looked familiar, and older than she originally thought. As the shadows around his face took shape from the depth of his hood, she stifled a gasp of recognition.

"Master Abib?"

The old weapons keeper had been in the Guild for as long as she remembered. His job of overseeing the crafting and care of the weapons made him indispensable, but for Kara he had always been more. Since childhood, he had been the man who understood her best. He was the one she had always gone to, with all her sorrows and frustrations, until the completion of her training distanced her from these feelings once and for all.

Abib approached the grate and peered inside, fumbling with the keys on his belt. He cursed as he undid the locks placed by the Jades, one by one. Then he swung the grate open and quietly slipped inside.

Kara watched him with wide eyes. Abib had the Guildmaster's ear and was the closest to what Oden Lan could ever call a friend. Had he sent Abib to spy on them? The thought made her heart quiver. She suddenly realized that the worst part of being expelled from the Guild was not the loss of her privileges and rank, but the knowledge that her old friends and comrades would now view her as an enemy and follow orders to fight against her.

Abib stopped in the center of the cell and set down his lantern, glancing around. His eyes paused on Mai, who lay still by the wall with no indication of whether or not he was awake. Then, Abib stepped forward and lowered to the floor next to Kara.

"I came to inspect your weapons," he said, "and to bring you this." He held out two throwing knives. "I heard you lost two of yours this afternoon. You'll need a full complement tomorrow."

She couldn't help feeling warmth flow over her as she took the knives from his hand. They were of the best steel, perfectly balanced. Probably even better than the ones she lost, which had already seen some action and had not been polished in over a week.

"Thank you, Master Abib," she said.

He nodded, reaching forward to pick up her weapon, leaning against the wall.

She stiffened. If he had come here with bad intentions, meddling with her weapon would be the best way to sabotage tomorrow's tournament. She watched him warily as he placed her black three-foot-long staff across his lap, pulling a narrow sword from each end in a smooth move that told of intimate familiarity with the weapon.

It was called a hagdala, a fighting staff that doubled as a sheath for two blades, making this weapon one of the most versatile amongst the Diamonds. Abib had personally overseen its crafting in the last stages of her training, months before her ranking tournament. Memories flowed as she watched his long fingers run along the edge of the blade. To her knowledge he wasn't doing anything unusual, just a routine inspection he had done so many times when she had left for an assignment or prepared for a serious fight.

"I spoke to Magister Egey Bashi," Abib continued, as if oblivious to the tension. "He told me that by morning Aghat Mai will make a full recovery." He glanced into the corner, where Mai's shape was barely visible against the wall.

"He did?" Kara was surprised. She was certain Egey Bashi wouldn't give this information to anyone he didn't consider fully trustworthy. She was surprised he would confide in Master Abib. Everyone knew how close Abib was to the Guildmaster. Was this a trap?

Abib tested the balance of her blades and sheathed them, reaching over to inspect her belt with the throwing knives. He frowned as he found a chipped one and replaced it with another he took from his own belt. Then he sighed, raising his face to meet Kara's gaze.

"Times have become twisted indeed, if you can look at me with such distrust, Aghat Kara. I came here as a friend."

"Why?"

He shook his head. A smile lit up his face, but the deep lines around his mouth also held sadness.

"Because I think what has happened to you is unfair. I have great respect for Master Oden Lan, and I am certain that when he awakes from his madness he will deeply regret all of this." He glanced around the cell. "I want to make sure his regrets are minimized."

Kara's lips twitched. "From what I saw yesterday afternoon, I believe he'll probably feel relieved when it's over."

Abib chuckled. "You don't know him well enough, Aghat. Trust me. Besides, regardless of his feelings, in these troubled times we can't afford to lose our two best fighters. Not over something stupid that shouldn't have ever happened." He threw a short glance over his shoulder. "You can stop playing dead with me, Aghat Mai. Magister Egey Bashi had a chance to tell me how his earlier treatment has made you more or less immune to Black Death. Your wound can't be that serious either. Not if Aghat Kara followed his instructions."

Mai sat up in one easy move.

Abib turned and measured him with an amused glance. "Much better."

"Glad to see you, Master Abib." Mai's voice seemed normal, fully recovered. Kara hoped it was really true.

"Likewise, Aghat Mai," the weapons keeper said. "You gave us all a nasty fright yesterday afternoon."

Mai leaned forward into the circle of light. Kara's skin prickled as she saw his shoulder, still bare where she had cut off his blood-soaked shirt. His skin was smooth, with no trace of a wound. The Keepers' cure was potent indeed.

Abib looked at the healed shoulder too, his eyes pausing on it for an extra moment before returning to his task. He lowered Kara's crossbow he had just finished tuning and handed it back to her, followed by a boot knife and a full set of bolts.

"I will inspect your weapons now, Aghat Mai. Your staff, please."

Mai hesitated only for a brief instant before passing him the staff, thinner and longer than Kara's, of the same polished black. She watched him with interest. Mai's weapon was very advanced, with a spring mechanism that could release two retractable blades hidden in its ends. It was nasty, as she recalled from her own experience. Even if you knew the blades were there, during the fight the eye could only follow the visible part of the weapon. To have a blade spring out when this staff was descending on you at high speed made it so much harder to avoid the additional foot's length of razor-sharp steel that could appear and disappear on his command. She shivered, suppressing the memory. Last time it had happened, the blade had hit her, sending her into a coma and making everyone believe she was dead. She hoped she would never have to face this staff in battle again.

Abib's fingers pressed the hidden triggers to release and retract the blades several times. He closed his eyes as he listened to the sound. Then he reached into his pack and took out a set of small brushes and picks, tuning and polishing the hidden mechanism.

"I also brought each of you a set of fresh clothes,

and told the lads guarding you to give you plenty of wash water in the morning. It could do wonders for the outcome of the challenge if you both look your best when you appear in the arena."

Kara nodded. It made sense. They were putting on a show, and every detail mattered, even if in the end it wasn't likely to make much difference.

"Do you think we have a chance, Master Abib?" she asked, before she could think better of it. This was a question from her childhood, when she was a little girl, driven too hard by her ruthless trainers, running to him for every bit of advice. She was grown up now and should never have to ask anyone for reassurance.

The weapons keeper frowned. "Nobody in the Fortress feels good about what has happened. Many are already mourning Aghat Mai. Rumor of your shadow throw has spread like fire, and everyone is in awe. No one is looking forward to fighting this unequal battle against you."

Kara's lips twitched. "I'm sure they'll still do their best."

Abib shook his head. "I have lived long enough to know that battles are often won or lost before they even begin. If Aghat Mai appears on the arena by your side in his best shape..." He spread his hands and fell silent.

Kara could see his point. Many ranked warriors viewed Mai as a hero, their admiration for him bordering on downright worship. To hear that he had been treacherously shot by a poisoned arrow after issuing an Ultimate Challenge to the Guild was bound to stir some response. And if he were to miraculously recover–

"Who are they sending against us?" Kara asked.

Abib shook his head. "I am not privy to all information. I know that Aghat Oden Lan spent time in his study with the Shadow Master before sending some men to his private training grounds. I can only tell you we have four active Diamonds in the Fortress right now."

Kara's eyes widened. "*Four*?"

"Not counting Aghat Raishan. We still hope his recovery will eventually add to the numbers, but not tomorrow, for sure."

Kara let out a sigh. *Raishan*. Another victim of the mess she had started.

"Which four?" Mai asked.

"Jamil, Lance, Rand, and Shebirah."

Mai nodded. "If the Guildmaster believes I won't be fighting, he will send Lance to spearhead the attack."

"Why?" Kara asked.

Mai's eyes slid over her calmly. "The only vulnerability in your fighting style one can exploit at short notice is the fact that you are more likely to back down under continuous, head-on brutal force. Lance is very good at this tactic."

Kara shivered. Mai had been trained as her shadow, a Diamond who knew her weaknesses and was more likely than others to get through her defense in single combat. This was the mechanism their Guild kept in place to ensure obedience, although before her and Mai it had not been explored in practice for many centuries.

"I know Shebirah well, too," Mai said. "I fought against her in her ranking tournament, three years ago."

Kara tried to recall. Shebirah was a tall, muscular woman, whose looks and fighting style resembled a man's. She did not know her at all. It was good Mai had experience with her, which may be explored for a fighting advantage. If only Kara herself had been old enough to have fought in others' ranking tournaments – but at nineteen, having ranked only last year, she was of course too young. And now, she had nearly no experience fighting other Diamonds. *Four.* She shivered. Even with Mai's help, what chances did they have against such numbers, with all the other Guild's gem ranks as backup?

"Why are there so many Diamonds in the Fortress?" she asked. "Usually we have one or two at most, with others on active assignments."

The weapons keeper's face twisted into a crooked smile. "Aghat Oden Lan has been recalling everyone from assignments to send them after you two. He did not believe Aghat Mai would answer his invitation."

Mai grinned. "No kidding."

"What did he write to you?" Abib asked.

Mai glanced at Kara.

"I think," she said, "there's no harm in telling me now, Aghat Mai. Things are unlikely to get any worse."

Mai leaned back. "He said he would torture me beyond recognition and hang me up from his tower to rot alive. It was... inventive, to say the least. Some of the inquisition terms were actually unfamiliar to me. I had no idea our Guildmaster was capable of such style."

Kara looked at him in shock. No wonder Mai had been prepared to do everything in his power not to let her see the letter.

Abib shook his head. "You made him feel very personally about it, Aghat Mai. You probably know why." He glanced at Kara. Mai answered him with an impassive look.

Kara wasn't sure what they meant, but just this once she thought it better not to ask. Inquisition terms... She shivered. They had to fight to the death tomorrow, to make sure Oden Lan had no chance to carry out his threats.

"And now," Abib said, "the way the two of you looked so good side by side yesterday afternoon did not make him feel any better. He is determined to throw everything he has against you. And he won't listen to reason."

Mai met Kara's eyes.

"Then I guess," he said, "we have nothing to lose."

21
ON THE VERGE OF DEATH

When Abib left, they polished their gear and laid out their clean outfits for later. There were still a few hours left before dawn, but Kara didn't feel like sleeping. Neither did Mai, it seemed, as he went through the preparations with the speed and efficiency that made every piece of his gear look as if it were clicking and sliding into place entirely on its own. It was good to see him back to his normal self.

"You are no longer poisoned," she said.

"It seems that the worst is over." He raised his eyes to her. "I hope I didn't do anything... improper."

She felt a blush creep into her cheeks.

Mai frowned. "That bad, eh?"

She held his gaze. "That good."

A quick smile slid over his face as he returned to his task.

"Do you remember any of it?" she asked.

His upward glance lit up with mischief. "Do you want me to?"

"I suppose not."

"Then I don't. Not a thing." He grinned. "I hope, though, it was better than going berserk and violent."

She couldn't help but smile. In a way, it was exactly like going berserk. The way he ripped her clothes when he stripped her. The way he claimed her, possessive like a conqueror savoring his prize. The way he drove into her, as if his life depended on releasing every bit of his strength inside her. It would have been frightening, if it hadn't answered her own need so well.

"Just don't get poisoned with Black Death again, all right?" she said.

"Not if I can help it." He turned away, repacking his throwing knives.

She sat against the wall and watched him, remembering everything that had happened. Her skin prickled with pleasure just by thinking about it. She could think of no better way to spend the last night of her life, on the eve of the execution that awaited them in the morning. And now, it was such a relief to know that he was alive and well and that they could fight side by side one last time.

He noticed her look and stopped, raising his eyes to her. "What is it?"

She took a breath. "You also talked."

Alarm stirred in his gaze. "I did?"

"Do you remember?"

He lowered his hands from his task and sat back, facing her.

"Do you want me to?" he asked quietly.

"Yes."

He hesitated.

"I remember everything that went through my head before I... went berserk. I hope I didn't say too much of it out loud."

"You said quite a bit."

"Did I?"

She watched him. "Did you mean any of it?"

His gaze drifted for a moment, his eyes becoming dreamy.

"I... I remember losing it at some point, when I was in pain and you held me so close. I spoke about your touch, the way it makes me feel... And yes, I did mean it. This is exactly how I feel when you touch me. Even the pain couldn't take it away."

She held her breath.

"That's when you started talking."

"*Started*?" His eyes widened in alarm.

"Yes."

He peered into her face. She saw him shiver as her gaze told him everything that had happened. She shivered too, remembering. In his delirium, he had said so much...

"I said everything I was thinking, didn't I?" he asked quietly.

"I believe so."

His gaze wavered. "Please forgive me. I never meant to say these things to you. The last thing I wanted was to let you know how I feel about you."

"Why?" she whispered.

"I have no right to burden you."

"*Burden* me?"

His gaze burned her.

"I'm probably saying this because I am still poisoned,"

he said. "But if I'm not mistaken, you're in love with another man."

She swallowed. *Kyth.* She *had been* in love with him. But she wasn't sure anymore. The last few days, since Middledale, had distanced her from him so much. And now, she was going to die, and none of this even mattered. But if, by some miracle, she were to survive and face Kyth again–

"Are you?" he asked quietly.

She hesitated.

"I… I don't know."

He lowered his eyes. "I'm sorry for prying. The times we were together – they've made my life worth living. I can't possibly ask for more."

"Yes, you can." The words came out so quietly that she barely heard them herself.

The intensity of his gaze made her skin prickle.

"If I asked you for more," he said, "I'd be forcing you into a choice."

"It's a choice I will have to make anyway, won't I?"

"Only if you want to."

She reached over and touched his cheek, running her fingertips down his skin. He shivered, a barely perceptible ripple of muscle visible on his bare, left arm. His eyes were dreamy as he looked at her.

She leaned forward and kissed him.

For a while, they lost track of time, their embrace so different this time from the violent passion before. He tasted so good, his pine scent clouding her mind, his tenderness as he held her making her heart quiver. *When you touch me, you make me dizzy, like I'm dreaming and never want to wake up,* he had said to her during his delirium. And now she realized that this was how she felt too. He made her dizzy when he held her like this, enfolded in a dream that was too good to last.

After a while she finally found strength to draw away from him and sat up straight, looking at him in the wavering lantern light.

"Let's live through this first," she said. "If we do, there will be time for choices later on."

"Fair enough." He turned, the defenses in his eyes clicking into place, hiding his feelings inside.

They finished repacking their gear, laying it out so that it would be easy to don.

"I suppose we still have time for some rest," he said, glancing at the dark sky outside.

She nodded and spread her cloak next to him, settling down. He reached past her to retrieve his staff. As he did, his hand brushed her forearm, inadvertently disturbing her wound, hidden under the sleeve.

Dear Shal Addim, how could she possibly have forgotten all about it?

She stiffened as his hand retreated, only for a brief moment, but he sensed it.

"You're injured," he said in disbelief. "All this time…" He grasped her hand and pulled up her sleeve to look at the long streak of red grazing her forearm.

"It's just a scratch."

He frowned.

It looked worse than she imagined. She couldn't believe that in the heat of things she could forget the pain. It stung now that he brought it out into the open, the damaged flesh on the inside of the deep cut packed with dust and dirt.

He shook his head. "I'm sure I made it worse by what I did to you... Why didn't you say something?"

She shrugged. She doubted if she had said anything he would have understood her in his delirium. But more than that, back then she hadn't wanted to risk that he would stop. "Sorry. I guess I forgot."

"How did it happen?"

"A crossbow bolt. It slid parallel to the skin. I didn't realize it had left such a cut."

He frowned, inspecting it more closely. "We need to treat it."

Wordlessly she rolled up her sleeve. She felt ashamed. Pleasure or not, she shouldn't have forgotten to treat a wound before going into battle. She hoped the Keepers' elixir was potent enough to take care of it in the time they had left.

He placed her arm over his bent knee as he crouched in front of her, thoroughly cleaning the cut with strips of bandage and water from his flask. It throbbed, but she braced herself, knowing that the worst was still to come.

He spread some disinfecting liquid over her cut and the skin around it. It stung as it evaporated, leaving behind a clean medicinal smell. Then, he reached for the Keepers' vial, carefully unscrewing the lid.

"This is going to hurt like hell," he said. "It feels as if someone is packing hot coals into the wound. Except that this pain doesn't go away until the healing is complete. Fortunately, it will only be minutes for a cut like this. You must keep your arm relaxed and absolutely still to make the healing effective. Are you ready?"

She nodded.

He leaned forward and used the small brush in his hand to spread the sticky liquid on the inside of the wound.

When the liquid connected with the flesh, it felt like a stab of a hot poker, except she had to force her muscles to stay relaxed as she took the pain, again and again, with every touch of the brush. The pain was searing. It took all she had to keep still, so that the healing elixir could work its course. Mai appeared to ignore it, slow and careful as he pulled the edges of the wound closed, making sure that no scar remained in its place.

Through clouds of pain she remembered how she had used this elixir on his shoulder just a short time ago. His pain must have been much worse with the penetrating wound he had. The poison must have made it even more unbearable. Now that she knew what it was like, she couldn't believe he had been able to handle it as well as he had.

When he finally put the brush back into the vial and screwed on the lid, she felt drained, grateful that his bent knee still supported her arm. He put the vial away and sat, looking at her with concern.

"I'm fine." She flexed her arm, surprised at how it felt completely undamaged, with only the memory of pain and no visible scar whatsoever.

"We have about two hours left before the break of dawn," Mai said. "I suggest we get some sleep. We can discuss battle plans in the morning on the way to the arena. I expect whatever they are planning will all go awry when they see me, anyway."

She nodded. She felt so drained that she found it hard to move. Too many things had happened to them in the past few hours, and they were beginning to take their toll. Sleep sounded like a very good idea right now.

Mai reached forward and pulled her into his embrace. Gently, he eased her down onto his spread cloak and stretched next to her. She relaxed against him, slowly giving in to the calmness he emanated. She knew he was stilling his mind, a technique they had both learned, and he was just so good at it.

As she slowly drifted into sleep, she felt complete like she never had before in her life. They may not survive what was coming tomorrow. But being with him made it all worth it.

22
THE TOURNAMENT

The arena in the center of the Outer Fortress blazed in the morning sunlight, covered with sand so white it was blinding to look at. Egey Bashi had never seen the arena so full. Many of the spectators looked like simple citizens from the outer grounds, but the majority wore Majat armbands without the stones, indicating their non-gem ranking prevalent among the regular fighters at the Guild. Egey Bashi knew that warriors of lower ranks were not asked to participate in the challenge, even though he had no doubt the Guildmaster would not hesitate to throw them into the action if required. However, looking at the display of battle-ready gems lined up for the fight made the very idea that the reinforcements may be needed seem ridiculous. Sitting next to Kyth and Lady Celana at the head of the arena, two rows behind the Guildmaster's seat, Egey Bashi was surveying the assembled ranks with a sinking heart.

A ring of Jade archers lined the top of the arena. They stood still, like statues, with their bows lowered. The ground below them, where the action was going

to take place, was surrounded by another ring of
men with rubies set into their armbands. Egey Bashi
counted thirty-six, evenly spaced along the edge of the
large oval space. His heart sank as he watched their
impassive faces, the only movement about them the
glint of their ranking gems as the sun slowly moved
higher into the sky.

Rubies were the second highest rank in the Majat
Guild, a deadly force in its own right. They also had
special training, fighting in groups so that they could
coordinate their actions and attack an opponent in
unison, which made them so valuable for the Royal
Pentade duty. Egey Bashi doubted even Kara and Mai
together could stand up to thirty-six of them, or even
half that number for that matter. But he also knew that
even this deadly Ruby force was there only for backup,
and that they were not expected to join the action
unless things got very far out of hand.

The Diamonds had not yet made their appearance,
but from a late-night conversation with his old friend
Master Abib, Egey Bashi knew that there were four,
all of them drawn to participate in the fight. The
Guildmaster had clearly spared no effort to ensure that
Kara and Mai had no chance in hell of winning the
challenge.

He hoped seeing Mai in top shape – his personal
contribution to today's challenge and a small present to
the insane Guildmaster – would stir some reaction. But
in the end, nothing short of a miracle could possibly
resolve this impossible standoff.

Egey Bashi settled into his seat, listening to the horn
blast followed by cheering that announced the arrival

of the defending Diamonds. They entered the arena at an unhurried walk, moving with the powerful grace of prowling tigers circling their prey, and stopped at its four sides. Egey Bashi recognized the taller one on the left as Aghat Lance, the man he had had some dealings with back in the past. The woman to his right, whose gender could be identified only by the way she wore her dark hair in a knot at the back of her head, was Aghat Shebirah, as far as he recalled. The other two, dark and lean men of average height, were unfamiliar, even though, like everyone else among the spectators, Egey Bashi was informed of their names and rank.

Another horn blast preceded the arrival of the Guildmaster, surrounded by a small group of black-clad men. Master Abib kept to his right shoulder, one step behind. The sight of the masked man on Oden Lan's left made Egey Bashi shiver. The fabled Shadow Master, the trainer who knew everyone's weaknesses and easily the most dangerous man in the Majat Guild, was here to personally oversee the battle and offer last-minute advice, if needed.

The Guildmaster exchanged greetings with the Diamonds at the arena and waited out the cheer before settling into his own chair. The fighters, and many in the audience, acknowledged him with a silent Majat salute, a fist to the chest, but to Egey Bashi's surprise quite a few others didn't join in, averting their eyes as they watched the Guildmaster take his place. He wondered briefly if punishment was warranted for such a display of disapproval, but he also knew that at the moment Oden Lan had other things on his mind. Could the sympathy of the crowd toward the

challengers be used as a wild card that could be played
to prevent the impending bloodbath?

A distant horn blast echoed through the arena,
followed by rising noise at the entrance at the far end.
Egey Bashi could guess rather than see the approach of
the challengers, surrounded by Jade guards in such a
tight ring that, from this distance, they were not visible
at all. The Magister wondered if this protection was
in place to prevent Kara and Mai from escaping, or to
ensure that the crowds wouldn't crush them in their
eagerness to see them up close.

People in the rows were standing up and gaping.
Many shouted, and Egey Bashi saw some of the faces
light up with surprise and relief. He could guess the
reason for this upheaval, but, once the challengers
came into full view, he got caught up in it anyway.
Even though he knew Mai would be there to fight,
the sight of him and Kara walking side by side was
captivating. Their faces were set into calm masks of
deep concentration, the air around them crackling
with charge. They looked so fit and ready that even the
Diamonds waiting for them in the arena did not seem
so impressive anymore.

Egey Bashi allowed himself a smile as he briefly
looked down the rows at the Guildmaster's contorted
face. Of all the times the Keeper had used their elixir
to save lives, this one possibly brought him the most
satisfaction. He could see the men around Oden Lan
stir in heightened conversation, and the fighters in the
arena exchange hasty glances. They had planned to
fight Kara alone, and they had assembled a ridiculously
large force to bring her down. And now, the stakes

had just doubled, and by the rules of the challenge no additional instructions could be issued to the fighters before the start of the action.

Kyth sat very still by his side, his eyes fixed on Kara. Egey Bashi felt sorry for the boy. He didn't deserve this messed up love affair with one of the best killers in the world, on top of the burden of being the heir of a turmoiled kingdom facing a powerful enemy. And now, he was going to witness the woman he loved being butchered for sport, with nothing whatsoever he could do about it. Egey Bashi squeezed Kyth's shoulder, exchanging a quick look with Lady Celana on his other side. The lady's smooth face held quiet compassion as she sat there with the composure of a queen receiving her court, a long Lakeland bow strapped over her shoulder. Egey Bashi reflected that this crowd was probably one of the few that found nothing odd in a refined seventeen year-old lady in an elaborate royal gown carrying a longbow. As far as the Majat were concerned, Lady Celana fit right in.

People in the audience cheered, many pressing their fists to their chests in the Majat salute as they watched Kara and Mai being led into position. Egey Bashi glanced at the Guildmaster's gloomy face, wondering if he was making a mental list of people to execute.

What a mess they were all in. Egey Bashi had an uncomfortable feeling that there was more to it than anyone realized as he inadvertently remembered the conversation he'd had with Mai back in Middledale. It was just as they discussed – all the Guild's top gem ranks down there on the chopping block. Had the Kaddim orchestrated all of this, like Mai suspected? And if yes, how?

With a sinking heart he watched Kara's and Mai's Jade escort dissipate, receding to the safe distance at a fast run. The challenge had begun.

Having witnessed many tournaments, Egey Bashi expected speeches and explanations, perhaps an exchange between Mai and Oden Lan, or at least an announcement of the rules to the spectators before the start of the action, but none of this ensued. The six Diamonds in the arena drew their weapons in one single move and sprang into action, so fast and violent that an unprepared observer would have trouble even understanding what was happening.

Kara and Mai moved in perfect unison. Having some experience with Majat training, Egey Bashi could immediately see that their very first moves had thrown all their opponents' carefully prepared tactics to the wind. He watched Lance's attempt to attack Kara smoothly averted as Kara and Mai changed places, leaving her opposite the lighter Shebirah, with two other Diamonds attacking from the sides. Their weapons, more versatile and exotic than the other Diamonds' swords, also made it more difficult for their opponents. While Egey Bashi knew that all the Diamonds in the Majat Guild were more or less equal in skill and it was only a matter of time before this four-on-two fight ended in disaster, it was clear that getting through to Kara and Mai would take a while.

It was captivating to watch how they acted together like a single being, as if anticipating each other's actions regardless of whether they were even in each other's line of sight. Absorbed in the gripping mêlée, Egey Bashi found himself thinking that he had never before seen such a perfect match, making him feel, against reason, that these two people were meant for each other. Of course, there seemed to be no possibility of them coming out of this alive, and that in itself was such a bloody waste.

The crowd were on their feet, holding their breath as they watched the deadly dance down below. Very likely in all the existence of this arena that housed the Majat top ranking tournaments and many of the historical challenges during past centuries, it had never encountered an audience so quiet. It almost seemed as if the outcome of this battle was personal to everyone, and nobody wanted to make a move or sound that could disturb the balance.

In the ensuing silence, the clashing of weapons rang loudly to Egey Bashi's heightened senses. He heard a screech as Kara twisted her sword out of a deadlock, trapped by two Diamonds while the other two attacked Mai side by side. She dropped down and bounced off the ground, coming up to her feet next to him. Their faces showed nothing but calm concentration, and only by knowing them well did Egey Bashi sense that they were both coming to an end of their strength and that any time now one of their enemies' weapons was going to come through.

A barely perceptible sensation pressed on his ears. He saw Lance in the arena stumble as Mai's staff connected with the side of his head, sending him to the ground. The crowd gasped as Mai went for the resulting gap, the tip of his staff hitting Shebirah in the chest. She fell flat on her back, releasing her weapon.

A roar swept the arena, everyone leaping and shouting. Egey Bashi marveled at the way the fighters continued without interruption, as if Mai's blow had not just reduced the odds by half. The Guildmaster was on his feet, barking orders. Egey Bashi saw the Rubies around the arena baring their blades, rushing forward into action.

The pressing on his ears was back, for another brief moment. A Ruby, rushing face-on at Kara, stumbled and fell on her blade, collapsing on the ground. And then, suddenly, too many people tumbled around in chaos, the action too dense to comprehend.

A hand grasped Egey Bashi's arm. He turned and met Kyth's gaze.

"The Kaddim!" the Prince said urgently. "They're here! I can sense their power."

"Where?" Egey Bashi's eyes darted around the arena.

"Please, Magister," Kyth urged. "We have to stop this! Quick!"

Egey Bashi nodded and rushed forward to the Guildmaster's side.

"Stop the mêlée, Aghat Oden Lan!" he shouted. "Now!"

The Guildmaster turned to him, his face contorted into a grimace.

"The Ultimate Challenge is to the death, Magister."

Egey Bashi shook his head. "We have detected foul play. The Kaddim Brothers are trying to interfere with the outcome of this tournament. Please, Aghat Oden Lan, we must stop it before all your best fighters down there kill each other."

The Guildmaster hesitated, looking back to the arena. More Rubies were now on the ground, with the Diamonds rushing in between. It no longer seemed like

a well-planned battle. As they watched, they saw one
Ruby stab another as a third one hit him on the back of
the head with the pommel of his sword.

"Stop the fighting, Aghat!" Egey Bashi shouted.
"Now!"

"Don't listen to him, Aghat Oden Lan," Shadow
Master said. "This is Guild business. He's an outsider."

Egey Bashi opened his mouth to respond, but at that
moment a movement caught his eye in the rows above.

Lady Celana stood up in her seat and raised her bow,
flicking an arrow out of a quiver at her belt. She took
aim and released it across the arena, toward a dark man
in an Anonymous mask standing on its other side.

Egey Bashi gasped.

The man was clearly not expecting it as he stood
with his outstretched hands pointing to the ground, in
a gesture that looked suspiciously like...

A Kaddim Brother, using his power.

Egey Bashi's skin prickled as he watched the arrow
hit, sending the man down.

A horn blast rang over the arena.

All the action stopped.

Egey Bashi glanced briefly at Lady Celana and turned
back to the Guildmaster.

"Have that man brought here, Aghat. Quickly. He
might still be dangerous."

For once, Oden Lan did not hesitate. He nodded,
giving quick hand signals to his men.

In moments the masked man with the green-and-
yellow Illitand arrow protruding from his chest was
dragged before the Guildmaster. He seemed barely
conscious as the Jades holding him pulled off his mask,

revealing a sharp-featured face with a halo of unruly brown hair standing around his head.

Egey Bashi froze, feeling a chill creep down his spine. *Nimos.*

"A Kaddim Brother," he said, "in the heart of your Guild, using his powers to affect the outcome of your tournament. Do you believe me now, Aghat Oden Lan?"

He felt a hand touch his sleeve and turned to meet Kyth's gaze. Lady Celana followed behind him, looking at the result of her archery with quiet interest.

"There's one more, Magister," Kyth said. He raised his hand and pointed at the Shadow Master. "Him."

Everyone froze.

"This is preposterous," Oden Lan said. "This man—"

"See for yourself, Master Oden Lan," Kyth said. "Have his mask removed."

The Guildmaster shook his head. "The integrity of our Guild depends on keeping this man anonymous, Prince Kythar. I don't expect you to understand our ways."

"The integrity of your Guild is about to go to hell," Egey Bashi blurted.

Oden Lan glared, but before he could say anything, Lady Celana stepped forward.

"I know a better way, Aghat Oden Lan," she said. "You don't have to reveal his face to test whether Prince Kythar is right. Have your men open his sleeve at the left shoulder."

"What?" Oden Lan stared.

"Members of the Kaddim Brotherhood have a brand mark on their left shoulder. It looks like an arrowhead with protruding corners, pointing downward. If Prince Kythar is right, this man should have one."

Egey Bashi let out the air he was holding, looking at Celana in surprise. "Smoke screen" indeed. This royal lady was far more intelligent than anyone realized.

He opened his mouth to confirm her words, but at that moment Shadow Master darted forward, drawing a knife from his sleeve. He grasped Lady Celana's shoulder and turned her around, pressing the blade to her throat.

"Back off, everyone," he said. "Or I'll slit her throat."

Kyth stepped forward past Egey Bashi, holding the man's gaze.

"This man," he said, "can use his mind control power to defeat any Majat. But I know he won't be able to stand up to the gem ranks in a fight. If anyone here would try to disarm him, I will protect them from the Kaddim mind control."

A black-clad shape appeared at his side.

"Allow me, Your Highness," Kara said.

She slid forward, shooting out her hand in a quick blow to the wrist that forced the Shadow Master to release his blade. Kara finished her movement by grasping Lady Celana and pushing her into Kyth's arms. Her other hand flew up, hitting the masked man on the side of his head, sending him down to the ground.

Egey Bashi let out a sigh. Compared to the action in the arena, her movements looked easy, almost casual. It was hard to imagine that this slender young girl could put such force into a blow that didn't even look as if it required any effort on her part.

Kara leaned forward and ripped off the fallen man's left sleeve. Everyone gasped, looking at the black down-turned triangle marring the man's skin.

Slowly, Oden Lan reached down and removed his mask.

Egey Bashi surveyed the fabled Shadow Master with quiet curiosity. Now that he was unconscious, he looked unremarkable, with gaunt features that seemed to be the Brotherhood's trademark, but without any other signs that could identify him as a Kaddim Brother. He probably had some Olivian lineage, his dark skin contrasted by pale bronze hair, cut closely to the scalp. Lying at their feet, he did not seem as imposing or frightening as rumors depicted him. In all respects but one, the Majat Shadow Master looked just like an ordinary man.

"Take them both away," Oden Lan said. Egey Bashi could not tell for sure, but it seemed that his voice was somewhat shaky.

"You should have them both killed right now, Guildmaster," he said quickly. "Keeping them alive will only make matters worse. The Kaddim Brothers are all able to communicate with each other. Besides, they can control your men's minds to disable them, or force them to attack their own. Look at the damage they've already done." He pointed to the battlefield. Now that the action had ceased, he could see medics rushing around, removing the injured men. The row of Rubies had reduced by half, if not more. The Diamonds were still standing, but Egey Bashi could see they were not in as good a shape as before.

"If I may suggest, Magister," Lady Celana said. Her voice was less steady and she looked shaky as she leaned on Kyth's arm, but her eyes gleamed with the same cool intelligence. "Alder's spiders would take care of these men once and for all. To my knowledge, the only Kaddim Brother who was ever killed by their venom was not able to be resurrected."

Kaddim Cyrros. The former Reverend of the Church. Once again, Egey Bashi admired the lady's wit. What an amazing Keeper Lady Celana would make. He searched around the rows, singling out Alder's towering shape. But before the young man could approach, a low whistle echoed through the arena.

Everyone turned to see a black-clad figure run down the rows, holding a round object in his hand that emanated thick smoke.

As if in a bad dream Egey Bashi recognized the man's gaunt features and his singular eyes, so light brown that they looked yellow.

Kaddim Tolos. Was this whole place creeping with the Kaddim?

"It's him," Kyth breathed out. "I could sense there was a third one, I just couldn't tell where."

Tolos stopped a few paces away from the Guildmaster's group and broke off pieces of his smoking substance, throwing them at his two fallen comrades. The substance popped as it hit the ground, sending showers of blinding sparks into the air.

A blast hit the arena, pressing on everyone's ears with smothering force.

Egey Bashi blinked. All three Kaddim brothers had disappeared without a trace. In their place smoke dissipated, leaving nothing behind.

"They're gone," Kyth said. "Just like before."

Like before. Before, the Kaddim had used a similar smoke to transport away a whole battalion, after

Kyth, with the help of three Diamond Majat, defeated them in the Illitand Castle. And now it had happened all over again.

Egey Bashi slowly released his breath.

"It seems we're out of danger for the moment," he said, "and in no immediate need of the spider venom." He turned to Lady Celana. "How did you know which one of them to shoot, my lady?"

"His Royal Highness pointed him out, Magister." She looked at Kyth fondly before turning to the Guildmaster. "Forgive me for opening fire in your arena, Aghat Oden Lan, but there was no time to lose."

Oden Lan only shook his head. His eyes traced Kara, who gave him a brief glance before returning to the arena and taking her place next to Mai. He watched her for a long time, then stepped forward and took his seat.

"Is every man accounted for?" he asked into space.

"Yes, Aghat," Abib said. "We lost over a dozen Rubies, but mostly to injuries. All the others are unscathed, I believe."

"In that case," Oden Lan said, "the challenge may resume."

23

GUILDMASTER

"You *can't* mean that," Egey Bashi said in disbelief. "This is insanity, and you know it."

Oden Lan measured him with a long glance.

"If you address me in that way again, Magister," he said. "I'll have you thrown into the dungeons."

"Forgive me, Aghat Oden Lan." Egey Bashi turned and retreated, seeking out Abib, who stood aside, watching the arena with an impassive face.

"We must stop this, Master Abib," he said quickly. "If they continue, more lives will be lost. Is there something in your Code that could possibly enable you to resolve this standoff?"

Abib didn't respond at once, his eyes drawn to the action below. Egey Bashi followed his gaze.

Once again all six Diamonds drew their weapons in what looked like one single move. But this time none of them rushed to attack. They didn't look as dashing anymore as they had at the start of the tournament. Sweat-soaked hair clung to their faces. Each of them had rips in their clothes, with cuts showing through.

Lance's face was blackened on the left side where Mai's staff had hit him near the temple. A nasty blow, Egey Bashi reflected, that could easily have been fatal even without involving a retractable blade, if Mai hadn't controlled his force at the very last moment.

The Diamonds stood, watching each other wearily, the crowds above them so quiet that every sound echoed clearly through the large space.

After a long pause, Lance lowered his weapon.

"Aghat Mai," he said. "You could have killed me when your staff came through. Yet, you didn't."

Mai shrugged. "I'm not here to kill anyone, Aghat. Not if I can help it."

"But–"

Mai's short glance stopped him. "My disagreement is not with you, Aghat Lance. We both know it. However, I am aware of your orders and don't hold any of your actions against you." He raised his staff.

Lance kept his weapon lowered as he threw a quick glance at the Guildmaster.

"Your integrity should be an example to all of us, Aghat Mai," he said. "As far as I am concerned, you have already won this battle." He threw down his weapon. "I surrender."

A gasp went through the crowd, and Egey Bashi saw Oden Lan rise in his seat, but before the Guildmaster could say anything, Shebirah stepped forward to Lance's side.

"Likewise, Aghat Mai," she said. "I am familiar with your staff. Your hand was right on the spring mechanism when you hit me in the chest. I expected you to release the blade. I thought I was dead when you hit me. Yet, you spared my life. I know I wouldn't have done the same in your place. You are a great man, Aghat Mai, one that our Guild cannot possibly afford to lose." She threw down her weapon next to Lance's. "I surrender too."

All eyes turned to the other two Diamonds. They stepped forward in unison and silently threw down their weapons.

Egey Bashi let out a sigh.

The Guildmaster's face contorted in anger.

"Very well," he said into the silence. "If no one in this Guild can stand up to your challenge, Aghat Mai, I will fight you myself." He drew his sword and stepped into the arena, approaching the group at a fast stride.

Mai lifted his head. "Master Oden Lan–"

"Draw your weapon, Aghat Mai!"

"But by the Code the Guildmaster cannot–"

Oden Lan charged.

He was an old man long past his prime, but Egey Bashi knew that in his day he had been one of the Guild's best. It showed, as he wielded his weapon with speed and precision that left everyone gaping. The Diamonds in the arena backed off, their faces frozen in shocked fascination.

Mai used his staff only for defense, dodging and parrying the blows without making any attempt to attack. He stood his ground, but, after the deadly mêlée he had just fought, it was clear that it was costing him a lot of strength. If they kept this up, the Guildmaster would eventually come through, Egey Bashi realized. Along with everyone else, he held his breath, watching.

"Fight me, Aghat Mai!" the Guildmaster barked. "Fight, or surrender."

Mai's movements accelerated as he dodged the blows. The air around him whistled as he spun around with a speed that made his slim shape blur. He swung his staff in a wide arc, a streak of black wood sweeping underneath the Guildmaster's blade, coming up in a spot where it was expected the least. It hit Oden Lan's wrist at full speed, sending his sword flying.

Mai kept his arm moving as he completed the spin, pressing the tip of his staff against the Guildmaster's throat.

Oden Lan's chest heaved as he steadied his breath.

"I *taught* you that move, Aghat Mai," he said in disbelief.

"You taught me many important things, Aghat Oden Lan," Mai said. "But the one I value most is standing up for what I believe is right."

Oden Lan's eyes flicked to the staff point at his throat. "Is *this* what you believe is right?"

Mai lowered his staff.

Oden Lan's lips twitched. "Do you wish to continue the fight?"

"I had hoped we could talk, Aghat Oden Lan."

"I thought I told you before. There is nothing for us to talk about. You've made your choice. And now, you are the one who issued the Ultimate Challenge. It is fought to the death."

Mai shook his head. "Not against the Guildmaster. Once you stepped into this arena, the rules changed. Please hear me out. That is all I ever wanted."

Oden Lan shrugged. "You have me at a blade point, Aghat. I don't believe I have a choice."

Mai held his gaze. "I was hoping I could make

you see that we have no quarrel, Aghat. The Kaddim Brotherhood orchestrated all this, and nearly destroyed our Guild's top ranks in easily the most senseless battle in our history. If they'd had their way just now, we would have lost all our on-hand Diamonds and Rubies in one blow. This must stop, before it goes any further."

Oden Lan's lips trembled as he glanced at Kara.

"I don't see a way to stop this, Aghat Mai," he said, "unless you surrender first."

Mai hesitated.

Please don't do anything stupid, Egey Bashi prayed. "We must do something, Master Abib," he said urgently. "Or else this will get out of hand again. If they surrender, their lives are forfeit. I know your Guildmaster enough to predict what he will do to them. This would be no solution at all."

Abib nodded. "You are right, Magister. This is our time to act."

He strode out to the arena and stopped in front of Oden Lan.

All eyes followed him, the expectation in the air so charged that it threatened to explode.

"This is the Ultimate Challenge, Aghat Oden Lan," Abib said, his voice ringing clearly in the silence around them. "You must surrender, or continue your fight. Given that Aghat Mai has just disarmed you–"

Mai moved to speak, but Abib stopped him with a short glance.

Oden Lan swallowed, his eyes darting among the fighters in the arena. Egey Bashi marveled at how everyone returned his gaze impassively, even though he could guess the turmoil within.

"If you won't surrender, you must continue the fight," Abib pressed on. "To the death. That is the Code."

Everyone held very still, watching Oden Lan. Despite his skill, he was no match for Mai. It was clear that if the fight continued and Mai chose to participate in it fully, it would be a very short one.

The Guildmaster's eyes slid over Abib with regret. He let out a sigh as he turned to his opponent.

"I surrender, Aghat Mai," he said.

For a moment, the arena and the rows around it kept deadly silent. Then, a hail swept over it. People were jumping to their feet, all eyes drawn to the group in the center of the arena.

Abib lifted his hands to signal silence and waited for the sounds to die out completely. Then, he solemnly stepped forward and lowered to one knee in front of Mai, bowing his head and pressing his fist to his chest in a Majat salute. All the Diamonds and Rubies in the arena followed suit, Oden Lan and Kara the only ones to remain standing.

"Hail, our new Guildmaster!" Abib shouted.

The roar that enfolded the arena this time was so deafening that Egey Bashi resisted the urge to cover his ears. Some stood up, pressing fists to their chests; many lowered to one knee, their faces showing such fervor that, against reason, Egey Bashi felt caught up in it. He looked down to the arena where Mai stood in the center of the action, with a stunned look on his face.

"What just happened?" Kyth asked.

Egey Bashi heaved a breath. "According to the Majat Code, the man who accepts their leader's surrender becomes the new Guildmaster."

Kyth's eyes widened. "*Mai*?"

"Yes. And by the looks of it, his people are just fine with this change." Egey Bashi looked at Abib with wonder. He had always had the utmost respect for the old weapons keeper, but had no idea what the man was truly capable of. The Majat Code was a tricky thing. It took a devious mind to navigate events and force Oden Lan to surrender, when it was clear that it was the farthest thing from the Guildmaster's wishes and from everyone's minds.

Oden Lan had made a mistake when he stepped into the arena. From what Egey Bashi knew about the Majat Code, this action halted the Ultimate Challenge, giving Mai the choice to follow the rules or to strike him down and face the ensuing consequences. Once Mai showed no intention of taking the Guildmaster's life, a normal turn of events would have been for the senior Majat to remind Oden Lan of his duty and persuade him to return to his seat, allowing the challenge to resume. If it had, everything would have come down to the Rubies and Jades, who hadn't yet surrendered and were likely up to the task of finishing the job.

Abib had played it differently, forcing everyone to overlook the fact that Oden Lan was in the arena in error and using the heat of the moment to make it seem that the fight must continue to the death. Even if the legitimacy of what he had done was very much in question, no one had called him on it, making Egey Bashi feel that more of the senior Majat were likely in favor of this change of command. And of course, none of it mattered now. Once the Guildmaster announced his surrender, it made the result as irrevocable as if the succession had happened in the most proper way.

Egey Bashi's skin prickled at this glimpse into the depths of Abib's mind. The weapons keeper had clearly seen Mai's potential before anyone else, and waited for the right moment to facilitate the takeover smoothly and without drawing any attention to himself.

By the stunned expression on Mai's face as he stood accepting his people's greetings, Egey Bashi knew the Diamond had no idea his challenge could end this way. But Egey Bashi was glad it had. For the first time in centuries the Majat Guild had a reasonable man in charge, one who could be trusted to do the right thing.

And now, for better or worse, Kyth had to negotiate his alliance with Mai. Egey Bashi hoped both men could put their feelings aside and wouldn't let their prior disagreements drive them to do anything stupid.

24
NEW COMMAND

Egey Bashi had never been to the Majat training grounds and now, standing at the edge of the large sunlit plaza, he knew that he was witnessing something not normally intended for outsiders. But above his curiosity about seeing the place which had trained so many unmatched warriors since the days of the Old Empire, he knew that what was about to happen was even more special. Watching the new Majat Guildmaster take command at a full parade was the event of a lifetime. During his long life, the Magister had seen many important gatherings, but he knew this was a memory he was going to carry to the end of his days.

The giant plaza accommodated row after row of black-clad warriors, separated into ranks identifiable by their armbands. The gems lined up in front, with thousands of non-gem ranks covering the rest of the large space behind them. They all stood perfectly still, like silent statues, the only movement about them the shifting folds of their long cloaks disturbed by the light morning breeze.

Egey Bashi gaped as he surveyed the assembled ranks. He had only a vague idea how many Majat warriors the Fortress housed, and seeing them all at once made his heart quiver. This force seemed invincible. If they could only get the Majat on their side, the battle with the Kaddim was all but won. He hoped that yesterday's display of Kaddim power had made it obvious to everyone here that destroying the Brotherhood must stand very high on the Majat's list.

It seemed unthinkable that a member of the Kaddim Brotherhood could occupy one of the highest posts in this Guild for over ten years. And now, this man was on the loose in the enemy camp, possessing full knowledge of Majat operations and the exact weaknesses of each of its top ranked warriors.

Egey Bashi was surprised to see that each rank, starting with the Diamonds, seemed more abundant than he had believed. Over thirty men wearing Diamond-set armbands lined up at the side of the courtyard closest to the gateway, through which the Guildmaster was about to make his entrance. Looking more closely, he realized that most of them were not that young. The top gem ranks retired in their forties but continued their duties at high command posts, which required experience rather than active weapons skill. They also made indispensable trainers, especially for those warriors who were going for the Diamond rank. Normally, the post of Shadow Master had also been selected from retired Diamonds. How could this Guild have become so messed up that they put a Kaddim Brother into the post?

The Keeper glanced at Kyth and Lady Celana standing at his side in the full regalia of their royal houses, and Alder and Ellah, one step behind. They all looked solemn, caught in this moment, easily one of the most historic ones in the existence of the Majat Guild. Mai's Ultimate Challenge not only made him legendary because of his unprecedented victory, but also because he was, by far, the youngest Majat Guildmaster in the history of the Guild, and the only one ever to assume this post in his prime.

A horn rang through the yard. None of the Majat moved or changed position, but Egey Bashi saw many eyes dart to the courtyard entrance, alight in anticipation that made the air over the giant plaza seem charged as if a thunderstorm were about to erupt. Even the Keeper himself couldn't help but gape as he watched Mai's entrance.

He looked so natural as he walked with swift, powerful grace at the head of his ceremonial escort. The Guildmaster's cloak, black with a Diamond Majat token embroidery over the back, draped all the way down to his boots, its folds wavering in rhythm with his measured steps. The cloak was thrown back over his left shoulder to expose his diamond-set armband shining against his black sleeve. Its gleam added to his aura of power, making all eyes watching him narrow, as if blinded by the glamor.

Mai still wore his staff, strapped at the back, with its tip protruding over his left shoulder. His calm face spelled confidence and quiet challenge, making every man in sight pull up, even though it didn't seem possible for anyone to stand any straighter. Eyes followed him with admiration and awe as he approached the assembled troops.

Egey Bashi held his breath. Dear Shal Addim, this man was born to command. He wore his mantle of station like a second skin, so natural in his new role as if he had always occupied it. By winning his challenge, he had found himself in charge of the largest military force since the days of the Old Empire, making him more powerful than the King. *He who commands the Majat commands the Empire.* Looking at Mai, this couldn't seem truer.

The sight of the men walking in parallel formation in Mai's wake made Egey Bashi's skin prickle. The Majat Guildmaster's Emerald Guard. He had read about it in old chronicles, but had never before seen them march at a full parade. Twelve men, clad in all black, stepping in perfect unison, their armbands glittering with clear green gems, their cloaks flapping in the breeze in fascinating synchrony. They were taught to fight in unison, too, or so Egey Bashi heard. It was nearly impossible to withstand their combined power.

Two more people walked by Mai's sides. Master Abib – on his right, three steps behind – looked solemn, but, by the way his lively eyes darted around, Egey Bashi could tell the man was very pleased with himself. And he damned well should be, with the way he'd managed to take advantage of the situation and put his man of choice in power without causing bloodshed.

Kara walked on Mai's left, cloaked and dressed in black like the rest of his escort, but without any Majat regalia. Egey Bashi was not sure if she had any official ceremonial role in this party, but her presence at Mai's side showed his intention to keep her around, at least for the time being. The Keeper saw Kyth's eyes narrow as he watched her walk by, enclosed in her aura of calm composure, not even glancing his way. Egey Bashi let out a sigh. Kara and Mai looked too good together as they marched side by side, their unison no less perfect than that of the Emerald Guards. Kyth couldn't possibly be happy seeing them this way. Egey Bashi just hoped the Prince would be able to put it behind him in the upcoming negotiations, scheduled to commence this afternoon.

Just their luck that one of the most historical undertakings in the kingdom of Tallan Dar had to be decided in a one-on-one talk between two hot-headed youngsters in love with the same woman.

When Mai reached the formation of the Diamonds, he slowed his steps and pressed his fist to his chest in silent salute. They responded in suit, and when the Emerald Guards walked past they fell into stride behind, extending his train by another impressive length. Egey Bashi noticed that Oden Lan was not among them.

Mai marched past the Rubies and the Sapphires and reached the Jades. He kept a slow pace as he walked, and Egey Bashi saw each man Mai's eyes fell on draw up with a fervor he had never seen in the presence of any commander before. These men adored him, and the Keeper found it fascinating to watch. Things in the Majat Guild were definitely going to change, and soon.

Mai turned and exchanged quiet words with Kara, walking in his wake. Her glance pointed him to a tall man in the front row, with a square jaw and full lips. Egey Bashi's eyes widened as he recognized the Jade who had helped him deliver the elixir to Kara and Mai the night before the challenge.

Dear Shal Addim. During his very first day in office Mai did not waste any time. Along with hundreds of people in the plaza Egey Bashi held his breath, watching.

Mai stopped in front of the Jade, his short glance pulling the man to attention, even though Egey Bashi could swear standing any straighter wasn't possible. He saw the man's lowered hand tremble as he stared ahead, doing his best to appear calm as Mai surveyed him. The Keeper had observed a similar effect back at court, when the Rubies of the Royal Pentade – as well as many of the court ladies – encountered the quiet interest of Mai's direct gaze. Here, at the Majat Guild, Mai's new authority amplified this effect many times over.

"Gahang Iver," Mai said, his words carrying clearly through the silent grounds.

The Jade lifted his chin, his eyes glassy with effort.

"I've examined your record," Mai said, "and spoken at length to your superiors and your peers. You are a man of exemplary character and, I am told, one of our Guild's best with a crossbow."

"Thank you, Guildmaster." The Jade continued to look ahead with an impassive expression, but Egey Bashi could see how much this praise meant to him.

"Walk with me," Mai said.

The Jade saluted and, as Mai and his train moved on, he fell into stride behind him. His face held an expression of awed disbelief, as if he thought he were dreaming and was afraid to wake up.

Mai stopped again when he reached the end of the row of Jades, opposite a dark man with piercing eyes, who saluted him with his fist to his chest.

"Gahang Khall." Mai's voice rose just a bit so that his words echoed through the plaza. "For the past eight years your record in the Guild has been spotless. I know that my predecessor always held you in very high regard."

The Jade saluted again, but his dark eyes watched Mai warily, waiting for the impending blow.

"However," Mai said, "when you gave the order to open fire on Aghat Raishan, you overstepped your authority and demonstrated a lapse of judgment, by firing on a man of a higher rank and a valued Guild member. While I am not privy to the exact orders you received, I believe this behavior was unwarranted. The lives of the top gem ranks are priceless to our Guild, and not to be risked in such a senseless way."

Khall continued to stand to attention. It seemed that he was about to respond, but Mai's glance cut him off.

"I also witnessed your lapse in leadership when you failed to keep your subordinate in line and prevent him from violating ceasefire," Mai said.

Khall's eyes narrowed, but he kept his silence under Mai's gaze.

"As I'm sure you know," Mai said, "such mistakes are gravely punished in our Guild. However, given your past record and the fact that you were under orders, I am willing to take only the necessary steps. I'm relieving you of command. You will join the ranks of the Guild's Jades."

Egey Bashi saw a movement ripple through the plaza. Khall had been in charge of the Jades for nearly a decade, and Egey Bashi had rarely seen a more ruthless and efficient man. His post, in charge of the

Guild's security, held a lot of power, keeping its affairs in perfect balance. And now, just a day after accepting his new post, Mai was upsetting this balance with his very first order.

"Gahang Iver," Mai said.

The Jade beside him stepped forward.

"You will take charge of the Jades in Gahang Khall's place."

Egey Bashi let out a sigh. This was a bold move. Yet, it was probably the right thing to do. Mai could not possibly leave his Guild's security to a man who had nearly shot him down, whatever orders he had received that enabled him to do that. As the new Guildmaster, Mai needed a loyal man in this post, and, having years of command experience himself, Egey Bashi had a good feeling that Mai was making the right choice.

Iver swallowed and saluted with his fist to his chest. "Thank you, Aghat Mai."

Mai nodded. "I need a man with good judgment, one who can be trusted to make the right decisions in a tight spot. I can't think of anyone better than you, Gahang."

"I won't let you down, Guildmaster." Iver looked stunned. Clearly, of all the consequences he expected for his disobedience and lending aid to convicted prisoners against the Guildmaster's explicit orders, this turn of events must have been the farthest from his mind.

As Iver took his place at the head of the Jades, Egey Bashi, once again, saw the magic working its way. Khall had been popular, but now that Mai had put a new man in his place, everyone's voices rose in a cheer welcoming the new Jade leader. Eyes fixed on their

new Guildmaster with such devotion that, had Egey
Bashi still been young and idealistic himself, it would
have brought tears to his eyes.

To his knowledge Oden Lan had never commanded
such loyalty in his men. Under Mai's rule, this Guild
would definitely have more chance to stay united.
Egey Bashi just hoped that this wouldn't make the
Majat more of a problem than they already were.

Mai and his escort made full rounds before finally
approaching the Keeper and his companions. Egey
Bashi heard breaths drawn all around him, men
standing to attention.

"Guildmaster." Egey Bashi bowed, his sideways
glance confirming that everyone around him reacted
appropriately as well. Lady Celana sank into a deep
curtsy. After hesitation, Kyth gave Mai a stiff bow. The
Majat Guildmaster outranked the Crown Prince – a
change Kyth would have to adjust to, if he ever hoped
to be successful in his negotiations.

Mai surveyed their group.

"Prince Kythar," he said. "Magister Egey Bashi.
I know we have both of you to thank for your help
against the Kaddim during yesterday's tournament."
He turned to Lady Celana. "And you, my lady. A
very impressive shot. I had no idea you were such an
accomplished archer."

And here was the magic again. The royal lady's face
lit up with color at his words. Egey Bashi had seen
her smoothly reflect court compliments before, but it
seemed that her composure didn't make her immune
to Mai's charms. Even Kyth squared his shoulders at
this casual praise from his rival.

"It was a joint effort, Aghat Mai," Egey Bashi said after a pause, which told him neither Kyth nor Celana was about to speak. "Please accept my sincere congratulations on your new post. We are all overjoyed at your victory in the challenge."

Mai nodded.

"Thank you, Magister," he said.

25
AMNESTY

Walking in Mai's wake, Kara couldn't help the feeling of quiet awe that enfolded her every time she looked at him. He had settled into his new role instantly, as if this high post was meant for him all along. She had always realized Mai was a natural leader, and it was so gratifying to see him in command, and to know the part she had played in instigating it.

She felt, above all, relieved that both she and Mai were still alive, and that their challenge hadn't ended in a bloodbath among the top gem ranks, as she had feared when she entered the arena the previous morning. Since the time, a few months back, when she had chosen to disobey her orders and save Kyth from being captured by the Kaddim, she had been on a death roll. And now, by a turn of events no one could have possibly anticipated, it was over, and at least for a time she could enjoy safety and peace.

She was amazed to see how well she was being received at the Guild. Being a challenger by Mai's side, helping his victory and fighting an impossible battle on his behalf, extended his aura of glamor over her as well. She saw it in the eyes of her former comrades as their expressions welcomed her back, dismissing earlier rumors that she was an outcast and a traitor and acknowledging her as one of the Guild's top warriors. That alone made it all worthwhile.

She was aware that she owed all these things to Mai, and that without his resolve to put his life on the line for her many times over, it never would have happened. The debt she owed him was far beyond something one could easily repay.

Whatever else she felt toward him – if anything – these other, personal feelings couldn't possibly be a match for what he had become: the leader of their Guild, the most powerful man on this side of the Eastern Mountain Range. She knew that, from now on, the best she could do was to admire him from afar and forget all about the confusion he had stirred in her during the last few days. They were no longer a match, two people of exceptional skill thrown together in a fight for their lives. He was in charge now, and his new role couldn't possibly go in hand with any personal bonds. She could live with it, she told herself again and again.

After the parade, Mai gathered his escort in the inner courtyard adjoining the training grounds. Kara was surprised when Mai's hand signs, thrown at high speed, rearranged the formation to leave her standing by herself, with everyone else facing her.

"Aghat Kara," Mai said, his calm voice echoing through the courtyard.

Against reason, she found herself pulling to attention. She wasn't a Majat anymore, but her hand inadvertently flew up, her fist pressing against her chest in a Majat salute.

"Guildmaster."

"I wish to express my gratitude to you for joining my challenge," Mai said. "You chose to stand by my side despite certainty that this action was going to get you killed. Your skill and resolve enabled our victory. I owe you my life, Aghat. I will not forget it."

She bowed her head. "It was my honor to fight by your side, Aghat Mai. And," she added before she could think better of it, "you know well that, before this challenge, you saved my life too, more than once. I am the one in your debt."

He held a brief pause.

"Your debt to me has just been erased. You don't owe me a thing, Aghat."

She nodded, at a loss for words. She knew she would never forget what she owed him, but having him dismiss it all in this formal conversation meant that nobody else would ever hold her to it. Against reason, this knowledge filled her with regret. He had just severed the connection that had bonded her to him for the past few months.

She kept her face still, hoping that her expression showed none of these thoughts.

"My new post," Mai went on, "enables me to give you something I always wanted you to have."

A gift? She raised her eyebrows. What could he possibly give her?

"Aghat Mai," she began. "You have no reason to–"

His glance stopped her. "Never refuse a gift before you know what it is, Aghat. I am certain you'd want to keep this one. I am giving you your freedom. And a full pardon from the Majat Guild."

Her mouth fell open. She was only vaguely aware of everyone else staring.

She shivered, overwhelmed with amazement and gratitude she couldn't possibly express. If Mai wanted to grant her full pardon, there was no better way to do it, and, knowing him well, she realized that he had given it a lot of thought. Bringing it up at the parade in front of all the troops might have stirred up a reaction. Saying it in a smaller gathering with all of the Guild's Diamonds present made it just as irrevocable, and much less likely to cause any uproar.

A lump rose in her throat. She looked at him wide-eyed as he continued calmly, as if nothing out of the ordinary was going on.

"I know that you have found yourself in a precarious position, Aghat Kara, pitched between your orders and your certainty that following them would be drastically wrong. You demonstrated exceptional integrity by choosing to do what you believed was right, while knowing that it would mean your execution. No one in the history of our Guild has ever survived the ensuing sanctions. This makes your situation unprecedented, not covered by the Code. As a result, it enables me to use my own judgment to decide your fate. As of now, you are formally free of your obligations to the Guild, and no Majat will pursue you because of your past. "

Against reason, she felt tears rise to her eyes and she bowed her head, pressing her fist to her chest again.

"It is also in my power as the Guildmaster," Mai went on, "to offer you a choice. If you wish to return to the Guild and resume your rank, I would be honored to welcome you back."

A choice.

She felt a flutter in her stomach that suddenly made it so hard to stand upright in front of him. In just a few words, he had thrown the world at her feet. He was offering her everything she could possibly dream of, as casually as if he were doing her a minor favor.

In all her life, she had never been in a position to make these kinds of choices. And now, she had no idea how to handle them. Looking into his eyes inadvertently brought to mind the *other* choice they'd talked about on the eve of the challenge – one she felt, with his new station, she'd do best to forget.

She swallowed.

"Thank you, Aghat Mai," she said. "No words could possibly express my gratitude. I am honored by your offer to return to the Guild, and will think on it very carefully before giving you an answer. And," she added quietly, "I will always be grateful for everything you've done for me."

Mai nodded, his narrowed eyes making it difficult to guess his feelings. He paused for a moment, looking at her. Then he turned away, and she felt the tension released as normal activity resumed around him. One by one, the Diamonds saluted to him and departed, followed by Master Abib, leaving the two of them in the courtyard, surrounded by his Emerald Guard.

"I am going to the medical barracks," Mai said. "You want to come with me?"

Kara nodded, unsure if she could find her voice, and fell into stride by his side.

Things around her were changing too quickly. Yesterday morning she had been an outcast, her life forfeit. And now, only a day later, she was free, the first Majat in history who had been able to leave the Guild without any obligations. From now on, she could do anything she pleased – including going back to her old life, if she wanted to. All this was just too much to deal with.

The arrival of the Guildmaster, marching in full regalia at the head of his Emerald Guard, caused a major upheaval in the medical barracks. Mai took it in stride as he made his way inside, past the saluting people lining the walls.

Raishan was sitting in bed, his back propped against a pile of pillows. His face looked drawn and very pale, with deep dark circles under his eyes. When he saw Mai, he moved to rise, but Doctor Lestor standing by his side placed a hand on his shoulder, forcing him to subside back into the pillows.

"Guildmaster." Raishan pressed his fist to his chest and bowed his head.

Mai nodded, responding with a brief salute before stepping up to the bedside.

"Aghat Raishan. I am so relieved to know that you are expected to make a fast recovery."

Raishan shot a glance at the doctor.

"Not as fast as I would like to, Aghat Mai. My place is by your side."

"And I look forward to you assuming it, Aghat. But only after Master Lestor releases you to active duty."

Raishan nodded.

"I am in your debt, Aghat Raishan," Mai said. "You received your wound protecting me. I feel responsible for what happened."

Raishan smiled. "Seeing you in charge makes it all worth it, Guildmaster. I cannot imagine a better man for the post."

Mai's face lit up with a quick smile. Then both men turned to Kara as she stepped up to Raishan's bedside.

"Welcome back, Aghat Raishan," she said. "For a moment, back in the courtyard, I feared we'd lost you."

"It's not as easy as you think." Raishan's eyes stirred with an affection that made her feel warm inside. He was such a good friend, and seeing that he had survived his ordeal made her feel so relieved.

"Well fought, Aghat," Raishan said. "Or so I heard. Your fame is spreading like fire, even here in the medical barracks. I wish I could have seen it. A shadow throw, eh?"

She smiled, surprised at how much this casual compliment pleased her.

"I look forward to seeing you on the training grounds soon, Aghat Raishan," she said.

Mai's next few steps took him to the rooms housing the Rubies injured at the tournament. Some of them were still in bad shape, but the doctors in attendance assured him that most of them were expected to recover completely, and within a reasonable time. As Mai made his rounds, stopping by the patients' beds and exchanging words of encouragement and reassurance, everyone's eyes followed him with fascination and reverence.

Kara watched this with mixed feelings. Some of these men had been wounded by her swords before she had realized, in the heat of the mêlée, that something was wrong. Fighting with a bare blade, as opposed to a staff with the blades one could draw or retract on command, could be a disadvantage in such a case. One of the Rubies had fallen right on her sword, and she hadn't been able to do anything to avert it. She was glad that none of them seemed to be holding it against her. In fact, they all smiled and saluted her, many eyes following her with expressions of awe.

Their last stop brought them to a smaller room at the end of the hallway. Kara's heart quivered as she followed Mai toward the freckled man with a bandaged chest, who shakily stood to attention beside his bed, watching the approaching group with a pale face.

She did not think she could ever look at this man again without a sinking feeling in the pit of her stomach. In fact, she hoped she'd never have to see this man again.

"Gahang Sharrim," Mai said.

The Jade saluted and sank down to one knee. "Aghat Mai. I—"

Mai's short glance froze the words on his lips. "You've disobeyed your orders and violated a ceasefire, Gahang. I believe you are aware of what kind of punishment is warranted. Do you have anything to say in your defense?"

The Jade's saluting hand trembled. "I am sorry for shooting you, Aghat Mai."

"It's not about me, Gahang."

Sharrim's lips quivered and, to her surprise, Kara saw tears standing in his eyes.

"I was guided by a foolish sense that my actions might somehow erase your past, Aghat Mai. I did not want to see you get hurt. The last thing I wanted was to hurt you myself. Not in a lifetime." His voice sank to a whisper as he looked at Mai with the devotion of a loyal dog waiting to be struck by its master.

Mai shook his head. "Once again, Gahang, this has nothing to do with your personal feelings. As you well know, the Majat Guild depends on the ability of its men to follow orders."

Sharrim lowered his eyes. "I am aware of how unforgivable my actions were, Aghat Mai, and will gladly accept my punishment. But... if you choose to spare me and give me an opportunity to prove my loyalty to you, I swear I will never again violate my orders."

Mai appeared to hesitate.

"I know that at heart you are a good man, Gahang," he said. "And I do realize that the circumstances that surrounded your actions were far out of the ordinary. I also know that you are the best archer our Guild has seen in decades. However, I need an assurance that I can trust you."

"You can trust me, Aghat Mai. I swear."

Mai nodded.

"I am placing you on probation. Any further incident will result in your permanent removal from the ranks, with the punishment determined by your superior officers."

Sharrim's lips trembled.

"Thank you, Aghat Mai. I will not fail you again." His voice sank to a near-whisper and Kara saw a tear roll down his cheek as he watched Mai depart.

He remained kneeling after Mai exited. Kara hesitated, wondering if she should call for help. With his recent wound, she wasn't sure he should be up and about, let alone kneeling down. Could he rise on his own without hurting himself even more?

He noticed her look and shakily got to his feet, watching her. Relieved, she turned to go, but his words stopped her.

"Aghat Kara?"

She paused, surprised that he had addressed her. She forced her face into a calm expression, unwilling to show how much this man unnerved her.

"That was a shadow throw, wasn't it?" Sharrim said, eyeing her with awe. "I thought it was impossible to perform. I didn't believe anyone had actually done it in the past, despite what the chronicles say. To my knowledge, no one in our Guild has been able to do it for centuries."

Kara's lips twitched. "I felt inspired, Gahang."

He swallowed. "I... I'm sorry for trying to shoot you down, Aghat Kara. And, I know I have no right to say this – not after what happened – but I am so glad Aghat Mai spared your life."

Kara couldn't help but smile. She suddenly saw this man for who he was, barely her senior, a talented archer who put his skill above all else. She also remembered the way he looked at Mai. In addition to the loyalty and admiration she had seen in nearly everyone today,

Sharrim's eyes held more. He looked at Mai as an object of his love.

Whether or not she shared the same feeling, she understood exactly how he felt.

She let out a breath.

"Yes, Gahang," she said. "Me too."

After the medical barracks, Mai left to attend to business in his office. Kara remained outside, striding along the grounds with unseeing eyes. It felt as if a burden had been lifted off her shoulders, and until it was gone she hadn't fully realized how heavy it had been. She was *free*, truly and unconditionally, and could do anything she wanted with her future. She could now go back with Kyth and live at court, and perhaps even work her way up into the line of prospective brides for the royal heir. She could also return to the Guild and resume her rank – a prized fighter, royalty in her own right, and a hero to her people. The Majat Guildmaster was a powerful man indeed to grant her all these things in one very short conversation. The only thing now was to decide what she wanted – and for some reason she was finding the decision harder than anticipated.

When she had lived on a death roll, with a firm understanding that every day could be her last, she became used to giving in to immediate impulses, without thinking of the longer-term consequences. This mind set, as she now realized, drove her to continue her relationship with Kyth, which was enjoyable and meant so much to him, despite being aware that it couldn't possibly end well. This same type of recklessness also drove her to explore her feelings for Mai, allowing herself the freedom she would have never considered if she hadn't believed they were both going to die. And now, the choice that lay before her was really the choice between these two men. Except that, even if she decided to stay at the Guild, any possibility of a relationship with Mai was off limits. Had he remained a regular Diamond, they could at least engage in occasional physical closeness, provided that they never allowed it to progress to an emotional level – which of course may no longer have been possible. But the Majat Guildmaster was not permitted to have personal bonds of any kind, definitely not with one of his subordinates.

Kara was surprised to realize that this thought kept returning to her again and again. Whatever she thought she felt for Mai, having him in her life was not an option, and she would do best to forget all about it. She was choosing between staying with Kyth and exploring her feelings for him, or staying at the Guild and admiring Mai from afar, like the rest of the Guild members. The first choice also involved trying to become someone else, fitting into a court life she had no idea about. The second, loveless choice, meant resuming the life she had been born to and learning to fully accept all its privileges and limitations.

One way or the other, it all narrowed down to Kyth. Did she love him enough to renounce what she was? Or did her rank in the Guild mean so much to her that she was willing to leave him behind?

Unwittingly, her feet brought her to the upper guest quarters, a low stone building with luxurious apartments inside that housed important visitors. She took a deep breath and made her way inside.

Kyth was sitting at a desk, buried in a pile of books and scrolls. His face lit up as he saw her, and when he rose to meet her she saw him shiver as he looked searchingly into her face.

"I am so glad you are alive," he breathed out. Then he stepped forward and swept her into his arms.

She relaxed against him. It was good to see him this way, after the painful days when he had looked at her with a hurt expression that made her quiver every time she met his gaze. It was good to know that he had finally forgiven her for what she had done and to realize from his welcome that the option of staying with him was open to her if she wanted it. He still loved her, that was clear. But how did she feel about him?

His hands caressed her and she gave in to it, searching for the feeling his touch used to evoke in her before. She felt strange that despite everything they had, she couldn't even fully relax in his arms, as if their previous closeness had never happened. It almost seemed that if she were to explore her feelings for him, she would have to start all the way back at the beginning of their relationship, when he, a naive boy, had worked so hard to break through her armor of a trained fighter and reach the woman inside.

His lips brushed hers, asking for a kiss. She hesitated. After everything that had happened, she wasn't sure she was ready. She needed more time.

She turned away, kissing his cheek instead, and glanced past his shoulder at the desk.

"What's all this?"

He held her for a moment longer, then dropped his hands and stepped away, hope in his eyes mixing with disappointment.

"I am preparing for the upcoming negotiations. I am supposed to read up on protocol, so that I can hold myself well enough to convince the Majat to accept our alliance."

She shook her head. "I'm sure Mai's head is in the right place about this. He wants the Kaddim destroyed as much as you do."

A shadow ran across his eyes at the mention of Mai's name.

"I'm not sure if I would rather have negotiated with your old Guildmaster."

She sighed. "Useless to think about it now. Besides, if you had negotiated with Aghat Oden Lan, it would have meant that I was dead."

He nodded, his shiver telling her how relieved he felt. She swallowed a lump, something that happened to her far too often these days.

How could she possibly hesitate, when this sweet, innocent man with a pure heart offered himself to her so unconditionally? Mai's closeness had confused her, but their brief and crazy relationship was over, with no possibility of return. She belonged here, with Kyth, didn't she? She *wanted* it to be this way, she realized. If she could rediscover her feelings for Kyth it would make her life so easy, offering her a safe haven of happiness, now that the threat of her Guild's wrath was no longer looming over her. Why couldn't she just settle for it? Why did the memory of her *other* feelings, the ones that weren't meant to be, keep haunting her even in another man's arms?

A creak of the opening door interrupted her thoughts. Magister Egey Bashi strode in, with Lady Celana in his wake. The royal lady's eyes flicked with swift displeasure that forced Kara to step away from the Prince even before she could give it any thought.

Egey Bashi greeted her with a quick nod. "Glad to see you well, Aghat – and congratulations on yours and Aghat Mai's brilliant victory. It was a sight not to be forgotten and such a relief to us all that it ended so well."

"Thank you, Magister," she said, wondering at how, despite her relief that things had turned out so well, she was having such trouble getting rid of an emptiness in her chest. She knew that long and strenuous battles often took a while to recover from. This was all it was, she told herself firmly. It had to be.

"Time to head for your negotiations, Your Highness," Egey Bashi said to Kyth. "Everyone's waiting."

Kyth nodded, picking up his coronet and royal cloak. Kara followed him, falling in stride with the Keeper in his wake.

"I wonder if I should be there," she said quietly.

Egey Bashi shrugged. "You'll be there, Aghat, whether or not you are in the room. I just hope both of them can look past it and focus on the more important things."

26
NEGOTIATIONS

Kyth knew that the Majat Guildmaster normally received visitors in his study, in the tower at the edge of the Inner Fortress. He was surprised when they were led a different way, through a gated archway, into an ornate stone building on the other side of the plaza.

The large hall inside rivaled the King's throne room in its age and grandeur. Walking over the flagstones toward the group waiting for them at the other end, Kyth realized that, in a way, this *was* a throne room. In this Fortress, as well as in the outside lands, the Majat Guildmaster had at least as much power as a king.

Kyth frowned as he walked. Ever since assuming his station, Mai had been running things on a grand scale, like a carefully prepared show. While Kyth supposed it was important for a new commander to assume his position with a certain ceremony, he had a feeling that Mai was enjoying all this glamor perhaps a bit too much.

Mai received the Crown Prince seated, with Master Abib and several senior Majat standing at the sides of his tall, massive chair. Kyth saw Mai's eyes narrow when he noticed Kara in his suite, and he couldn't help feeling just a bit smug about it. She had fulfilled her obligation to Mai by standing at his side through his difficult battle. And now, this man couldn't possibly have any claim to her.

Kyth stopped five paces away from the chair, bowing to the exact extent he believed was warranted by protocol.

"Aghat Mai," he said formally.

"Prince Kythar." Mai's eyes bore into him, and Kyth imagined a touch of quiet challenge in his gaze.

He had gone through an extensive talk with Egey Bashi that afternoon on how, in this conversation, he should dismiss any thoughts of their personal rivalry, but he couldn't possibly help it. Mai was a showoff and a ruthless man, with no respect for anyone who did not share his rank. He was also a man who could seduce a woman for sport and use her to his own ends. Kyth swallowed this last thought, glancing at Kara standing a few steps behind.

Kyth knew that Mai was aware of his exact mission, but he now realized that this man was not going to make it easy by facilitating the conversation. Kyth had to go through all the formalities with no help whatsoever from the other side, and embarrass himself to the full if he missed any of the protocol details. Not that he expected it to be any other way.

Kyth lifted his chin.

"Guildmaster," he said. "My father, King Evan, has sent me here in the hope that we can forge an alliance between the Majat Guild and the kingdom of Tallan Dar in our fight against the Kaddim. This request is backed by Magister Egey Bashi of the Order of Keepers," he indicated Magister Egey Bashi, "Lady Celana of the Royal House Illitand, and Alder, the emissary from the Forestlands." *And Ellah, the truthseer who will see right through your scheming.* He glanced at his friend, standing quietly at Egey Bashi's side. Mai knew she was a truthseer, which somewhat reduced the advantage they'd hoped for when they originally planned the negotiations with the old Guildmaster. Still, Kyth willed this man to tell a lie. Ellah would see right through it, and she would signal him as she stood there with her hand resting against her thigh. If he was telling the truth, she would hold out one finger. If a lie, two.

Mai's eyes slid over Kara again. Kyth was willing to bet the man was wondering why she was here as part of his suite, and he couldn't help letting out a small smile of triumph. *She is mine*, his eyes told Mai. *Not yours.*

Mai leaned back in his chair.

"As I'm sure you are aware, Prince Kythar," he said, "the Majat Guild has retained its high standing through the centuries by maintaining full political neutrality. A formal alliance between the Majat and your kingdom is impossible."

"*Impossible*?" Kyth's eyes widened. Hadn't this man learned diplomacy? Didn't he know that even in the heat of an argument an ambassador should never be met with a straight rejection?

Mai held his gaze, an annoying smile playing on his lips. "Through the entire history of our Guild, the Majat has formed no alliance with anyone. Doing so would violate everything we are."

"But…" Kyth continued to look at him in disbelief. Was Mai going to throw away everything? Had they traveled here in vain?

He struggled to steady his voice.

"The Kaddim are your enemies too," he said.

Mai nodded. "Yes. And we intend to deal with them, I assure you. On our terms."

"On your terms?" Kyth still couldn't believe what was happening. In a few words Mai was destroying everything they had been fighting for. He *knew* what was at stake, didn't he?

"Yes," Mai said, seemingly undisturbed. "The Majat will deal with the Kaddim the way we believe is warranted. You may join our forces, if you wish, but it must be done under our command."

"Your command."

"Yes."

Kyth took a breath. Was Mai out of his mind? For Shal Addim's sake, Kyth had saved him from the Kaddim, once. Had he forgotten?

"You know, Aghat Mai," he said, "that I am the only one who can resist the Kaddim power."

Mai smiled. "That is hardly true, Prince Kythar. I can resist it too. As well as Aghat Kara." His eyes hovered on her again, and Kyth saw a brief expression of regret in his gaze. Was he feeling sorry he couldn't force himself on her again *in the heat of a fight*?

Kyth forced down his racing thoughts. This was exactly what Egey Bashi had warned him about. He was here as an ambassador, and ambassadors had to distance themselves from personal feelings when conducting a negotiation.

"I can protect others from their power, Aghat Mai," Kyth said. "Before you acquired your... resistance to them," *because of your feelings for her,* "I was the one who protected you, once. If I remember, you even mentioned that you felt indebted to me after that time, didn't you?"

He saw Egey Bashi by his side shift uncomfortably from foot to foot and realized that he must have said something inappropriate. But he was *right*, wasn't he?

Mai glanced at him calmly.

"You remember correctly, Prince Kythar," he said. "I am in your debt. However, this personal debt does not extend to the lives of my men."

"If we march against the Kaddim together, I can *protect* your men."

Mai held his gaze, and this time Kyth definitely caught the expression of irony.

"I know of the current extent of your ability in some detail, Prince Kythar. So far, you can protect *one* man. The rest is theory, and I cannot stake my men's lives on a theory, can I?"

Kyth took a step back. All around him people were shifting and exchanging glances. He was aware that somehow he had messed things up, but he had no idea what to do now. Worse, he didn't want to appear as if he was looking for advice from anyone. Mai was talking entirely on his own, and the men of his suite hadn't even changed their positions since the negotiations started. Was Kyth any worse?

"So," he said, "you will only agree to join forces if we surrender ourselves to your command?"

"Yes," Mai said.

"But…" Kyth began, but paused as he saw Egey Bashi by his side briefly lower his head and pinch the bridge of his nose.

"Perhaps, Prince Kythar," the Keeper said, "we can reconvene these negotiations at another time? I feel it might be prudent to give it a day or two. With Aghat Mai's permission, of course." He glanced at the Majat group.

Mai's gaze hardened. "At any time, my answer will be the same, Magister. The Majat will not act as part of an alliance or join forces under anyone's command. If Prince Kythar wants our help, he must surrender to our terms."

Kyth continued to stare. He was aware that diplomats were not supposed to swear and storm out of negotiations, but this was exactly what he felt like doing. Mai clearly had no intention of helping, and there was nothing he could do about it. The only thing Kyth couldn't understand was why Mai had insisted on this charade in the first place, and brought them into this formal audience hall – unless, of course, his only purpose had been to embarrass Kyth and show him his place. Knowing the man, Kyth wouldn't put such a motive beneath him.

He glanced around at his followers, noting Ellah holding out one finger to indicate that Mai was telling the truth, and Kara standing so still that she appeared like a statue.

In the ensuing silence Lady Celana's voice rang clearly like a bell.

"If I remember correctly, Prince Kythar," she said, "the only way the Majat Guild can ever be forced into unconditional cooperation is through the Ultimate

Challenge. Such a thing has never happened before, but if one were to challenge the Guild and win, the Majat would have no choice but to follow."

Kyth stared. "The Ultimate Challenge?"

She nodded. "Much like the one issued by Aghat Mai just a short time ago. A fight to the death against the entire Guild."

Kyth's eyes widened. He knew that, for some reason, Lady Celana seemed to hold him in high regard. But to suggest that he could issue an Ultimate Challenge and fight the entire Majat Guild to the death?

"Do you believe, my lady," he asked slowly, "that I would be able to stand up to such a challenge?"

She smiled. "You don't have to fight them yourself, Your Highness. You can choose a champion to fight in your stead." Her eyes briefly flicked to Kara.

Kyth's skin prickled. What she was suggesting was devious. Yet, this did give him a way to get out of this situation without losing face. Kara was a worthy champion, one Mai would consider a threat. And given that she was the one who put him in command, given his *feelings* for her, he would surely do everything possible to avert this fight?

Kyth glanced at Mai, noticing with satisfaction how the man was sitting very still, his eyes focused on Kyth as if he were a snake about to strike. It was captivating to see this wary expression in Mai's eyes that bordered on fear. *Didn't think I could do anything against you, eh?*

"By the rules," Lady Celana continued calmly, as if oblivious to the tension, "your champion cannot be an active member of the Majat Guild. There are no other restrictions."

Kyth's skin prickled as he turned and met Kara's gaze. She gave him a barely perceptible nod.

Kyth drew himself up.

"Aghat Mai," he said. "I wish to issue an Ultimate Challenge against the Majat Guild. If I win, the Guild must promise unconditional support in our war with the Kaddim. I choose Kara as my champion."

Mai's eyes narrowed. His gaze darted to Lady Celana and rested briefly on Magister Egey Bashi. He did not look at Kara at all, and the way his glance excluded her made Kyth's heart quiver. What had he done?

"If you lose," Mai said. "She will die."

Kyth swallowed. "I know."

Mai slowly relaxed his shoulders and finally turned to Kara.

"You can refuse," he said. "If you do, I will allow Prince Kythar to withdraw his challenge, given that you probably did not have a chance to discuss this plan with the Prince in any detail."

She lifted her chin.

"I accept, Aghat Mai. I will champion Prince Kythar's cause."

Mai went so still that for a moment he appeared inanimate.

"Why?" he asked quietly.

She looked at Mai with such deep regret that Kyth's heart quivered again. *What have I done…?*

"I believe, Aghat Mai," Kara said, "one way or the other this alliance must happen. If you and Prince Kythar cannot agree on the terms, I see no other choice. I believe it is the right thing to do."

Mai nodded. His eyes became glassy.

"Very well. The challenge will take place tomorrow morning at the main arena. I will not restrict your whereabouts before that time and will grant you access to all the Guild's resources. You may prepare in any way you wish."

Kara nodded, watching him with wide eyes. Everyone else turned to Kyth, as if expecting something.

He shook off his stupor.

"I believe there is nothing else to be said, Aghat Mai. So, if you have no further words for me, I wish to take my leave."

Mai nodded, his expression distant as if he was deep in thought. Kyth had never seen him like this. Not that he gave a damn.

He turned and strode out of the room, with his companions in his wake.

"I did not think Aghat Mai would accept," Celana said quietly as she fell into stride next to Kyth in the outside courtyard.

Kyth looked at Kara, walking on his other side. Her lips twitched as she turned to Celana.

"For once, my lady, you underestimated him. He always does what he believes is right."

"But in this case…" Lady Celana's glance at Kara told Kyth how deeply she understood the emotions involved.

"He is protecting the entire Guild," Kara said. "Regardless of his personal feelings, he cannot stake everyone's lives to save mine."

Celana raised her eyebrows. "But if you knew he would do that, why did you agree to be the champion?"

Kara sighed. "It seemed to me the negotiations had reached a standoff. I believe in this alliance, and despite my utmost respect for Aghat Mai's judgment, I don't think he is giving it a chance. I am hoping my actions will prompt him to give it another try."

"You think he will call off the fight?"

Kara didn't respond, and Kyth's heart sank as he looked at her distant expression.

"Do you think you can win this challenge?" Kyth asked quietly.

She shrugged. "Only one way to find out. We didn't leave Mai with many choices. I know one thing for sure. If he decides to go through with the challenge, he will do everything in his power to win."

27

RESOLVE

Once again, Kara was striding unseeingly through the Majat grounds. No matter how hard she drove herself, she couldn't seem to find any rest. She tried to think of any reason she should be feeling good about what had happened, and failed.

Mai's look, when she had accepted the challenge, haunted her. One of his very first actions as he took command was to grant her freedom and erase her debt to him. She was alive and free, thanks to him. Was *this* how she was repaying him for everything he'd done for her?

When Kyth's desperate glance back in the audience hall had begged her to accept the challenge, she couldn't possibly refuse. Kyth's negotiation skills were not in the same league as Mai's, leaving the Prince cornered and trapped with nearly no escape. Worse, to Kara's sense, Mai wasn't about to offer him any way out. If Kyth had stormed out of the hall in the presence of the senior Majat – as she felt he was about to do – it would have been nearly impossible to mend affairs.

By accepting the challenge she hoped, above all, to

gain some time that might help Mai reconsider and find a possible exit from this stalemate. They all needed this alliance to happen, one way or another, even though Kyth had done a very poor job of phrasing his request. She knew that Mai understood that too. She couldn't help admitting that ultimately Mai was right and it would be best to do everything on Majat terms, but negotiations were all about compromises, and the way things had gone hadn't left room for any. She was hoping that her willingness to put her life on the line might help everyone else involved see how important it was to take steps in the right direction.

If Mai allowed the challenge to proceed, he would have no choice but to put his best warriors against her. She was certain he wouldn't want to do it if there was any possibility of avoiding it. Mai had a devious mind. Perhaps this additional time would enable him to find a solution. Of course, afterward he would probably never want to see her again. But despite how much this thought disturbed her, she told herself again and again that it was a necessary price to pay to defeat an ultimate enemy. There were bigger things at stake here than her confusing feelings toward a man who wasn't available anyway.

More than once she wandered to the Guildmaster's tower, hoping for a chance to catch Mai and at least attempt to explain herself, if not help him devise a way out of the situation. But his doors were firmly shut, and the Emerald Guards standing outside showed no intention of letting her through.

Having given up on Mai, she tried to see Master Abib, but the weapons keeper could not be found anywhere on the grounds. She checked every corner, every secret place she knew the old man favored, but could not find a trace of him. Even his associates, scurrying around the weapons stands and attending to the forges below, seemed to have no idea of his whereabouts.

Mai had kept his word to grant Kara access to the entire grounds. No one barred her way even when she ventured into the very heart of the Inner Fortress, the place off limits not only to outsiders but also to Outer Fortress trainees. Her feet had inadvertently brought her to the very distant secluded area, that housed the apartments of some of the senior members of the Guild.

She was surprised to see two Emeralds standing guard outside one of them. Her heart raced as she stepped closer, realizing who they were likely guarding.

The old Guildmaster, Oden Lan, had not been around during Mai's parade and had been prominently excluded from any ensuing activities. She knew his position was precarious. A normal change of command occurred when the previous Guildmaster died, and it was rare to have a man around who had surrendered command under pressure, without prior intention to lay down his power. Things must have been tough between them, and Kara was aware that Mai couldn't possibly let Oden Lan wander the grounds until the man was fully ready to accept his successor.

As she approached the door, the Emeralds didn't bar her way like they had at the Guildmaster's tower. Surprised, she glanced at them with question, but they stared firmly ahead, showing no intention of even acknowledging her presence. She pushed the door and, finding it unlocked, cautiously stepped inside.

In the large, dimly lit room she didn't see Oden Lan immediately. He was sitting so still in his tall armchair that he appeared inanimate – an ability that came with the stealth all Diamonds possessed. Yet, as she crossed the room toward him, she was surprised to realize that he was not doing it on purpose. He was so absorbed in his thoughts that the stillness came naturally.

She stopped several paces away, unsure what to say, or even what it was that brought her here, to face the man who had ordered her death.

His lips quivered. His upward glance stirred with a deep longing that made her feel instantly uncomfortable. He didn't speak, and after a while she realized that she had to either leave or break the silence.

"Master Oden Lan," she said.

"Kara." His voice came out at a near-whisper as he fought to control his trembling lips.

She shivered. This man had been the closest she ever had to a father. Having him turn against her had left a deep wound, but she had never fully realized how bad it was until now, when she stood in front of him after having helped to bring about his defeat. It suddenly seemed so important to talk to him, to bring things to a closure between them.

"I am sorry for everything that happened, Aghat," she said. "While I do not regret any of my actions, I truly wish things had gone differently." *I wish you'd understood why I violated my orders, and why Mai violated his. I wish you hadn't ordered my death. I wish you hadn't unleashed our entire Guild on the two of us.* She was surprised at the force of her emotions as she looked down on him.

He continued to watch her, the longing in his eyes that she found so unsettling now mixing with bitterness.

"You broke my heart," he said quietly. "Ever since you came into my care, I loved you... like a daughter I never had. And then you..."

She stared. Hearing Oden Lan talk about his love for her frightened her, affording a glimpse of the dark pit that harbored his emotions and had driven him to the verge of madness. He said he loved her like a daughter. But that was not the way he was looking at her.

With a sinking heart she remembered all the meaningful glances exchanged around her whenever Oden Lan's name came up, the way everyone kept saying how *personally* her decision to disobey her orders made him feel. Was *this* what they all meant? Did this man truly think he *loved* her?

Against reason, she suddenly felt sorry for him, a man whose unresolved feelings had blinded him to something that was so obvious to everyone else. She now realized that his resolve to kill her, the way he was willing to fight Mai to the death no matter what, stemmed from the feeling he had just confessed. In his mind, Oden Lan possessed her, and knowing that she was off limits to him despite that, forced him into a mad jealousy, a willingness to destroy anyone who had so much as touched her. He may never come to terms with Mai, just for that reason. Not while she was still around.

Her pity for him, her sudden awareness of how he felt about her, made her want to run away and never see him again. But another, wounded part of her kept her in place. She needed to make amends, to remove this dark shadow from her life.

She sank down to the floor at his feet and covered his hand with hers. He didn't withdraw it, but she sensed a shiver go through his body at her touch.

In all his years as a Guildmaster she would never have dared to touch him. And now, having emerged on the other side of death, facing one deadly challenge after another, having betrayed the trust of the man who had done everything for her, she didn't feel these things mattered anymore. She was free, no longer bound by Majat rules, and she was going to do what she damned well pleased.

"I've always felt you were the closest I had to a father, Aghat Oden Lan," she said. "Living up to your expectations has always been my highest goal. The decision I made when I disobeyed your orders... I had no choice. I want you to understand this."

His eyes darted to her hand covering his, the longing in his eyes so overwhelming that she suddenly felt afraid. She forced herself not to move, to keep her hand in place. She wasn't afraid of him anymore. She wasn't afraid of anyone or anything.

Oden Lan shook his head.

"Yes, you did have a choice. You could have done your duty. You disobeyed me because of your love for that boy, didn't you?"

Her lips quivered. "No. I did it because I knew it was the right thing to do."

"But you do love him, don't you?"

She hesitated. He was the second man who had asked her that in a very short time. Inadvertently her thoughts drifted to that other time she'd had to answer this question, locked in a cell with Mai. Thinking of it made her shiver. She suddenly realized that on that night, despite what she believed awaited them in the morning, she had felt unconditionally happy for the first time in her life.

And now, in one move, she had just thrown it all away.

"I thought I loved him, at the time," she said. "But I believe I was wrong."

"Still." Oden Lan paused to control his twitching lips. "You acted on your personal feelings. It goes against everything you were trained to be."

So did you. She held his gaze. "The Kaddim are our enemies, Aghat. You've seen what they are capable of. That time... they played on your sense of righteousness by forcing you to accept my assignment, with full knowledge that I would do everything possible to refuse. They had spent considerable efforts prior to it to make sure I knew exactly what they were and how disastrous it would have been if they had their way. Normally you would have seen it too. But you didn't listen to me back then, because you believed I was acting on my personal feelings. That was part of their plan too."

He didn't say anything as he watched her.

"They played you," Kara went on, "and Aghat Mai saw through it, despite the fact that he wasn't even there when it happened. He staked everything, including his life, to interfere with their plan. It takes a great man to do what he did. You must see that, don't you?"

"Aghat Mai." Oden Lan's expression once again became bitter. "It's all about him now, isn't it?"

She sighed. "He's in charge now, so, yes, it's all about him. He staked everything to set things right – and he won. And it's hard to imagine a more capable man in dealing with the Kaddim. Can't you just accept it?"

His gaze wavered as he looked down at her hand, still covering his. After hesitation he covered it with his own, gently caressing her skin.

She stiffened. This was a fatherly gesture, she told herself. She had just done a similar thing to comfort him. Except, she didn't caress him like this, his touch trying to evoke a response, promising more. She didn't *love* him, not the way he professed to her. She didn't love him like a father, either, she realized. This man had dominated her life. He had made her the way she was – first training her as a top killer and bathing her in glory, then ordering her death when she dared to disobey him. And now, having gone through all that, she was finally free of him once and for all.

She watched his caressing hand, then glanced to his face again. Despite everything, she couldn't stop feeling sorry for him. Her heart quivered at his wounded look as he saw the rejection in her eyes and dropped his hand away.

"Aghat Mai is capable all right," Oden Lan said. "Too capable for his own good."

Kara shook her head. "I hope you can resolve your feelings toward him, Aghat Oden Lan. The Guild still needs you, even if you are no longer in charge. And… you should feel nothing but pride at seeing how well Aghat Mai fits his new station. You must realize that, like me, he learned most of what he knows from you."

Oden Lan looked at her searchingly.

"You are not telling me everything you feel toward him, are you?"

She looked away, angry at the color that crept into her cheeks. Why did he keep talking to her about her feelings?

"Whatever else I feel toward him, or anyone else, is irrelevant."

Oden Lan's lips twitched. "Is it?"

She sighed. "It is, for this conversation, Aghat. And you would instantly see it too, if only you could truly think of me purely as a father would. If you did, it would make things so much easier for everyone."

His gaze wavered with deep feeling as he looked down on her.

"Why?"

She took a breath. "Because, this is the way I feel about you – as a father I never had – and it would never be otherwise."

His lips twitched.

"I thought that boy took you away from me. And now, it looks like Mai has taken you away from him, hasn't he?"

She shook her head. "It's not like that, Aghat Oden Lan. No one took me away from you. You did it yourself. As for Mai – I would be dead many times over if it wasn't for him. I'm sure you understand that something like this would create a bond not to be easily broken." *Except, I did break it. Just like that.* She forced the thought away.

He nodded slowly.

"I heard he granted you freedom and full pardon."

She tried to smile. "He was very generous. I am

certain he felt a reward was warranted after I stood by him during his challenge, even though I am really the one who should be feeling grateful."

"Is this the feeling you settled for? Gratitude?"

Her gaze wavered.

"He is the Majat Guildmaster. You should know better than anyone what this post entails. Would it ever be possible for me to feel anything else toward him?"

Oden Lan reached forward and once again covered her hand with his.

"I know how it feels," he said. "And since I am not the Majat Guildmaster anymore, I am finding myself on another side of this scale. My feelings for you... Keeping them to myself has been tormenting me all these years, until it finally drove me mad. I know now that you would never be able to return them. I used to dream that you would, one day, despite the impossibility of it. But I understand now that this was never meant to be... In my desire to give you only the best, I've caused you much pain. I hope you can forgive me."

Her lips trembled as she felt tears rising to her eyes.

"I forgive you, Aghat Oden Lan," she said. "And in expressing the way I feel about you, I couldn't possibly put it better than the way Aghat Mai said it to you at the tournament yesterday. You taught me many important things, and I will always be grateful to you for that. With the way you trained me, I couldn't have possibly acted otherwise. You taught me to stand up for what I believe is right. I intend to do it every time, even if it costs me everything I hold dear."

She let out a breath, her own words sinking in until she truly realized this was indeed how she felt.

She and Mai shared this training, this belief, and they both learned it from this man. This was what drove her to agree to champion Kyth's challenge, with full knowledge that it would destroy anything she had with Mai, aware of the terrible position she was putting him into. It hurt beyond measure to know that standing up for her beliefs would harm the man she cared for and sever their bond that she cherished so much. And yet, she also knew that Mai had given up more when he forfeited his life to save hers. If she were to die at the tournament tomorrow, she would die with full knowledge that she had done her duty. And that meant so much more than anything else.

She smiled as she held Oden Lan's gaze, and he smiled back, gently patting her arm. It was truly a fatherly gesture this time, and it felt so comforting as she sat on the floor by his feet. For the first time Kara saw the man she had known him to be, ruthless in pursuing his beliefs, but also wise and experienced like no one else. He had taught everyone around him these high values. And now, even though his command had been ripped from his hands by a man less than half his age, these values remained, and would always be there for as long as their Guild stood.

"Thank you, Aghat Oden Lan," she said. "Whatever happens to me, I will always be grateful to you for the part you played in my life."

28
IMPASSE

Egey Bashi couldn't stop swearing. He no longer felt bothered by the surprised glances of the people next to him as he took his seat at the head of the arena. Bloody hell. Important negotiations had to be conducted by adults, not by adolescents having too much trouble thinking with their heads.

It had been the wrong decision after all to bring Kara into the room. Egey Bashi had originally thought her presence might be calming to Mai, who obviously shared a deeper bond with her than anyone cared to see. But to have her march in as part of Kyth's suite had been a mistake, and Egey Bashi held himself fully responsible for it. He could see how the outcome of the negotiations had been decided in a few short glances before the talking even began. Lady Celana's famous knowledge of history and politics hadn't helped either. And now, the dung was flying, and everyone without exception was on the receiving end of it.

He watched the spectators settle into their seats around the arena, and the ring of Jade archers take their places along its top. He had no idea who Mai was putting against Kara, but the presence of the Jades showed that he was not going to just throw the fight, as Egey Bashi had secretly hoped after he realized that the Guildmaster had no intention of reconsidering and resuming negotiations.

The order of things was somewhat different this time. The first horn blasts announced the arrival of the challenger and his champion. Kyth and Kara approached the arena side by side and exchanged a few words. Then the Prince was led to a seat at the end opposite the Guildmaster's, and Kara proceeded alone, stopping in the center of the large oval space. She looked so small down there, her slim black-clad shape sharply contrasted by the gleam of the white sand.

Another horn blast announced the arrival of the Guildmaster and the defenders. Egey Bashi narrowed his eyes, watching the approaching Majat, a dozen men walking with fast strides. Mai was among them, but to Egey Bashi's surprise he did not take his chair, but instead strode past it and into the arena. The Keeper's skin prickled as he belatedly realized that Mai wasn't wearing his cloak of station, and that another man wearing this cloak was taking the Guildmaster's seat. With a sinking heart he recognized Master Abib.

Bloody hell.

The arena went deadly still as everyone watched Mai stride across and stop in front of Kara. Her eyes widened in surprise.

"You can't fight in the Ultimate Challenge, Aghat Mai," she said, her words ringing clearly over the silence. "You're the Guildmaster."

Mai drew his staff.

"I'm not," he said. "I have renounced my post."

He did not give her a chance to respond as he sprang into action, forcing her to draw her blades and defend. She had no time even to compose herself for the attack. Egey Bashi saw her stumble under his shower of brutal blows, and for a moment he feared the fight was going to be a very short one.

The Keeper watched, holding his breath. The action unraveling in the arena in front of him was far beyond anything he had ever seen. The fighters whirled so fast that their movements were difficult to trace, even in the blinding sunlight. Their skill, matched down to the impossible, made their deadly fight seem like a dance, so fascinating that Egey Bashi found it unthinkable to look away.

He knew that Mai had been trained as Kara's shadow, a fighter who knew her exact style and weaknesses, and he could tell that Mai was using his knowledge to the full. Several times Kara wavered and lost her footing. Twice she had to scramble to avoid his blade, which was springing out of the tip of his staff and retreating without trace. So far she was holding her own, but Egey Bashi knew it was only a matter of time.

He knew that, while Diamonds channeled their entire passion into their fight, they were also trained to maintain a certain detachment, so that the fight did not get them emotionally invested enough to throw them off balance. Mai had clearly overstepped this boundary. He was fighting to win, and, by the looks of it, he had put his entire self on the line to achieve it. Egey Bashi realized that he was witnessing the full power this remarkable man was capable of – a sight one couldn't forget in a hurry.

He could see that Kara realized it too. It was also obvious that, unlike Mai, her heart wasn't truly in this fight. As she parried and dodged his blows, Egey Bashi saw her face set into the grim determination of a person who knew her doom was not far away.

All the audience were on their feet, gaping. The only people who seemingly kept their presence of mind were the Jades lining the top of the arena. They had their arrows resting on their bows, ready to fire. But it seemed that, no matter what orders they had received, even with their skill it would be difficult for them to find a gap.

Shaking off his stupor, Egey Bashi rushed forward through the rows to the Guildmaster's seat.

"Master Abib! What the hell happened?"

The weapons keeper tore his eyes away from the arena and turned to Egey Bashi. His face held regret.

"Aghat Mai asked me to take over his post – with the strict understanding that this is a temporary measure until the challenge can be resolved."

"And you agreed?"

Abib's gaze wavered.

"Believe me, Magister," he said. "I did everything I could to dissuade him. Aghat Mai can be very headstrong. He made it very clear to me that if I were to refuse this post he would find another man to take his place. Under the circumstances, I felt I may be doing the least damage by obliging him."

"You have to stop the fight before it's too late. We

both know that, whoever wins, there is no possibility of a good outcome to this senseless battle."

"I wish I could, Magister, believe me, but this is the Ultimate Challenge. It's fought to the death."

Egey Bashi's thoughts raced. He forced himself to avoid looking, but the speed of the clashing sounds at the center of the arena told him the fight was at its height.

"Can you call a recess?"

"If warranted."

"Let me talk to him, alone... And while I do, I hope to hell you can find something in your Code that would enable you to end this stalemate. I know how good you are at these things."

Abib hesitated, then signaled. A horn rang clearly over the silent rows.

The fighters completed their movement on the same beat and sprang away from each other, coming to a standstill in one single step. Not for the first time Egey Bashi admired how the Diamonds could go so instantly from fast action to stillness.

Mai strode to them across the arena, his eyes flaring with anger. His hair was caked with sweat, his shirt ripped down the left arm to expose an oozing gash inside.

"This'd better be important, Master Abib," he barked.

"Magister Egey Bashi needs to have a word with you, Aghat Mai."

Mai spun toward Egey Bashi with a murderous look.

"You interrupted the fight to have a *word* with me?"

Egey Bashi took an inadvertent step back. He had never seen Mai so far over the edge. For once, he was glad of the presence of Abib and his men who could protect him if needed – or so he hoped. He had no idea what Mai was capable of in the heat of his battle rage.

"I've formally requested this recess from your Guildmaster, Aghat Mai," he said slowly and distinctly, hoping that, despite evidence to the contrary, Mai could actually comprehend his words. "He deemed it warranted."

Mai's chest heaved as he steadied his breath. Egey Bashi was glad to see some reason return to his eyes.

"Magister Egey Bashi asked for a private conversation, Aghat Mai," Abib said. "You may conduct it in the guard room over there." He gestured toward a gateway that, as Egey Bashi knew, led to a small courtyard adjoining the arena.

Despite his best effort, he had to break into a trot to keep up with Mai's purposeful stride. He secretly wondered if he should have asked for a Majat backup during the upcoming conversation, in case things got out of hand. The last thing he wanted was to find himself on the receiving end of one of Mai's famous blows.

The guard room was bare, furnished with plain wooden tables and benches. Mai strode between them with the restless power of a caged tiger, pacing back and forth several times and finally coming to a halt a few steps away from the Magister. Egey Bashi had the feeling that Mai was trying to keep a distance to avoid the temptation of harming him. Used to nothing but calm composure from this man, Egey Bashi couldn't stop staring.

"Forgive me for interrupting your fight, Aghat Mai," he said. "I hoped to have a conversation that might help us all find a way to stop this challenge without any losses on either side. Seeing your resolve, I was not certain it would be possible if I waited any longer."

Mai's lips twitched. "You think I haven't considered all other possible options, Magister?"

"You certainly gave us quite a surprise by appearing in the arena."

Mai glared. "Bloody shame. Forgive me for being so damned inconsiderate of your feelings, Magister."

Egey Bashi lifted his hands soothingly. "Please, Aghat Mai. I know that, deep inside, you are a reasonable man."

"Is there a point you wish to make, Magister?"

"You *need* Prince Kythar's alliance."

"I repeat, Magister. Is there a bloody point?"

Egey Bashi edged back. A Majat backup was beginning to seem like a very good idea right now. The only consolation was that, had Mai indeed chosen to strike him down, he probably wouldn't feel a thing. Given the options, it was definitely one of the better ways to go.

He took a breath. "The Kaddim infiltrated your Guild, Aghat Mai. For Shal Addim knows how long, a Kaddim Brother had been in charge of your shadow training, a post that made him nearly as important as the Guildmaster himself. And now, this man is out there, with knowledge of the exact fighting styles and weaknesses of every member of your Guild. Don't you think action from the Majat against the Kaddim is warranted in response?"

"It is," Mai said. "But not on Kyth's terms."

Egey Bashi narrowed his eyes. "It's not about you and Kyth. You should know best that your disagreement

with him, if you indeed even have any, cannot be
decided in battle. Would you let your foolish rivalry
drive you to destroy everything we're fighting for and
play right into the Kaddim's hands? Would you put
Kara's life on the line to prove a point to him?"

Mai's gaze wavered. "Her life is not on the line. I
have renounced my post to ensure it."

"A bloody stupid thing to do, if you'll forgive the
expression. You would do best to resume your post as
soon as you can. You were *born* for it, damn it."

Mai's chest heaved again, and Egey Bashi saw some
of his normal self finally surface through the rage. It
was a welcome sight, even though he was still a long
way from feeling relieved.

"I see no way out of it now," Mai said. "The Majat
Guild must win this challenge. I will do everything I
can to ensure it."

"Even kill Kara?"

"I told you, Magister. I am not going to kill her. If
you hadn't interrupted the fight—"

"You think you can do your 'viper's kiss' on her again?"

"I've done it before. Except now, I have more Jades
to back me up."

Egey Bashi shook his head. "How do you think it
feels to her to receive a foot of steel in her chest? What
if your blow goes bloody wrong this time? Even with
your impressive backup, you cannot be sure, against an
opponent of her skill."

"What do you suggest, Magister?"

"Perhaps, if you can communicate to Kara your
intentions to fight the Kaddim, she can be persuaded
to surrender?"

Mai's face darkened.

"She is doing it for Kyth. If she surrenders, he will think she betrayed him. I don't want to put her into that position."

"Perhaps you can at least give her a choice?"

Mai's gaze stirred with such deep pain that Egey Bashi shivered.

"I *am* giving her a choice. I have been, all this time. Not that it's any of your bloody business, Magister."

Egey Bashi sighed. "I am impressed by your willingness to sacrifice everything to let her pursue her feelings for another man, but aren't you taking it a bit too far?"

"Like I said, Magister, none of your bloody business."

Egey Bashi raised his hands soothingly again. He couldn't help feeling as though he were trying to tame a wild and dangerous beast – not talking to someone he had always held among the most controlled and level-headed men he knew.

"Perhaps you can talk to Kyth again, Aghat Mai? Last time your conversation got a bit out of hand, but I feel if you two could perhaps meet in private, you can find a way that would enable him to surrender his challenge without cutting off all his other options?"

Mai shrugged. "Kyth doesn't trust me. I can't say I blame him."

"Bloody shame. Well, I have news for you. To defeat the Kaddim, you *must* reach an agreement, one that ideally involves no more weaponry. You need his ability to resist their power in order to protect your men."

"We have a considerable gap to overcome in these negotiations, Magister. He wants the crown to lead the attack. I can't possibly allow it."

Egey Bashi sighed. "By the old saying you yourself quoted to me once, after you resume your post, you will be in command of a force that equals everything they had in the Old Empire. Perhaps this high post warrants, shall I say, a change of command style on your side?"

"What do you mean, Magister?"

"You are too used to deciding all matters in combat. I also know your tendency to make it single combat, driven by your reluctance to risk other people's lives. However, as the leader of your people, you are bound to realize that, at this level of command, things are normally decided by words rather than by one's skill with the blade."

Mai hesitated. For the first time in the conversation Egey Bashi could finally allow himself a small sigh of relief.

"You are the first person who ever said such a thing to me, Magister."

The Keeper smiled. "Like I told you once, Aghat Mai. I pride myself on being the first in many things."

"What do you want me to do?"

"If you're ready to promise me you won't murder anyone on the spot, I suggest we talk to Master Abib and possibly consider bringing Prince Kythar into the room. As far as I understand, during a recess, the Majat Guild can do this without losing face."

Mai's face darkened again.

"I can talk to Master Abib. Briefly. I can't promise the rest."

Egey Bashi let out a breath. "That would be a start, Aghat Mai."

As they descended into the small courtyard, a group of the Majat was waiting for them, with Abib in the lead. He was holding the Guildmaster's cloak over his arm. Mai stopped, looking at him warily.

Abib stepped forward.

"Forgive me, Aghat Mai," he said. "I must apologize to you for acting in error, due to my poor knowledge of the Code."

Mai raised his eyebrows. Egey Bashi knew Mai didn't believe this any more than the Keeper himself. There was likely nobody in this Guild with better knowledge of the Code than Master Abib.

"When I accepted your resignation as the Majat Guildmaster and agreed to temporarily bear this title," Abib continued, seemingly unperturbed, "I overlooked one very important detail that was later brought to my attention by other members of the Guild." He glanced around at the assembled people, which included, as Egey Bashi now noticed, Gahang Iver, the new leader of the Jades, and Aghat Lance, fully armed and battle-ready.

"It appears, Aghat Mai," Abib said, "that, by the Code, the Guildmaster cannot lay down his command to fight in a challenge. Therefore, technically, your resignation never took effect." He stepped forward and flung the Guildmaster's cloak over Mai's shoulders. "You cannot appear in the arena again. You must name your champion, and while this is of course your decision, I feel obliged to let you know that Aghat Lance is available and has volunteered, with your permission, to represent the Guild in this challenge."

Mai took a step back. His eyes flared in anger that quickly turned to alarm as he ran them over the silent faces of the assembly. Egey Bashi could guess his thoughts. Kara was already exhausted by the mêlée. Lance, famous for his brutal force tactics, would likely have no trouble getting through.

"I took the liberty of informing Prince Kythar of this turn of events," Abib said. "And he is willing to meet with you, in the hope that the impending outcome of the fight by his champion against the entire Guild can be averted. In fact, he expressed his willingness to discuss things on your terms when we explained to him that there is no possibility of you continuing the fight in the tournament yourself."

Mai measured him with a long glance.

"Very well," he said. "I will meet Prince Kythar in my study."

He turned and strode away.

Egey Bashi let out a breath. Once again, Abib had demonstrated not only his ingenuity, but also his ability to make quick decisions by devious manipulations of the Code. Egey Bashi had trouble believing that he and Mai could have overlooked such an obvious thing before, or ignored any other provision that could have made Mai's resignation anything but legitimate. However, when Abib had just challenged that decision with such authority, in the presence of senior Majat, he had left no room for Mai to question him on the spot. This confirmed what the Keeper had been suspecting all along. The Majat Code was not absolute, and the decision of the Guild's seniors could twist it like a weathervane, when needed.

And now, their purpose had been achieved in just a few words. Mai had resumed his post and agreed to meet with Kyth.

Egey Bashi had the utmost confidence that, knowing the stakes, Mai would find a solution and come up with a good plan – especially if Abib could ensure that he and the Prince talked things out in private, and for as long as necessary. He didn't envy Kyth going into this conversation. But at least he hoped that Mai was over his violent stage and the Prince was in no immediate physical danger.

"Well done, Master Abib," he said. "However, I feel it may be prudent to ensure that for the duration of this talk the Guildmaster's study doesn't harbor any weapons."

29

DIPLOMACY

Kyth ascended the stairs of the Guildmaster's tower at a fast walk. At the end of the fifth flight he had to stop to catch his breath before entering the open door of the study.

Witnessing the fight at the tournament had greatly demoralized him. When he had issued his challenge, he never believed Mai would actually go through with it. When Mai had appeared in the arena, Kyth felt as if the ground had been kicked from under his feet. Watching Mai's resolve and seeing him throw everything into the fight had finally made Kyth fully realize that this ruthless man was not going to back down, whatever the stakes. Mai obviously took the whole thing very personally, and despite the fact that Lady Celana, Alder, and Ellah had done their best to assure Kyth that Mai was not going to kill Kara even if he won, Kyth couldn't feel convinced. He wanted nothing more than to find a way out of this situation.

He knew that bigger things were at stake that rested on this alliance, and if he had been told he must risk his

own life in these negotiations with a reasonable chance
to win, he would have gladly agreed. But throwing
Kara's life into the bargain was too much, and he was
deeply regretting it. Mai had called his bluff, and even
though admitting it put Kyth at a big disadvantage,
he strongly felt he had had enough of these games.
If Mai agreed to meet one-on-one, Kyth was more
than willing to listen to everything he had to say and
do his best to bridge the gap between them. Back in
the audience hall, he had probably said a few things
he shouldn't have. He had gone too far, and he was
willing to admit it. He was determined to do his best to
remedy the situation, even if it included apologising to
Mai, privately or in public.

Mai was sitting at his desk when Kyth entered,
watching him calmly. He had changed his shirt and
combed his hair, but the wear of battle still showed in
the tense set of his shoulders, in the way he kept to
the edge of the chair, as if ready to spring into action.
The knuckles of his right hand, resting on the surface
of the desk, were grazed, with the skin peeled off from
what must have been a near-hit by a very sharp blade.
Kyth shivered.

"I..." he hesitated, not sure where to begin.

Mai's short glance stopped him.

"Sit down."

His eyes pointed to a chair on the opposite side of
his desk. Kyth felt his feet inadvertently carry him
forward toward the seat. He lowered onto the edge of
it, keeping Mai's gaze.

"Your challenge," Mai said, "was by far the most
stupid thing I've ever seen happen in our audience hall.

Closely followed by everything else you said. What the hell were you thinking?"

Kyth's mouth fell open. He had expected, if not an apology, perhaps an acknowledgement that things had gone wrong on both sides and that Mai was willing to take steps to close the gap. He had not expected *this*.

He considered taking offense, but quickly decided against it. They were alone in a closed room, with no one to overhear them. This man was not supposed to do him any physical harm – or so he hoped. What better chance would he ever have to speak his mind?

"You left me no other choice," he said. "You refused my alliance. What else was I supposed to do?"

Mai let out a sigh. "I assume you haven't had much schooling in diplomacy, have you?"

Kyth frowned. "Oh, and you have?"

Mai measured him with a quick glance. "More than you, obviously."

"What makes you say that?"

"I didn't refuse. I named my terms. You named yours. That is where a negotiation usually starts."

"But you said..." Kyth was taken aback. He was indeed beginning to feel like an idiot. Had he put Kara's life on the line for nothing? "You told me right off that an alliance was impossible."

"I *told* you," Mai said, "that a strike against the Kaddim must be done under the Majat's command. And yes, a formal alliance *is* impossible. But that's not what you really need, is it?

"Isn't it?"

Mai sighed. "You didn't come here to put on a bloody show of being the first in history to violate the

Majat's political neutrality. I know King Evan couldn't possibly have put you up to that. He knows better, even if you don't. All you need is for us to help you kick the Kaddim's ass."

Kyth hesitated. He was fairly certain all these expressions weren't a part of any diplomatic talk he had ever learned. Obviously the schooling in diplomacy Mai was boasting about was conducted differently here at the Majat Fortress compared to the King's court.

"And your offer to take command was supposed to make me *agree*?" he asked.

"Yes, if you were smart enough to listen."

Kyth stared at him with disbelief.

"You want me to join the Majat attack force and serve under *your* command?"

Mai regarded him with irony. "You don't expect me to serve under yours, do you? You're not that bloody stupid."

Kyth bristled. "Why not?"

"Do I look suicidal?"

Kyth swallowed. This conversation was not going the way he expected. Yet, he knew that pushing this kind of argument any further wouldn't help things.

"It's not about who is in command," he said.

Mai let out an exasperated sigh. "Yes, it is. That is exactly what it's all about."

Kyth stared. "Do you put your pride so far above everyone else?"

Mai shook his head. "It's not about pride. It's all about instant decisions that need to be made on the spot by someone who knows exactly what they're doing. The timing lost in an improper chain of command could lose you a battle before you realize it. Do you have any idea how to lead a force in a strike against the Holy Monastery?"

Kyth shook his head. "No. But... if you remember, I didn't start by asking you to surrender your forces to us. You will still lead your men. All I asked for was an alliance. In diplomacy," he added nastily, before he could stop himself, "it means that the sides are equal in standing and join forces against the same enemy. Aren't you supposed to know these things, with all your schooling that is apparently so much better than mine?"

Mai's face held an annoying smile. "Equal standing?"

"Yes."

Mai laughed. "Same question. Do I look suicidal?"

Kyth's eyes narrowed. He knew he shouldn't be giving in to anger, but it was so hard to control it. Mai was laughing in his face, taking full advantage of the fact that Kyth had no choice but to listen. Mai had always been an arrogant asshole, and now that he was in command this became a lot more of a problem. Kyth found himself wishing that the old Guildmaster was still in charge – if, of course, that could have been achieved without Kara perishing in the tournament.

"You think you are so much better than everyone else," he snapped. "Don't you?"

Mai relaxed his shoulders, settling deeper into his chair. Kyth saw him wince as a casual movement must have disturbed his injured arm. *At least she showed you she can kick your butt in a fight.* The last thought inadvertently brought back memories of the challenge, the way Kara nearly lost her footing, the way Mai's blade, more than once, swept far too close to her face. She must be harboring some injuries too, waiting alone in the arena until they could resolve this argument. Kyth swallowed, trying to distance himself from the annoying smile that played on Mai's lips.

"I *am* better," Mai said, "when it comes to fighting. I am infinitely better than all the forces you have at your disposal – if you can even call them forces. Everyone sees it, why can't you?"

Kyth subsided into his chair. Grudgingly, he had to admit that Mai was right. He *was* better, especially if he didn't have to be so annoying at the same time.

"I will not agree to join an attack hindered by such a handicap," Mai went on. "If you want the Majat's help, *I* will decide who can join us and in what role. You have to do it my way. Unconditionally."

"Aren't you driving a bit too hard of a bargain? In diplomacy, people make compromises. Or so I heard."

Mai crossed his arms on his chest. "I *am* making a compromise, by agreeing to take outsiders into our force. If you'd troubled yourself to read up on history, you would have realized how big a compromise it is. If you want this to happen, you'll have to cover the rest of the gap. Take it or leave it."

Kyth drew a breath. "And you are willing to gamble Kara's life on it?"

Mai's eyes flared, as if Kyth had struck him.

"I am not gambling," Mai said. "You are. And if you show any intention of doing this again, I will go after you myself. She is far too precious to be used in this way, and I cannot even begin to wonder how it is possible that you don't see it. I attribute it to your stupidity."

Kyth went very still. He wasn't going to get angry again. He wasn't. Mai said it because he cared. Not because he was trying to get him off balance.

"You could have refused the challenge," he said.

"And surrendered my men to your command?"

"It's not like I was going to kill them or something."

"If we agreed to the attack on your terms, it would be as good as killing them. Do you think I had a choice?"

Kyth wanted to respond, but a retort froze on his lips at the sight of the deep pain that stirred in Mai's eyes.

Kyth's skin prickled. He suddenly saw everything that had happened from the other side. Mai had renounced his post as the Guildmaster to be able to appear in the tournament, despite the fact that even Kyth could see how well this post suited him. He had put everything he had into the fight and then, when things got out of hand and Mai was faced with the necessity of putting another Diamond in his place who would likely finish the job, he opened negotiations again, despite the animosity Kyth knew he must have felt for him.

His feelings for Kara. For the first time since he had learned about them, Kyth thought about what this truly meant. Whatever had happened between Mai and Kara in the heat of a fight, he knew that right now they weren't together. He recognized the signs by the way she had resumed her aura of detachment as soon as their joint challenge was over and Mai went on to accept his high post. She was the same way with Kyth now, detached and closed off, not letting any emotions through. It hurt to see her this way, except that Kyth had also known happiness with her, when she had shown him how much she cared. What they'd had before made him hope she could return to him again some day, when she was ready.

Like it or not, these feelings for Kara were something they both shared. On some level, this knowledge made it possible for Kyth to bypass his animosity and truly relate to Mai.

I don't own her, Mai had said to him once. *Neither do you.* Kyth suddenly realized that, until now, he had, in a way, believed that he had a claim to her, based on their prior relationship. But in truth, he didn't own her at all. She could come and go as she pleased. When she was with him, it felt like a dream. When she was not, it hurt like hell.

Was this how Mai felt *all the time*?

Kyth raised his head and met Mai's gaze.

"You were trying to do your 'viper's kiss' on her, weren't you?" he said quietly. "You renounced your post to fight in the tournament yourself, so that you could save her life."

Mai's eyes briefly flicked to his grazed knuckles, and to his left arm, hidden by the sleeve. Then he raised his gaze to Kyth again, his tranquil expression more impenetrable than the walls of the Majat Fortress.

"None of your damned business," he said. "And yes, I was. Somebody had to save her from the trap your stupidity drove her into."

"And what would you do," Kyth asked slowly, "if I accepted your terms and surrendered to your command?"

Mai leaned back into his chair.

"As the first order of business, I would put you through a proper set of training to defend against multiple opponents."

Kyth raised his eyebrows. He hadn't thought of that at all. Yet, it made a lot of sense. Perhaps placing Mai in charge had something to it?

"And then?" he prompted.

"Once I believed you were ready, I would lead a small Majat force for a surgical strike against the Monastery."

"Small?"

Mai sighed. "How many can you protect from their power?"

Kyth receded into his chair. Now that emotions were out of the way, he was beginning to realize how good Mai was at these things. He had always thought Mai's proficiency with weapons was his main skill. But in his new post, this man continued to surprise him.

"How many do you think I would be able to protect after your training?" he asked.

Mai shrugged. "With the limited time we have... maybe a dozen? It all depends on how good you are."

A dozen. It sounded good, if nearly as unattainable as the moon.

"And then?"

"I heard," Mai said, "that the Holy Monastery is a fortress of its own. It's very difficult to take it with a head-on attack. I believe infiltrating it would be our best option. A dozen of our top gems would likely be up to the job."

Kyth sighed. He was beginning to feel more and more like a fool. If only they could have had this kind of conversation yesterday in the audience hall–

"I've made a mess of things, haven't I?" he said.

Mai nodded. "You certainly have. Although I admit I didn't make it easy on you. We were both... blinded, I guess."

Here it was. An apology. Or at least the closest he could ever hope to get from Mai.

"Is there a way out?" Kyth asked.

"There are several ways out," Mai said. "But the one I suggest would be for you to return to the arena with me and formally surrender your challenge."

Kyth nodded. If this was the only thing he had to do, it seemed easy.

He suddenly became aware of Mai's intent gaze.

"I've said it once," Mai said, "and now I will say it again, in the hope that repeating it will help get it through to you. Don't ever put Kara's life on the line again. She's very devoted to your cause. Don't take advantage of it."

His eyes glinted with steel. Looking at him, Kyth suddenly realized another thing. Mai cared for Kara so much that he was willing to surrender her to Kyth. He was willing to do anything to make her happy, including laying down his life. Only after witnessing their Ultimate Challenge against the Guild did Kyth understand what it truly meant, and what Mai had been giving up when he had made his original decision to spare Kara's life.

"I'm glad your challenge against the Guild ended the way it did," he said quietly.

Mai's lips twitched into a brief smile as he nodded his acknowledgement.

"When I issued the challenge to you," Kyth went on, "I did not think for a minute you were going to go through with it. After you and Kara fought side by side, I didn't think you would find it possible to turn against her. If I had known what was at stake–"

Mai's brief glance stopped him.

"When you inherit your throne, you will soon realize that your responsibility to your people goes far beyond any personal feelings and bonds. Just hope that no one ever forces you into the kind of choice you threw at me yesterday afternoon."

Kyth continued to stare. For the first time he saw through his hatred, through Mai's glamor, down to the core. He was a man of exceptional integrity, who always did what he believed was right. And, he truly loved Kara. Whatever her feelings for him, whichever one of them she chose in the end, Kyth now understood exactly how Mai felt.

Neither of them had the right to stake Kara's life on this negotiation. In the end, all that mattered was the success of the war, and Kyth suddenly realized that there was no better man than Mai to lead the attack.

If it had to be done on his terms, so be it.

"I would like to formally withdraw my challenge, Guildmaster," he said. "I hope, despite everything that has happened between us, you will permit me to do it and to surrender to all your conditions. And... I am grateful for your help."

Mai nodded, his brief glance of acknowledgement making it seem as if there was nothing to it.

"Let's go back to the arena," Mai said, "and finish the show."

30

SYNCHRONY

Kara spent the next few days avoiding Mai. She trained with Raishan, who was thankfully back on his feet, even if still not quite at full strength. She also watched Kyth, and talked to him after his practices to offer advice and comfort. His trainers were driving him very hard, and sometimes she secretly wondered if Mai had made it just a touch more difficult on him than necessary. Still, they needed Kyth to be fit and ready for action, and in the end there was no better way.

It was nice to see how Kyth was progressing, wielding a light training saber against six men at a time after only a few days of practice. He had come so far from the sensitive, idealistic boy she had first met, in awe of her fighting skill and head over heels in love with her. She knew he could tell that her heart was no longer with him. She could see how much it hurt him, and she felt guilty about it. But it was useless to give in to guilt and regret. Past deeds could not be revoked. Past feelings were even harder to manage.

She often strode through the grounds with Magister Egey Bashi, whose down-to-earth wisdom felt so soothing to her turmoiled feelings. She caught a glimpse of Mai from time to time, and tried to stop herself from looking his way.

Kara couldn't help feeling amazed at how Mai's presence on the training grounds energized everyone, sending ripples of activity down to its every distant corner even when he was not in sight. No Majat Guildmaster in history had ever trained side by side with his men, and the mere knowledge of it inspired devotion far greater than anything she'd ever seen.

"You can't avoid him forever," Egey Bashi said to her once, on the way to the practice floor.

Kara's shoulders stiffened. One of the reasons she valued the Keeper's company so much was because he never forced her into difficult conversations, even though she was certain he had a deep understanding of everything involved. And now, his casual comment reached straight to the bottom of her heart, hurting more than she cared to admit.

"You are going to march together against a common enemy, Aghat," Egey Bashi said. "The least you can do is to make amends."

Kara hesitated. He was right, of course. Sooner or later, she would have to face Mai. Whether or not he could forgive her for what she had done, he could use her skill in the upcoming fight, and she couldn't allow her own insecurities to stand in the way.

"You are right, Magister," she said. "I'll go talk to him."

Egey Bashi nodded. "I think I saw him at the indoor range this morning. He spends most of his time there – or so I heard."

Indoor range. The secluded area on the east side of the grounds was used for training in synchrony, teaching fighters to anticipate each other when fighting in groups. If Mai spent most of his time there, no wonder she caught such rare glimpses of him.

When Kara approached the gated doorway at the edge of the training field, her ears caught the sound of the drum inside. Synchrony was taught to a beat, which initially helped the fighters to pick the same rhythm. Later, during a fight, they could actually call these beats by name. Hearing the call, everyone could change in mid-stride, without any possibility of the opponent keeping up.

Of course, in real life no fighters in action moved in unison. But this training in large groups, learning to sense each others' actions, created a unity between them that enabled them to act as a single being in battle. Emeralds, from which the Guildmaster's personal guards were drawn, specialized in this technique, making them indispensable because of the way they acted together as a force that could ensure the safety of the most important man in the Guild.

The drumbeat grew louder when Kara stepped inside. Her eyes widened, drawn to the large wooden platform in the center of the practice floor.

Mai was training with his Emerald Guards. A drummer at the edge of the floor was beating varying rhythms, and the Emeralds, with Mai at their head, were moving in such unison that Kara felt her skin prickle.

It looked exactly like a dance. The beat was fast, with complex syncopations, one of the more advanced ones.

Mai moved to it so perfectly that for a moment she forgot he wasn't doing it for show. His natural grace, added on to his skill, made even the Emeralds at his sides look clumsy by comparison, despite the fact that Kara knew them to be the best.

Mai was wearing a blindfold and held a practice sword in each hand. Every once in a while his blade swept against one in his neighbor's hand, and each time Kara saw him frown, clearly displeased with himself. He was obviously driving himself very hard to bring himself up to speed with his new guards, and she didn't blame him. The Emerald Guards were a powerful resource, and in order to fully utilize them he had to learn to fight by their side.

The beat ceased, thirteen men coming to a stop in perfect unison. Mai tore off his blindfold and strode to the edge of the practice floor, grabbing a towel to wipe the sweat off his face. His hand paused with the towel halfway down his neck as he saw Kara. He lowered it, watching her.

She stepped forward, feeling like a little girl caught peeking.

"Aghat Mai," she began and stopped, unable to go on. What could she possibly say to him? That she was sorry she fought against him in Kyth's challenge? That she felt bad about throwing away everything they had? Talking about it was no use. He probably knew she didn't feel good about what she had done. He also knew that she had done it anyway. His look, back in the audience hall, when she had told him she was accepting the challenge, would haunt her forever. It was as if she had stabbed him in the back.

"We could use you in the formation, Aghat," Mai said.

Kara's eyes widened. That was the last thing she had expected him to say.

"Me?"

He frowned. "I assume you will be coming with us to Aknabar. Won't you?"

"Yes. But..."

"I want you to train with me so you can fight by my side."

She swallowed. She would like nothing better than to fight by his side. This was probably the best she could hope for, after everything that had happened. But she hadn't expected he would offer it to her. She had thought he would never trust her again.

Mai pointed to a stand with the practice swords. Wordlessly, she laid down her hagdala and took two, choosing the lighter ones and quickly testing them for balance. He watched her with an unreadable expression.

When she was ready, he threw down his towel and signaled, assembling the Emeralds back into formation.

"Start with the Om," he told the drummer.

Kara nodded. Om was one of the easier beats, mid-pace, without syncopations. She could do Om, couldn't she?

Mai didn't put his blindfold back on. Moving next to him, she quickly realized the exercise was not as easy as she thought. The fighters' movements were nearly unpredictable, except for the rhythm, and she had to both anticipate and follow, while keeping up the speed. After a short sequence she felt that her head was about to explode. She was glad when she heard the drum cease, and lowered her swords, trying to steady her breath. She couldn't imagine how Mai, after only a few days of practice, could do such a perfect dance at a fast syncopation, while wearing a blindfold.

"You are too tense," Mai told her. "You have to relax when you're doing this. You're trying to watch us. All you need to do is listen, and let go."

Listen. Yes, that's probably how it worked when she and Mai fought side by side and could anticipate each other's moves without even seeing each other. But to do it with twelve men whose fighting style she barely knew?

"Just keep at it," Mai said. "You'll improve faster than you think."

She shook her head. "I don't understand how you could possibly do it blindfolded."

Mai smiled. "There's another trick. You are trying to follow all of us. While eventually you'd need to do that, you should get used to us first. Start by following one."

"One?"

"There's always a leader in each formation. But even if the leader is not in your line of sight at each particular move, you can follow someone else, assuming he's moving in unison with the others."

She hesitated. "I'll try."

"I know you can do it, Aghat. Trust me."

She looked up at him. He seemed calm and friendly, discussing the exercise in a way he always did at the practice range. But she could also see the guarded look behind the friendliness that made her heart quiver every time she caught his gaze. He would probably never look at her the same way again. She forced the thought away.

She could see the Emeralds around them dissipate, catching a break and wiping off sweat. Mai was driving everyone very hard to prepare for the attack.

"Who are you bringing?" she asked, trying to support a normal conversation.

"Lance and Raishan," Mai said. "Sixteen Rubies, thirty Sapphires, and fifty Jades. As well as twelve men of my Emerald Guard."

She nodded. These seemed like perfect numbers – a force strong enough to withstand a small army, yet light on the march and flexible enough to enable Mai to improvise on the spot. She realized that he was also being careful by leaving enough top gems behind to make sure that if things got rough in action it did not deal a crippling blow to the Guild.

Watching his face, the way he glanced at her sideways as if expecting a blow, she suddenly realized she wouldn't be able to go on this way. Knowing how she had hurt him hindered her practice too. It would be a handicap in a fight, unless she could resolve everything between them and know exactly where they stood.

"Aghat Mai," she said. "I... I know it probably won't make any difference, but I wanted to tell you how deeply sorry I am for everything I caused you by agreeing to champion Kyth's challenge."

A shadow passed across his face. His gaze softened.

"I know you did what you believed was right, Aghat," he said. "I also know you were thrown into a tight spot with no time to consider your options."

"Yes, but–"

His glance stopped her.

"In the end, it was perhaps all for the best. Your resolve to throw your life into the negotiations was a timely reminder to both of us to keep our minds on the goal. Without it, we would have been unlikely to be training for the march right now, would we?"

She let out a breath. "It seems that I find myself in your debt once again, for going to unimaginable ends to save my life."

"I told you," he said. "I have erased your debt with me. Permanently. I hope this way you will never feel obliged to do anything because you feel you owe me."

"You know I'll do anything for you anyway," she said, "debt or not."

His glance made her cheeks inadvertently light up with color. She was aware the words came out more personally than she had meant them to be in a casual conversation. But they were out there now and she couldn't possibly take them back, even if she wanted to.

He regarded her for a moment.

"I sincerely hope we never have to put this to the test. Not after you've nearly laid down your life to fight by my side."

She tried to smile. "I hope you don't feel indebted to me for that, do you?"

"How could I possibly not?"

Her smile widened. "I am not a Majat Guildmaster," she said. "But I can grant you some small favors of my own. I hereby permanently erase your debt to me, if indeed you ever had any. From now on, I hope you never feel obliged to act because you feel you owe me. That makes us even, doesn't it?"

He smiled. "I suppose it does. And, as you probably

know, debt or not, I'd do anything for you too. No matter what, you will always have my friendship. Just now, I saw you doubt that. You should not."

Friendship. She felt relieved. He had forgiven her for what she had done. She couldn't ask for anything more. And yet, she couldn't help also feeling a pang of disappointment, which she tried very hard to force down. Whatever he had said to her in delirium, on the eve of what they had both believed to be their execution, could not possibly hold up in real life. He was the Majat Guildmaster now, the most powerful man in the kingdoms, whose life was devoted entirely to the affairs of his Guild. She would have to be crazy to think of him in any other way.

She smiled, glancing past him onto the practice floor. That syncopated beat he had been moving to when she walked in, so graceful and fast that he took her breath away. How could he possibly do it so well?

"That was the Hai beat, right?" she said.

"Yes. You want to try it with me?"

She nodded, following him to the floor.

This time he didn't assemble the Emeralds as he took a place by her side, signaling to the drummer. The beat started slowly and built up rhythm after a few steps. She concentrated, trying to match his moves, aware of the way she was lagging behind.

Don't watch. Listen.

She tried to recall the way they did it in battle, when they fought side by side. Back then, they acted in perfect unity, aware of each other's moves without really seeing them, and that, above all, had made them so invincible. Moving next to him was so easy, his style and rhythm

326 THE GUILD OF ASSASSINS

such a good match for hers. Once she remembered, it took little effort to let herself go, sliding her mind into that half-entranced state when everything he did by her side evoked an instant response, so that she didn't even have to look at him to make sure of their unison.

She felt almost disappointed when the beat stopped, too soon for her to savor the sensation to the full. She lowered her swords, only now realizing how tired her muscles felt after the strenuous exercise.

Mai was watching her, as well as, she realized, all the Emeralds and the trainers nearby, everyone's distracted expressions so different from the usual concentration on the practice range. She slowly let out a breath.

"That was... easy," she said.

Mai smiled. "Now, shall we try the blindfold?"

31
DEFENSE

Kyth lowered his saber, feeling every muscle in his body moan in response. According to his trainers, he was still a few days away from the completion of his training set, and he did not think he could possibly live through it. He knew he was improving, able to face ten men in a light practice fight – something he would have sworn to be impossible only a week ago. Mai had said that by the end of the practice he should be able to handle twelve. But right now, Kyth was wondering if he would die first, making it all unnecessary in the first place.

Had it been a mistake to surrender command to Mai after all? Was this man trying to kill him? He dismissed the thought. Mai surely had far easier ways to kill him without engaging twelve trainers day and night in the process. Most likely, he just wanted to thoroughly humiliate Kyth and show him once and for all who was a better man.

He limped to the side of the practice floor and collapsed on the bench next to Alder and Ellah.

"That was... good," Ellah said with encouragement in her voice that Kyth found somewhat forced. He knew his last practice session had been miserable, when he stumbled and almost fell onto a trainer's sword. He didn't bother to respond, leaning his elbows over his bent knees, hanging his head in between.

"You're just tired," Alder said. "It will be easier after you give it a rest."

Kyth glanced at him sideways. The only way he imagined being able to rest was if he actually died. Barring that, sitting here on the bench for a short break was all the rest he was going to have. Even when they let him go for the night his dreams were dominated by the same nightmare he lived through every day, making it impossible to find any peace.

What could have possibly possessed him to agree to all Mai's terms so unconditionally?

Alder was a good one to talk. He was also receiving training, since his presence, and especially his spiders, were incorporated into Mai's battle plan. But his training was of a more normal kind, with fitness sessions in the morning and sword practice in the afternoon, to ensure he could protect himself to a reasonable extent and not become a handicap to the rest of the attack force. Kyth's practice sessions were different, with ruthless men attacking him from all sides with various weapons until his tiredness made them all a blur and he succumbed to someone's blow. He had many cuts and bruises to show, but it wasn't like anyone would even offer any sympathy. Kara had been the only one showing concern, but after the whole mess with the challenge, he didn't think she had enough influence with Mai to change the way he was doing things. Worse, seeing Kyth and Kara sitting side by side at the practice range was likely to drive Mai even more insane, not that Kyth cared. Despite his aches and pains, the thought that Kara's sympathy for Kyth would make Mai displeased brought satisfaction, and the knowledge that she cared enough to spend time with him was one of the few things that kept him going day by day.

He sensed stillness around him and lifted his head. His heart sank.

Mai was striding toward him, dashing and fit, wearing a spotless black outfit. The Emerald Guards in his wake stepped in such perfect synchrony that they all seemed like Mai's shadow, amplified many times over.

Great. Just what I need right now.

Mai stopped right in front of Kyth, looking down on him with the calm interest of a child examining a bug he had just squashed. His eyes paused on Kyth's sweaty forehead, his disheveled hair, the shirt, ripped at the shoulder, the sore knuckles of his sword hand. It seemed that he savored each of these details to the full before looking Kyth in the face.

Kyth felt past caring anyway. He just sat there, looking into the distance as if Mai wasn't there at all. He didn't want to know what Mai wanted with him this time. In his spent state, there wasn't anything he could possibly do anyway.

"How's the practice going?" Mai asked.

It took Kyth a moment to realize Mai wasn't even talking to him. His eyes were directed to a trainer who had silently appeared by Kyth's side.

"We're up to ten, Aghat Mai," the trainer said. "Prince Kythar is making good progress."

Mai nodded. "Let's try."

Despite his tiredness, Kyth couldn't help but lift his head. "*Try?*"

Mai kept a calm face. "Yes. We're marching in five days. I want to know where we stand."

Kyth opened and closed his mouth wordlessly. Did Mai expect him to stand up and *fight*?

As a matter of fact, did he really expect him to *stand up*?

"Perhaps," Alder said carefully, "this can wait until tomorrow morning? It's getting late. I hope you can see for yourself that Kyth's very tired right now. He has just gone through five hours straight."

Mai regarded Kyth for another long moment.

"He can do it."

"The hell I can." Kyth lowered his head again. He couldn't help it if Mai was insane, delusional, and cruel. There was no way he was going to get up right now and pick up a saber.

He was surprised when Mai dropped in a quick move, kneeling in front of him and peering into his face.

"You're too tense," he said. "This is not the way to do it at all. It's a wonder you progressed this far in your state. Look at you." His eyes slid over Kyth again, taking in every detail as if enjoying his rival's misery.

Yes, I am your rival. And she likes me better than you. The thought made Kyth feel a bit better, even though he knew he would never say anything like that out loud.

Mai shook his head. "If you can't let go, your training is never going to work."

Despite his tiredness, Kyth found himself bristling.

"I can already defend against ten."

Mai's eyes flickered with calm pity. "And in the process, you become so exhausted that you can't even sit up straight. Are you also planning to do this in battle? Do you expect that after you spend yourself somebody will just sweep in and carry you away?"

Kyth hesitated. "The battle won't last for five hours."

"Battles can last for days."

"But–"

Against reason, Kyth found himself pulling upright, so that his face was level with Mai's.

"I can't risk you giving up in the middle of a fight because you are too damned tired," Mai said. "If you spend your entire strength defending against ten, how can I possibly rely on you holding up for as long as it takes?"

"As long as it takes?" Kyth's heart sank. Up until now, he felt he was making good progress. And now, Mai had just destroyed all that with a few short words. Did this man ever know where to stop?

"Stand up."

Mai's short command was so unexpected that before Kyth could even think about it he found himself on his feet.

Dear Shal Addim, he'd had no idea he could even stand upright.

"Good," Mai said. "Now, pick up your saber."

Kyth picked it up, eyeing him warily.

Mai leaned forward and grabbed his shoulders, peering into his eyes.

"Relax your arms," he said.

Kyth did. It seemed impossible to disobey.

"If you wield your weapon with a stiff hand, you will never be able to use it at full power."

"What?" Kyth was having trouble thinking through his tiredness.

"That's why we made you practice with a rope before," Mai said. "Think of your blade as if it's a rope, soft and relaxed until you drive its end into a target. Don't think of it as hitting. Try to *reach* instead."

His intensity drove through Kyth's stupor, a hypnotising combination that, against reason snapped him back to alertness. Still, how could he possibly think of a saber as if it were a rope?

Mai let out a sigh. "You once told me that when you use your gift, it works better if you completely relax your mind, right?"

"Yes," Kyth said slowly. He'd had no idea Mai could actually remember such things.

"Do it now. Relax your mind."

Kyth did. In his tired state it seemed easier than he thought it would.

"Now, go to the practice floor."

Kyth followed, feeling like a sleepwalker.

Mai signaled with his hand and twelve men responded, flooding the floor in Kyth's wake.

Kyth snapped out of his trance. "Your *Emerald Guards*?"

Mai nodded, as if there were nothing to it. "They're good at fighting in unison. The best technique for an attack force composed of top gems. This is your chance to see what an actual fight with the Kaddim might be like."

Kyth swallowed, looking around the twelve motionless men standing around him, each far more fit and impressive than he ever hoped to be. Was Mai *insane*?

Mai shook his head. "Don't be afraid. They won't harm you."

"I'm not afraid," Kyth blurted. He was, but there was no way in hell he was going to show it. He supposed Mai's assurance should make him feel better, but he just couldn't feel it in his heart.

"They won't be attacking you," Mai said. "Just moving next to you. All you need to do is touch each of their blades with yours. Once. Can you do it?"

No. There was no way in hell Kyth was going to lift his saber again today. Yet, the challenge in Mai's eyes drove him. Against reason, he felt he really wanted to show this man that he was not a failure, that he was up to the task.

He nodded, gripping his blade.

"Good."

Perhaps it was because Kyth was so tired he couldn't possibly think anymore. Or, maybe because he could sense Mai watching him, even though with the way he had to keep twelve men in sight at the same time he couldn't possibly be sure. The Emeralds' feet were tapping a rhythm, and Kyth's tired mind drove him to slide into this rhythm, moving between the men, touching their blades.

Just when he felt it was beginning to get easy, he heard Mai shout a short command and the rhythm changed, acquiring a complex pattern with syncopations. Kyth cursed silently as he almost lost his balance when the men next to him changed their entire movement style in an instant. He tried to adjust, but the new beat was just too fast. He panted, trying to match, forcing his mind into a calmer state, calling in the wind. There was no way he was going to give in to this, whatever games Mai was playing with him.

The beat changed again, sliding into a slower step Kyth found easier to follow. He was just beginning to think he was getting a grip on it, when Mai's voice sounded again. This time, the beat broke down. *Bloody hell*. Every man on the field was now moving to his own rhythm, no longer in synchrony, and that made their fast moves impossible to trace, let alone follow. How the hell could *anyone* stand up to that?

Kyth darted for a gap and threw down his saber, striding off the floor. A part of him was wondering how he could possibly have the energy to be so angry, after he had already been feeling so tired just a little while ago. But he was too angry to care as he strode up to Mai.

"Are you bloody out of your mind?"

Mai had the same look again, the quiet curiosity of a child who had just squashed a bug. There was also just a touch of challenge in his gaze as he surveyed Kyth's sweaty face, his disheveled clothes, the way he swayed on his feet as exhaustion finally started taking its toll.

"Not bad." Mai met Kyth's gaze, then looked past him to the group of trainers standing at the side of the field. Kyth noticed how they all visibly relaxed after this quick praise.

"Give him a good rest," Mai said. "Starting tomorrow, increase the number of trainers by one each session, until we march in five days."

He briefly nodded to Kyth and strode off, followed by his Emerald Guards.

Kyth stared after him, too tired even to feel upset. It was his own bloody fault, for agreeing to surrender all command to this man, who clearly knew no boundaries in showing his superiority to everyone in sight.

He found himself wishing that some day, when this was all over, he could have it out with Mai once and for all, but he knew it was probably never going to happen. In any case, nothing seemed as important right now as sleep. At the very least, he could thank Mai for affording him the opportunity to take the rest of the day off, or whatever was left of it, anyway.

Kyth waved a weary goodbye to his friends and stumbled upstairs to his sleeping quarters.

32
AKNABAR

The Majat force consisted of over a hundred men, a small group by the standards of an army, but far more powerful than anything an average kingdom could muster at short notice. Egey Bashi couldn't help feeling awed at being in the midst of it, one of the very few in history to be allowed to march into battle along with the Majat. Whatever mistakes Kyth had made, whatever mess they had found themselves in during his childish negotiations with his rival for the same woman's affections, this event would be recorded in the chronicles as his achievement, aiding his recognition as a worthy future king.

Mai kept a moderate pace, setting camp early each day, so that he and his men could practice for at least two hours before sunset. That, in itself, was an impressive sight. Everyone except the Jades had to move in formation to a synchronous beat, and Mai often had Kyth join the exercise, teaching him to anticipate everyone's moves and positions. Egey Bashi had great respect for the Prince, but he kept wondering if Kyth was going to hold up till the end. He seemed on edge, and the only lasting benefit of this arrangement was in the way all the women flocked around him afterward, each offering sympathy in her own way. Ellah's quiet conversation visibly calmed him; Lady Celana's open praise, the way she blushed every time she encountered the Prince, boosted his self esteem. But in the end, it was Kara's casual talk, the way she made him lighten up just by briefly sitting at his side with a few encouraging words, that kept the Prince going. Egey Bashi couldn't help noticing also how Mai's eyes rested on the pair in between his numerous duties, and each of these times he prayed that both men could continue to keep their minds on the goal and not to repeat the same mistakes over again. He had higher hopes for Mai, the older and more responsible one, but the quiet triumph in Kyth's eyes every time the two men met didn't help at all.

Even at this pace, Egey Bashi was surprised to find that their march to Aknabar took no more than two weeks. This was probably due to the enormous influence the Majat Guild had over the lands, so that fresh supplies waited for them at every stop, men from nearby settlements joining them at each campsite to help set up and cook, and then quietly departing back to their homes. Egey Bashi believed that the Majat term for this was "camp relay", as opposed to a simple relay when men traveled day and night changing mounts every fifty miles. Watching this made him understand how true was the old saying about the Majat's power rivaling that of the Old Empire. In all the lands the Empire used to cover, from the northern

snow caps to the distant tips of the Shayil Yaran
southern deserts, the Majat had but to say a word to
get anything they wanted.

What amazed the Keeper most was how Mai was
able to take on all this power in such a short time. It did
seem as if this man was born for his post and in some
mysterious ways, unbeknownst to himself, had been
preparing for it all his life – as if this knowledge of the
Majat ways, up to the ultimate heights of their power,
coursed in his blood. Watching him in command, Egey
Bashi couldn't possibly understand how any of them
hadn't seen this before. The glamor that surrounded
this remarkable man made the very idea that he could
have been killed on his Guild's orders, or commanded
anything but full surrender at the tournament, seem
preposterous.

At the sight of the domed roofs of the Holy City, the
Majat regrouped, dismounting and flipping their cloaks
inside out, speckling them with dust. In just a few short
moments the impressive military force reduced to a
group of weather-beaten travelers, breaking into small
groups that entered the city from different gates. Egey
Bashi couldn't help but stare. He felt more and more
glad that anyone he cared for was highly unlikely to find
themselves on the receiving end of the Majat wrath.

The hundred-men attack force swept through the
city like flakes of dust, seamlessly blending into the
Aknabar street crowds. Even for the scouts on watch,
it would have been difficult to detect that their city had
just been invaded by a nearly invincible military power,
about to strike at the very heart of the former capital of
the Old Empire: the Holy Monastery of Aknabar.

The party reconvened in an inn, one that Egey Bashi knew well, even if he didn't cherish the memory. Its weathered sign with a faded image of a wild flower identified it as Wild Aemrock. Run by the Majat Guild, located within an easy walk from the Monastery walls, this inn had been the base for every recent operation Egey Bashi had been involved in on his visits to Aknabar. Before, he had stayed here because of the fact that he was accompanied by a Majat bodyguard. And now, as part of the retinue of the Majat Guildmaster, he was amazed, even if somewhat nauseated, at the welcome they received.

The innkeeper, Mistress Yba – a shapeless middle-aged woman with the voice and physique of a troll – knelt as Mai walked in, touching the floor with her forehead. The reverence in her face resembled that of a newly converted priest who had just encountered the Lord of Heaven himself. Her large knobby hands shook as she clambered back to her feet, ushering the inn's servants through last-minute preparations. Mai's quick greeting sent her into a fit of gasps as she scurried around, finally retreating out of sight.

Mai had clearly sent word ahead to warn the innkeeper to prepare for their arrival. The inn had been completely transformed, from a dull and not-too-welcoming accommodation for the pilgrims to the Holy City, into a camp for an armed force. The large common room had been set with enough tables and benches to accommodate the entire party, and all available space upstairs and downstairs outfitted with cots and beds, arranged with efficiency that made perfect use of the limited space. The back yard connected to a sizeable paddock, large enough to house all the horses. Grudgingly, Egey Bashi had to admit that, despite her obvious shortcomings, Mistress Yba knew her job. Of course, if she hadn't, there was no way the inn would have remained on the Majat payroll for long.

Mai laid out maps and charts on the central table, bending over them in calm concentration, while his men outside were putting together the final touches to transform the inn's back yard into a training ground. After a while the other three Diamonds joined him at the table. Egey Bashi regarded Lance, the least familiar of the group, a tall, cocky man with a dark tan, near-white short hair and pale arrogant eyes. Every Diamond was unique, but many of them shared this air of superiority, an ability to relate equally only to their fellows in rank. To Egey Bashi's knowledge, Raishan and Kara were so far the only happy exceptions to the rule, even if Mai carried this quality with a flair that made it all but forgivable in his case.

As the Keeper approached the table, Lance's eyes slid over him with a mildly annoyed look, which quickly receded as he saw the other three Diamonds acknowledge the Keeper with welcoming nods, moving over to make room for him. The map they studied was the layout of the Monastery grounds, far more detailed than Egey Bashi believed was possible to procure for anyone outside the Church. He looked at it with interest, connecting some of the geography to the place he had previously known mostly through action on the inside.

"What's the plan, Aghat Mai?" he asked.

"We'll march tonight, Magister. I'm taking a small force, Diamonds and Rubies to the numbers Kyth can protect."

Egey Bashi nodded. It seemed like a sensible plan. Diamonds and Rubies could do very serious damage to the enemy, if not land a victorious strike with only minimal effort. And if worst came to worst, this force would at least enable them to access the enemy's numbers and key positions without creating too much havoc.

"Do you think they already know of our arrival, Aghat Mai?" he asked.

Mai shrugged. "If they don't, we can consider ourselves lucky. But I'm not counting on that. I expect them to be prepared, especially if our late Shadow Master is with them."

Egey Bashi nodded. Knowing that the man leading the defense had intimate knowledge of all the weaknesses and fighting styles of their attack force significantly worsened the odds. He hoped no surprises were forthcoming.

"If my knowledge of the Monastery grounds can help, Aghat Mai, I would be glad to join you."

Mai shook his head. "No, Magister. We're already extending to protect Kyth. I don't want to stretch it even more."

Grudgingly, Egey Bashi nodded again. He had never thought of himself as a person who needed protection. But things obviously looked very differently to a Diamond Majat.

"Aghat Raishan's knowledge of the Monastery is fairly extensive," he said. "We've been there together more than once. And, I believe Aghat Kara knows her way around as well. I'm sure you'll do fine without me, Aghat Mai."

Kaddim Tolos strode through the Monastery grounds with a frown on his face. He only vaguely registered the hooded figures scurrying out of sight at his approach: priests, the unimportant and soon-to-be-extinct kind of the Monastery's inhabitants.

Things at the Majat Guild had not gone as planned. The challengers were supposed to use the advantage the subtly applied Kaddim power had given them to go for the kill, eliminating the Diamonds and the Rubies, and in the process exhausting themselves enough to let the Jades shoot them down. Kaddim Xados, posing as the Shadow Master for the last ten years through an ingenious mind control scheme devised and executed by Nimos, had laid out a perfect plan. It would have worked too, if not for that man, Mai, who not only was annoyingly resistant to the Kaddim's power, but also managed to stop his hand in time to avoid killing two of his fellows in rank. Tolos still couldn't get over his disbelief at seeing it in action. The man had been handed a perfect opportunity to even the odds, and he simply blew it. He showed a weakness that made it very clear to Tolos that in the long run he couldn't possibly be a strong leader, even if his boyish charm had proven to be a temporary advantage in putting him in command. Men, women, they were all the same, eager to indulge in a fantasy over a pretty face. Tolos, with his centuries of experience, knew better.

And now, the Majat were coming in force, with Mai in charge, and the only thing to hope for was that the man would indeed prove a poor leader and blow his chances at the Monastery as well.

Tolos felt fortunate that the scouts they had placed on all the roads out of the Majat Guild had been able to send news quickly, relaying every detail about the Majat force marching against the Monastery. Even more so, Kaddim Xados was in charge of their defense, and there was no one better suited to deal with the situation. Who could possibly know more about the Majat and their weaknesses than their recent Shadow Master?

He pushed open the doors of the Great Shal Addim Temple and stepped in. The giant space inside looked airy and light. Vaulted stone archways protruded from the ceiling, trapping sunbeams from the tall windows in the space around the altar in the center, shaped like a four-pointed Holy Star. The light shrouded the star in intricate golden lace, making it gleam, as if floating in the air. It was the holiest place in the kingdom of Tallan Dar, the apex of the Old Empire, soon to become the womb for its rebirth in full glory under the new rule. Very few could possibly stand in the way of the Kaddim Brotherhood, poised to reunite the lands and instigate the Reincarnate as the Emperor for ages to come. Once they dealt with their small Majat problem, nothing else could possibly stop them.

Tolos strode toward the four silent men waiting for him around the altar – a place of worship, where heaven and hell clashed in constant turmoil. Only opposites could ensure the wholeness of things, and ever since the fall of the Old Empire these opposites had been thrown too far out of balance for things to work as they should.

He felt pride as he surveyed the assembled Brotherhood: five of their Cursed Dozen – a force that could surely rival the Majat and the rest of the kingdom, if recent events hadn't allowed several Diamonds with their devilish fighting skill to escape the Kaddim's mind control. Still, even with this handicap, the force in front of him was not to be ignored. In addition to Nimos, with his superb Power to Control, and Farros, whose Power to Command extended to a unique ability to kill a man with a highly targeted blast, there was also Haghos, a man with intimate knowledge of Monastery affairs and a unique skill to preserve bodies for resurrection. On top of that, Xados, who had, until recently, occupied the notoriously fabled post of the Majat Shadow Master, possessed unique knowledge of weapons and military tactics. Added to Tolos's own proficiency in leading large cohorts of Kadan Warriors, this force alone should be perfectly enough to deal with everything they had in the Kingdom of Tallan Dar, once the Majat were out of the way. In addition, their Bengaw Outpost harbored more Brothers, as well as the Reincarnate himself.

"Adi Kados," he greeted as he approached, acknowledging the assembly with a brief bow.

As similar greetings echoed among the group, he kept his eyes on Xados.

"The reports I've heard have been vague, Kaddim," he said. "When we left the Majat Guild in a hurry, I assumed everything was set. What went wrong?"

Xados shrugged, his light, graceful movement making him look almost like a Majat. He had always been a superb fighter, securing the choice of his candidacy for the Majat infiltration as soon as it became clear Nimos's mind magic was likely to work on their Guildmaster.

"We can only guess," Xados said. "Mai has always been a wild card. Given a choice, I would have staked more on people like Oden Lan."

Tolos frowned. "We staked everything we could on Oden Lan. But he wasn't going to bring down their Guild alone, without any help. He is, after all, one man."

Xados sighed. "For better or worse, Mai is now in charge and we will have to deal with him. I don't think this is necessarily bad."

"How so?"

"He's still very young. Much too young for his post. However good he looks in command, he lacks experience and, if pressed hard, he might make mistakes a more seasoned commander would never succumb to."

"Shouldn't we think in more immediate terms?" Tolos asked. "In the current situation, shouldn't we be targeting his fighting style?"

Xados shook his head. "Mai's fighting style is nearly flawless. In fact, the Guild has not even been able to train a shadow for him."

Tolos waved his hand in dismissal. "These Majat terms mean little to me, Kaddim."

"It means," Xados said, "that no one, even in their own Guild, possesses enough skill to defeat him one on one."

Tolos frowned. "In my experience with warrior training, Kaddim Xados, I have learned one important thing. No man can possibly be flawless."

A smile slid across Xados's lips. "You are right, Kaddim Tolos. While I couldn't easily name an advantage we could use in a direct confrontation with weapons, Mai has distinct character traits that could perhaps be explored as a weakness."

"*Character* traits?"

"On many occasions, he has demonstrated remarkable resolve to spare lives."

Tolos sighed. Were they desperate enough to call this an advantage?

Xados eyed him calmly. His disconcertingly purple Olivian eyes made him look strange among the group. Yet, Tolos reflected, distinct-looking eyes seemed to be a trait among the Kaddim brothers. Purple did not look nearly as exotic as Farros's speckled gray, or Nimos's iris-less dark disks that made him look like an owl. The only man here with more normal eyes was Haghos, but the devilish gleam in his gaze did nothing to comfort a casual observer.

"The signature style of Mai's command," Xados went on, "has always been in the way he tends to lead his people in action, rather than staying behind and giving orders like many other commanders prefer to do. This style makes him very inspiring to his men, but it also harbors certain weaknesses. Perhaps we can play on them."

"How?"

Xados smiled. "Our compound affords very few opportunities to fight in an open field. Whatever force he brings, he will likely begin his attack by personally leading a small group in the hope of dealing a quick surgical strike. You can count on this group to be nearly invincible, nothing we can possibly handle in direct confrontation. However, if we lure them into a spot where we can gather enough fighters to distract them all for a short time, we could target him personally through a highly coordinated ranged attack. If all of us here can use our combined power to do it, he won't even see it coming."

Tolos thought about it. A combined mind power of five Kaddim Brothers could make them all act like one, if they fully lended themselves to it. It could also amplify their skills through this shared mind link. He knew about Majat's synchronous training, but no training could possibly compare to five people truly driven by one single mind, on top of the exceptional weapons skill of the Cursed Dozen, rivaled only by the Majat.

He hesitated. "He's bringing several ranks, including Rubies, Sapphires, and Jades. Each of these ranks can outperform our current warriors in training."

Xados shook his head. "In fact, I would put our best warriors against their Sapphires with no hesitation. And their Jades, of course, are good only in ranged weapons and cannot stand up to a direct attack. However, the Ruby and Diamond ranks are continuing to present a challenge to our men."

"So," Tolos said, "even if we take him down, we'll still have three other Diamonds to deal with – not to mention whoever else he brings. He has sixteen Rubies in his force, assuming our scouts got it right."

"They did," Nimos assured, breaking his silence for the first time. Tolos slid a brief glance over him. He knew he could take this man's assurances at face value.

His mind control was superb, the way he could not only communicate with his men at great distances, but also seemed to be aware of their thoughts. Fortunate that they were able to revive him after the blow he received last time they had all faced their enemy.

"Only Mai and Kara are immune to our mind control," Nimos went on. "And, last time I saw them, I couldn't help noticing the bond they share. If we manage to hit him, she will be shattered."

"Enough to succumb to our power?"

"Enough to do something foolish, perhaps."

"Something foolish can hardly be relied on as a tactical advantage, Kaddim."

Nimos shrugged. "Even barring that, their attack would be blunted without him. The Majat would be greatly demoralized. We would not only have one less Diamond to deal with, but also leave them without a leader."

"Would one of the other Diamonds be able to take his place?"

Xados shook his head. "These are fine issues, Kaddim. Lance would probably step in, but their men would not follow him as eagerly as Mai. He's a bit too arrogant for his own good. Raishan is the opposite, if anything, too mild to be an effective leader. And Kara, of course, has no formal authority to command. Not unless she resumes her rank in the Guild. I'd say, short-term we would have nothing to worry about."

Tolos nodded. It made sense. Except, any attack plans seemed shaky after the way things had gone at the Majat Guild. Above all, the incident made Tolos realize how little they still knew about powers at play in that enigmatic fortress, despite the fact that their man had been so close to their command for the past ten years, freely sharing all inside information.

"Let's plan a ranged attack," he said.

33
FLYING DAGGERS

Kyth felt clumsy and slow as he moved in the midst of the Majat force, twelve men whose stealth and power surpassed anything he had ever seen in action outside the training grounds. The four Diamonds kept to the front, and the Rubies formed a tail in their wake, positioning themselves on Kyth's sides so that they could protect him from any attackers and benefit from his power at the same time. Kyth felt nervous as he walked. Up until now, all his training had been theory, never tested in a real fight. And now, he was going to determine once and for all if this training worked. He hoped he was not going to let anyone down.

Under the cover of dusk, they approached the wall at an inconspicuous spot indicated by Raishan. Mai and Kara went first, their grappler hooks flying up the wall in perfect unison, sleek shapes pulling up and over like two darting shadows. After a long moment he heard a click of hooks retracted from the other side, indicating that the way was clear.

Kyth's heart raced as he wielded his own hook. He had tried it before, with variable success. He hoped he could do it now, without appearing ridiculous to the men at his sides who clearly didn't consider the task of scaling the smoothly hewn wall, over two men's height, difficult enough to train for. He put all his force into the throw, trying to mimic the brisk moves of the Majat by his side. His hook caught, but when he pulled, it released and fell down, landing very close to Kyth's foot. He cursed under his breath, bending over to pick it up, aware of the shapes disappearing from his side one by one. Were they just going to leave him behind?

Raishan reached over and took the hook from Kyth's hand. "Here, let me."

Kyth nodded gratefully, feeling like an idiot for not being able to do it himself.

"We'll go together." Raishan flung the two hooks up with a smooth movement, catching them on the wall perfectly, with enough distance in between for both of them to scale the wall side by side. Kyth only nodded as he took the thin rope from the Diamond's hands, focusing on climbing up without making even more of a fool of himself. *Of course* Raishan could catch two hooks on the wall with one throw, so confidently that he didn't even need to check if they held before putting his weight to it. No surprise at all that Mai thought so little of the task that he went ahead without bothering to consider whether Kyth, their main protection against the Kaddim, would have any trouble following behind.

The courtyard connecting to the other side of the wall was large and rectangular, and completely empty. Being here brought back bad memories. Last time,

Kyth, Alder, and Ellah had been marched in here at the orders of the old Reverend Haghos, later found to be a Kaddim Brother, who had planned to use Kyth in his elaborate plot to take over the throne. And now, through several turns of events no one could have possibly foreseen, Kyth was coming back to pay the debt. Hopefully, the Majat force they had brought made it possible to ensure that this particular debt was paid in full, once and for all. Last time, Haghos had forced a sword through Kyth's chest. Even though the wound had not been as bad as it seemed, Kyth did not cherish the memory.

He caught himself when he realized Mai was looking at him.

"Are you ready?" he asked.

Kyth nodded.

"Just make sure," Mai said, "your mind doesn't wander the way it did just now. And, try to keep up."

Without waiting for a response, he turned and slid off into the gateway ahead, moving so smoothly that his black-clad shape melted into the shadows.

From the moment they entered the Monastery, Kara couldn't escape the feeling something was wrong. The way each empty courtyard in their path yielded to another, without so much as a man in sight. The way the entire Monastery grounds stood eerily quiet, as if devoid of life. They were being led, into whatever trap the Kaddim had prepared, and, for better or worse, they had no choice but to follow.

Mai led the formation known as a spearhead, a powerful strike force that was very hard to resist for warriors of any skill when led by the top gems. Kara and Raishan stepped side by side in his wake, with Lance bringing up the rear. The Rubies fanned out at their back, completing the spearhead and keeping Kyth closely in their midst. Such formation could quickly and efficiently take out a focused enemy force, but had its flaws when faced with vast numbers. Of course, the amount of men Kyth could protect with his power made their choice of attack plan very limited anyway.

Kara knew they should likely have nothing to worry about. Four Diamonds were a formidable force, and the Rubies nearly doubled the odds. Together, they were infallible even with such small numbers. But she also knew the enemies were led by their own Shadow Master, who knew each of their weaknesses in great detail. The thought was just too disconcerting to dwell on.

Edging deeper into the Monastery grounds, they finally heard a movement up ahead. Mai signaled with his hand before slipping into the next space, a large rectangular courtyard adjoining the side wall of the Great Shal Addim Temple.

The courtyard was flooded with men. A wall of hooded shapes rushed forward at once to meet them on all sides, as soon as the Majat formation cleared the courtyard gateway. They were wielding orbens – spiked balls hanging on long chains, the ancient weapons Kaddim warriors favored – such an annoyance in a sword fight. Kara whirled her blades, dodging, thrusting, and slashing, protecting her side of the spearhead. She was facing two dozen, a manageable number if no distractions were sent her way.

She sensed the waves of Kaddim mind control power sweeping the space and spotted five hooded figures standing at the edges of the courtyard behind the wall of action, their spread palms facing downward, as if drawing strength from the ground under their feet. She was immune to them, and she briefly swept a glance around their group to make sure everyone was fighting and Kyth was able to handle his part.

She focused on her opponents, noticing in passing how Mai was left facing much larger numbers than the rest of them, as if the majority of the enemy attack was aimed entirely at bringing him down. Her skin prickled as she realized this might indeed be the case. The Shadow Master was bound to know enough about Mai to realize how inspiring he was to his men, how dangerous he was in his new post. If they lost Mai, the Majat attack would lose its edge. She put extra energy into dealing with her share of enemies, hoping that after she was done she would still have enough time to join the fight by his side.

A Ruby beside her fell to the ground, hit by an orben. She side-stepped, slicing at his attacker, sending him to the ground as well. This was not good. The orben wielders moved better than she remembered from when she had faced them last time. They also moved more synchronously, as if someone had been giving them Majat synchrony training. Damn it. They had to find the Shadow Master in this Monastery and take care of him once and for all. Was he one of the five figures standing by the wall?

Her skin prickled as she glanced at the figures again, realizing that they were no longer maintaining their poses with downcast palms. They stood at a half-crouch, in attack positions, each holding a dagger. Their eyes were focused on the fight going on at the end of the courtyard.

Mai.

Kara's heart raced. Only now did she realize how Mai's numerous attackers did not fan around him like they did with the other Majat, instead engaging him only from the front, leaving his back open…

She gasped, her momentary loss of concentration letting an orben sweep too close to her face. She parried it, only half focused on the action around her.

The five hooded figures raised their hands in terrifying unison, blades flying from their palms, spiraling in the air with a synchrony far beyond any skill; a synchrony, she realized, driven by Kaddim magic which enabled five different men to act as if controlled by a single mind. A form of shadow throw – not with two daggers thrown in unison by one person, but with five, thrown by different people with no less unison and so much more impossibility to deflect them.

There was no way in hell Mai was going to be able to do anything about them. Fully engaged in his fight, he couldn't even spare enough attention to see them coming.

It was a split second decision that didn't really take any thought. As she dove into the path of the daggers, she tried to tell herself that she would have done the same for any commander, that it was the right thing to do. Her swords whirled faster than conscious thought, deflecting three of the flying blades. She spun around, kicking another one aside with her foot. She did far better than she expected, but there was nothing she could possibly do about the last one. It hit, burying deep into her chest.

In her battle state, she didn't even feel any pain. The only strange thing was the way her body suddenly stopped obeying her the way she was used to, her legs folding from underneath her, making her stumble and lose her footing.

Her darkening vision noticed the Kaddim fighters give in under Mai's attack, retreating into the next courtyard. She realized with sudden clarity that they weren't fighting to defeat him. They were only distracting him, so that the daggers could reach their target.

Time slowed as she saw Mai spin around and rush to her side.

"*Kara!*"

His voice had a strange echo, as if coming from a distance. She wanted to look into his eyes, but couldn't quite force her head to turn. Pain descended, its waves washing through her, making it so difficult to think.

How stupid of me to get hit.

"Bloody hell!" For a moment, Mai's contorted face made him almost unrecognisable. He sheathed his weapon in an instant and scooped her into his arms.

"Retreat!" he barked.

34

PAIN

Kara floated on waves of pain, only vaguely aware of the action going on around her. Orders, barked at high speed. Men regrouping, retreating back to the wall. Two Rubies were on the ground, but the numbers lost by the enemy were far greater as the Kaddim defenders ran off toward the gate on the other side. It couldn't be any other way in a fight against a Majat spearhead.

How could she be so stupid as to get herself hit? She should have tried harder with the last dagger. She knew she couldn't have done anything about it, but thinking that way meant giving up, and if she did, she would be as good as dead.

Probably nothing to be done about that, either.

If she had deflected all the daggers they could have pressed the attack, even though it wasn't clear if that would have been the best choice. But without her skill, they couldn't possibly risk it. Besides, she was now dead weight, and she knew Mai was never going to leave her behind.

Mai held her to his chest as he ran, and she was aware that he was doing his best not to cause any more pain, but with the dagger sticking out of the wound it was all but impossible. She did her best to distance herself from it, wishing she wasn't such a burden as he flung his grappling hook on top of the wall, carrying them both over to the other side with a power that made her feel as if they were flying.

She couldn't remember the entire way back, the run along the cobbles that made her, once or twice, pass out from the pain and return to her senses only to be met with new waves of it. It eased as they reached the inn and Mai finally slowed to a walk, shifting her into a more comfortable position in his arms as he strode though the door into the inn's common room.

She struggled to remain conscious, half aware of the gasps around her, of Mistress Yba scurrying around, of the servants following her hushed commands to sweep everything off a table and cover it with a white sheet. It became too bright as lanterns were lit all around, and Kara saw Magister Egey Bashi rush forward, and Kyth standing in his wake with a frozen face. She ran her clouding eyes along the concerned wall of people, hoping that everyone who came with them was accounted for and that, besides the two Rubies they'd lost at the start of the attack, she was the only casualty.

Mai lowered her onto the table, his movements brisk and efficient as he cut her shirt away from the wound. Mistress Yba rushed forward with clean bandages and bowls of water.

Kara drifted off again as they cleaned the wound, the throbbing becoming worse as she returned to her senses. Part of her wished she hadn't, but that would mean giving up, and there was no way in hell she was going to let everyone down.

She saw Mai's face leaning over her.

"I'm going to remove the dagger," he said.

She tried to focus on his face, but couldn't. It was just too hard.

He placed a hand on her shoulder, holding her lightly but with a grasp that told her he could apply any force if needed. She felt other hands over her arms and head and did her best to stay relaxed. She had known worse pain.

It hurt almost as an afterthought as he pulled the dagger in one quick smooth move. Warmth trickled in its wake, the metallic smell of blood floating to her nostrils with nauseating clarity. She felt more throbbing as someone pressed cloth to the wound, holding tight to ease the blood flow. For a brief moment she drifted off again and came to, the face leaning over her taking shape to become Magister Egey Bashi.

"We're going to have to use the elixir on your wound."

It took her a moment to comprehend his words.

"Do you understand me?" the Keeper said urgently.

What was he asking? Oh, yes. It was going to hurt like hell. She remembered the searing pain when Mai treated her scratch on the eve of the tournament at the Majat Guild. She also remembered how Mai had shivered in her arms when she had used it on his arrow wound. With the wide dagger gash penetrating deep into her chest, this one was going to be so much worse.

"Do it, Magister," she said. *I need to be back on my feet so that I can fight.*

For a moment she wasn't sure if she actually said any of it out loud as she saw his hesitation. Then he nodded, his face receding to the background and she heard more running and more cursing around the table.

"We're going to have to hold her down." She wasn't sure who said this, probably Egey Bashi.

"Maybe knocking her out would be best?" *Raishan.* He sounded calm, probably the most composed of the group.

"We can't risk it, Aghat. Her wound is too grave."

"If she bloody dies from the pain it wouldn't be much better, would it?" *Mai.* She could hear the strain in his voice.

"Please. We have very little time, Aghat Mai."

That bad, eh? It didn't feel that way, if only the pain would stop. *If I die, I won't feel it anymore.* She drifted off with the thought and came back again, reflecting how the pain didn't feel any better at all.

The conversation floated in again.

"...obviously you've never had it used on you, have you, Magister?"

The Keeper's voice, as it boomed in response, had a different edge from Mai's, but her strangely heightened senses told her the Keeper was no less agitated.

"I know you won't want to stand by and watch her die, Aghat Mai. Not when we could have done something about it."

"Don't you Keepers have any bloody substance that doesn't hurt as much?"

A pause. "None that is nearly as potent, Aghat Mai."

More words rustled in response, but she was having trouble catching them. She sensed movement as looming shapes formed beside the table on each side. She focused. Mai and Raishan, their faces set into calm masks. She tried to turn her head, seeking out Mai's gaze.

I'll be all right. She hoped her lips actually formed the words. She couldn't hear them coming out. She was having trouble hearing anything at all through the throbbing in her chest.

She could feel hands on her: Mai's and Raishan's, resting lightly on her arms and shoulders, toned to brace for the impact if needed; Egey Bashi's, cleaning the skin around the wound. Mistress Yba stepped up behind, reaching over to cover her forehead with a wet towel. Kara wished she hadn't, but they probably needed to hold her head down too. Besides, after they applied the elixir, she probably wouldn't care anymore. She flicked her eyes to Egey Bashi, who had cleaned the dagger and was now coating it with the sticky liquid from his bottle. Like hot coals, packed into the wound. Right.

The Keeper leaned over her and she felt Mai's and Raishan's hands flex as they closed their grip, steadier than iron shackles. She was grateful for it. She had to keep absolutely still for the cure to work, and she wasn't sure she could do it on her own.

"Ready?" Egey Bashi said.

She nodded. At least she hoped she did.

His hand holding the dagger hovered over her for one extra moment, his face reflecting deep concentration. *Taking aim.* The cure worked best if he could push it into the wound in one move, making sure that the substance instantly covered all the damaged flesh inside.

A dagger into the wound. Dear Shal Addim, even without the elixir it was going to hurt like hell.

She braced for it, but anything she imagined couldn't possibly compare to how it felt – like a white-hot iron inserted into her throbbing chest in a slow, drawn movement that never seemed to end. She wasn't going to scream, but the pain was past anything she could possibly control. She heard her own voice as if coming from afar – or perhaps she was only dreaming it?

She knew some lucky people passed out from the pain and woke up only when the worst was over. She wished it could happen to her, but it didn't. She could feel Egey Bashi's hands slowly working their way around the wound, pulling the edges together, every touch sending new waves of searing pain through her every nerve. Mistress Yba was pressing the towel over her head, and on top of everything else it was simply too much to take. Kara tossed her head in a powerful move, throwing the woman's hands off.

She could see the fear in Yba's eyes as she stumbled backward away from the table. Mai's and Raishan's fingers dug into her skin, their muscles tensing in an unwavering hold. She could feel their strain as they held on with what seemed like an effort far greater than it should be for two men of their strength. *Dear Shal Addim, am I going berserk?*

Egey Bashi was shouting, and she couldn't understand his words. She concentrated.

"Relax!" The Keeper's voice seemed distant, even though she could see he was right next to her. "Stop fighting us, damn it!"

She tried. Every nerve in her body was shooting, making it impossible not to respond. She forced her thoughts back to her training. The pain they were taught to endure without a flinch was nothing like this one, and she had never had to take it on top of a serious wound. Still, she felt angry with herself for slipping so far out of control. She should know better, damn it.

She called up calmness in her mind like she had during her training, willing her twitching muscles to still, embracing the pain that threatened to consume her. She gave in to it, waves of it washing through, clouding her mind, penetrating every inch of her body. *This must be what it feels like to be burned alive.* Except that when you burned you were allowed to scream and fight, instead of forcing your searing muscles into deadly stillness. When you burned, you eventually died, and then the pain stopped and never came back. It seemed that in her case she would receive no relief at all as the pain went on and on, robbing her of reason, and eventually of any conscious thought. She drifted into a semi-trance, wishing that she could at least pass out, so that she'd have a short break from the pain.

She didn't remember how it ended. Gradually, she realized Mai and Raishan were no longer holding her down, the absence of pressure on her shoulders and arms making her feel light, as if she were flying. She started hearing sounds again, the argument going on seemingly very close to her head. In her exhaustion, she winced at the force of the sound.

"...what else do you think I should have done?"

"Maybe go back to your White Citadel and work on a better damn cure?"

"We *are* working on it, Aghat Mai. And, you are welcome, by the way."

She turned her head, aware of how the argument had stopped when they saw her watching.

Mai's eyes fixed on her, as if they were alone in the room. He stepped forward to her side, slowly, like a sleepwalker. His drawn face made him look feverish, sick.

Her shoulders ached, and she followed his gaze to the finger-shaped bruises blackening on her upper arms. *Dear Shal Addim, did I get so far out of control?*

"Sorry." She hoped the word actually sounded outside her head.

Mai slowly relaxed, as if recovering after a very strenuous fight.

"You took a dagger for me," he said. "What the hell were you thinking?"

She felt a lump in her throat from the way he looked at her, his relief so overwhelming that it caught her too. She understood exactly how he felt. If he were here, lying in her place, she would feel the same. She probably would have said the same thing.

"I thought I could deflect them all," she said.

His eyes showed that her attempt at deception hadn't fooled him at all.

"When I asked you to fight by my side," he said, "this was not what I had in mind. In the future you should bloody well remember that. And... thank you for saving my life."

She nodded, feeling her face, despite everything, relax into a smile. It was so good to see him alive and well, and not struck down by the devilish five-dagger blow sent from different directions by five different

ANNA KASHINA 365

men. It was also good to know that she would likely recover and be able to fight by his side again, even though at the moment even the idea of changing position seemed completely out of the question.

"We should move her to a room upstairs," Egey Bashi said. "She needs rest."

Mai turned to him.

"Sorry, Magister. I shouldn't have said all those things."

The Keeper nodded. "I think we all felt a bit stressed, Aghat Mai. This was by far the most serious wound I've ever had to treat on the spot. Given a choice, I would never have risked it." He turned to Kara. "Well done, Aghat."

Her eyes flicked to her bruised shoulder again, noticing in passing how the wound had closed completely, leaving no trace.

"I could have done better," she said.

"I don't think so. Not with that wound. For certain, you could have done a lot worse."

Worse. She could have, if she had allowed her berserk state to take hold. They would have had to call Lance to hold her down too, as if two Diamonds weren't enough. Given the damage, she could have strained herself and died, before the cure ever had a chance to work. What the hell was she thinking, fighting like that? The fear in Mistress Yba's eyes as she stumbled away from the table haunted her. Through all her training, she had never imagined something as simple as pain could send her so far over the edge.

She relaxed her muscles, glad that for the moment she didn't have to do anything at all. They were going to move her to a room, but she hoped they would just leave her alone for a while, so that she could rest.

She realized she was dozing off only when she felt Mai's arms enfolding her, lifting her off the table, carrying her upstairs. She rested her head on his shoulder, quietly inhaling his scent, savoring it while no one could possibly catch her at it. His hold was so calming, and leaning against his chest she felt her stress slowly release, forcing the memory of pain to the back of her head. She wished he could stay with her, hold her like this until she drifted off to sleep. But there was, of course, no possibility of it, with all the other people that flooded the room behind him and then slowly departed one by one, throwing concerned glances over their shoulders. Kyth was among them, and she did her best to reassure him with a smile. She must have scared the hell out of him, both by taking the hit and by going berserk from the pain afterward.

Mai remained, kneeling by her bed.

"Are you going to be all right?" he asked quietly.

Yes, if you stay with me, she wanted to say, but she only nodded, responding to his concerned look with a quiet smile. His eyes told her so much, how afraid he had been to lose her, how relieved he was to see her alive. She would have done the same for anyone else in his place. But the fact that it was him had made the stakes so much higher.

"Sorry for causing so much havoc," she said.

His gaze wavered. "Just promise me you'll never do anything like this again."

She smiled. There was no way in hell she would ever give him such a foolish promise. If she had to do this over and over again, she wouldn't hesitate.

"I'll see you at practice," she said. "Tomorrow morning, I hope."

He nodded. For a moment it seemed to her that he was going to say something else, but he kept his silence as he rose to his feet in one quick move, stepping through the door and closing it behind him.

35
NUMBERS

Kyth paused in the doorway, looking through at the inn's back yard transformed into training grounds. Kara was practicing in the corner, doing a complex exercise routine on a horizontal bar that involved one-handed pull-ups, hand-stands, twists, and somersaults. It looked far too strenuous for someone who had nearly died less than a day ago, and so breathtaking that he found it impossible to look away. Kyth could see how she was testing each of her muscles, her reflexes, making sure she was fully fit for action.

Several servants from the inn stood at the sides, gaping. Kyth didn't blame them. Diamonds could move like no one else, and Kara's grace and beauty made the sight that much more spectacular.

He leaned against the door frame, allowing himself a moment to enjoy the view. The events last night had been far too much. Seeing Kara get hit felt as if the dagger had hit him too, even before the look on Mai's face told him how serious it was. Watching her writhe in agony as the cure worked its course left him nearly as exhausted as she looked afterward. And now, seeing her back on her feet made him realize anew how much he cared about her, how important it was for him to see her well, even if she didn't belong to him anymore. While she was around he had hope, and this hope was one of the very few things that kept him going.

He started as he suddenly became aware of another figure standing by the wall across the doorway, looking outside. Mai, his black-clad shape so still that he blended with the shadows. Kyth took a breath, forcing down his racing heart. Damn this stealth that enabled Diamonds to appear all but inanimate, like statues, nearly invisible at a distance of only a few feet. He glanced sideways, but Mai was not looking at him, his eyes focused on the action in the courtyard.

Kyth's gaze was inadvertently drawn to Mai's face, noting the paleness, the dark circles under his eyes, the strain in the set of his shoulders, usually so easy and relaxed. His heart quivered. Now that he fully understood how Mai felt about Kara, he could also relate to what Mai had lived through last night. Watching Kara get hit, taking a dagger that was intended for him. Calling off the attack and rushing back at full speed, knowing that even putting every bit of his strength into the run may not be enough to make it on time. Holding her down during her agony, fully aware that he was causing more pain, powerless to do anything at all to ease it. Watching her ordeal had been draining, her recovery such a big relief for Kyth. But for Mai, so closely involved in every step, these feelings must have been amplified many times over.

And now, as the commander of their force, Mai had to take Kara back into action, with full knowledge that something like this might happen again and he may not be able to save her next time. Kyth knew Mai enough to realize that, despite everything, Mai wouldn't hesitate to do it, and that if she died next time it would shatter him. Hell, the Kaddim were probably counting on that, having a man on the inside who knew every detail about the Majat Guild. Kyth had seen the effort they had put into taking Mai down. They'd probably put in the same effort, if not more, next time.

He thought about his own part in the attack last night. After all the training he had received, protecting twelve men in action had seemed easy. In fact, he realized that wielding his power had been far easier for him than wielding a blade. It all came down to details. His power wasn't exactly like a weapon, even if he envisioned it that way. It was more versatile, and he could handle it much better than he could ever master a sword. Treating his skill like an extension of his weapons practice was a mistake, a costly one that reduced his power to only a fraction of what he was capable of.

He turned and stepped up to Mai's side.

He expected a reaction, but the Diamond just kept still, watching the action outside. He was exhausted, Kyth realized. Despite everything, he probably hadn't had any sleep last night. And he couldn't possibly afford to show it.

Would Kyth ever be able to lead his people as well as this when his time came?

"Mai..." he began.

The Diamond turned to him, his look so weary that for a brief moment Kyth felt worried. Then Mai shifted, a barely perceptible ripple through his body making him look like a statue coming alive.

"What?" Mai said briskly.

Kyth did his best to ignore the impatient undertones.

"Use more men for your next attack. I can protect them."

Mai's eyes slid over Kyth with quick appraisal. "How many?"

"As many as you need."

Mai shook his head. "I've seen you fight. You can maybe handle fourteen, fifteen if you extend yourself, but–"

"It's not about my skill with the blade."

"Yes, it is."

Kyth clenched his teeth. A short time ago he had been feeling sorry for this man. And now, with just a few quick words, he had snapped back into his old irritation. He could already see this conversation going down the drain, like many of their previous ones.

"No, it's not, damn it," he snapped. "Why don't you just *listen* for a change?"

Mai raised his eyebrows.

"When I defended you in the Grasslands," Kyth went on, "when I protected Raishan in the Illitand Hall, I couldn't even pretend to follow all your moves. Hell, I couldn't even *see* some of them when you moved very fast. Yet I did it just fine. The same applies here. I realized it last night. My skill *resembles* sword fighting, but it's not the same. I don't have to be able to follow the moves of your fighters to defend them. When I protect your men, all I need to do is keep them in sight. I can extend it to any visible distance, covering any numbers."

Mai's eyes narrowed, and Kyth was relieved to see a shade of doubt in his gaze. "You can?"

"Yes."

"How can you be so sure?"

"I just am."

"Not good enough."

Kyth sighed. "Your spearhead attack is not working very well, you saw it yourself. The Kaddim are too sneaky to defeat with a small force, even one as good as yours. Besides, the man leading them knows all your weak spots. The only way you can overcome them is with numbers, and you know it."

Mai's smile lit up with sarcasm. "Since when are you so proficient in military tactics?"

Kyth took a breath, reminding himself of the strain Mai had been under and of the uselessness of breaking into an argument.

"Send everyone," he said. "Besides evening the chances on the battlefield, the Jades alone would make all the difference. If they're around, no one else would be able to go for a ranged attack."

"There is no way in hell you can protect *everyone*."

"Look," Kyth said. "You do want my help to kick the Kaddim's ass, don't you?"

Mai glanced at him with amusement. "I see you've been learning diplomacy."

"I have a good teacher." Kyth ran his hand through his hair with an exasperated gesture. "Can you just please stop being so bloody stubborn about everything? You have nothing to prove to me, and you know it."

Mai shook his head. "Perhaps. But you have a hell of a lot to prove to *me*. It's the lives of my men we're talking about if you bloody fail."

Kyth didn't want to get upset, but he couldn't help it. Why couldn't Mai just stop being such an asshole about everything? They were on the same damned side, weren't they?

"The lives of your men?" he demanded. "You should be the last one to talk about that. I did my part last night, and you... It's a bloody miracle you are still alive. If it wasn't for Kara, you'd be dead. You lost two Rubies. You think after what happened I'm the one to prove something to *you*?"

Mai's eyes flared, but as Kyth held his gaze, the Diamond slowly relaxed his shoulders. His face darkened. Kyth knew he had hit the most sensitive spot, but was past caring.

"Do you think," he pressed on, "now that you've shown weakness, the Kaddim are going to leave you alone? If they think they have a way to take you down, they'll come after you again and again, until they finish the job. You'll still face the same choice, but on their terms."

Mai's short glance stopped him. "Are you trying to make a point?"

"Yes, damn it. I want you to *trust* me. As a commander, you were hopefully taught that to win a difficult battle you have to take risks."

Mai looked at him sideways. "How the hell do you know a thing like that?"

Kyth sighed. "I've been reading... Does it really matter?"

"No." Mai appeared to hesitate. Then, a barely perceptible ripple went over his body again, shifting away any signs of strain, snapping him back to his graceful and arrogant self.

Damn, this man could shift between modes as if flipping a deck of cards. How could Kara possibly find him trustworthy? Kyth dismissed the last thought as he looked at Mai expectantly.

"All right," Mai said. "We'll try it your way. But you'd better be bloody sure."

Kyth looked at him wearily.

"Of course I'm bloody sure," he said. "I wouldn't have it any other way."

36
INSIGHT

Egey Bashi paused in the depth of the inn's common room, watching Kyth and Mai by the doorway engaged in a conversation that looked more like an argument. The Keeper shook his head. He needed to talk to Mai, but the topic he had in mind was too delicate to break in amidst this kind of disagreement, whatever it was this time. Perhaps it was better to wait until both of them ran out of steam. By their looks, it was likely to happen soon. Both men were clearly exhausted. Egey Bashi hoped that, whatever attack plans Mai was harboring for the next try, he would have enough sense to give everyone, especially himself, at least a day's rest.

Last night's events had taken an alarming turn. The Kaddim's tactics had been devious, the way they lured the attackers into the first available space that could accommodate enough men to resist the Majat, the way they focused their entire attack on Mai. Had they taken him down, it would have been disastrous, but even with Kara's interference the Kaddim nearly succeeded in dealing an irreversible blow. Kara's death would not only have reduced their Diamond force by a quarter, but would have destroyed morale once and for all. Worse, the effect her wound had had on Mai demonstrated a weakness the Kaddim were likely to explore next time.

Egey Bashi was probably the only one who truly understood how close it had been with Kara's healing. Under normal circumstances Egey Bashi would never have agreed to use the elixir on her until he could be certain she was in no immediate danger. So many things could have gone wrong, even with someone of Kara's training and self-control. For a moment, when she went berserk, Egey Bashi was afraid the strain would kill her before the cure could get a chance to set. Anyone else in her place would likely have died. Only her strength and resolve enabled her to regain control in time to allow the healing to take its course, and, even with that, Egey Bashi could not be certain until the very end if the pain was going to kill her despite the elixir's incredible potency.

The conversation showed no signs of stopping, and Egey Bashi was beginning to contemplate whether he should join it anyway. Just then, soft footsteps behind him announced the arrival of Lady Celana, emerging from an inner doorway. She stopped by his side, following Egey Bashi's gaze to the two arguing men.

"May I join you, Magister?" she asked.

"I would be honored, my lady." Egey Bashi turned, studying her with curiosity. The royal lady could blend in well. In her dark pants outfit, with hair tucked into a smooth arrangement around her head, she still looked refined and beautiful, but also inconspicuous, making her all but unnoticeable in the inn's busy routine. So different from the times when she donned her splendid royal gown, making all heads turn as she passed by.

"There is something I wanted to discuss with you about the Kaddim, Magister," she said.

"The Kaddim, my lady?" Egey Bashi raised his eyebrows. This was not what he'd expected her to say.

"I have been reflecting on everything I've learned about the ways of the Kaddim," Celana said calmly. "Both from the chronicles and from personal accounts of various people who have seen them in action. Prince Kythar's comments have been most insightful as he appraised me on his observations."

Egey Bashi crossed his arms on his chest. He couldn't wait to hear what the devious mind behind this smooth porcelain forehead was able to conjure with the help of Prince Kythar, whose mere mention brought a faint color to Celana's cheeks. At least somebody here was smitten with the Prince, and he couldn't even imagine what fruit this affection had produced this time.

"From my reading," Lady Celana said, "I know that the Kaddim Brotherhood is headed by twelve men, who report directly to their leader. They are called a 'Cursed Dozen'. These men are the only ones referred to as Brothers, unlike others that serve more of the utilitarian functions, such as fighting and servitude. As such, without the Cursed Dozen the Kaddim wouldn't even be a brotherhood anymore."

Egey Bashi nodded. He knew it too, even if this knowledge didn't seem to be of much use in their current attack plans.

"Thinking back on everything I have recently learned about the Kaddim," Celana went on, "I believe that the members of the Cursed Dozen possess different, complementary powers that secure their roles among the twelve and provide a range of abilities that makes the Kaddim much more capable than anyone realizes. Perhaps these different powers have enabled them to survive through centuries, when everyone believed them to be extinct."

Egey Bashi raised his eyebrows. Her glance showed that she acknowledged his surprise. It also showed a glimpse of hidden satisfaction. Egey Bashi's skin prickled. Even with his knowledge of how smart she was, he apparently hadn't been giving her enough credit. It seemed that she was aware of her "smoke screen", fully utilising the fact that no one expected much from a seventeen year-old beauty. Furthermore, she was likely using it for her gain, where possible. Like now, when she had disarmed him by throwing in a topic of the conversation he completely hadn't expected.

"Different powers?" he asked.

"Yes."

"How so?"

"Do you recall the time when Kaddim Nimos encountered us on the road to the Majat Guild?"

"What about it?"

Lady Celana smiled. "It seemed that his only goal that time had been to seed rivalry in our midst, by hinting at certain… personal feelings that he knew would bother Prince Kythar and put him at odds with Aghat Mai." She blushed again, briefly glancing to the two men in question, still arguing. "Remarkably, Kaddim Nimos demonstrated amazing knowledge of the relationships involved and seemed to know the exact words to say and what information to hold back to produce the maximum effect."

Egey Bashi listened with captivation. She was right. She was also showing exceptional insight, even if he still wasn't sure what she was driving at.

"Prince Kythar," Celana went on, "also told me that Nimos did similar things during your last trip to the Majat Guild. That time, Nimos seemed to be more focused on making sure that everyone was aware of his bad intentions toward the Prince and of how unthinkable it would be if he had his way. He made several appearances, as I heard, each of them greatly disconcerting Aghat Kara and demonstrating to everyone that he and his men could, if needed, take down Aghat Raishan."

"Yes," Egey Bashi said slowly. He had been there both times Nimos interfered with their trips. Lady Celana was recounting it right, even though he still couldn't make the connection.

"I feel," Celana went on, "that Kaddim Nimos has been acting this way because he was likely appointed to the task. It also struck me that the things he said – especially about Aghat Mai – are not commonly known." She blushed again, glancing briefly toward the arguing men. "This made me wonder whether Nimos might somehow possess an innate ability to sense feelings, and whether this ability may involve a special form of mind magic, different from the Kaddim's regular skill common to all the Brothers."

Egey Bashi's eyes widened. What she said was true. Mai's self-control made it nearly impossible for anyone to guess his feelings toward Kara. At the time of their recent encounter with Nimos, Egey Bashi had been easily the only one aware of these feelings, and this knowledge had required studying Mai very closely – a task the Keeper undertook precisely because he believed it to be essential to understand the reasons for Mai's resistance to the Kaddim.

"Mind magic?" he echoed.

"Yes," Celana said. "I thought of it when I realized that Nimos's knowledge of feelings and emotions, the way he was playing on it, couldn't have possibly come from any information he might have obtained by regular means. Of course, mind control is already a Kaddim trait, which also gave me a clue, even though his type of magic is different, I believe. I haven't observed the same qualities in any other Kaddim Brother."

Egey Bashi's skin prickled. Now that Celana was laying it out, it seemed so obvious.

Damn it, this lady was a born Keeper.

"I couldn't help wondering," Celana went on, "if this power may also be used to subtly cloud people's judgment. Aghat Raishan told me that once or twice he had experienced brief confusion when Kaddim Nimos was in sight."

Egey Bashi's mind raced. She was right again, of course. Once, Raishan had been holding Nimos at sword point and then, for an inexplicable reason, let him go. Was this all a part of Nimos's unique power Celana was talking about?

"Such power, if it exists, could be used for devious mind manipulations," Celana said. "For example, to instigate a Kaddim Brother at a key post in the Majat Guild."

Egey Bashi hesitated. Even for her wit, this seemed a bit far-fetched.

"Wouldn't the Majat appointment likely be to the credit of the Shadow Master himself?"

She shook her head. "Not if I am right. A Shadow Master at the Majat Guild is a difficult post, requiring an entirely different set of skills. Given that this man likely had no Majat training, I couldn't help wondering if he was able to acquire these skills through a sort of magic power. I thought of it in the last few days when I was observing the Majat in action. A man in his post needs an eye for people's physical skills – perhaps a unique spacial memory that allows him to point out weaknesses and strategize the defeat of all their fighters. My guess is, his special talent enables him to do that – and Nimos, knowing that, took care to instrument his appointment at the Guild. I may be wrong, of course." She lowered her eyes.

Egey Bashi leaned forward. "Please go on, my lady."

She glanced up again. "I also thought of Kaddim Tolos. If you remember, during the tournament at the Majat Guild he was the one to summon the time vortex and make him and his comrades disappear. Prince Kythar believes he was also the one to do it back at the Illitand Hall, when the Prince's magic granted us victory." Her cheeks lit with color again. "If my theory is right, Kaddim Tolos is the only one able to do that, while Nimos's mind powers, and the Shadow Master's spacial skills, are essential to orchestrate the battle."

Egey Bashi watched her, wide-eyed. Celana smiled at his expression.

"Based on these three, I couldn't help wondering if everyone on the Cursed Dozen has a distinct skill. Aghat Raishan told me once how another Kaddim Brother, Farros, nearly killed him, when you and he infiltrated the Monastery on a prior assignment. He seemed to believe Farros had been specifically called for the task."

Egey Bashi let out a sigh. She was right, yet again. When that had happened, Egey Bashi had been standing right there, watching it with his own eyes. Kaddim Farros possessed what was known as the Power to Kill, an ability to focus mind control magic into one person to explode the heart. That time, he had focused a near-lethal blast on Raishan to prove a point, and the rest of the Kaddim were very specific that Farros be the one to do it. How could Egey Bashi not have thought about that back then?

"Prince Kythar," Celana said, "told me he saw five Kaddim Brothers during their attack last night. As I thought more about it, I couldn't help wondering if knowing their special powers might give us an additional advantage in overcoming them."

Egey Bashi frowned. If Lady Celana was right, focusing on the Kaddim Brothers, rather than the warriors, could hold the key to their victory. More, if they targeted the *right* Brothers, they could cripple the enemy once and for all. For instance, taking out Tolos could guarantee that none of the Kaddim would be able to transport out of the fight, so that in the long run they wouldn't resurrect, like Nimos. Getting the Shadow Master would lose the Kaddim their source of inside knowledge of Majat affairs. Of course, targeting any of them, individually or together, was not an easy task.

"The fifth one Prince Kythar spoke about," he said, "is likely Kaddim Haghos, who performed the duties of the Reverend Father some time ago." Deposed by Egey Bashi himself, in a chain of events that led to King Evan's coronation. *Damn it, why couldn't I have finished the job?* "I am not certain of his special power, but he surely knows his way around this Monastery in great detail."

Celana nodded. "As I understand from Prince Kythar, when faced with the Kaddim power he is sometimes able to sense... a *flavor* in their force? At least, he described it this way to me, once. I felt knowing that there might be differences in their magic could be useful to His Highness in his fight. I have given it a lot of thought. But I wasn't sure how to approach him about it." Her eyes trailed to the two arguing men again. As they watched, Mai turned and strode off, while Kyth continued to look at Kara practicing in the courtyard.

"Well done, my lady," Egey Bashi said. "I do believe Prince Kythar, as well as others on our attack force, will find this information invaluable. We must gather everyone in charge to discuss it. If you don't mind informing Prince Kythar, I will talk to Aghat Mai."

She nodded, throwing a doubtful glance at Kyth and back at the Magister.

"I was hoping you could facilitate the conversation."

Egey Bashi smiled. It was fascinating to watch all this cool wit dissolve into uncertainty when faced with the object of her affections. In some ways she was still just a child.

"You'll do just fine," Egey Bashi said. "I am certain Prince Kythar would be glad to hear it from your own lips."

Egey Bashi caught up with Mai in a passage leading through the back stairs to the second floor of the inn. He panted as he struggled to catch up with the Diamond's smooth stride.

"Aghat Mai," he called.

Mai spun around, coming to an abrupt halt.

"Magister?"

Egey Bashi's heart quivered as he looked at the Diamond, noting the paleness and dark circles under the eyes.

"I hope you are heading for some rest," he said.

"Is this the reason you stopped me?"

"No. I wanted to have a word with you."

Mai's tensely set shoulders slowly relaxed under the Keeper's gaze as he shifted impatiently from foot to foot. *Dear Shal Addim, the man is barely holding up on his feet.*

"If this is about what I said to you last night–"

Egey Bashi shook his head. "It's already forgotten, Aghat Mai. I also said a thing or two I regret, and I know none of us truly meant any of it. We were all a bit on edge. Right now we have a different issue. Lady Celana Illitand has made a critical observation, which I feel may be important in planning your next move. I'd like to ask you to include her when you meet to discuss attack plans."

Mai looked at him with silent question.

"She believes," Egey Bashi went on, "the Kaddim Brothers you are facing specialize in powers, and Kyth may be able to use this to identify them. I'm not sure yet if this could be useful, but I thought you might have ideas – after I hope, you get a few hours' sleep."

A quick smile slid through Mai's lips. "You're speaking like a doctor, Magister."

"I am, in this case. I hope I convinced you last night that I know something about healing."

A shadow ran across Mai's face.

"Yes, Magister. We are all indebted to you."

Egey Bashi sighed. "This brings me to another topic I wanted to discuss with you, Aghat Mai."

The Diamond regarded him with a guarded expression.

"I couldn't help noticing," Egey Bashi went on, "that during your attack last night, Kara was not the only person wounded by that dagger."

Mai didn't respond but Egey Bashi noticed the way he receded into the shadows, his fatigue suggesting that the damage was more serious than the Keeper thought.

"I feel very fortunate," Egey Bashi went on, "that the Keepers' treatment proved so successful in Kara's case. However, I cannot help feeling concerned that *your* injury, while perhaps less deadly, might prove considerably harder to heal."

Mai leaned against the wall. Egey Bashi found himself resisting an urge to support him.

"Are you afraid I'll make mistakes, Magister?" Mai asked quietly.

Egey Bashi shook his head. "No. I have the utmost confidence in your leadership, Aghat Mai."

Mai's smile touched his lips but left his eyes in shadow. It looked... bitter? Defeated?

"Thank you, Magister."

Egey Bashi took a breath. "Despite that, last night left me worried. We are fighting a war, not a battle, and your enemies are now aware that you have a weak spot. Sooner or later they'll find a way to exploit it further."

Mai was watching him wide-eyed – afraid, Egey Bashi realized as he struggled to find the right words.

"I know," the Keeper said quietly, "that you would never allow your personal feelings to jeopardize the lives of your men. However, I am also aware that under certain circumstances you wouldn't hesitate to jeopardize yours."

Mai's lips twitched. "Are you suggesting I stand by and let them do whatever they want with her?"

Egey Bashi sighed. "I am *asking* you – for this campaign – to treat her like everyone else on your force."

Mai's gaze became distant.

"Believe me," Egey Bashi said, "I know what's involved. A young man like you probably cannot imagine someone of my years understanding these kinds of feelings... and sacrifices."

Mai's eyes followed him with the captivation of a child. Egey Bashi's heart ached at his expression.

"I am asking you," he said, "to look past that. With the pressure you are already under, I know I'm asking a lot. Perhaps you might find inspiration in the way Kara was able to distance herself from her pain last night to enable her healing. I haven't told you that this was the only thing that saved her life, narrowly. If she had allowed her pain to take control, she would be dead. Since you have some idea what it feels like to be treated by this elixir, I am sure you can understand the strength and resolve it took on her part. I know you are capable of the same, if not more."

Mai's face paled as he receded deeper into the shadows.

"I know," Egey Bashi said, "that you are aware of the burdens of your post. I also know that on one occasion you've recklessly laid it down to defend Kara's life in a tournament that should never have taken place at all. Now, the stakes are increased many times over. I hope you can keep this in mind."

Mai held his gaze.

"I know my responsibilities, Magister," he said. "And I'm good at what I do. But, personal feelings aside, Kara is a quarter of our spearhead force. If they take her out–"

"True, Aghat Mai. Just think of her equally to everyone else. That's all I'm asking – with full knowledge of what it means to you."

Mai continued to watch him and once again, like he had a long time before, Egey Bashi could glimpse through his glamor to the young man inside, barely an adult, who had been unexpectedly burdened with power and responsibility that surpassed everything in the kingdoms. There was no room for love in Mai's new role – and he knew it. And now, for the sake of the greater good, he was being asked to give it up.

Egey Bashi reached forward and patted Mai on the shoulder.

"I wish I could help you carry at least a part of your burden," he said quietly. "We often have to make impossible choices when loaded with more than one man could possibly bear. You are holding it admirably. You are a great man, and I will always be proud to have fought by your side."

Mai smiled, but his eyes had a guarded look.

"Thank you, Magister," he said. "And... likewise."

37

ATTACK PLAN

The war council reconvened in the evening. In addition
to the four Diamonds, it included Kyth, Lady Celana,
Alder, Ellah, and Egey Bashi. Kyth couldn't help feeling
out of place as he sat at the command table across from
Mai and Kara, watching them put small pins into the
map, shifting them around in response to comments
from Lance and Raishan. They looked as if they were
playing an elaborate game.

Mai looked refreshed and relaxed, back to his usual
self. Watching him, Kyth couldn't help wondering if
this change was due to the fact that the Diamond had
gone to his room upstairs to catch a few hours of sleep,
or to the fact that Kara was now back at his side, sitting
so close that their sleeves touched as they moved their
hands over the map. Part of him wished to be in Mai's
place. Another part couldn't get rid of an unsettling
feeling he couldn't quite name. Watching the effect
Kara had on Mai made Kyth wonder, for the first time,
what would happen to Mai if she chose Kyth in the
end. Would Mai ever be able to come to terms with it?

Or, would it shatter him once and for all?

Would Kyth be the one she chose...?

He dismissed the last thought. With the impending battle, these things should be the farthest from his mind.

He focused on the information relayed to him earlier by Lady Celana. If she was right, the different magic of the Kaddim Brothers should indeed be distinguishable to his inner eye as he wielded his power against them. He thought it was possible. Except, he didn't seem to be able to put his hand on how to do it.

"With the force we're bringing this time," Mai said, "they will likely assemble their men further in, probably in the main courtyard at the back entrance to the Shal Addim Temple." He pointed to a large rectangle on the map, accented with pins around the perimeter.

"Unless they try to break us up," Lance said.

"We shouldn't let them. If we want our increased numbers to make a difference, we must keep together."

The four Diamonds drifted into a discussion that involved too many military terms for Kyth to follow, eventually shifting into the language of their Fortress, sharp words with hard consonants he couldn't possibly reproduce. He spent the time watching Kara, so beautiful and radiant now that she was well again, sitting at the table among her fellows in rank. She looked so natural in their midst that Kyth couldn't help wondering if the life with him at court could possibly make her happy. He forced this thought away too, turning to Alder instead.

"Can you send your spiders to strike on command?" he asked.

Alder hesitated.

"They do listen to me, at times, but I haven't ever tried to ask them to *strike* anyone. Why?"

Kyth shook his head. "I thought… if I could indeed spot the Kaddim Brother we want to destroy, it could be a good way. Lady Celana thinks the spiders' venom would prevent them from resurrecting." He briefly glanced at the lady by his side, who blushed and lowered her eyes.

He was just beginning to feel he was actually good for something, when he caught Mai's gaze from across the table.

"*Can* you spot the right Brother?" Mai asked.

Kyth shrugged. There was nothing wrong with the question, but he couldn't stand the look, mocking and challenging at the same time.

Here we go again.

"I'm trying to figure it out," he said.

"Figure it out?"

Kyth sighed. "Don't you have a map to look at or something? I thought you were busy planning the attack."

"Yes, and you're in it. Unless you have second thoughts about how many men you can protect."

"Do you have second thoughts about how many men you can lead?" Kyth bit his tongue. He was aware how everyone was looking at him now, with surprise and concern. He had let his dislike for Mai get the better of him, again. If only Kara wasn't sitting so close, Mai towering over her as if he owned her. *He doesn't. No one owns her. Not him. Not me.* For some reason, the thought brought no comfort whatsoever.

"Perhaps," Egey Bashi put in, "Prince Kythar and I can try to analyse the specifics of what he can sense about their power?"

Kyth let out a breath, watching Mai recede back into his seat as the tension around the table slowly released.

"Do it, Magister," Mai said.

He is in charge. I wanted it this way. I can deal with it. Kyth took another deep breath.

"I'm not sure I can feel a difference when I defend against them," he said. "But as I recall, I could sense distinct flavors of their powers on occasions when I tried to use them instead of the wind." He paused, aware of the puzzled looks from around the table. It made no sense, the way he said it. Nobody could possibly understand it.

"Tolos's power," Kyth went on, "was *bitter*. It left a taste on my tongue I couldn't possibly mistake for anything else."

"Good," Egey Bashi said. "That's a start. What about the others?"

Kyth shook his head. "All the other times I have been using their combined powers without trying to tell them apart. When done this way, it leaves a... muddle of sensations, really – none of them pleasant, but all different."

"Perhaps," Lady Celana said, "recognising Kaddim Tolos's power would be a good start? If he can be targeted, the Kaddim would have no means of escaping – assuming that Aghat Mai's forces can finish them off."

Mai hesitated, then nodded. "True. Besides, if Prince Kythar cannot distinguish the rest of them, Tolos is the only one we can even consider."

Kyth shook his head. "It's more of a problem than that."

"A problem?"

Kyth paused, watching Mai. He tried to convince himself the Diamond was just being efficient, not trying to mock Kyth deliberately and show everyone who was a better man. He also tried to tell himself that the way Kara was sitting, so easy and relaxed next to Mai, had nothing to do with the way she felt about him. She just chose a good spot to be close to the map, nothing more.

He swallowed. "I can only sense their power when I'm not protecting anyone."

Mai's shoulders slowly relaxed. "Not much use to us then, is it?"

"Actually," Kara said, "it could be, if we do decide to target Tolos."

Mai turned to her. "How?"

She smiled. "You and I can go in with Kyth and target whoever he points out. We're both resistant, aren't we?"

Egey Bashi shook his head. "Too risky. The Brothers would likely be very heavily protected."

"Still," Kara said. "If our attack is successful, Tolos is the one who can pull them out. To prevent that, we must target him, one way or another. If Kyth can identify him early on when they least expect it, in theory we could take advantage of it."

"In theory."

"Yes."

Mai appeared to consider it.

"Possible," he said, "but not something we can plan for in advance."

"Perhaps we can keep it in mind, then?" Kara said.

"If we do," Mai said, "I think we have a better option."

He turned to Kyth. "I'll put a Jade next to you. If you spot Tolos, tell the Jade and he'll shoot at him. With the way the Brothers are protected he'll likely miss, but this way he can mark the target for us – just like Lady Celana did so brilliantly, back at the Majat Guild."

His short glance made Lady Celana's cheeks light up with deep crimson. Damn, how did he manage to have such an effect on women?

"You are too kind, Aghat Mai," Celana said.

Mai smiled. "You should know me enough by now to realize how far from the truth that is. It was an ingenius move, my lady, one I would never have expected from an outsider to our Guild."

Kyth bit his lip. This was how Mai did it. Some flattery, some attention, some showy looks. Was this what it took to get women on your side?

Weren't both Kara and Lady Celana smarter than that?

"You *are* kind, Aghat Mai," Lady Celana said, "even if for some reason you choose to pretend otherwise. And, my shot back at the Majat Guild was Prince Kythar's idea. So, the praise should really be due to him."

Mai looked at her in quick surprise. So did Kyth, feeling his eyes widen as he turned to the lady by his side. Was she actually *praising* him to Mai?

For the first time he looked at the royal lady with new eyes. Her attention, which he had believed to be a part of her political ambitions, suddenly acquired a new color. The way she was willing to spend time with him when no one else was around. The way she always seemed so interested in his stories as he recalled his travels to the Grasslands and his previous encounters with the Kaddim. Could it be that she actually *cared*?

He couldn't help but smile.

"Thank you for your confidence, my lady," he said. "While I agree with Aghat Mai that your shot was brilliant, I do appreciate your resolve to speak on my behalf."

She nodded, her blush so captivating that he couldn't help gaping. It took him a moment to realize that the conversation had moved on and that everyone was bending over the map again, the Majat drifting into a lengthy exchange of military terms with Magister Egey Bashi.

He looked at Alder again, and at Ellah by his side, both of his friends as out of place here as he felt.

"How about your truthsense?" he asked Ellah. "Can it be used to distinguish the *flavors* of somebody's powers?"

She hesitated. "I suppose. If they're using their joint power while their specialty is in something else, it could have some flavor of a lie. Or... not a flavor. A color."

Kyth nodded. She wielded colors in her mind to enable her truthsense. Perhaps if he tried to learn it from her...

"Can we join our powers somehow?" he asked. "We—"

He paused abruptly as he realized Mai was looking at him again. *Damn.* Did this man have two pairs of ears?

"We're not taking Ellah into battle," Mai said.

Kyth sighed. "Of course not." *What the hell was I thinking?*

Mai shook his head. "If you can spot Tolos, it would help, but in the upcoming fight it doesn't guarantee us victory. Preventing their escape is more of a strategic move to make sure they're not a problem later on. Don't sweat over it. Your main task is still to protect everyone."

Kyth nodded.

"You're not having any second thoughts, are you?" Mai asked.

A retort froze on Kyth's lips as he realized grudgingly that the question made sense. As a commander, Mai had to know.

"No," he said.

Mai's gaze softened. "Just remember. We're taking a risk, betting on your ability that has never been tested before. Don't try to impress anyone. If you feel – at any point – that you may not be up to the task, you must tell me at once."

"*Tell* you?"

"The Jade archer will shadow you. He'll know how to give a signal."

Shadow me. Kyth's skin crept. In the Majat Guild, shadowing someone meant being able to kill him. He hoped that wasn't what Mai had in mind.

Lady Celana had just said that Mai was kind, even if he did a good job of hiding it. Kara was sitting so close to him. Even Ellah at some point had been infatuated with Mai, along with dozens and dozens of court ladies of all stations. The Diamond had this effect on people that made them follow him even when there seemed to be no special reason to trust him. Was Kyth the only one mistaken? Or was it possible that Kyth was the only one with the ability to see through Mai's glamor to the man inside?

Was it the man Kyth was prepared to trust with everything he cared for?

Was it the man he could accept as a successful rival for Kara?

Was Kyth prepared to step aside and let him have her?

He forced these thoughts away. He had made a decision to trust Mai fully with this attack, and so far the Diamond had given him no reason to doubt his honesty, or his intentions. It may be different when it came to women, but the upcoming battle plans should not be driven by such considerations. If they all survived and defeated the Kaddim, there would be time for rivalry later on.

For now, all he hoped was that Mai's attack plan would not put Kara's life in jeopardy again.

38
ATTACK

The Majat force marched in full daylight, a hundred men fanning around the tall Monastery wall. Kyth kept to the center of the formation, next to Egey Bashi, Alder, and a tall Jade archer Mai had assigned to him for the duration of the attack. Gahang Torr.

Four Rubies surrounded them, Kyth's protection throughout the operation. One of them threw a grappler hook for the Prince, as a hundred hooks flew up around them in near synchrony. Kyth did his best to keep up as a row of black-clad shadows slid over the wall beside him in one single move. The attack had begun.

The Majat's tactics were different this time. The party paused in each courtyard, sending scouts to the gateways on all sides and waiting for their signals before proceeding. Like last time, they met no resistance as they ventured deeper into the compound.

Mai called an all-stop at a large double gate, tightly shut. His quick hand signs rearranged the formation in the blink of an eye. Several men scaled the walls, sending more hand signs as they peered over into the courtyard beyond and noiselessly dropped back to the ground.

"From what I understand of this language," Egey Bashi said quietly, "our welcoming party is behind this gate. Or the best part of it, anyway."

"Do you think they are capable of defeating us, Magister?" Kyth asked quietly.

"Hard to tell," Egey Bashi said. "They will likely send reinforcements, again and again. They will probably also try to separate the attackers into smaller groups. I know that Aghat Mai is prepared to resist these attempts. Just focus on your part, Your Highness. The rest is in capable hands."

Kyth sighed. He wished he could fully believe that.

Two men pulled the gates open. The Majat hid behind it, waiting for a wave of arrows to sweep out and hit the wall on the opposite side of the courtyard before rushing inside. Kyth shivered. Last time they had encountered no ranged attack. Clearly the news of the Jades in the Majat party had reached the defenders.

He sensed waves of Kaddim force flow in through the open gateway. He focused on countering it, his invisible blade rising up to protect every man in sight. The task was far more challenging than last time, when he had only twelve to worry about. Fully absorbed in it, he didn't even notice how the fight started, the clashing of weapons reaching his ears as if from a distance as he put his entire mind into wielding his defense.

He saw a man at the edge of his vision waver under the Kaddim's force and increased his efforts, expanding his invisible shield. Damn. It was taking everything he had. He felt dazed as his Ruby bodyguards ushered him forward. He followed them like a sleepwalker, unable to spare any attention even to the movement of his feet, feeling as if he was handling far too much.

Was Mai right all along? Had Kyth taken too much upon himself in a misguided attempt to impress him?

He kept the best of his effort on the Diamonds and Rubies, aware that this was the tip of the attack force they couldn't afford to lose. He had the most trouble with the Jades, who stuck to the edges behind the fighters and scaled the walls and roofs to shoot from above. He could tell the Jades were doing less damage than they could as he struggled to focus his power over a larger distance. If only the wind was stronger, so that it could aid his magic...

The wind.

Last time he was fighting a Kaddim battle, he didn't have the wind at all. He used the Kaddim power instead, wielding it as if it was an elemental force. Perhaps it *was* an elemental force of sorts, tainted with unpleasant flavors, bitter and destructive by nature, but potent nonetheless. Should he try to tap into it again?

Could he use it to defeat the Brothers?

He tried to take his mind back to the time in Illitand Hall when he had managed to intake the combined power of four Kaddim brothers and throw it back at them. He was dealing with five now, but shouldn't that make it even better?

He searched them out, five hooded figures standing in the deep shadows by the far wall. He couldn't tell which one was which, but he could sense the pulsing power they emanated, its net targeting everyone in sight, breaking against his invisible blade. One blade seemed hardly enough. He should have asked Mai to teach him to fight at least with two, maybe it would double his defense capabilities?

He could see that, despite their spectacular moves, the Majat were making less progress than they could expect with their kind of force. Worse, even the Diamond spearhead wasn't doing so well, surrounded by vast numbers of the best fighters the Kaddim could put forth. As he watched, he saw Lance waver as an orben hit him in the arm, a wound that was surely going to cripple his attack. His heart wavered.

Damn it, why couldn't he do better?

He concentrated.

Think of your blade as if it's a rope, Mai had said to him once. *Soft and relaxed until you drive its end into a target. Don't think of it as hitting. Try to reach instead.* Back then, exhausted and defiant, he hadn't wanted to listen. But now, suddenly, it made perfect sense.

He extended his invisible blade, imagining a rope with a knot on its end reaching deep into the enemy line. It cut through the waves of Kaddim power like a flash of lightning.

He could sense the effect as the battle picked up, the Majat attack instantly acquiring more speed. He continued to lash out in every direction, making sure his rope-like blade reached equally to every fighter on their force.

He could sense it working by the way the clashing of the weapons around him suddenly rang with a new beat, the Jades' arrows whizzing by, picking out the attackers. The Kaddim Brothers by the wall huddled closer, clearly spending more effort than before. He tried to target the source, cutting off their force as soon as it left their outstretched palms, breaking it before it could even reach the battling men.

It felt so easy as he mastered it that he suddenly felt he could do more. Keeping his blade at work, he used another part of his consciousness to extend forward, tugging at the strings of power from the Kaddims' hands, testing them one by one. A metallic, thick smell that had a gagging quality of infected blood. A choking sensation, like a cloud of dust thrown in the face. A gust of wind that made his eyes itch, like smoke. A smell of rot, like dead fish at the pit of a shallow pond. There. The bitter smell that left a taste on his tongue, like bile.

Tolos.

"Gahang Torr," he shouted. "Shoot that one!"

The attack wasn't going as smoothly as Kara had hoped. She could tell that Kyth was having trouble. Most of the men around her were doing nothing more than holding their own. At this rate, the outcome of the battle was very much in question, especially if Kyth didn't improve very soon.

The only people fighting with full might were herself and Mai. They needed every bit of it, too. It seemed that at least half of the Kaddim fighters were honing in on them, as if determined to take them down no matter what.

Despite all that, she was surprised at the energy and excitement she felt, fighting next to Mai. The way she sensed his movements, the way he responded in perfect synchrony as they both yielded to their ability to anticipate each other's actions, made it feel like a dance, deadly and perfect – an attack nobody could possibly resist. Despite the strain of battle, she felt perfectly balanced, a calmness singing inside her as she hacked and parried, the pile of bodies at her feet growing so tall it hindered new attackers as the Majat spearhead cut deeper into the enemy line. Fighting next to Mai, she felt invincible, like never before.

She could see the huddled group of Kaddim Brothers by the far wall. Kara hoped she and Mai would have a chance to break through and take them down. Given the trouble Kyth was having, this step seemed essential to guarantee victory without losing too many men.

She saw Lance by her side take a direct hit, his left arm hanging limply as the orben likely dislocated the shoulder. She cursed, marveling at the way Lance continued the attack, doing nothing more than dropping his off-hand blade and changing his stance, putting his right foot forward to protect the injured arm. He was an amazing fighter, but he wasn't going to be able to hold like this for long. Worse, the very fact that the attackers got through to him wasn't a good sign.

She sensed a sudden change in pace and dared a quick glance toward Kyth and his group, noting that the Prince was now standing straighter, with a more confident look. He was finally getting a grip on it. She hoped it was in time to turn the advantage to the Majat.

As she glanced at him again, she saw Kyth pointing and shouting, followed by the low hum of an arrow whistling through the air toward the group of Kaddim Brothers. Torr's sound arrow, signaling the identity of

Kaddim Tolos. Her heart raced as she glanced at Mai, realizing no help was forthcoming from his end, the line of his attackers so dense that it rivaled the densely packed stones of the Monastery wall at their backs.

She swept through her own attackers, no longer bothering with clean blows, using all the dirty moves she had ever learned to cripple, injure, and disable everyone in sight, even if temporarily. Her eyes darted to the far wall, noting the hooded man who ducked Torr's arrow, throwing a murderous look at the archer. As he raised his head, she caught the gleam of the man's yellow eyes – eyes she would never forget from the time he and Nimos had cornered her in the Illitand Hall.

She slid between the attackers, putting her entire force into moving fast enough to transcend the enemy line. She whipped up two throwing daggers as she ran, weighting them in her hand. Could she do another shadow throw?

She felt inspired enough to try.

She didn't stop running as she sent the two blades flying in perfect unison toward the yellow-eyed man. He made no attempt to deflect them, but tried to dodge instead, his frantic moves telling her he knew all about this kind of throw and how dangerous it was to attempt to alter its course. She heard a thud as the daggers hit, sending the man down to the cobbles. In the next moment the other four Kaddim were around her, each drawing two curved sabers from the sheaths at their back.

She swallowed, feeling as if she were reliving a bad dream. Back in Illitand Hall, when she had faced

Nimos and Tolos side by side, she'd had no weapons except a captured orben and was handicapped by the weight of a child in her arms – Princess Aljbeda, whose protection got her into the ordeal. That time, only Mai's interference had saved her from imminent death. And now... could she handle four, all by herself?

She could see carnal triumph in their eyes – Nimos's dark and owl-like, and others, speckled, and purple, and snake-gray. She tried to distance herself from them as she focused on parrying their attack. They formed a tight circle around her, thrusting simultaneously from all sides, moving in perfect unison, as if controlled by a single mind. If there was such a thing as a five-dagger shadow throw, could there be a technique called "shadow attack"? *Dear Shal Addim, our Shadow Master is one of them, and he knows all my weaknesses and can relay them to the others.* She dismissed the thought, putting all her strength and speed into the fight.

Her peripheral vision caught a movement behind her. Tolos, the man she had wounded, rising to a crouch, making passes with his hands. She smelled a bitter wisp of smoke. *He's summoning a time vortex.*

It dawned on her how the Kaddim Brothers were crowding in, putting more effort into containing her within their circle than into the actual attack... The smoke was enfolding her, making her eyes tingle, blocking her vision...

Are they trying to take me with them?

A chill in the pit of her stomach caused her a moment's lapse in concentration, a saber whizzing too close to her face. She forced herself to distance her mind from what was going on behind her, from the way the cobbles suddenly felt uneven, buckling and caving under her feet.

Pulling...

A dark shadow darted behind her attackers' line. A black polished staff cut into the circle of the Kaddim, a blade springing from its end, hitting one of them in the chest.

Mai.

Relief washed over her as she watched him sweep past the falling man, clashing weapons with another one by her side. He was shouting, and in her daze she couldn't make out the words, but she could see the action erupt in his wake as the Majat regrouped, forming an impenetrable line. The enemies fell to their blades left and right, the Jades' arrows blocking the waves of new reinforcements at the side gates. Thick furry shapes darted by her feet. *Spiders.* They launched upon a hooded man at her side, his scream as they stung him echoing to every corner of the courtyard. Then, waves of thick smoke enfolded her and she felt Mai's hand grip her arm, pulling her out of the way as the cobblestones under her feet finally caved into a bottomless pit.

Time vortex.

She held on to Mai, grasping with all her might as he pulled her away, watching the cobblestones pop back into place. Sounds returned, the clashing of the ending battle, the gusts of the wind. The courtyard around her stood level, far more solid and somewhat emptier than moments ago.

The Kaddim Brothers were gone, as if they had never existed.

"Bloody hell," Magister Egey Bashi said, striding up to her side.

Dazed, she ran her gaze around the courtyard. The battle was dying out, the Kaddim fighters crumpling under the Majat attack. Without their leaders and the mind power to back them up, they were demoralized. Jade arrows whizzed by, joined by the swordsmen, cornering the remaining men, picking them off one by one until the large courtyard was strewn with bodies, hiding the cobblestones.

The Kaddim fighters made no attempt to surrender. But even if they had, Kara knew they would be shown no mercy.

There seemed to be no reason to rejoin the fight, which appeared to be all but over under the overwhelming Majat force. She let out a breath, her death strain slowly giving way to fatigue as she steadied herself against Mai, finally finding the strength to disengage from his grip. His stunned look answered so well the way she felt inside.

"Are you all right?" he asked.

She nodded. "Thanks."

"No problem."

She shivered, surprised at the way she felt like crying. Facing the Kaddim Brothers again after what happened last time seemed like too much. Having been nearly caught in the middle of their time vortex...

She shivered. Why were they trying to take her with them? What did they want with her?

All around her the fighters were stopping and lowering their weapons. There were no standing enemies in sight. She watched Kyth approach with his group, and Alder swept past her, bending down to pick up his spiders.

"Have we… won?" he asked.

"Yes," Kara said slowly. "I think."

"We have definitely succeeded in freeing the Holy Monastery," Egey Bashi said, "as well as in taking down a major number of Kaddim warriors. This ends the Kaddim rule within these walls, and the takeover of the Holy Church that, to my knowledge, had been in progress for at least decades. I'd call that victory. The King will be so pleased."

Mai shrugged, his look suggesting he didn't give a damn about the King's pleasure.

"Let's survey the grounds," he said. "I, for one, would like to make sure there are no Kaddim left."

Egey Bashi glanced at Kara. "Did you see which one of them the spiders bit?"

She shook her head. "No. Sorry, Magister."

"It's fine," Mai said, "as long as they bit at least one of them."

"They did." Kara swallowed, feeling an unpleasant weakness in the pit of her stomach. She would probably never know how close it had been, but one thing was certain. If it hadn't been for Mai she would likely be out there right now, trapped in the worst nightmare that had ever haunted her dreams. He had told her he had permanently erased her debt with him. But it was impossible in her situation not to feel at least a little bit grateful.

She realized something else too. Whatever else she felt toward him, she was certain that this gratitude would never prompt her to act differently toward him. The way she felt about him surpassed any simple feelings like debt, gratitude, and duty.

She would do anything for him, even if it meant staying by his side without ever being able to let him know how she felt.

39

THE HOLY MONASTERY

Kyth was amazed at how quickly and ruthlessly the Majat dealt with their defeated enemies, searching out and killing all survivors and making quick arrangements to dispose of the bodies, which were piled into carts and taken away Shal Addim knew where. In less than two hours the courtyard was empty again, its blood-stained cobbles gleaming with rusty red in the afternoon sun. In all the centuries of the Monastery's existence it had probably never seen such a blood bath. Hopefully, it never would again. Watching the way the Majat operated, Kyth could finally fully understand how this formidable force was the one that truly commanded the kingdoms that had emerged out of the ruins of the Old Empire. No one else he had ever seen could possibly lead such a quick and efficient strike that finished the job once and for all.

It was nearly as impressive to see the way the Majat dealt with their own wounded and dead. While the disposal of enemy bodies was still underway, Mai personally led a small group that approached every man, examining their injuries, saluting the dead. Despite everything, Kyth had to admit feeling nothing but admiration at the way Mai genuinely cared for his men as he mourned his fallen comrades and gave aid to the survivors before arranging for their transportation back to Mistress Yba's inn. Mai personally set Lance's dislocated shoulder, bandaging his wound with the help of Egey Bashi. Watching Lance, weak with pain, barely able to sit up against the wall, Kyth wondered for how long he had been fighting after the orben hit him and how he was able to sustain the attack despite the injury.

The losses on the attackers' side were fewer than Kyth had feared. Only six of the Majat were dead, with thirty or so wounded, their injuries ranging from light to severe. No one had an injury nearly as grave as Kara's had been, leaving hope that everyone would recover, and soon.

After arrangements were made for the dead and wounded to be sent under escort back to the inn, half of the Majat attack force stayed behind to survey the Monastery grounds. Kyth used the time while Mai was occupied with dispatching orders to stride over to Kara's side.

She looked dazed and appeared startled when she saw Kyth.

"Are you all right?" he asked.

A tense cord in her neck slowly relaxed, as if it had taken her a moment to recognize him. He hadn't seen her so shaken in a long time.

"Yes," she said. "You?"

Kyth shrugged. "I'm fine. I just feel I could have done better."

She reached forward and patted his arm. "You did fine."

Kyth shook his head. "If I had done everything right from the start, we would have had fewer casualties. Lance wouldn't have been hit."

Kara held his gaze. "In our training, we are taught never to give in to self-doubt or relive other possible scenarios. Battles don't always go as planned. The only thing each of us can do is our best. You did yours, and admirably. Without you we would likely all be dead, no matter how well everyone could fight. You made this victory possible – that's the most important thing."

Kyth let out a sigh. How could she always make him feel so good with so few words?

"They were trying to pull you into their vortex, weren't they?" he asked.

Her face darkened. "They nearly succeeded too. Mai came in the nick of time."

Kyth nodded, his eyes trailing to Mai giving orders at the other side of the courtyard. He saw what Mai had done to save Kara, and what would have likely happened if he hadn't mounted an inhuman effort to break through his attackers' line and reach her side. Despite everything else he felt toward Mai, his gratitude to the man couldn't possibly be expressed in words.

Was it enough to step aside and give Kara up to him?

It isn't my choice, he reminded himself. *Not Mai's choice either. It's Kara's.* He realized with sudden clarity that whatever choice she made, he would trust it to be the right one for her. Mai was a worthy rival; he saw that now. If Kara chose him over Kyth, it would be shattering, but he would be able to accept it and wish her happiness from the bottom of his heart.

He turned back to her, his face relaxing into a smile at the sight of her beauty and radiance. She had been through a lot, too much for a nineteen year-old. She deserved to be happy, whatever path she chose for herself.

"I am so glad you're fine," he said.

She smiled. "So am I."

They turned and walked toward Mai side by side, just as the first of the scouts he had sent out started trickling back into the courtyard, herding groups of disheveled priests.

Kyth gaped as he watched the Majat lining the holy men along the far wall and ushering them to pull off their robes, leaving them wearing only flat shoes and crude sleeveless undershirts that draped to mid-thigh like flaxen sacks.

Kyth had never seen a priest without a robe before. The sight was terrifying in its misery. Removal of their garments of authority reduced the spiritual leaders of the kingdom to a huddled group of shivering men, eyeing the Majat in terrified fascination as if beholding devils themselves. They looked so ordinary, perhaps more pale and drawn, twitching from the sunlight, covering their tonsured heads with their hands.

"*What* is going on?" Kyth asked.

"Aghat Mai wants to make sure none of them are branded with the Kadan sign," Egey Bashi said, coming up to Kyth's side.

"By *stripping* them?"

The Keeper shrugged. "The Majat have their ways. Can't say I blame them, either. While this is a bit heavy-handed, you have to admit it's efficient."

414   THE GUILD OF ASSASSINS

"I suppose," Kyth said slowly, watching more men ushered forward into the line. Some wore iron shackles, dragging their feet on the cobbles. A few needed to be half carried. Kyth guessed they must have been taken out of the Monastery dungeons. He shivered. He had heard a lot about the inquisition, but had never before had the chance to see the fruits of its labors.

The large courtyard was filling up. By Kyth's estimate the Majat scouts had brought out nearly four hundred men.

Mai strode up to them, talking to a group in his wake.

"Is this everyone?" he asked.

"Nearly everyone, Aghat Mai," said a man walking on his right, wearing a sapphire-set armband. "My men are still breaking down some of the doors at the back of the compound."

Mai nodded. "Keep looking, Keilar Bart. We can't afford to miss anyone."

Kyth ran his eyes along the rows, suddenly realizing who was missing.

"Mai," he called out.

The Diamond paused abruptly and glanced up at him, his expression making Kyth suppress the urge to scramble out of the way. Mai's commander's face – the one he wore when he sent people to their deaths – could be terrifying to behold. Kyth stood his ground, reminding himself that he was a crown prince and a man in his own right, even if just now he had spoken more casually than was proper when addressing a Majat Guildmaster.

"Father Bartholomeos," he said. "He's not here, but he should be. The letter my father received from the Kaddim said he was in the dungeons."

Mai glanced at the Sapphire at his heels.

"We searched through the entire dungeons, Aghat Mai," the man said nervously. He pointed to the group in shackles, some standing, some sitting and lying on the cobbles of the courtyard.

"Perhaps," Mai said, "the Kaddim took him with them?"

"No," Kyth said slowly. "I think I know where he is."

Kyth shivered as he led the Majat through the passages underneath the Monastery compound. Last time he was here, a prisoner of the late Reverend Haghos, he had been locked up, waiting for his execution in the most secure prison cell the Monastery could boast. The Circular Chamber.

The same chamber had served as a prison for the renegade priest who had rescued Kyth at birth to secure the Dorn dynasty's right to rule. Father Bartholomeos, a Dorn house priest back then, had spent seventeen years locked in that chamber, paying for his role in the plot. And now, Kyth had a feeling he was there again. Where else would Haghos, who knew exactly how the man felt about the place, put his rival for the position of head of the Church?

His heart raced as he counted the turns of the endless passages, hoping he remembered it right. Last time, he had been here with Alder and Ellah, but Alder, walking by his side now, didn't seem to remember much. Kyth had to rely only on his own memory.

He felt utterly lost and was considering a retreat back to the surface where they could probably find a priest to help them – assuming anyone would cooperate after the treatment they had received – when he felt a familiar draft from the side hallway, a waft of scent bringing a memory that made his hair stand on end.

Torch smoke.

"Here," he said, pointing at the wall.

The Sapphires in his wake looked surprised but said nothing as they stepped forward, feeling around the blind wall ahead. Kyth focused, trying to remember *that* time, when he was here on Reverend Haghos's orders.

Two priests, setting their torches into the sconces, running their fingers along the left side of the wall...

"Put your torches into these sconces," he heard himself say, marveling at the way the Majat obeyed him without delay. He stepped forward, running his fingers along the wall beside the left torch, trying to recall the way he had seen the priests do it back then.

A barely perceptible click echoed even before he felt a hidden spring yield to his touch, forcing a section of the wall to slide aside, revealing the chamber inside.

In the flickering torchlight, he watched familiar sights float into his vision even as they floated up in his memory in nauseating detail. The smoothly hewn walls that had a way to absorb sound, hitting on the ears with a ringing stillness. A pile of hay in the corner, serving as a bed and a shelter. The bald man with bushy eyebrows and pale shiny eyes, rising to meet them...

"Father Bartholomeos!" he exclaimed.

"Prince Kythar," the old priest said. "It's about time."

Kyth was glad that Father Bartholomeos seemed to be well enough to walk back to the courtyard on his own, even if slower than the speed picked up by his rescuers on the way down. The old priest winced as he emerged into the sunlight, and another time when he saw the rows of half-naked Monastery inhabitants lined outside. As he approached Mai and his group, he wordlessly rolled up the left sleeve of his robe.

"Aghat Mai," he said. "I hope you can personally ascertain I have no brand mark – unless, of course, you want me to disrobe anyway."

Mai looked upon the priest's shoulder before nodding.

"Thank you, Father Bartholomeos," he said. "Disrobing won't be necessary. I'm glad you are all right."

The old priest ran his eyes around the courtyard again.

"Quite a havoc, Aghat Mai. Prince Kythar appraised me on the details as we walked. I daresay the Majat will be remembered within these walls for generations to come."

"I hope so." Mai's face was almost serious as he said it, but Kyth noted amusement in his quick glance. "If you're well enough, Holy Father, perhaps you can go over the Monastery plans with Keilar Bart," he indicated the Sapphire by his side, "and make sure we missed nothing when looking for leftover Kaddim warriors."

Bartholomeos nodded. "Of course, Aghat Mai, anything I can do to help." His eyes reflected the same amusement, as if he and Mai were sharing a private joke. Kyth couldn't help admiring the old priest, who had endured imprisonment in this Monastery for decades and had just been sealed into his old dungeon for weeks, but was still able to maintain his sense of humor and presence of mind.

Egey Bashi cleared his throat.

"Perhaps, Aghat Mai," he said, "before taking any further steps we could first ensure that Father Bartholomeos indeed has proper authority within these walls? Last time I was with the King, he had received quite a rude letter from the Conclave, suggesting that the Holy Father's appointment may not be as legitimate as we all believed. Signed by the Kaddim – or so I hope."

Mai nodded and raised his head, narrowing his eyes as he ran them over the cowering rows of priests.

"Any members of the Conclave here?" he asked, putting extra force into his voice to make it carry easily through the large space.

A few hesitant nods followed.

"Everyone on the Conclave, step forward," Mai commanded. "You may put on your robes. The rest – as you were."

Kyth was amazed how military discipline seemed to work so well without any prior training for the holy servants of Shal Addim. In moments, a line of black-robed shapes formed in front of the half-naked throng.

"Keep your hoods off."

The priests hastily obeyed as Mai ran his eyes over them.

"Eight," he said. "Aren't there supposed to be twelve?"

Egey Bashi spread his hands. "I guess the rest were Kaddim Brothers."

Mai nodded and turned to Bartholomeos.

"You may elect four more, Holy Father."

Kyth sighed. There it was. Just like that. The holiest posts in the Church, elected under sword point on a military platz. One had to be a Majat to imagine such things could work – and to have an extra dose of glamor, like Mai, to ensure they actually did.

It took only minutes of huddled conversation between Bartholomeos and the robed Conclave members to point out four more priests, who were then led forward, hastily pulling on their garments.

"Good," Mai said, watching the assembled priests pull up into a straight line under his gaze, as if lining up for a parade. "And now, Holy Fathers, I would like you to vote for electing Father Bartholomeos as the Holy Reverend of the Church. All in favor, raise your hands."

Twelve hands shakily rose up. Mai held a pause, running his eyes along the entranced faces.

"Capital," he said. "Elected by unanimous vote. I will make sure to inform King Evan how enthusiastic the Conclave was in supporting His Majesty's choice. Congratulations, Reverend Bartholomeos." He actually bowed to the priest this time, making Kyth stare. Did Mai still remember how to bend his back to anyone?

Kyth let out a sigh. This was likely the shortest and the most unanimous meeting in the history of the Holy Conclave – and definitely the only one conducted in such a public setting. Mai was probably the only person in history who could actually pull this off.

"Now," Mai said, turning to the rest of the ranks. "As soon as the Holy Fathers here ensure that my men haven't missed anyone on the grounds, you may all put your robes back on and resume your duties." He turned to Bartholomeos. "I can leave a small force behind to assist you, Holy Father."

Bartholomeos smiled. "Thank you, Aghat Mai. I appreciate the thought, but, as long as no Kaddim are here, I'd prefer to do things my way. We priests don't feel comfortable around weapons."

Mai nodded. "Just let us know if you need anything, Holy Father. We will remain in Aknabar for a few days to tend to the wounded before continuing on to Tandar to meet with the King."

"After I settle things here," Bartholomeos said, "I might join you on your trip, Aghat Mai. With your permission, of course. I understand from Prince Kythar that your victory on these grounds still leaves open questions on whether our enemies might recover enough to come back in force one day. I've heard a thing or two during my imprisonment that might come in handy when you and the King discuss further steps – as I assume you will."

"Definitely," Mai said. "And, thank you. We'll welcome your company and appreciate any information you can give."

40
THE CHOICE

Mistress Yba's inn had been transformed once again, from a war camp into hospital grounds. After making funeral arrangements for their fallen comrades, five Sapphires and one Jade, Mai had personally joined the improvised medical team that also included Raishan, Kara, Ellah, and Egey Bashi. Majat field training in caring for the wounds, combined with Egey Bashi's experience and the healing properties of the numerous substances carried in the pouches at his belt, did wonders for everyone's speedy recovery.

Only a few grave injuries were treated by the elixir, and in each case a quick consultation between the Keeper and the Diamonds in the group resulted in knocking out the patient for the duration of the healing. Kyth marveled at the quick efficiency with which they could hit one or two pressure points to cause a wounded man to pass out for a specified amount of time. He realized now why Mai and Raishan had been so upset when Egey Bashi forbade them to do it to Kara, whose suffering would have been so much

less if they had been allowed to. Seeing the dazed looks
when the patients came to, he also understood why
the Keeper had refused that time. With the gravity of
Kara's wound, she would have been unlikely to have
awoken at all. He shivered, watching the potency of the
substance that could make serious wounds disappear
without a trace in mere minutes.

It took five days to get everyone back on their feet and
into travel formation. On the morning of the sixth, they
bade farewell to Mistress Yba, who walked them out
into the street, bowing so deeply with every few steps
that Kyth secretly wondered if she was finally going to
tip over. The large woman finally stopped by the inn's
doorway, watching them with tears in her eyes. Kyth
realized that she had been viewing the entire operation,
which in his mind bordered on a nightmare he hoped
soon to forget, as the honor of a lifetime, when she, a
simple innkeeper, got to host a Majat Guildmaster and a
hundred of his top men. In a way, Kyth could understand
her feelings. Mai, in his dashing outfit, surrounded
by his Emerald Guards, could certainly give anyone
enough to remember for years and years to come. As he
stopped in the doorway and personally thanked her for
the help, putting in some of the charm and eloquence
he was capable of, she finally dissolved into sobs and
nearly fainted on the spot. Kyth was surprised to see that
even this woman, whose gender distinctions required a
careful observer to notice, seemed to be smitten with
Mai. He also wondered at the way the Guildmaster took
it in his stride, as if expecting nothing else.

Despite the abundance of inns on the road from
Aknabar to Tandar, Mai chose to camp, which was

perhaps wise, considering the size of their party. After some discussion he grudgingly conceded to erect small tents for Lady Celana and Father Bartholomeos on every stop to observe the protocol. Celana had offered for Ellah to share her tent, and the two girls spent a lot of time together, chatting by the fireside.

Kyth could only wonder. While both of them were among the smartest people he knew, he never realized either girl was prone to forming easy friendships, especially given the gap between their ranks – a royal lady from an ancient Lakeland fortress, and a commoner from a Forestland village. But here they were, spending most of their time together, and welcoming Kyth and Alder into their company after every evening meal.

Sitting next to them by the fire, Kyth was beginning to feel that, if he wasn't ready to develop any special feelings for Lady Celana, he definitely was ready to enjoy her friendship and the affection she showed him when they sat together side by side. Her looks, the way she blushed when she met his gaze, made his self-esteem soar, even if he took care not to lead her to any assumptions he was not ready to back up with his confused feelings.

In all this time, he found no opportunity at all to be alone with Kara. She was always in the middle of the Majat. Kyth had no doubt that she fully deserved the way all of them, even the arrogant Lance, regarded her with affection and admiration. He could tell how much it pleased her to be welcomed back into their company after being an outcast for such a long time. He was happy for her, even if each of these gatherings distanced her from him more and more, with nothing whatsoever he could do about it.

One evening, after a few days' travel, he felt he couldn't take it anymore. He rose abruptly in the middle of one of Lady Celana's stories about the history of the Westland Royals of his clan and walked off into the forest, aware how the conversation behind him trailed to a stop as his friends watched his retreating back. He felt guilty about doing it, but he couldn't help it. Watching Kara laughing, sitting next to Mai on the other side of the camp amidst the Majat, suddenly seemed like too much.

Kyth strode through the forest until the voices by the campsite reduced to a distant echo, and settled on a log at the edge of a small moonlit glade. No matter what, he could never stop thinking about Kara. During the past weeks, she had been very friendly toward him, but he could tell something was missing. He had experienced it once before when, after her near-death experience back in the Grasslands, she had retreated into her private Majat world and spent weeks training alongside Mai and Raishan, before emerging back to her old self. That time, she eventually returned to him of her free will and they spent the most amazing time getting to know each other better and exploring their new closeness. She had made Kyth so happy that he believed they had both found love. Back then, it seemed so natural to submerge into that wondrous feeling without giving any thought whatsoever to what lay in their future. And now, he still felt every bit as strongly about her, but he wasn't sure about her feelings anymore.

When she retreated into Majat company this time, it seemed similar to what had happened before, and yet he could also sense differences: the way she only seemed fully comfortable when Mai was nearby; the way the two shared private glances and moved in unison, as if sensing each other's thoughts; the way Mai sprang to alertness every time she was in sight. It was unsettling to watch.

He heard a rustle of footsteps behind him and turned around to see Kara.

Her face was in shadow. Moonlight touched the molten gold of her hair resting against the dark skin of her cheek, making it gleam. She looked so exquisite that Kyth's breath caught in his throat as he watched her approach.

"Can I join you?" she asked.

He rose to meet her. Before he knew it, he stepped forward and swept her into his arms, holding her close, inhaling the faint floral scent of her skin and hair. His lips found hers in a kiss, and she responded, the sensation echoing through his body, clouding his mind. It took him a moment to realize her reluctance, the way she held back. Her lips closed as she turned her face away, brushing his cheek with hers.

His hands fell away, releasing her.

"Kyth," she said quietly.

He stood, his arms lowered by his sides, his heart sinking as she slowly disengaged from him.

"I'm sorry," she said quietly.

Kyth froze.

During the last few weeks, he had been living through this moment again and again in his mind, preparing for the worst. He thought he was ready to accept her decision, even if it shattered his heart. He thought he could take it, and wish her happiness, whatever path she chose to follow.

He didn't expect this sinking feeling that rose in his stomach before she had even said anything, making his legs so weak that suddenly even standing upright seemed like an effort.

"Can we talk?" she asked.

He nodded, giving in to the weakness in his knees as he sank back to the log he had been sitting on before she arrived.

She sat next to him, so close that he could feel her warmth by his side.

"I..." she said, "I never meant to hurt you. I guess, in this situation, it couldn't be helped."

Kyth nodded again. He felt so drained that he wasn't sure he would ever be able to speak again.

"I should never have given you hope in the first place," Kara went on. "The way I was brought up, the way I was taught to respond to men... it left no room for the feelings that are so natural to you. At some point, I felt I could become like you. You were the first one who ever made me feel so special. It was... intoxicating."

Kyth opened his mouth. He could speak, he discovered, if he tried hard enough.

"You *are* special," he said quietly. And yes, intoxicating was the right word. It *had* been intoxicating. It still felt that way as she sat next to him, so beautiful that all he ever wanted to do was watch her face.

She smiled sadly. "Not in the way you mean it. What I realized lately, after thinking about it a lot, is that if I stayed with you I could never be fully myself.

Regardless of my feelings for you, I don't think I could live with that. Sooner or later, I would be bound to hurt you even more."

He nodded. Through the numbness of his grief, he did understand. He could see it too. However happy she made him feel, court life was not for her. And he – even if he renounced his birthright for her sake, he could never fit into her world.

"What are you going to do?" he asked quietly.

She kept silent for a while.

"Mai offered for me to resume my rank at the Guild," she said.

"Are you going to?"

She paused again. "I haven't decided yet."

"Do you love him?" The words came out before he could think them through. He regretted it immediately, but it was too late.

She kept silent for so long this time that he was afraid she was never going to speak again.

"I do," she said. "But my feelings toward him are irrelevant."

"*Irrelevant*?"

She shrugged. "He's the Majat Guildmaster. His post makes it impossible for anyone even to *look* at him that way."

"You can't forbid anyone to *look*," Kyth protested.

"Perhaps not. But there is no possibility of ever acting on it."

Kyth turned to look at her face, still in shadow. He recognized the air of detached calmness, her personal form of armor she receded into every time her feelings became too involved.

"So, you're deciding whether to return to the Guild so that you can stay by his side and admire him from afar, or to leave and pursue another kind of life?"

"Yes," she said quietly. "At the moment, I am not sure I can live with either."

"You deserve so much more."

"I deserve," she said, "whatever comes my way. I was born to be a Diamond, even if resuming my post at the Guild may become unbearable with the way things have turned out. The question is: can I ever be anything else?"

Kyth continued to watch her.

"He loves you, you know," he said.

"How can you possibly know that?"

"I just do. Trust me. For someone who shares these feelings it is always possible to tell."

Her lips trembled and she quickly looked away.

"Whether or not he does, he also knows the limitations of his position. If he truly feels this way about me, I would be torturing him too by staying at his side."

"Shouldn't you at least give him the choice?"

She sighed. "There *is* no choice."

"He could step down from his post. He did it once before for your sake."

She shook her head. "I would never ask him to do that again, not for my sake. This post fits him so well. But even if he did step down, it wouldn't make it any more possible for us to be together. If he did, he would become a regular Diamond with all the restrictions applied by the Guild to this rank."

Kyth shivered. All this time, he thought he was the one being miserable. And now, facing her grief, the trap she found herself in, made him feel as if his own suffering couldn't possibly compare to what she had to endure.

She was the most amazing woman in the world. All this time, he thought she was choosing between two men who loved her with all their hearts, and that whatever choice she made would bring her happiness. And now, the choice she was making was breaking her heart, and Kyth was powerless to do anything to help.

He reached over and put an arm around her. She leaned into him, relaxing against his shoulder.

"Whatever happens to you," he said, "I will always be there for you. You can always count on having a place at court, and on having a devoted friend who will go to great lengths to make sure you can lead a good life."

She turned her face into his shoulder and he enfolded her with both arms, gently stroking her hair. Her breath came out in a short gasp that felt like a stifled sob. Yet, when she finally disengaged herself, her voice came out calm and even, showing nothing of the turmoil going on inside.

"Thank you, Kyth," she said. "I couldn't wish for a better friend than you. And... I am very sorry for causing you pain."

41

AMENDS

The streets of the Crown City of Tandar were lined with people, waving flowering branches and throwing petals under the horses' hooves. Riding in Kyth's wake, Egey Bashi couldn't stop wondering which member of their large and impressive party caused the most turmoil. The Reverend Father of the Church, attended by the twelve priests of the Conclave, certainly stirred a reaction, as well as the Crown Prince, riding next to the heiress of the Royal House Illitand, both in formal garb, looking as good together as if they were a couple. But perhaps the most unusual sight was the Majat Guildmaster with his impressive suite that easily outnumbered the rest of the procession and made the whole train look like a minor invasion into the heart of the kingdom. The fact that this force could indeed turn into an invasion and achieve easy victory on Mai's whim was too unsettling to dwell on. Perhaps this was the reason a Majat Guildmaster had not led an embassy into any kingdom in over five hundred years.

The front courtyard of the King's castle was appropriately rearranged to receive the high guests. The King himself stood at the entrance, with Mother Keeper by his side. Egey Bashi felt warmth wash over him as he briefly met her eyes. She curtseyed to Mai, who dismounted in the middle of the courtyard and approached the King with the Emerald Guards in his wake. The Majat Pentade instantly sank to one knee, each man saluting with a fist to the chest. Mai signaled for them to resume their posts as he stopped in front of the King.

The two men exchanged brief nods, acknowledging their equality in rank. Quite a change, Egey Bashi reflected, from the time when Mai left this court just a short while ago.

The King stepped forward and extended his hands in welcome.

"Aghat Mai," he said. "Congratulations on your new post."

Mai bowed his head, his brief glance of amusement answered by the King's smile.

"Thank you, Your Majesty," he said.

"We've received a brief report of your victory at the Monastery," the King said. "And wish to extend our profound gratitude for your help in dealing with a very dangerous enemy."

Mai smiled.

"I appreciate your kind words, Your Majesty. However, it would be unfair for me to take all the credit. Our attack would have been impossible without Prince Kythar, whose talent and courage not only saved my Guild from infiltration, but also protected my men, enabling them to fight. I think I can speak for everyone here when I say we wouldn't be alive and victorious if it wasn't for him."

Egey Bashi was aware of the entire courtyard going still. The Prince's mouth literally fell open, and the Keeper felt about to mirror this expression. What Mai had said seemed so unlike the arrogant and ruthless image he maintained, so different from the way he and Kyth had been at each other's throats ever since Middledale. And, he was right, of course. Without Kyth's ability to protect Mai's men from the Kaddim, without his willingness to surrender all the command to Mai and face the ensuing hardships and humiliations, the whole operation would have been impossible. Without the Prince's resolve to put his entire self on the line, the Kaddim would have won.

"My men and I," Mai went on, "are indebted to His Royal Highness. We all owe him our lives, as well as the lives of our comrades back at the Guild."

He bowed his head to the Prince, saluting him with a fist to the chest.

Egey Bashi continued to stare as all the Majat in the courtyard followed suit, saluting the Prince.

The sight of a hundred Majat saluting an outsider was something he had never imagined seeing in his lifetime. He hadn't even known this salute could be extended to a non-Majat.

He thought he knew Mai reasonably well, but this man had just surprised him yet again.

Kyth stood with a dumbfounded expression, and Egey Bashi could just guess what was going on in the Prince's head. All this time his rivalry with Mai had driven them to the point where they couldn't be trusted to remain civil in each other's company, let alone have a constructive conversation. Whatever Kyth's part in this interaction had been, Mai hadn't made it easy on him at all, taking full advantage of his superiority, forcing the Prince to back down and publicly acknowledge it whenever possible. Egey Bashi knew that on Mai's part this animosity was driven by the fact that he considered Kyth to be his successful rival for Kara's affection. Even the most remarkable of men could be blind when it came to women. And now, even though to Egey Bashi's knowledge Mai still believed it to be the case, he had just handed Kyth all the credit, with the gallantry and chivalry that Egey Bashi had never thought him capable of.

The Prince shifted from foot to foot and Egey Bashi saw him make a visible effort to regain his composure.

"Thank you, Aghat Mai," he said. "You are most kind in saying these things. However, I am sure you know that without you this attack would have been impossible. I will always remember everything you taught me and cherish the honor of having fought under your command. And," he added quietly, "I hope that some day I can be half as good a leader to my people as you are to yours."

Mai held his gaze.

"You make your people proud, Your Highness. And, while I believe you understand now that we can never be formal allies, I hope on a personal level you can accept my friendship." He stepped forward and extended his hand.

Kyth swallowed, looking at Mai in disbelief, as if suspecting a trap. However, nothing but good-natured

434   THE GUILD OF ASSASSINS

honesty showed on the Guildmaster's face. After a
moment, Kyth took the offered hand and shook it.

The courtyard went very quiet. Egey Bashi could
actually feel his mouth falling open this time, and
closed it with a snap.

This was easily a first for any Majat Guildmaster
– the man whose post notoriously discouraged any
possibility of friendship. And of course, with this one
gesture the alliance between the kingdom of Tallan Dar
and the Majat Guild was sealed, without taking any
official steps that could possibly pose a risk of finding
their way into the chronicles.

Did Mai do these things on purpose? Or did it just
come naturally to him?

The King cleared his throat.

"You've just made a father very proud, Aghat Mai,"
he said. "Your praise of my son means so much to me."

Mai bowed his head. "Praise well deserved, Your
Majesty."

The King smiled, and Egey Bashi imagined he saw
tears standing in his eyes.

"In addition to everything else you have done for us,
Aghat Mai," the King said, "I'd like to thank you also
for rescuing Father Bartholomeos. I am rejoiced to see
him safe and well."

Mai nodded. "It was no trouble at all, Your Majesty.
Actually, we have Prince Kythar to thank for the
part he played in the rescue. Importantly, however,
I wanted to let you know that I took steps to ensure
that the Reverend's election by the Conclave cannot
be disputed this time. Just in case, we have brought
the entire Conclave here to confirm this in person."

He gestured to Father Bartholomeos's suite. The priests acknowledged his attention with uneasy glances.

The King raised his eyebrows. "I appreciate this, Aghat Mai," he said. "But isn't this quite unprecedented?"

"The Holy Fathers assured me it would be no trouble."

The priests averted their eyes, studying the courtyard pavement with forlorn expressions.

"I can confirm, Your Majesty," Bartholomeos said into the awkward pause, "that the Holy Fathers were more than happy to abide by Aghat Mai's wishes. He and his men made quite an impression at the Monastery, not to be easily forgotten."

The King measured Mai with an amused glance.

"I have no doubt of that," he said. "Aghat Mai makes quite an impression everywhere he goes."

That, he does, Egey Bashi thought. While Mai's act at the Monastery wouldn't be forgotten in a hurry, he continued to be worried about the impression Mai had made on their enemies, transported Shal Addim knows where. He had no doubt that in any future attack plans Mai would be the primary target. They had to form a plan that would prepare them for that.

He cleared his throat.

"If I may suggest, Your Majesty," he said, "after the festivities, which I've heard you planned in honor of your high guests, we should perhaps convene a council to discuss further plans?"

"Further plans, Magister?"

"Despite the success of Aghat Mai's attack, I am afraid some of the Kaddim Brothers have escaped. We must consider the possibility that they might still pose danger in the future."

The King nodded, the irony back in his eyes.

"Of course, Magister. I'm sure this couldn't possibly wait."

The festivities took the form of a state dinner, at which Mai was offered the honor place at the head of the table on the King's right, next to Mother Keeper. Egey Bashi settled for a place down the line on the left, a few seats away from Kyth, who would have looked out of place at the high table if it wasn't for Lady Celana by his side, radiant and seemingly determined to keep the Prince company. Egey Bashi was relieved at the way the Prince laughed at her jokes, his cheeks actually lighting up with color as she threw some of her admiring glances at him. He knew that Kyth's heart wound was deep, but watching the scene he could imagine a recovery, and a speedier one than originally seemed possible.

Egey Bashi realized that with the deep understanding Kyth had for Kara, with the remarkable empathy the Prince showed for everyone he cared for, he was likely able to see the obvious, no matter how much it hurt him. Kara and Mai were meant for each other. Forcing them apart was impossible on so many levels that no one should even consider it seriously. Kyth was bound to understand that in the end, and Egey Bashi was glad that the Prince not only had, but was prepared to move on in due time.

From his own experience the Keeper realized that it was impossible to stop loving someone who had been your whole world, as Kara had been for Kyth. This kind of love never went away. But it was possible to find another place in your heart for someone else, who could bring you comfort and match with you in different ways. He was confident that, given time, Kyth would find the happiness he deserved.

Egey Bashi tore his eyes away from the Prince, surveying the rest of the gathering. Father Bartholomeos and his priests took the entire left side of the high table, opposite the Diamonds and Rubies from Mai's retinue. The other Majat could be seen further down the table, but no matter how hard Egey Bashi looked, he couldn't find a very important member of their group. Kara was not sitting anywhere at the high table. In fact, as Egey Bashi searched further, he realized she wasn't in the room at all. He had no doubt she had been invited, and had been offered a place of honor next to her fellows in rank, not in the least because her participation had been so instrumental in realizing all their plans.

His heart quivered. Unlike Kyth's, Kara's heart wound might take some interference, and he hoped he knew the remedy. He also knew he had to hurry. Kara was unlikely to be inactive for long. With her training and resolve, Egey Bashi was sure she would not delay taking matters into her own hands, and not in a good way – simply because she likely believed her happiness was impossible. In fact, he felt he could do more good if he left the table and looked for her right now, but he couldn't leave just yet without offending the King, so he tried to distract himself by watching the interactions around the high table.

By now he should have stopped feeling surprised every time he saw Mai embrace yet another aspect of his new role as naturally as if it were his birthright, but he couldn't help reflecting on it once again. Mai had spent four years at the King's court in servitude, present at all the official functions only in his role of bodyguard. And now, only weeks later, he looked so natural as an equal by the King's side, easily supporting the conversation that contained enough politics and etiquette to overwhelm most men groomed into such posts. This seemed especially surprising given that Mai was easily half the King's age and possessed no known ancestry or the upbringing of a noble. Some things in life just worked out, and this was one of its most amazing examples.

By the time dessert was served, Egey Bashi felt he couldn't wait any longer. He made his excuse to his neighbors, scowling in response to Mother Keeper's ironic gaze as he hastily retreated through the large double doorway.

The castle seemed emptier than usual, and became all but vacant as he reached the outer hallways. Strange, how every servant and courtier gravitated toward the festivities even when they had other things to do.

Speeding through the blessedly deserted passages, Egey Bashi found his way outside into the Majat training grounds. He was certain he would find Kara here, but, despite looking very carefully, he nearly missed her. She was sitting by the wall in the corner of the main training platz, hugging her knees pulled up to her chest, so still that she looked like one of the carved stone ornaments protruding from the wall.

As Egey Bashi approached, her striking violet eyes surveyed him with a calmness that he knew had been carefully put into place to conceal the turmoil inside.

"Mind if I join you, Aghat?" he asked.

She nodded, but didn't move, her eyes watching the Keeper warily as he lowered onto the paving stones by her side.

"I was surprised not to see you in the King's dining hall," he said.

She shook her head. "I know I was supposed to be there, Magister, but I just wasn't in the mood. I hope my absence didn't cause any problems."

The Keeper sighed. "I know Aghat Mai, among others, would have liked to see you there."

The quick smile that slid over her lips looked bitter.

"I'm not part of his official suite."

Egey Bashi turned toward her, watching her intently.

"I heard you could be, if you decided to. He made his offer for you to return to the Guild very public."

She lowered her eyes. "He was most kind. No other Guildmaster would ever have done a thing like that for me."

Egey Bashi slowly shook his head. "I'm sure neither of us should pretend that he is like any other Guildmaster. Nor could you possibly ignore the fact that there is very little Aghat Mai wouldn't do for you."

Her shoulders stiffened.

"I've always valued your tact, Magister, but I heard that, on occasions, you've demonstrated surprising resolve in prying into people's personal feelings. If you feel inclined to do this to me, I hope you can choose a better time."

Egey Bashi shook his head.

"I hope, Aghat," he said, "that in addition to my reputation as a meddler, you might also have heard at least something about my skill as a healer. Sometimes to heal a serious wound one must prod deeply into it, even if it hurts like hell."

She raised her eyebrows. "I fail to see the relevance, Magister."

"I'm sure you are smarter than that, Aghat. You are wounded, even if this fact may not be obvious to everyone. If I thought you could deal with it on your own, I wouldn't be here, believe me."

Her lips twitched. "Like I said, Magister. I'm not in the mood. Perhaps we could have this conversation another time?"

"You mean, after you deal with the worst of your pain on your own and do something foolish with your life for no reason whatsoever?"

"No reason?" Her eyes narrowed. "Do you presume to know everything about everyone, Magister?"

Egey Bashi sighed. "I wish. And no, of course I don't. However, I believe I know something you don't about the situation you find yourself in."

"Really?" Her lips twitched into an ironic smile, but Egey Bashi could also sense the strain behind it.

He leaned back into the wall.

"Something not commonly known about this castle," he said, "is that it possesses an amazing library – alas, greatly under-used. I couldn't help thinking that with your current desire for solitude you might find that place... comforting. In particular, their section on the history and customs of the Majat Guild rivals the one you have back home, and is especially rich in those chronicles that your Guild prefers to keep from circulating too widely among its members."

"*Library*?" she echoed. "But I..." her voice trailed off as she continued to watch him warily.

"You might find interesting things in there, Aghat, especially regarding the post of the Majat Guildmaster and the kind of privileges it affords." Egey Bashi paused, relieved to see the way her eyes widened as she listened. "I hope you read on it as soon as possible. It breaks my heart to see you like this, even if it is, in a way, none of my business. Perhaps you'd find my motivations easier to understand if you consider them as purely pragmatic. If we are ever to expect a strike back from the Kaddim, your presence would be instrumental to our success, not only because of your unique resistance to their power, but also because of your efficiency and brilliance – which, I cannot help noticing, might be somewhat hindered if you were to remain in your present state of mind. For all these reasons I feel that if you, for instance, decide to go to the library right now and spend, oh, a day or so searching, you might just be surprised at the information that section has to offer. You'll find it in the east cloister, under 'M'. Some of the chronicles are stacked deeper inside, on the second row on the shelves. You might want to start with those. I especially recommend the one stashed into a hidden compartment on the left side of the shelf. The latch that opens it looks like a griffin head, different from the rest of the ornaments. I don't think you'll need my help with it, but, if you do, please don't hesitate to ask. You know where to find me."

He held her gaze for a moment longer, making sure all the information settled in. Then he got up and walked away.

42

SURRENDER

The Majat Guildmaster had the rank of a king, entitled to his own apartment in a prime area of the castle, with a complement of servants and enough room to accommodate all his men. But Kara knew that Mai had rejected this arrangement and chose to reside in the Majat grounds, occupying the old room that had belonged to him when he had been leader of the Pentade. When Kara approached it along the bare stone corridor, she felt her heart quiver, echoing with a weakness in her knees a fighter of her rank was not supposed to have.

She took a breath before raising her hand and knocking on the door.

Mai's eyes lit up with quick surprise as he saw her standing in the doorway. She swallowed, hoping that her voice would not betray her nervousness.

"Aghat Mai," she said. "I came to have a word with you, if this is a good time."

He silently stepped aside, letting her into the room, and closed the door, watching her with a wary expression. He wore no weapons, clearly unprepared for visitors. The absence of his staff tip protruding above his shoulder made him look strangely open, as if caught off guard at a very private moment. She glanced around to see the staff leaning against the wall within easy reach, its black polished wood giving off a quiet, suffused gleam.

Kara had never been in this room before. Its simple furnishing mirrored her own quarters, but some additional touches indicated Mai probably cared about comfort more than she did. His low bed by the far wall was much wider than hers, covered by spotless white sheets. A curtain adorned the window, which overlooked the lake, admitting a spectacular view. A shelf in the corner next to a massive desk held books and scrolls, as well as an elaborate writing set gleaming with heavy silver carvings. The latter was likely an addition required by his new station, but she glanced over the books with interest, finding them mostly related to the topics of history and military strategy.

She looked back at Mai, feeling his gaze burn her as he continued to watch her. She swallowed.

"I came to give a formal answer to your very generous offer to allow me to resume my rank in the Guild."

She waited for a response, but it didn't come, so she went on.

"I have given it very careful consideration and I have decided to decline."

His gaze wavered and she saw his shoulders sag just a bit, as if a tense string inside him had suddenly given way.

"I understand," he said. "This is a big loss to our Guild, but I respect your decision... And I am happy for you.

As I mentioned before, you are free to do whatever you will, and no Majat will ever pursue you because of your past." His gaze softened. "After everything you've been through, you deserve to live out your life in peace and to pursue your happiness."

"Thank you, Guildmaster," she said. "This means a lot to me. Because of your generosity, I now find myself the first in the history of our Guild with freedom to pursue personal happiness. No words could possibly express my gratitude."

His gaze hovered on her with a glimpse of feeling that receded before she could catch what it was. As she peered, his eyes became tranquil, like the summer sky.

She took a breath. "One of the most important reasons for my decision was that my freedom now enables me to have a conversation with you that would have been impossible if I were your subordinate."

He lifted his eyebrows in a silent question.

"Once, you asked me if I was in love with Kyth."

He went very still.

"Forgive me," he said. "I shouldn't have."

"I'm not."

His eyes widened. His face showed hesitation as if he wasn't sure he had heard her right.

"I'm very fond of Kyth," she said. "He will always have my friendship. I greatly admire him for what he has become, and value his role in our fight against the Kaddim. But I don't have any feelings for him beyond that."

Mai stood so still that he appeared inanimate. Only his eyes continued to follow her, their look so intense that it burned.

"For some time," she went on, "I have mistaken my feelings toward Kyth for love. But I now know for certain that I was wrong."

"Were you?" Mai asked quietly.

"He… he was the first person in my life who ever made me realize that I can be more than just a prize fighter for our Guild. He taught me to see myself as a woman, as well as a deadly warrior. I am grateful to him for that. But I know for certain that he is not the man I want to spend my life with."

She swallowed, his captivated look making her skin prickle.

"I have resolved my feelings with him. As a friend, he was very understanding and wished me happiness. I also informed him of my intention to leave the court."

"Where will you go?" Mai asked quietly.

She met his eyes.

"I hoped you would be able to help me with that decision."

"Me?" His widening eyes suddenly made him look young and vulnerable.

She paused to steady her voice. "Yes. Thinking about my future, I took advantage of the royal library, which apparently contains a wealth of information about the limitations – and privileges – afforded to you by your post as the Majat Guildmaster."

He frowned, peering into her eyes, and she quivered at the hope she saw in his gaze.

"My findings surprised me," she went on. "They also gave me hope, which prompted me to approach you with this conversation."

He was watching her in hypnotising stillness.

"I found that the post of the Majat Guildmaster leaves a man with much more personal freedom than we have all been raised to believe. A man in this post cannot pursue any personal relations with his subordinates, or anyone whose allegiance may be exploited as a basis for a political alliance. However, nothing in the Code precludes a Majat Guildmaster from having a lasting relationship with an outsider to the Guild, who has pledged no loyalty to anyone else. This, of course, makes it nearly impossible to find a match – which is probably why, historically, the Majat Guildmaster has been perceived as a person off limits to everyone else."

Mai continued watching her, the quiet fascination in his gaze sending her heart racing.

"I've even found a precedent," she went on, "when a Majat Guildmaster married a woman from outside the Fortress. While the legality of this marriage is strongly debated in the chronicles, she shared his quarters, had full access to all the Guild's grounds, and accompanied him on all assignments."

"To no good end. He was unable to protect her."

Kara's eyes widened. She would never have found this particular chronicle if not for Egey Bashi's tip about the secret compartment. She was certain that, even if copies existed elsewhere, the Majat would have made every effort to ensure that they would be equally hard to find. The Guild couldn't possibly afford for such things to be publicly known.

"You read this chronicle too?"

"Do you think I haven't considered the possibility?"

She felt as if he had just kicked the floor from under her feet, sending her into freefall.

"You have?"

He smiled. "A man can always dream. There's nothing in the Code to prohibit that, is there?"

A thrill echoed in the pit of her stomach.

"In our conversation you just referred to," Mai said, "I also told you about my feelings."

"You did." Now it was her turn to be hypnotized as the emotion she had glimpsed in his gaze earlier torrented to the surface, trapping her like an invisible bond.

"I didn't mean to, back then. But in retrospect I'm glad it happened that way, if my confession has anything to do with your motivation to do your... research."

She swallowed. "You never said anything since then. If you knew your post allowed it..."

He shook his head. "I said that I would never force you into a choice. I knew you had feelings for Kyth. My closeness had inadvertently confused you. I didn't want to take advantage of it."

Kara looked at him with wide eyes. Dear Shal Addim, up until this moment, she hadn't fully realized the sacrifices he'd made for her. He had opened up to her down to the very core, and then quietly stepped aside, giving her all the time she needed to make her choice. He had lain down his entire self to protect her, without any intention to benefit from it.

"It wasn't a hard choice," she said. "And I'd made it a long time ago. You are the man I love. This is why I came to you today for a decision."

He frowned. "A decision?"

"Yes. You can let me stay by your side. Or, you can dismiss me."

He stepped forward and pulled her into his arms.

"There," he said. "You're by my side. And I am never letting you go. How's this for a decision?"

"Good," she whispered.

His hands slid up into her hair, cupping her head, drawing her closer. Her breath caught as she lifted her face to meet his kiss.

It felt like homecoming, his taste instantly going to her head like a sip of strong wine. As he held her, she remembered the last time he had held her this way, on the eve of their tournament. Back then, it felt like saying goodbye. And now, it felt like a new beginning, the force of her happiness bringing tears to her eyes as she savored his taste, his smell, the way his arms around her made her feel so complete.

An eternity swept by in a single instant, the world around them shifting to become a brighter, better place. They spent a long time just standing there, savoring each other, immersed in the new closeness she had often dreamed of but never felt possible to experience.

She felt dizzy as he finally drew away from her, just enough to see her face. The tenderness in his gaze made her head spin.

A smile glimmered in the corners of his mouth as he looked down on her.

"Do you intend to wear your weapons all the time?" he asked.

Wordlessly, she stepped out of his arms and unstrapped her knife belt, placing it at his feet, followed by her boot dagger, her grappler hook, and, finally, her hagdala.

It looked like a formal surrender, and this was exactly how she felt, surrendering to the man she loved, body and soul. The way he looked at her made her shiver, his fascinated expression sending her heart racing to new heights. She had never imagined anyone could make her feel the way he did, like a rare treasure a man could only dream of.

All this time, they had been fighting the impossible – two people meant for each other, a perfect match. And now, nobody could possibly do anything to keep them apart.

She kept his gaze as she took off her clothes, laying them down at his feet next to her weapons, standing in front of him stark naked. She watched him a moment longer, letting the surrender settle before she stepped into his arms again.

He swept her into his embrace and carried her to his bed, stretching next to her, still fully clothed. His hand circled her wrists, holding them above her head as he leaned over to kiss her. His free hand caressed her in a long, drawn movement that made her entire body respond with arousal, his touch sending shivers down to her most intimate parts. The fighter in her felt panicked about being so helpless in his arms. With his fighting skill he could do *anything* to her when she lay like this in his hold, her arms over her head, his tongue claiming her mouth, his light, toned body trapping her underneath with no possibility of escape. She was amazed how this thrill of fear in the pit of her belly added to her excitement, until she felt she could release any moment, before he even took his clothes off.

She knew what he was doing, and how important it was for both of them to experience this in their new closeness. Despite the enjoyment he had given her before, every time she had been with him this fighter's fear had been there at the back of her mind, driving her to match his strength, to compose herself, to keep at least partially in control even during the ultimate closeness. This fear, as she now realized, had also precluded her in the past from ever enjoying her body to the full, making her teachers in the Guild feel so exasperated with this particular side of her training, making it so difficult for Kyth to get close enough to awaken the woman in her. The only time she had been able to at least partially let herself go was with Mai during his delirium, when her belief that he was not aware of his actions had temporarily released her fear, making her feel that despite his strength she was the one in control. She remembered how this knowledge that she was letting go with full awareness of the possible consequences added to her excitement, her release that time even stronger. And now, when he was fully in control and had her in his power, the thrill of it built to an arousal she had never experienced before.

Giving in to his caress, she also realized more. She no longer felt she had to match him or maintain her own in their closeness the way she did in a fight. She was ready to give herself to him fully and unconditionally, to do with as he willed, and this was a feeling she had never believed possible for her to experience with any man.

She could sense his need that matched hers, and the way he held back, stretching the moment, giving her time to surrender completely into his control. She knew that, being a fighter of the same training, he fully understood what it meant for her, and how much it meant to him that she did. She could also sense his control slipping as his movements became more powerful, savoring her, possessing her like a prize beyond his wildest dreams.

His slow caress built her excitement to the impossible. She floated on the waves of her arousal, so ready for him as he finally released her and drew away to remove his clothes, catching her in his arms. She grasped him, her hands now free to explore him, savoring every inch of his light, toned body moving against hers. She felt carnal in her passion as she claimed him, bit by bit, losing herself in every delicious moment as he, in turn, claimed her for his own. A moan escaped her lips when he entered her, her head rolling to meet his kiss. He drove into her and she dug her fingers into his back, his powerful rhythm driving her to the edge, holding her there for an impossibly long time. She screamed and shuddered in his arms as he accelerated, his release inside her sending her to new heights which clouded her mind completely, making her feel as if it was never going to end.

Later, when she finally came to her senses enough to be aware of her surroundings, she turned to look at him, weak and lightheaded, with a tingling sensation of happiness rising in her stomach threatening to overwhelm her. He was lying on his side, leaning on one elbow, watching her. His gaze stirred with a tenderness that made her heart quiver.

"Did you mean everything you said to me?" he asked.

She smiled. "As far as I remember. It all became a blur at some point. You tend to have this effect on me... Why?"

He took a breath. "I know this is not how marriage proposals are supposed to go, but you did mention the possibility."

She held his gaze. "I surely made it sound that way, didn't I?"

He frowned, peering into her face. "Is it something you would really consider?"

"Is there a reason I shouldn't?"

"You would marry me?"

"If you asked me to."

"Will you?"

"Yes."

His eyes widened as he held her gaze, his chest heaving in a breath that quivered like a suppressed gasp. He briefly closed his eyes. When he opened them again, she saw a smile glimmer in their depths, mixing with the same fascination she saw before.

"I did hear you right," he said. "You just agreed to marry me, didn't you?"

She smiled at his stunned expression. "Yes, I did. Is there something in this decision that you find surprising?"

"Everything. And no, surprising is not the word. Astounding. Unbelievable. Impossible."

"Why?"

"This decision," he said, "would bond you to me. In everyone's eyes, it would give me a *right* to you."

She laughed. "It goes both ways, doesn't it? In everyone's eyes, it would give me a right to you too."

He shook his head. "It hardly changes anything on my part. I am bonded to you already. I have been, for quite a while. For me, there could never be anyone else."

She melted at the tenderness she saw in his gaze. Dear Shal Addim, he had felt this way about her despite his belief that she belonged to another man, despite his certainty that they could never be together. The realization of it was so overwhelming that she felt tears in her eyes.

"I am bonded to you too," she said quietly. "I have been, since..." She paused, suddenly unsure. When had she first realized they were meant for each other? Was it the time when he talked to her in his delirium and everything he said matched the way she felt? Or was it before, when their fighting incident got out of hand and despite the impossibility of it she felt so good about their closeness? Or perhaps even earlier, when he had put his life on the line to save hers and she first got a glimpse of this remarkable man who always did what he believed was right? She had always been drawn to him, she realized. Ever since she was a girl, watching him rise in the Guild's ranks like a shooting star, five years her senior, so glamorous that all she could do was join the crowds of his admirers without any hope of getting close. All the time they trained together in the Inner Fortress she hadn't even talked to him for any length of time. And now, seeing him look at her this way, she felt surreal. Was she going to wake up and realize it was all a dream?

She remembered what he had said to her when they first made love. Being together was worth dying for. She now realized that she felt this way too. If she were to die right now, she would die with no regrets.

She reached up to his chest, tracing every sculpted muscle with her fingertips, watching his skin prickle in response. It was just so difficult to keep her hands off him.

"When I think back on it," she said, "it feels like I've always been in love with you. I just never considered a possibility of acting on it."

"Neither did I," he said, "until that time, during our fight, when I simply couldn't help it."

She frowned. "I always thought I was the one who took all the steps."

He grinned. "You are so innocent." The mischief in his eyes melted as he held her gaze. He slowly ran his fingers down her body, making her shiver with pleasure.

How could he make her feel so good with a mere touch of a hand?

"Are you sure being with me is what you truly want?" he asked quietly.

She raised her eyebrows. "Are you having second thoughts?"

He leaned down and kissed her.

Time stopped again as they lay in each other's arms, submerged in their new closeness that went so far beyond simple desire. Even if they spent every waking moment with each other for the rest of their lives, would she ever get enough of him?

She noticed how much time had passed only when she realized that the light coming from outside had acquired a reddish tint of early sunset. She had come here late morning. Had they really spent most of the day together? It felt like only an instant had passed since she had taken off her clothes and stepped into his arms.

He drew away from her again, watching her with a mix of tenderness and laughter.

"I still can't believe this is happening," he said.

She grinned. "You'd better start believing it because I am not going anywhere. And by the way, with the distractions we encountered, I failed to mention that if you do want me to stay with you in the Guild, I have some terms."

"Terms?" He raised his eyebrows.

"Yes. I'd like to have the full privileges of an active Guild member, outside formal command. I did check that all this is permissible by the Code, if the Guildmaster approves it."

He appeared to consider it seriously, but she saw the mischief in his gaze.

"I can meet those terms," he said. "But I also have some terms of my own."

"Yes?"

"I'd like to be the one to oversee your safety."

"My safety?"

"Being this close to me will make you a target for all my enemies. If you did your research well, you probably realize why so few of the Majat Guildmasters have ever been married long enough for this fact even to find its way into the chronicles."

Her eyes widened. "There were more?"

"Oh, yes – despite the fact that normally this post is expected to be filled by an older man. However, the sad ends of these marriages, the impact it had on Guild affairs, eventually led to instigating the current belief that the Guildmaster is off limits."

She smiled. "Don't you think, in my case, even if your enemies wanted to deal you this kind of a blow, they would have trouble finding anyone up to the job?"

He measured her with a quick, appraising glance. "True. But..."

"But what?"

"Keeping you at my side has already harmed you before. That time when you took a dagger aimed at me, you nearly died. So did I, when I thought that no matter how fast I ran I could never be fast enough to bring you to safety. And again, when I had to watch you take pain beyond any possible tolerance, which should have been mine. That healing took only half an hour, but it lasted an eternity. If you are ever harmed again because of me..."

She smiled.

"I'm sorry you had to go through that on my account. However, you must understand that you're not alone. Once, you took a poisoned arrow for me with full knowledge that, healing or not, it meant certain death. I knew that too. Have you ever considered how it felt, before I realized you could be saved?"

His eyes widened.

"I survived."

"So did I. And yes, sometimes that's what it takes when two people fight side by side. I guess we'll both just have to come to terms with it and leave the rest to our skill."

He shook his head. "The Kaddim hate me. And they're still out there."

She looked into his eyes, an inadvertent smile sliding over her lips. "Are you going to dismiss me because of that?"

"Hell, no. But... I can't even think of what will happen if I lose you."

"You are not going to lose me," she said. "Unless you want to, of course. If you ever do, you have but to say the word."

He reached over and pulled her into his arms in a powerful move that bordered on roughness, his force echoing inside her with new arousal.

"You must be joking," he said.

She inhaled his scent, briefly closing her eyes so that she could savor it.

"I must be dreaming," she whispered.

ACKNOWLEDGMENTS

This novel would never have been possible without the support and inspiration from many important people in my life.

First and foremost, I will always be grateful to my grandfather, Vladimir Keilis-Borok, who enjoyed the world of the Majat warriors even more than any of my other writing, and felt so personal about Kara and Mai that he found strength to discuss their lives and motives with me until his very last days. He was among the first people who saw their potential for being together during my early work on the *Blades of the Old Empire*, and our conversations about it yielded some of my favorite scenes. The majority of the first draft of this novel was written during my trips to his bedside in the last months of his life, and this book will forever bear the mark of his magic.

I thank my lifelong friend Olga Karengina, who has always been my number one beta reader, and whose encouragement and support drove me on during the work on this book. I am grateful to several friends and fellow authors for their helpful critique, especially WBJ Williams, who read the full draft of this novel in a very short time and gave me some critical encouragement and suggestions on the story, and J. M. Sidorova, whose comments and inspiration shaped a lot of my writing in this book. I also thank those multiple readers and fans who urged me, after reading *Blades of the Old Empire*, to explore the idea of physical closeness between Kara and Mai, which ended up getting out of hand and developing into a full-blown romance.

I am grateful to my husband for sharing my passion for fantasy and martial arts, and for his tips and suggestions that underlay some of the advanced Majat techniques. I also thank my parents for being supportive of my writing for all these years, ever since I turned six.

Last but not least, I am very grateful to my agent, Michael Harriot, and to the publishing team of Angry Robot Books, especially Lee Harris, Caroline Lambe and Michael Underwood, for their support and all the hard work that went into bringing my book to publication.

THE MAJAT CODE · BOOK 1

BLADES
OF THE
OLD EMPIRE

ANNA KASHINA

**Knowledge is power, and power
must be preserved at all costs...**

A swashbuckling tale of assassination, inventions and families at war, from a secret corner of history that is more familiar than you know.

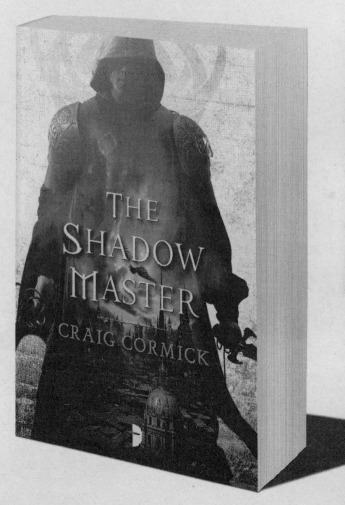

War is the only reality.